MW01125280

By Joanne Meschery

In a High Place

Truckee: A History

A Gentleman's Guide to the Frontier

Joanne Meschery

Simon and Schuster
New York   London   Toronto   Sydney   Tokyo   Singapore

Simon and Schuster
Simon & Schuster Building
Rockefeller Center
1230 Avenue of the Americas
New York, New York 10020

Copyright © 1990 by Joanne Meschery

Designed by Levavi & Levavi
Manufactured in the United States of America

1   3   5   7   9   10   8   6   4   2

Library of Congress Cataloging in Publication Data

Meschery, Joanne
A gentleman's guide to the frontier/Joanne Meschery.
p.   cm.
I. Title.
PS3563.E777G46   1990
813'.54—dc20   89-26157
ISBN 0-671-46369-1

Lines from "Western Country" by W. S. Merwin reprinted with
permission of Atheneum Publishers, an imprint of MacMillan Publishing Company, from The Carrier of Ladders by W. S. Merwin.
Copyright by W. S. Merwin.
Excerpt from "Good Morning, America" in Good Morning, America, by Carl Sandburg, copyright © 1928 by Harcourt, Brace, Jova-
novich, Inc. and renewed 1956 by Carl Sandburg, reprinted by
permission of the publisher.
Lines from "One More, The Round" copyright by Beatrice
Roethke, administratrix of the estate of Theodore Roethke. From The
Collected Poems of Theodore Roethke by Theodore Roethke. Used

(continued on page 349)

*To my father
and
To the memory of my mother*

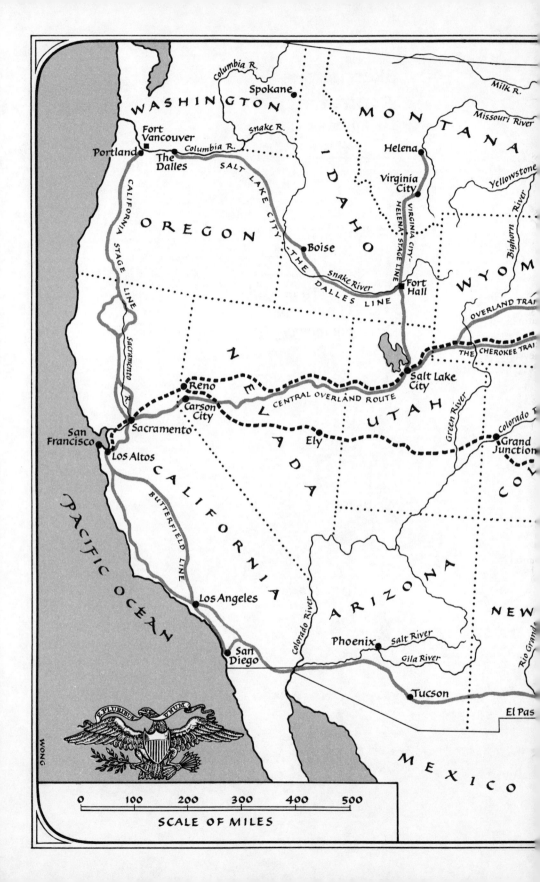

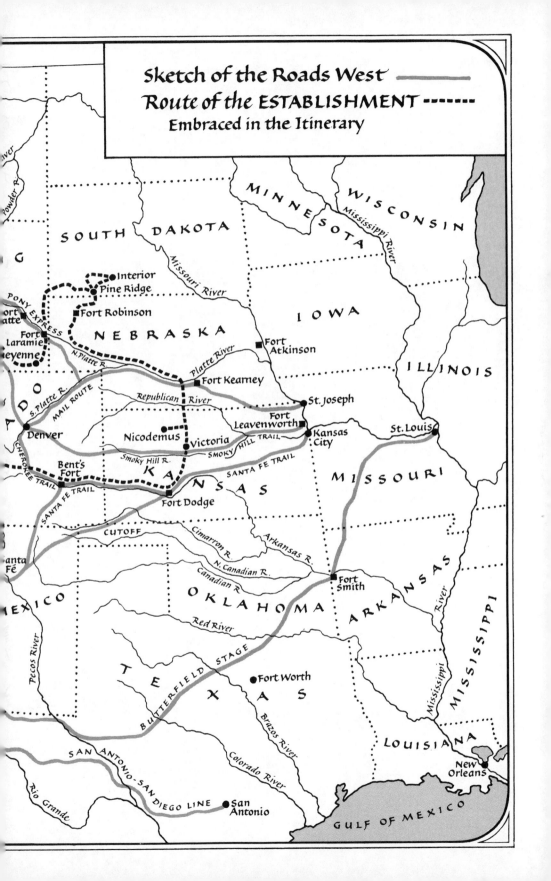

Sketch of the Roads West ⎯⎯
Route of the ESTABLISHMENT ------
Embraced in the Itinerary

WISCONSIN

MINNESOTA

SOUTH DAKOTA

Powder R.

Mississippi River

Missouri River

IOWA

Interior
Pine Ridge
Fort Robinson

NEBRASKA

PONY EXPRESS

Fort
latte

Fort
Laramie
eyenne

N. Platte R.

S. Platte R.

MAIL ROUTE

Platte River

Fort
Atkinson

ILLINOIS

Fort Kearney

Republican River

St. Joseph

Fort
Leavenworth

Denver

CHEROKEE TRAIL

Nicodemus

Victoria

SMOKY HILL TRAIL

Kansas
City

St. Louis

Smoky Hill R.

Bent's
Fort

SANTA FE TRAIL

KANSAS

SANTA FE TRAIL

MISSOURI

SANTA FE TRAIL

Fort Dodge

CUTOFF

Cimarron R.

Arkansas R.

N. Canadian R.

Fort
Smith

ARKANSAS

anta
Fé

MEXICO

Canadian R.

OKLAHOMA

Red River

Mississippi River

MISSISSIPPI

Pecos River

BUTTERFIELD STAGE

T E X A S

Fort Worth

Brazos River

LOUISIANA

SAN ANTONIO-SAN DIEGO LINE

San
Antonio

Colorado River

New
Orleans

Rio Grande

GULF OF MEXICO

I heard that you ask'd for something to prove this puzzle the New World . . .

—Walt Whitman
Leaves of Grass

Whither Thou

Each no doubt knows a western country
half discovered
which he thinks is there because
he thinks he left it . . .

W. S. Merwin
"Western Country"

1

On July 25 Andrew Marsh sailed his sloop past the starting-line buoys and swept beneath the Golden Gate Bridge and out of the bay. For most of that sharp, gusty morning he could still catch sight of the fleet, thirty-nine racers, some with their colorful spinnakers already flying. But just beyond the final light station Marsh turned 190° and headed the *Whither Thou* south, away from the others into the open gray seas of the Pacific.

For three days he sailed with a strong northwesterly wind. He ate very little during these first days and slept only in snatches. He dozed in the cockpit, waking with a start to check the lines and self-steering gear which he always found to be working well without him.

When he hit light winds he began to worry he'd sailed too far south. Still, he remained within a few miles of the course he'd charted in those weeks before the race. "The People's Race," local newspapers called it—only one sailor entered who might qualify as a star in the racing world. The rest were hardly more than weekend yachtsmen, without a custom-designed boat among them. Just regular people in regular boats. That's how Marsh's son had put it the day before the race. Except Richard's voice held a hard edge, and he'd glared at Marsh across the white formica table, then blinked as if the trouble was only the brilliant sun filling the breakfast nook. He raised his coffee mug to Marsh. "Just regular millionaires." "I'm not a millionaire," Marsh had answered quietly.

For eight days the light winds continued, and Marsh kept his spinnaker flying, hoping to pick up speed. He figured at this rate it would take three weeks to reach Kauai and the finish line in Hanalei Bay—a last place in his division, last in the fleet. Not that losing really concerned him. He told himself what mattered was the journey—San Francisco to Hawaii alone under sail. He needed this break, this boundless solitude without a shore in sight.

And if it made any difference, he probably would've been a millionaire. He'd come very close. So he could afford a modest shrug for his son that morning. "I guess if I hadn't sold the firm . . ."

Richard had nodded toward the kitchen, the sound of a running faucet. "So please tell me—" He leaned forward and spoke in a whisper. "Tell me why a man would quit working to devote himself to his dying wife—*my* dying mother—then turn around and join some crazy sailboat race across the ocean."

"Listen, Richard—" Marsh looked to the kitchen, keeping his voice low. "Do you have any idea—I mean, what it's been like all this time?"

But then he doubted Richard would ever understand. In the same way he longed for his wife to get over cancer, Marsh sometimes found himself wishing his son would recover from being a prosecuting attorney. Of course, Richard had problems of his own—problems Marsh didn't grasp either. But who could? "I'm experiencing difficulty with my wife," Richard told him recently. This didn't sound like a worried husband, but reminded Marsh of a television announcer cautioning the viewing audience. The trouble is in the transmitter. Do not adjust your sets.

Nobody talked this way about human troubles. Except Richard, and maybe doctors. Specialists, surgical oncologists. They spoke of carcinomas, necrosis, metastases. Or in comparisons. *The malignant tumor will extend into normal tissue like a crab.*

One night twelve years before, Marsh found the lump in Virginia's right breast. It had been that long ago. In the dark he came upon that unfamiliar place as if he'd discovered a secret. After all these years there could still be some part of her kept unknown from him—another mystery. He felt the lump hidden like an egg and explored it first with his mouth, then probed with his fingers. And for just an instant he was filled with both excitement and dread.

Even before her illness Marsh had been thinking of early retirement. He'd also owned the boat before. But he'd never really planned on entering this race. During Virginia's last hospital stay he'd brought a few books home from the library—just out of curiosity. *Single-Handed Passage, Voyage Alone, Voyage Unafraid.* Evenings, he plotted the charts in his den simply as an exercise. And for how long can a person be said to be dying? Twelve years, and no doctor had ever mentioned dying—

at least not to him. They talked only about what to do next until it seemed there would always be something they could do.

He'd christened his sloop the *Whither Thou* just to tease Virginia. She hated sailing and refused to go anywhere with him on the boat, claimed she couldn't step aboard without feeling sick to her stomach. Now it seemed she was sick almost every night. Once she told him that she vomited tears. "I swallow them, and then what do you know—" She snapped her fingers. "Up they come."

The day he painted the name on the sloop's bow, Virginia arrived at the marina with a bottle of champagne. From the pier she frowned at the bright blue words. "Ruth never said that," she called down to him. She shook her head as he shattered the bottle against the bow. "Everybody knows the Bible's a man's book."

So he sailed alone, and once in a while crewed for somebody else at the marina. All his real friends were still working. Sometimes it seemed the whole world was at work except him. Not that he didn't have certain jobs. He gave their housekeeper notice and took over her chores. He vacuumed meticulously, loaded the dishwasher, shopped for groceries, and tried his feeble hand at cooking when Virginia was having a bad day. The first months after he retired they went out often. They ate at the best restaurants, attended the theater, symphony, and more movies than Marsh had seen in the accumulated years of their marriage. Sometimes he felt they were courting all over again. And as in their prim, long-ago courtship, sex had once more become taboo.

It almost seemed they'd traveled together full circle. But Marsh knew better. They'd set a backward course, like ships turning about, beating into the wind when they might've been running before it. To live with Virginia these past years was to witness the Creation in reverse. He could recite it line by line, by heart—this man's book, a story he alone might survive to tell.

In the beginning her right breast was taken from her and all the flesh seared. And there was evening and there was morning, one day. On the second day her remaining breast was cut from her and her young girl's chest shone with a radiant light. The third day she gave up her womb and ever after felt a scalding hot flash and dreamed she was falling from a high place. On the fourth day a small oval gland was drawn from the darkness behind her eyes, and she forever lost desire. The fifth day the roots of her nerves were severed where they sprang from her spinal cord. After this day she no longer felt the great pain.

And on the sixth day, with Marsh over a thousand miles out in the vast blue Pacific, she turned from the kitchen sink, feeling faint and leaning into the arms of her daughter-in-law, and she said, "Oh my."

It was also on this day that Marsh finally caught the warm, brisk trade winds. The *Whither Thou* leapt before these winds, nudged even faster by the steady surge of the following seas. Marsh was now two weeks into the race. He recorded this in the boat's log, all business. But after a moment he smiled and added an exclamation point.

At 0500 hours he took a star reading in the damp dawn twilight, then moved below. He stood leaning over the gleaming teak chart desk and yawned into his plotting sheets. He hadn't used the self-steering much since he'd hit the trades. The days had grown increasingly warmer and the sea turned azure. He'd stowed his wind cheaters, shed his Levi's and cable-knit sweaters, and puttered around the cabin wearing only his roomy gray sweat pants and a pair of rubber thongs.

As he waited for the kettle to boil on the galley stove, he untied the cotton cord at the waist of his sweats, then knotted it again—looser, so the pants rode below his navel, a trace of light brown hair. The cord reminded him of the pajama strings that had given him fits as a child, the ends frayed and always hopelessly twisted, tied in impossible knots— terror for a small boy stamping madly in the cold morning bathroom to keep from wetting his pants. Marsh fixed himself a cup of coffee, wondering why the memory of pajama strings would cause such sadness in a man. How did the world ever hope to operate sensibly when people who endured sickness, pain, hunger, and war could still be brought close to tears by the sight of an article like pajama strings.

Marsh climbed through the hatch, impatient with his thoughts, his own company. It seemed his mind had begun taking up more space, grown loose and blowsy on the open sea. He checked the self-steering, then wandered the boat, making his usual rounds. He tightened the mainsail and noticed the line had begun to chafe. He made a mental note of this, then dropped two trolling lines over starboard and port side. For a moment he thought maybe he should haul the lines back. He didn't want to slow the *Whither Thou;* she was making very good time now. The faster she sailed the more aware he became of the race. But it would take a whale to stop her, and he hadn't seen any of those creatures yet.

He roamed the deck, dragging the line to his safety harness behind him. He did nothing topside without snapping into the belt, his only connection if he should suddenly find himself overboard in those lumpy waves, watching the *Whither Thou* skitter away from him on the wind. So he wore the harness, but kept neglecting to secure the rope end to the metal eyes he'd fastened everywhere on the boat.

He wasn't usually a man to tempt fate. Nor someone given to mulling over childhood traumas. He considered himself a doer rather than a thinker—an active man, on and off the job. "Nobody special," he once said in a speech to his Rotary Club. "Believe me, I don't leap any tall buildings." No, he'd built them. Up and down the peninsula you could spot the crisp complexes erected by Marsh Engineering, Inc. Nothing bold, just solid strength—prestressed concrete, steel and glass. Virginia claimed she saw something of him in every building. She doubted even the next great earthquake could topple them. "Like you," she declared not long ago. "Here to stay."

Marsh unsnapped the belt and moved below. He lay back on his bunk, his hands laced behind his head. It was true, he'd reached fifty in better shape than most. He'd escaped the middle age afflictions of his friends—ulcers, booze, pot bellies, younger women, divorce, hemorrhoids, boredom, failure . . .

For a minute he closed his eyes, listening to the steady thunk of the boat moving faster. And from somewhere aft, a low creaking—that noise heard only at sea. This bunk like a cradle rocking. Too much solitude, Marsh thought. But he'd prepared himself, he'd read the library books. *A critical point of fear during a solo voyage often occurs near the point of no return (PNR). This is the moment beyond which it is easier to go on than turn back.* Today he'd reached that place and the trade winds were already sweeping him past it.

Yesterday when he made his radio-telephone call to Virginia, he mentioned this. "I could turn around now, sail right back." But she paid no attention. "Have you seen any whales?" she wanted to know. "Don't let them come up close to the boat. If they do, grab the camera. That'll get rid of them. Whales hate to have their pictures taken."

Marsh opened his eyes, looked down at his watch. Half an hour and it would be time for their daily talk. It occurred to him that he'd never loved Virginia so much as in these long days and nights on the *Whither Thou*. Nothing to do with the old notion about absence, the heart growing fonder. Out here he could simply think about Virginia without the presence of a third party—that cancer which had made them a triangle. Now it seemed he'd sailed all these miles for no reason except to love her again in the old way, without that other hand forever tapping at his shoulder trying to cut in.

Richard was wrong about this trip, he decided. He shifted onto his side, smelling the damp in his pillow, the sea salt in his coarse and unfamiliar beard. The movement of the boat lulled him. The cabin air turned warm and still around him. He heard the creaking as if it were music, faint scales on a cello drifting from another room. Outside this quiet the *Whither Thou* sped. And Marsh imagined himself closing the distance, racing past the point of no return toward his wife.

He dozed only a few minutes, then moved to the chart table and the radio-telephone. For once he had no trouble reaching the shore station at Point Reyes. As the marine operator dialed his home number, Marsh smiled at the row of instruments above his desk—radios, barometer, clock, chronometer, speedometer-log, depth sounder, wind indicator. All systems said Go, pointed to success. He'd tell Virginia, he might win this race yet. She'd get a kick out of that. Tell her, batten the hatches and full speed ahead.

But the shore operator broke onto the line saying no answer. Marsh glanced at the clock—only a little after ten in California, the hour he and Virginia had agreed on. Maybe she'd slept in this morning. But then, Richard's wife would've answered the phone. Alexandra knew he'd be calling.

"Maybe if you try later for messages," the marine operator put in, and Marsh realized he'd been thinking out loud, rattling off the possibilities within earshot of the crackly voiced stranger on the other end.

How many days have I been talking to myself, Marsh wondered. Just when did his thoughts turn into monologues? He had no idea he'd become that lonely. "I've been out here too long," he mumbled into the phone.

"Everybody's been out there too long," the operator replied, then signed off.

At 1100 hours Marsh called the shore station again. He drummed a pencil over squares on his plotting sheet as a dispatcher matter-of-factly reported, "We have traffic for the following vessels . . ."

Marsh often listened to this broadcast, the dispatcher reading down a traffic list, ticking off names of boats—names that reminded him of a day at the race track: Gilda's Choice, Home Free, Varuna . . .

"Able Leader, Whither Thou—"

Please call your home. Not much of a message, but Marsh tried the house once more without luck. Then slowly, carefully he peeled two oranges. He set them aside, unable to eat, to think. Finally he pushed from the chart table and climbed on deck. He'd give it till noon, then put the call in again.

He slipped into his safety harness, making sure now that the rope end was snapped to an eye on the side deck. He walked the length of his tether, forward, then aft. He leaned out over the life line—that cable strung high for protection—and the rails, too, holding him there, his knuckles white around the hand grips. The *Whither Thou* pulled on the beam wind, leaving its foamy trail. Spray beaded in his beard, sizzled over his toes. His baggy sweats whipped around his legs, clinging in the breeze. And Marsh clung, too, suddenly aware of the danger.

Virginia had made him aware. All along she'd done this for him. Twelve years, and at each event of her cancer he'd been alerted not only to her jeopardy, but his own. He gave up smoking, cocktails with lunch, fried eggs and bacon, late nights, refined sugar, and almost all starch. He started playing tennis again, sailed his sloop like a demon. He stopped following the stock market and hired a financial advisor. He swallowed a potent multi-vitamin every morning, poured lecithin on his cereal. And it had worked. Whatever Virginia lost, he salvaged. One night in bed he held her and told her that she'd saved his life. But she just smiled against his cheek and whispered with that wry, husky trace in her voice, "Behind every great man . . ."

So once again Marsh felt on guard. He repaired the chafed line on the mainsail, then hurried below and ran the engine just long enough to recharge the sloop's batteries. Except for this, the engine was illegal, and he didn't want to be disqualified from the race. In the closet-sized head he splashed fresh water over his face, then shaved for the first time in days. He noticed his hair had lightened a little from the southern sun and he'd begun to grow tan. For once he used the pump toilet rather than aiming a casual piss overboard. Then he pulled on a pair of crisp-pressed khaki shorts and stepped to his chart table.

Noon sharp, he reached for the radio-telephone. Somehow he felt less worried sitting there in his clean clothes, his hair carefully combed. As the marine operator dialed, Marsh's fingers moved with the numbers, forming circles, semicircles on the teak desk. He saw that his finger trembled now. And it was true. He'd never loved her more.

His daughter-in-law answered, her voice halting and faint. He heard her clearing her throat. "I have a cold," she said. "I hung around the hospital for hours, but they wouldn't let me in her room. This damned cold. Well, probably hay fever is all. I mean, it's July, Marsh. How long have you been gone?" Alexandra sounded confused, as if it had been years. "Yesterday we were in the pool. Mom swam three laps. Then this morning she—" Alexandra stopped. He heard her breath catch. "Where are you?" she said. "Oh God, Marsh, you better turn around."

He looked down at his desk, the place where those lines intersected on the plotting sheet. He stared at that spot as he spoke to his daughter-in-law, and again when he talked to Richard. "My position at 0500 hours . . ." But that had been dawn, a sight taken from three morning stars.

"She's comatose," Richard said.

For a moment Marsh could only shake his head at the receiver. Comatose. In his quick fear it seemed he'd forgotten words.

"A coma," Richard said. "She's sleeping with her eyes open. Dr. Greenberg calls it a coma vigil. He says she could come out of this any time. Or maybe never. Just no telling."

"I'll be there as fast as I can," Marsh said.

"Don't rush on her account," Richard answered. His voice broke then, turned high like a child on the verge of tears.

Marsh strained to make out his son's choked words. Finally he said, "Don't worry, Richard. Please."

"Sorry," Richard whispered. Then there was just a hum on the line.

Marsh sat kneading his clean-shaven chin. He shut his eyes, rested his forehead in the heel of his hand. He tried to think why he'd shaved. Whatever possessed him in the first place—coming out here, the middle of nowhere. Had he confused all these cockeyed efforts with her struggle, believing he could eventually make some difference? Now he felt only a weariness from these days alone. He'd hardly slept, refused to stay below, cook himself a proper meal. He and Virginia had stocked the galley with enough food to last for months.

"Go," she'd told him that night in the den. They sat surrounded by supplies, each item sealed in plastic to keep out the damp sea air. Bags of freeze-dried stew, dried apricots, powdered egg yolks and milk, a pound of trail mix. Fresh fruit and vegetables in a laundry basket. His clothes, plastic-wrapped. A first-aid kit containing everything from paregoric to a black cloth eye patch. She gave him a box of sanitary napkins called "Safe and Sure"—those soft white pads she no longer needed. "In case of a deep cut," she said. She swiveled in his leather chair, wearing his fluorescent orange life jacket. The jacket swamped her, billowed around her chest, her face. Teasing, she strung the black patch over one eye and grinned down at him on the carpet, on his hands and knees packing a carton with canned tuna, her marmalade, a jug of white wine. He would swear she'd never looked better, her hair shiny and cut straight like a boy's, cheekbones high with color that could've been health. The one mischievous eye, her rakish grin. "Go. By all means."

Marsh stood in the stern pulpit, steadying himself against the wind and the boat's roll. The sextant shook in his hand. The sun shimmied as he tried to haul it down to the far horizon of sea and sky. Below him a patch of sea suddenly swelled with color. Marsh watched a school of dorado glowing like rainbows, swing eastward. They broke the surface, so near it seemed they were sliding out from under his feet, forming a wide luminous shoal stretching back the way he'd come. And he had only to leap onto that color, ride it like a moving sidewalk, let it carry him home. Marsh pressed at the rail, gazing down at the bright path, watching till it grew ragged and disappeared. Then he crawled below.

Again he bent over his charts, figured his position. Thirteen hundred hours, six minutes, forty seconds. Twenty-seven degrees latitude . . . He reached for the radio-telephone.

He talked to Alexandra who gave him Dr. Greenberg's home number and a time to call the doctor that evening. Then he radioed the *Aikane,* the race committee's escort boat which he knew was sailing somewhere out here, probably close to the middle of the fleet.

"My position," he began. Then he explained about the trouble. "An illness in the family," he said. "I could divert."

"Divert where?" the man's voice demanded. "You're exactly where you're supposed to be, no way faster than the course you're on. So keep coming, buddy. Watch for squalls, though. You've got one sitting off your starboard bow. But you're doing great. Just keep coming."

Marsh grabbed another orange and hurried above. He felt better. He was on course, the man said. Doing great. He slipped on his safety harness and fastened the metal clamp near the cockpit. Then he sat at the wheel, not steering, but searching through his binoculars.

He couldn't see the escort boat. He didn't spot any boats at all. But the *Aikane* must've seen him. Exactly where you're supposed to be, the man told him. Just keep coming. It seemed the fellow was rooting the *Whither Thou* on, as though he understood something Marsh didn't. Marsh slid the binoculars back inside the case. That man not only knew where he was, but the positions of the others as well. For an instant Marsh was stirred by a secret excitement, a thrill he couldn't name because the larger part of him would not allow such an idea—that he might think of winning even now, at a time like this. That he could imagine island girls wreathing him in orchid leis, and later the awards dinner, a lavish luau where the trophies would be given. Place, win, or lose, Marsh thought. I will definitely miss the dinner.

Then he saw the squall—in a pure blue sky, clouds gathering like smoke from an explosion. Not more than a mile off starboard, just as the *Aikane* had said. And moving fast his way. Marsh dodged below, set his coffee cup in the galley sink where it wouldn't spill and shoved his charts into a drawer. He zipped up his windbreaker and hustled back on deck.

The sea was already turning choppy, the mainsail backwinded with each shifting gust. Marsh released the self-steering and took the wheel. Too late to run before this weather. He headed the sloop up into the wind, then set the self-steering gear and scrambled to lower the spinnaker. He hated hauling the big chute down. This squall would cost him time.

As the sky darkened overhead, the *Whither Thou* tossed harder, but not going anywhere. Marsh gazed across the churning waves, debating whether he should douse the mainsail as well. Then reluctantly he released the main halyard. As he moved to furl the sail he glanced up, seeing the halyard whipping slack around the mast, now catching—the line tangled on the radar reflector high above him. From below he pulled hard at the line, but it only snagged tighter. He jerked the halyard one way, then another. He kept yanking till his fingers throbbed from trying and he heard his breath turn ragged and grunting beneath the wind.

For a moment he rested, letting his arms drop to his sides. His fingers bloomed with blood blisters, pinpoints of red like little decorations. His hands looked strangely small to him—small as the hands of a dwarf. Even his legs felt shorter, weak and quivering as he started up the mast.

He fastened the end of his safety harness at the first step, then pulled himself higher. Halfway up the mast he paused, holding tight against a crashing blast of wind. The *Whither Thou* ducked her nose under a wave, then reared on her stern. And Marsh dipped and rose with her. The ocean climbed before him, dashing his face with spray. Now the sky reeled past, and the black clouds opened. Warm rain splattered him. He heard the cry of a gull, but no bird flew this far from shore. The sound came from him. He glanced down. His stomach turned. Far below him an orange rolled crazily in the cockpit. He should've eaten that orange, eaten something. All that time he'd been taking such good care of himself, arriving in excellent shape. Had he done it for this? The finish just ahead?

"My position," he whispered as he climbed higher. When he reached the radar reflector he grabbed the line with one hand and yanked. The halyard sprang free, simple as that. So simple that tears welled in his eyes.

Marsh clung there a minute. He gazed into the wind, then over his shoulder. He saw no escort boat, no shore. This can't possibly be the fastest course, he decided. How is it that a man can sail farther and farther from home and still get there in less time than it takes to return the way he's come? He'd kept his course west by southwest. West, the direction that had always been his true bearing. But the compass no longer pointed toward home. Marsh shook his head. Rain pelted him. The sweet, fresh water washed his salt tears, the salt sea.

As he descended, the wind slackened and the boat stopped thrashing. Marsh watched the storm cloud scudding across the sky like some lumbering black bear on a rampage. He glanced at his watch, surprised. The squall had lasted only twenty minutes.

The *Whither Thou* sailed into sunshine and the warm trades blew steady again. Marsh turned the sloop downwind. He felt better steering, as if it might make a difference—move the boat faster. But he could not sail swifter than this wind. The islands were still three, maybe four days away. Too far. He couldn't rush below and radio the airport—tell them, Hold the plane. Call the doctors, nurses, whisper in Virginia's sleeping ear, Hold everything.

You just can't face it, Richard had accused him that morning at home. Marsh slid lower in the cockpit, remembering his mother sighing about men, as if he himself would never grow up to be one. They're never around, she said, when you need them. Never at home unless they're miles away, never at peace unless they're at war.

Marsh moved to the rail, watching the sun dip lower on the horizon. "Hell," he mumbled after a minute. "I can face it."

Below him, the trolling line stretched taut, then jerked as a fish leapt from a wave. Marsh grabbed the line, relieved to feel the strong tug in his fingers. The fish ran a straight pull, just beneath the surface. Marsh saw that it was one of the dorado, fins glittering like fool's gold. The dorado turned and Marsh gained a little. Tired old fish. No telling how long it had been on the line, maybe since that school passed earlier. The dorado leapt once more, then veered, this time toward the sloop. Marsh reeled until he could see the leader wire and the dorado below him. He hauled the fish onto the deck, feeling weakened by this small exertion just as when he'd fumbled with the snagged halyard.

"Look who's calling who tired," he said to the fish.

Against the white decking the dorado appeared even more brilliant. It looked a good three feet, flapping there with its big blunt head, mouth working. Marsh had never caught such a fish, though he'd eaten it at the marina. He'd also read that dorado were known to bite. He stared at that gaping bulldog face, inched his big toe a little closer, testing. Then he bent nearer. He saw the bright colors of the fish beginning to fade. Slowly the shining blue and green disappeared, the golden fins paled. Marsh looked away, blinking to clear his vision. When he gazed down again the dorado had turned a solid gray. He touched the dull scales and felt instantly sick. He lurched to the rail, heaving on an empty stomach, nothing but a scalding clear spray.

And still the fish was turning, transformed by air from gray to silver-white. Turning like those time-lapsed nature films he'd watched as a kid—a whole life cycle witnessed in a minute. Marsh leaned over the dorado, rushing to cut the line. He lifted the big fish flapping and silver in his hands and dropped it over the rail.

"Not on my boat, you don't," he called.

He sank behind the wheel. At his feet, the orange rolled in the cockpit like garbage. It seemed he'd peeled a hundred oranges over these past days and eaten none. He was falling apart, he'd read too many library books. Yes, he'd read the words of those old Egyptians. *His life time used up, Went to hell in his own boat, Having no need for the ferry boat of the dead.*

But she had said Go. I'd truly like to know you can do it. And he'd gone willingly, all those years traveling the distance of her disease, losing track of months and days, of Richard—her illness becoming the safe and familiar course he'd taken toward his own survival. He'd left everything behind, yet failed to look down that road where illness leads. Not always to recovery, but to a dusky ocean horizon—the very curve of the Earth falling into twilight and an end called terminal.

It seemed his hand hadn't stopped shaking since he'd last used the sextant. With difficulty he found his stars—Altair, Vega, Fomalhaut. Then he moved below. He lit the kerosene wall lamp in the companionway and turned to his radio-telephone.

"My position," he said, reporting again to the *Aikane*. Then he called the shore operator and gave him Dr. Greenberg's number.

"There's been no change in her condition," Greenberg told him. "We're doing everything possible."

"Is she—" Marsh stopped, unable to ask. He looked down at his charts, saw his progress, lines moving through pale blue squares. The *Whither Thou* had made 175 miles today. That much farther from home.

"Dying? She might rally, Andrew. I can't say. But when it happens, this is probably how it will be."

Marsh shut his eyes, let his breath out slow. The rhythmic movement of the boat rocked in his mind, that creaking like a gate opening, closing. "Do I have time to get back there?"

"Just where are you?" Greenberg asked. But before Marsh could answer, the doctor said, "Yes, absolutely. You've got time."

After he hung up, Marsh sat trying to figure exactly how far to the islands. Granted, he wasn't much of a navigator on land or sea. The night Richard was born, he'd missed the freeway exit driving Virginia to the hospital. They'd gone as far as Candlestick Park before he realized. Later, Virginia gave him a Boy Scout compass. She'd held it due west. "The way home," she said.

Marsh told himself to eat something. He would need all his strength, take every advantage of the following seas. This was the night for that stew. But instead he found a box of crackers and climbed above to the cockpit. Evening fell around him as he sat munching one Triscuit after another. The crackers tasted like nothing to him, trivial but somehow better because of it. He didn't take the wheel, thinking he should nap before the long night's watch. *The single-handed sailor must try to sleep,* one of his books had stated. *Only a few minutes' sleep may save his life.*

Doctor Greenberg hadn't said, *If* it happens. For the first time in all their conversations, he'd told Marsh *When* it happens. "It will be like this," Marsh whispered, closing his eyes. Not if I die, but when I die before I wake. And in that hospital, up five floors and down the corridor—in that place he knew so well—not as a second home, but more like another job to which he'd commuted on a regular basis, a schedule maintained, hours kept in the Relatives' Lounge. There he'd seen all manner of family and friends come and go clutching gifts for the ones in the hushed, shade-drawn rooms along the hall. He'd noticed the brisk turnover in nurses, could never learn their names fast enough. He'd watched the jade tree in the corner grow. And God knows the jade will take its time. He'd been there that long—hadn't missed much in that place where Virginia lay sleeping with her eyes open. And yes absolutely, the doctor said. You've got time. "So wake up, Ginny," Marsh hollered. "Wake up!"

He jumped in the cockpit, startled by the sound of his own voice. He squinted out, trying to adjust to the darkening air, to the black ocean hissing by and the snap of sails he could barely distinguish. Then he blinked and let out a cry. Directly in front of him, just above the bow, a light shimmered and blazed so bright it stung his eyes.

"Watch out!" he shouted, forgetting all his sailor's words as he grabbed the wheel. He cranked hard to port side, hearing the spinnaker shudder and collapse, losing wind. But still that brilliance bore down on him from a height that could only be a steamer. He tried not to breathe, strained to hear the big churning turbines. He shielded his eyes, looking for the dark slamming wall of the hull coming closer, some faint lofty gleam from the bridge. He spun the wheel all the way to starboard. Again he shouted up, then threw on the broad spreader lights and the strobe flasher at the masthead. He clanged the bell which had seemed only a decoration. He ducked at the wheel, the loud beep of the off-course alarm dinning his ears. And still the light drew nearer—dead ahead. He glanced up, hollering, then dove through the companionway. He held himself stiff, jammed below, waiting for the booming jolt, the brute bow of the steamer, a splintering crash. But he felt only the roll of the wallowing sloop, heard nothing except that lunatic alarm sounding from the cockpit, and a man—who but him—chanting his wife's name over and over in the quickness of a panting, terrible breath.

Cautiously Marsh pulled himself up. His legs trembled as he climbed from the hatch, his teeth clattered. He crawled toward the cockpit and gripped the wheel. The alarm stopped. In the darkness he felt a sudden and immense silence. Nothing out there. Yet he couldn't bring himself to look. Nothing and nobody but him. Oh, he'd asked for this getaway. But it was one thing to choose to be alone, quite another when you'd been cast out. After all these years, it had come to this. In a room far away she lay sleeping with her cancer, her face turned to a white wall, turned from him.

"Ginny," he said, shaking his head. "Don't do this."

Then Marsh raised his eyes. Just beyond the bow he saw Venus shining low in the western sky, so bright and dazzling it seemed square in his path. He stared out thinking, My God. He'd been steering all over the ocean trying to avoid collision with a star.

He reached to switch off the powerful strobe flasher and the spreader lights above. The shakiness had left him except for a small tremor in his hands. He checked the sails, full of wind again, then returned to the cockpit.

Night deepened, the moon shed a vast gleam over the ocean as if each wave held a little light. Marsh could make out the most pale far-flung stars. He found Canopus, brightest in the constellation called The Ship. He spotted the Flying Fish, and Furnace, the River Eridanus. Before him, Venus blazed on, the evening star, a star for all men to steer by. All castaways, Marsh thought. Those who sail apart and adrift.

And then Marsh saw the Southern Cross shining over the horizon— a cluster of stars never glimpsed in the latitudes of home. That cross, a reason to rejoice for explorers of old, set their feet dancing to have ventured so far.

Marsh stood behind the wheel and gazed at the Southern Cross. He watched it into the early hours, thinking of the great distance he'd come, the journey still ahead. Toward dawn, he could still see the Cross, higher on the horizon. "A sight for sore eyes," he said to the dusky air. But even as he spoke his vision blurred. He leaned, groping for the sextant, then pushed straight to take a reading from this new and impossible sky.

2

Four nights later on a Thursday, Marsh flew home. The flight from Honolulu to San Francisco had been mobbed. Returning vacationers pushed toward the terminal gate. Marsh spotted his son standing back of the waiting crowd—some already waving, smiling.

But Richard was shaking his head. "You look awful," he said. He didn't seem to be complaining, only voicing his approval as if his father had finally done something right.

Marsh shifted his duffel bag to his other hand and frowned down past three leis hanging limp over his knit shirt, to wrinkled linen slacks, white deck shoes. He'd packed these clothes for the awards dinner in Hanalei Bay along with a brass-button blazer, now wadded inside his bag. But instead of the luau he'd scrambled from sea to airborne in less than forty-five minutes, stopping just long enough for a phone call to Dr. Greenberg. "I'll be there tonight," he'd told the doctor. "That will be fine," Greenberg had replied in such a pleasant tone they might've been arranging something simple, like an after-dinner drink.

As Richard turned with the crowd heading for Baggage Claim, Marsh caught his arm. "No luggage."

They moved through the south terminal, the duffel bag bumping at Marsh's legs. From the corner of his eye Marsh spotted a men's room. He could've used a stop there, but passed it by, feeling a greater urgency in this rush through the airport with Richard.

They crossed a corridor and hurried into an elevator going down. Somehow it seemed to Marsh that Richard had grown taller while he'd been away. Maybe it was only the sharp cut of the gray suit, the crisp blue shirt and tie. Ten-thirty at night and Richard looked ready to stride into a courtroom. A man on the job—on the scene. In my absence, Marsh thought. For an instant he felt like knocking at that hard shoulder. Are you the man of the house?

But he hadn't been gone that long. Marsh put a hand to his unshaven face, he could still smell the ocean in his fingers. It was only this afternoon—a dinghy sent from shore to meet him. Not the throng of island maidens he'd imagined, but a lone blonde woman from the race committee rowing steadily toward him. Too exhausted to wave or holler a greeting, he'd watched from the sloop's rail as the woman drew closer, then alongside. As he stepped off the *Whither Thou* into the rocking dinghy, the woman cupped a hand at his elbow, steadying him. She scooped up orchid leis, shook them into bright rings. Dry-mouthed and speechless, he bent to receive them. "You've made a fine crossing," the woman said.

But it seemed no crossing, only this race never ending—through the parking lot, car doors slamming, tires squealing onto the freeway. And Richard in the driver's seat, whisking him without a word in the wrong direction, farther still. He wanted to blurt, Home's back there. Turn around! But instead he kept quiet. He stared out the dark passenger window, clutching the duffel bag tight on his lap like a stranger traveling through some troubled foreign country.

Richard sighed, slowed automatically for an exit up ahead. As they left the freeway and braked at a four-way stop, he muttered, "You haven't even asked about her." He looked at Marsh, then at his watch, as if he'd been timing his father's silence. "Go ahead, ask. I'm the one who can tell you—*I've* been here."

Marsh looked away. He gazed across the intersection to high-rising hospital lights on the hillside. He thought of her there, so close after all the distance—those last days and nights on the *Whither Thou* without a single conversation, just an occasional voice crackling over miles, reports that seemed less real to him from out there, his position. He cleared his throat, feeling the fear suddenly heavy in his chest, heavy as the flowers bunched around his neck, the air sick with their sweetness, his shirt clammy from their dew.

Richard shut off the ignition, threw the keys on the dashboard. "Ask me, dammit!"

Across the intersection a car approached, then paused at the opposite stop sign, waiting. Beyond it the hospital rose banded in light. Marsh counted five floors up.

"Richard . . ." he began, but that seemed all he could say.

Cautiously the other car moved into the intersection, then past them. Marsh looked over at his son who'd become so like a father, stern and glowering, still waiting. But from what harsh parent had Richard learned these lessons? And how could a man be expected to speak, when she might die even as he sat struggling to form the words in a car stalled not more than six blocks away.

Marsh flung open the Volvo's door. He pushed from the car, rushing through the unyielding headlights and the sudden blare of the horn demanding, Ask me.

For days this had been his only question. From every latitude, How is she? Afraid to ask, he had asked. He broke into a run, his sea legs surprised, stiff and ramming too hard on the pavement. He swerved onto a sidewalk, past dark houses. The orchids bounced, rustled along his neck, turned cool in the night air. He lurched back into the open street, dodging a lawn sprinkler's fanning splat. And here the Volvo screeched around him and stopped.

Marsh stood in the street, leaning for breath, his hands braced on his knees. He glanced from the car to the hospital entrance—the word Mercy glowing in white neon just ahead. For an instant it seemed he could still escape all of this, backtrack across a hundred front yards and down the hill to breaking coral reefs and a safe anchorage in a deep sandy bottom. Because there would be no mercy on this shore. Then Richard rolled down the window, called him. Marsh tucked in his shirt and trudged to the car.

They drove in silence under the arching neon sign, past the broad steps leading to the hospital entry. At the rear of the building Richard pulled beside the big double doors marked Emergency.

"Room 501," Richard said. He nodded at Marsh. "I'll be along as soon as I park."

Marsh felt for the door handle, then hesitated. He glanced down, unable to look at Richard. "How is she?"

"Go on," Richard said.

Marsh lingered on the curb a moment, then turned and walked into the brightly lit lobby of Emergency. Before he moved into the elevator he looked back, watching for Richard. Then he pushed the button for Up. Never mind, he told himself as the numbers blinked overhead. He didn't need his son to lead him by the hand. A hundred times and more than a hundred—mornings, afternoons, evenings, he'd done this by himself. So here he was again. Another time. Virginia.

He stepped off the elevator onto the fifth floor and walked down one corridor, then another. This enormous east wing—all of it—Oncology. Over the years he'd watched the ward expand, occupying more rooms, spreading through the wing like the disease for which it was named.

And as always here, Marsh smelled popcorn. On this ward only—someone, somewhere seemed to be continually popping corn. He'd heard they ate it in the Doctors' Lounge, the Nurses' Lounge. Behind closed doors—bushels of it. At all hours. The staff changed, patients came and went, but the aroma of popcorn remained like a tradition—the trademark of oncology. Not that visitors ever glimpsed so much as a kernel. But nobody cared. At least there wasn't any smell of sickness here. Marsh had seen patients brought up from surgery, still half asleep on their gurneys. Along this hallway you could watch them open their groggy eyes, hear their first whispered word: *popcorn*. Why, even Virginia—

"Can I help you?" a nurse asked, looking up from the formica counter of the ward station.

Marsh glanced over, not about to stop. But the young woman leaned out, waving him down. As he stepped to the counter, she smiled at the leis. "Which island were you on?"

"Please," he said. He frowned past the nurse to the panel of video screens endlessly monitoring patients—lines rising, descending, like distant and mysterious mountain ranges. "I have family in 501. My wife—"

The young woman slid a clipboard onto the counter, flipped pages.

"Andrew Marsh," he said, hurrying off. "Husband of Virginia."

Halfway down the corridor he found her room. The door was wide open, inside a ceiling light blazed. He stood at the doorway, suddenly unable to just walk in. Across the large private room Virginia lay on her side, her back toward him so all he saw was a shock of her cropped dark hair, one arm crooked over the white sheet, tubes running from her wrist.

In that bed her body scarcely made a difference, the sheet undisturbed. Beside the bed his daughter-in-law sat in a straight chair, her face upturned, watching a late show on the wall-mounted TV. In her lap she held the television remote control. She wore a blue paper mask over her nose and mouth. A TV headset flattened her hair, covered her ears. Marsh frowned at the quiet, the room mute as the television, his wife lying insignificant surrounded by machines and long-stemmed roses, two house plants. And Alexandra sitting there like some solemn pilot flying a dangerous mission.

Marsh stepped through the doorway and cleared his throat. His noise frightened him, the terrible brightness of the room. "I'm here," he said, but no one heard. Virginia slept on, his daughter-in-law remained fastened to the controls. High in the corner a man looked out from the TV and smiled, then spoke without a sound.

"It's me," Marsh whispered.

He waited, running a hand through his sea-tangled hair, touching the leis on his chest. Then he rushed. As he strode toward the bed Alexandra glanced up, her eyes astonished above the mask. She pulled off the headset. Marsh paid no attention to her hand stretching out to him, his name. He bent over Virginia, her blue eyes also wide but not for the long-awaited sight of him—not for anything. He kissed her face, bumping a plastic tube strung from her nostril. His orchids brushed her chin. He felt the softness of her cheek and the crescent bone beneath grown sharper, almost a sliver along his lips. The flowers trailed across her mouth. "Wake up, Ginny." Petals swept past her eyes. He kissed her forehead, her pale lips. And this is how the story goes . . . For a hundred years she lies sleeping on a bed of flowers. Until she is awakened by a kiss.

Marsh lifted the leis and placed them at the foot of her bed.

"They're beautiful," Alexandra said, stepping beside him. It seemed she'd grown taller, too, standing with her arm settled strong and solid along his back.

Marsh nodded, gazing down at Virginia. This is how the story goes. She awakens. But who believes in fairy tales forgotten for years, then returned to memory out there on a long night's watch—a yarn retrieved as if from the sea itself. Alone out there—away from it all—a man might believe anything. He could imagine his wife still lovely. Sick, yes, but lovely. Imagine her sick and asleep, waiting only for him. Now, seeing her here, just a slip of a woman lost inside a blue hospital gown, and a bruise already old, yellowing on her wrist from the needle feeding her vein, these orchids wilting at her feet—now who would believe?

"Once in a while you'll see her move," Alexandra said, tightening her grip on his shoulder. "It seems like something, but it isn't. Just involuntary."

Marsh bent over his wife, watching for that movement which meant nothing. Then he heard Richard entering the room and stood straight. Richard moved beside him, dropped the duffel bag at his feet. "I thought you might want your things."

"Yes," Marsh said, trying to recall what could be inside that bag other than his blue blazer.

Richard crossed the linoleum floor and opened a door opposite. "Private bath." He gestured around the room. "Closet there. The day bed's made up. You'll find a blanket in that dresser, bottom drawer."

Marsh listened, following his son's hand waving here and there. In this room Richard appeared the only person able to speak in a normal voice.

"It's a pain having both cars here," he was saying now.

Alexandra shrugged. "We could leave the Volvo for Marsh. He might need it."

Marsh turned back to the bed. He looked at his wife lying silently on her side. She seemed such a minor presence here, like a child curled in a corner where adults sit talking. He shook his head at her. A thousand rooms and more conversations than he could remember, it had always been Virginia in the middle of everything. And if not Virginia, then her sickness at the center, relieving him of everything else. And so Marsh waited now—waited for Ginny to sit up and tell this son of theirs that they didn't want his damned Volvo.

But Richard was already sliding the car keys onto the dresser. "Fine," he said, sounding like he didn't mean it.

"If you think of anything you need, call us," Alexandra said, her voice muffled behind the mask. For a moment her arm was around him again. Then she stepped away with Richard.

Marsh followed them into the corridor and almost smiled as Alexandra ripped the paper mask from her face.

"Thank God," she said, crumpling the paper in her fist. "Still, it's the only way they'll let me see her. Not that I've got much of a cold left. But Dr. Greenberg says Mom's very susceptible. He says—" Alexandra frowned off, her face flushed from the mask. She pulled a Kleenex from her jeans pocket and touched it to her nose, then her eyes.

"He says a cold could kill her." Richard nodded at Marsh as he spoke, his gaze steady with anger.

Alexandra rested her hand on her husband's arm. "Richard, please," she said softly.

Marsh watched her, how she turned to Richard, her face quiet against his shoulder, her hand stroking. What would a man do without a wife, he wondered. Whatever in the world would he do.

"So," Alexandra said, suddenly brightening, looking around at him. "I'll be back in the morning. Dr. Greenberg usually stops by before ten." She dug into her pocket and handed him a folded page of stationery. "I've kept track of everybody who's phoned or sent cards, flowers. Marjorie Eberline, the Hanvilles, Julia Oakes . . ." She paused, squinting to recall, then waved a hand. "And dot-da-dot-da-dah," she said, as if that completed her list. "Oh, and somebody asking for you—here in the hospital. Norman Vickers. Says you'll remember him from last time. He's awfully sick, Marsh. He—"

"Talk about it tomorrow," Richard said. He looked at Marsh. "Call if anything happens—*anything*." He started down the corridor, then stopped, waiting for Alexandra.

Marsh glanced over at her, waiting, too. She stood fidgeting, screwing her mouth. Her nose looked raw from her cold and Kleenex. He saw the tiredness in her eyes, shadows ringing them. "Don't worry, Alex," he said. "Go home and get some rest."

For a moment she gazed down the hall where Richard lingered. Then she turned to Marsh, tucking a strand of long brown hair behind her ear.

"Who won?"

Marsh stared at her.

"You know—Hawaii. The race."

"Oh, the race." He frowned at his deck shoes, then shrugged. "Everybody has to cross the finish line before the committee can post the results." He tried to think back. Had he crossed the line? "I don't know," he mumbled. "They need to look at the times. There's actual time and adjusted time. They make allowances."

"Good," Alexandra said. She clapped him on the shoulder like an old pal, then she was off, dashing after Richard.

When they'd disappeared around the far turn of the hallway, Marsh moved back inside Virginia's room. From the corner of his eye he saw the wall TV still silently blazing color. But it could wait. He glanced over at Virginia, then hurried into the bathroom.

Ever since he'd left the *Whither Thou* he'd felt the constant need to urinate. Not a simple urge, but a pressure he could barely hold. On the flight from Honolulu he'd beaten a path between his seat and the cubbyhole restroom. But then, as now, when he finally relieved himself— almost nothing. What he felt to be gallons about to burst was no more than a trickle running down the side of the toilet bowl from his tired, limp penis. Nerves, Marsh decided, zipping his linen slacks. Or maybe an infection, some bug picked up at sea.

"Least of my worries," he said as he turned to the sink. Then his breath caught and he slammed his hand to his mouth. He leaned nearer the mirror above the sink and stared at the startling shambles of his face. His eyes were swollen as if he'd been crying for days. Marsh drew his hand away. Out there—yes, he had cried a little. Or some. He'd cried some. His lips were swollen, too, cracked from the salt air, the sun. His bearded face didn't look tan anymore, only dirty. He touched the dark places under his cheekbones—not smudges, but hollows. He nodded at the mirror. Down to skin and bones. But he'd eaten the oranges. He'd eaten some.

Marsh stumbled from the bathroom. Richard was right—he looked awful. He turned off the TV, then scooted a chair beside Virginia's bed. He reached between the metal bars of the side rail and touched her shallow cheek. Sitting here it seemed he and Virginia had truly grown old together—but in a matter of days. Such a short race to the finish line.

At this moment they were gathering on the island, boats anchored safe in harbor, all the bright dinghies beached on the sand. Marsh slipped his arm beneath Virginia's head. "There's a committee," he said. Around a table members were meeting with pencils, paper, stopwatches. They sat tallying results, deciding the winners, losers. They were making allowances. March cupped his hand at Virginia's temple. He sat very still, his finger resting there until—yes, now he felt the fragile pulse. He cleared his throat. "You see, this committee can adjust the time."

He fell silent then, listening to the rhythmic sigh of the respirator breathing in and out, breathing for her. It seemed he listened for hours with the ceiling light still burning harsh above them, his arm growing numb beneath her head, the pressure in his bladder building, painful as a cramp. He believed he should be doing something for her now that he was here. But he couldn't think what. After all his panic, the alarming rush, just to sit with his legs crossed . . . So he was glad when a nurse poked her head around the doorway, then stepped inside.

She walked briskly to the bed, bending across from him. "You must be Mr. Marsh," she said. She tucked the sheets tighter under the mattress. "It's time to turn your wife. If we leave her in one position, she'll develop bed sores." She glanced over. "You'll need to move your arm."

Marsh nodded, trying to work his wrist out from under Virginia's head. He stared at his fingers paralyzed in her hair. "I think my arm's asleep."

The nurse came around to where he sat. She clucked her tongue as she massaged his bicep. "I've heard of giving your right arm, but this is ridiculous."

Marsh flexed his tingling fingers. "I'll turn her," he said.

"Next time," the nurse said. She slid a hand beneath Virginia's shoulder and eased her onto her back. Then she took a small bottle from the bedside cart and squeezed the rubber dropper over Virginia's eyes, first one, then the other. For an instant those blue eyes shone, welling as if with tears. She blinked.

"Did you see that?" Marsh glanced to the nurse, jiggled Virginia's hand. "Look—she did it again."

The nurse smoothed the cotton gown over Virginia's legs, then drew the top sheet around her waist and her flat chest sprouting only the yellow wires monitoring her heart.

"Sometimes they blink," the nurse said. "Sometimes they don't. So it's best to irrigate. Next time you can do it." She paused at the foot of the bed, fingering the orchid leis. "Your friend Mr. Vickers is here again. He told me you were coming from the islands." After a minute the nurse stepped away. "I suggest you get some sleep. Or a hot meal. The cafeteria's on the main floor."

Slowly Marsh took his gaze from Virginia. "I know where it is." He moved to switch off the overhead light, then followed the nurse to the door. "I was on Kauai," he said, lingering in the dim glow from the corridor. "Just briefly."

Before he returned to Virginia's bed he dashed into the bathroom and a minute later stepped out shaking his head. I am a sick man, he thought. He sat down then, peering over the side rail to make out Virginia's face. Except for the soft light from the hallway, the room was dark.

He felt his way, slipping his arm under her head again. Her face fell toward him. Her cheek rested in the crook of his elbow. Marsh nodded. "They're still eating popcorn up here. That nurse just now—I think I spotted some between her teeth." He smiled. "Either that or she's been spitting tobacco."

In the darkness he patted Virginia's shoulder. His fingers buzzed, growing numb. "You probably don't remember when I chewed tobacco. First year in Rotary—summer league slow pitch. Don't know why I chewed it. Just for the guys, I guess. Just the game."

For a while he was quiet. He gazed around the room, uneasy with the silence. Finally he began to hum. He sang soft snatches under his breath.

> *R-O-T-A-R-Y on land and on the sea.*
> *From north to south, from east to west,*
> *He profits most who serves the best.*

"Now there's a song I never sang you," he said. Then he frowned, thinking how ridiculous—that scrap of nothing. But it occurred to him at a time like this he should be telling Virginia those things she hadn't known.

Marsh sighed with the respirator, wondering where to start. He searched his mind for secrets until it seemed he was the one in need of absolution, this unburdening his dying confession. But the harder he tried to uncover whatever he'd concealed, the worse he felt. His secrets were trivial, his sins minor—she would've said dull. He had no great crimes to dredge up, not one forbidden night, no other woman. For a moment it seemed Virginia's sickness hadn't just kept him out of trouble. It had kept him from life. Except for her, he was a man without a past.

Finally he glanced over. "Forgive me," he said.

But she had told him there would be other women. She'd said, "Just wait. After I'm gone you'll be surprised." He'd touched a finger to her lips. "Hush up. You're not going anywhere." Then he'd look away, keeping his voice casual. "What women?" She shrugged. "My friends—

ours—some we've known for years. You have no idea." She cocked her head, her eyes full of mischief. "I could make you a bet, write their names and seal them in an envelope . . ." She nodded at him, grinning it seemed with triumph, as if she was relishing the idea that she might win even after death, still keeping her hand in. "Of course I wouldn't do that," she added quickly. She'd giggled, then laughed full out, unable to stop herself. "Oh Marsh, my poor man. Are you in for a shock."

Now he slumped in the straight chair, thinking what a terrible tease—this Virginia, this girl. Even in her sleep she leads me on. She refuses to close her eyes. She blinks and my heart jumps. What a tease, Virginia. You lie with all the secrets. And I've sailed an ocean. I have given my right arm.

He dozed then, his head slack and lolling into his chest, mouth open, his breath a whistle in the quiet. Toward dawn he was awakened by his bladder, a pain worse than ever. He squinted across the room, for a moment unsure of where he was. It seemed he might still be on the *Whither Thou,* crammed in the cockpit watching day begin, the dusky light rising like mist from the sea. Then he heard the respirator. He saw the dark Druid shapes of those machines standing upright and vigilant around her bed.

Marsh shifted in his chair, unable to budge his arm. From his shoulder down he felt nothing at all, not even the small weight of her head at his elbow. He would wait for the nurse. Someone was bound to come along soon. Then he would turn his wife. He'd irrigate her eyes. Marsh tried to think what else—what more would this day bring. Where to start, he wondered. In the quiet he sat waiting and wondering. He watched the gray light lifting, revealing her face. He leaned closer. With his free hand he clutched the rail. "To tell you the whole truth," he whispered. "I have never liked Rotary."

3

In the hospital cafeteria Marsh wolfed three cinnamon rolls, sticky with frosting and still warm. Over the years he'd managed to resist this breakfast special. But his sense of emergency had turned him reckless. In the midst of his fear, he felt somehow charmed. He drank a fourth cup of coffee, ignoring the pressure in his bladder. Then he wrapped another cinnamon roll in a napkin and headed for the elevators.

Earlier, he'd stopped at the ward station and asked Norm Vickers' room number. He considered dropping by there now, but as he started up the corridor he spotted Dr. Greenberg stepping from Virginia's room. Richard and Alex had also arrived, trailing the doctor into the hallway. Their little huddle was a familiar sight, a private conversation carried outside. Although it struck Marsh as peculiar that sooner or later things should be aired like this—the worst brought to light, every secret revealed in a hallway—in public.

"Where's your boat?" Dr. Greenberg glanced over Marsh's shoulder as if expecting to see the sloop dry-docked on the fifth floor.

"I left it," Marsh said, glad he'd had the sense to hire a delivery skipper even before this trouble. He'd never planned to leave Virginia any longer than the actual race. At least he could say that much for himself. He ran a hand through his uncombed hair, then down his whiskery cheek. It seemed his hair had also turned excessive with this emergency, on some kind of spree over his body. He wished he'd shaved, brushed his teeth. But his duffel bag contained nothing except his blue blazer.

"I left everything," he mumbled.

Richard nodded at Alex, speaking in a tone he might've used for his secretary. "Make a list and see that he gets whatever he needs."

Alex looked up, her eyes narrowing, mouth clamped. For just an instant Marsh felt some other danger hovering. But in the next second it was gone, passing them by.

Greenberg hadn't stopped smiling, his gaze on Marsh. "One of these days we'll have to sit down so you can give me some pointers on sailing." The doctor chuckled. "Far as I know, mizzen is just another word for lost."

Marsh tried to smile, his mouth so dry his lips felt hooked to his teeth. He'd known the doctor since Virginia's first surgery, strictly on a medical basis. But as often happened with these isolated meetings, Greenberg had become what Marsh called, "something like a friend." Greenberg was also the best, so confident in his field he could joke about his ignorance in another. It seemed a kind of tip-off—some man-to-man signal meant to inspire trust rather than doubt.

And sure enough, Greenberg was already drawing a folded paper from the pocket of his starched white medical coat. "We call this a no-code order." The doctor spread the paper open for Marsh. "Richard and I have gone over it, but your signature's required. Your son couldn't sign."

"Besides which I wouldn't," Richard snapped. His eyes darted around the hallway and he was chewing gum, something he rarely did.

Marsh watched him sliding the gum from one side of his mouth to the other, flattening it with his tongue. What's come over us, Marsh wondered. He felt the doughy weight of the cinnamon rolls he'd bolted down, the extra one still hoarded in his hand. He had an urge to stuff it into his mouth as he studied the paper.

I, _____, the undersigned, do request that no effort or procedure be implemented which would artificially sustain the life of . . .

Dr. Greenberg glanced to the open door of Virginia's room. "She'd want you to have a choice. I know her. Unless we have an order from you, we'll try to keep her alive in any state. If she goes into cardiac arrest we'll be in that room with the crash cart and Thumper before you can blink."

Marsh read from the top again where it said (Please type or print).

"We're not fighting the disease anymore," Dr. Greenberg said. "From now on it's pure mechanics."

Marsh fumbled for his jacket pocket and slipped the paper inside. Against the blue blazer, his fingers—a shine of knuckles and sea-weathered skin—appeared to belong to somebody much older. His tremor felt elderly. His thoughts, feeble. He touched his pocket—how could he be expected to decide? A man in his condition, hardly sound in his own mind and body. No one should hold him responsible. Wasn't there something called diminished capacity?

He looked over at Greenberg. "Could I speak to you privately?" He turned to Richard. "I'd just like a minute alone."

"Of course," Alex said.

The doctor turned Marsh away, then leaned back to Alex and Richard. "I hope both of you will think this over. You'll feel better if it's a family decision."

Richard glanced at Marsh and shook his head. "I want no part of this."

The doctor steered Marsh up the corridor and around a corner into the empty Relatives' Lounge. He motioned to a blue vinyl sofa, then eased his lanky frame down beside Marsh. He crossed his arms.

"Listen Andrew, I know this is rough."

Marsh gazed around the narrow room. Nothing much had changed since his last time here. Except somebody'd replanted the jade tree. Its leaves had spread wider, filling the corner. Marsh brushed at his wrinkled jacket. He folded his hands, then opened him. "Probably nothing," he said so quietly that Greenberg leaned closer. "At a time like this—"

"Go ahead," Greenberg said. "I need to know how you feel."

"Well, it's about my bladder," Marsh said. He settled back against the sofa, relieved to be sitting here voicing such a minor problem. Just for a minute—something small. "I think maybe I've picked up some kind of infection. Nothing serious, but every ten minutes I feel like I have to go. Then when I do . . . Pssst—that's all it amounts to."

The doctor cocked his dimpled chin and stared.

"When I was on the race, no trouble whatsoever." Marsh shrugged. "I mean, you've got the whole ocean whenever you feel like it."

Greenberg sighed, as if resigned another time to these random problems broached wherever he went—a doctor in the house. "Could be anxiety," he said. "But it sounds more like a breakdown in conditioning. Make a habit of urinating at the slightest urge and that's what happens. Your bladder gets lazy."

The doctor stood, his hand at Marsh's back as they moved to the doorway. "Of course urology isn't my specialty, but I'd say you've lost a little control. Try holding yourself as long as possible. And you might want to see somebody. Who's your doctor?"

As they walked along the corridor, Marsh tried to think who. But office visits, hospitals, prescriptions, X rays, lab tests—all of medicine seemed Virginia's territory, like a club only she belonged to.

For a moment Greenberg lingered outside her room, then he started to move on.

Marsh caught his sleeve. "You're my doctor."

"Then as your physician," Greenberg said quietly, "I advise you to give some thought to that no-code order. And soon."

But Marsh couldn't put his mind to it, not with Richard and Alex in Virginia's room. They sat at either side of her bed, Richard bent over an open briefcase on his lap, Alex sorting through index cards in a box labeled Native Wildlife Research.

"I think Mom looks better today," Alex said, studying a card.

Marsh moved to the foot of her bed, his orchid leis already browning at the edges. Virginia had lain here nearly a week, and in that time Richard and Alex appeared to have established a routine for themselves, tending to business as usual. Life goes on, Marsh thought. He gazed at his wife for whom everything had stopped—but not absolutely. In those sheets it seemed she existed like the monotonous static snow on a television screen after the picture had vanished.

But no matter. Marsh thought his daughter-in-law might be right. He smoothed Virginia's stubborn cowlick, then turned away. As he headed for the door Richard glanced up.

"Don't sign that form. If anything happens to her—"

Marsh wheeled around. He wanted to say, Something *has* happened! Instead he started for the door again, feeling suddenly dazed. "She looks better," he said.

In the corridor he drew the paper from his pocket. . . . *and do hereby assume full responsibility*. He walked past the Doctors' Lounge, the aroma of buttered popcorn like the lobby of a movie theater. Nobody'd handed him such a paper when his father was in the hospital. No form for his mother, three years later. His parents had left the world without anyone's consent, nobody's signature.

When he reached Norman Vickers' room, he stopped. He stuffed the form into his pocket and stepped inside.

"Hi, Norm," he said loudly, not sure whether the big black man was dozing over the book on his lap or simply engrossed in it.

Vickers' head came up slow. His hair curled like smoke against the pillows. He gazed at Marsh through heavy eyes, his mouth parted for air, his dark skin slick with sweat. He looked much worse. But then, Marsh could only compare with the last time he'd seen Vickers here. Norm's hospital stays never went unnoticed. Part of it was his size. And always a jumble of balloons bumping the ceiling above his bed—balloons Vickers sent to himself, making nurses and doctors smile whenever they walked into his room.

Along with Dr. Greenberg, Marsh considered Norm Vickers something like a friend. Vickers was also the only black man Marsh could count among his acquaintances, though he had the vague impression of knowing many more. He'd first met Vickers in the waiting room of Dr. Greenberg's office. He'd driven Ginny for a checkup and while she was with the doctor, he and Vickers started talking, passing time. Marsh felt an instant connection. He and Norm shared a common interest—cancer. The next time Virginia entered the hospital, Marsh ran into Norm again. Ginny lost her pituitary gland and Norm gave up a lung. But it appeared now that the big man had suffered even greater losses.

Norm tilted his head against the pillows and stared at Marsh through his smoker's squint. He fumbled at his throat, pressing a finger over the open end of a tracheal tube. For a moment his lips moved without sound. Then his deep voice wheezed. "Please . . . Sit."

Marsh pulled a chair closer to Norm's bed. He leaned forward resting his arms across his knees, his hands folded between them. After a moment he said, "Virginia's in again. I guess you knew."

Vickers nodded, shutting off the hole in his throat. "Can't keep us away." His words faded in and out, leaving gaps like a phonograph needle skipping over a record.

Marsh gazed down at the floor. "I think she's dying, Norm." There— he'd said it. His eyes welled, blurring the green linoleum.

"Virginia, too," Norm whispered. He sat a little straighter, looking almost pleased, as if he'd just bumped into somebody going his way and was glad for the company. He nodded up at his balloons. "I am not here for my health."

"That's no way to talk," Marsh said. But he felt oddly relieved. There was something about the sight of Norm sitting in bed with his hospital gown untied at the neck, the blue cotton loose and falling over one flabby sweat-glistening shoulder—something about illness, even in a large man like Vickers, that struck Marsh as feminine, almost seductive. He guessed Virginia was the reason, her strong female presence overpowering even sickness. But this business of dying was different. More like man's work. It seemed men died for real reasons.

Marsh nodded toward the door, recalling the short pleasant woman who'd popped in and out of here the last time. "Where's your wife?"

"Divorced," Norm said, as if it were some geographical location.

For a minute they fell quiet, the only noise the suck of the tracheal tube. It was a sound so ragged and webby, Marsh caught himself inhaling deeply, afraid for his own breath. Finally he said, "What about your father? Somebody must've told him you're sick."

"Dying," Vickers corrected. He let his book fall closed, its pages dog-eared and loose without a cover. Then he smiled. "My father taught me to set a table. Properly," he added.

"Your father's a fine person," Marsh said, though he didn't really know the man. He'd seen Norm's father only once, a springy little man perched like a bird on the edge of the hospital bed. But it was clear that Norm felt a surprising, almost unnatural affection for his father. He'd followed his father into the refrigeration business. Marsh couldn't imagine Richard following him anywhere. But Norm loved both his father and his father's work. "Refrigeration has been good to us," he'd once told Marsh. And Marsh thought it must be so, judging from this sunny private room.

"My father was always a gentleman." Vickers closed his eyes, speaking as if he was already reminiscing from some far remove. "And a man of the true West. He was that, too. But this . . ." Norm roused himself on the pillows, tapped his chest. "This time it would kill him, he mustn't come. But if you could see him, go see him. Tell him that I remember everything . . ."

Norm let his head fall back. Sweat ran from his dark shining face. His mouth worked for air. Marsh looked away, reminded of the fish gaping and flapping on the blazing deck of the *Whither Thou.*

"Tell him it has been a pleasure. Tell him . . ."

"I should leave," Marsh said. "You need rest. Virginia—"

"A moment," Vickers gasped, raising one finger like a sales clerk temporarily busy with somebody else.

Marsh leaned back. He crossed his legs, uncrossed them. After a while he said, "If it's all right, I'll just use your bathroom." Without waiting for an answer, he dashed from the bed.

As usual, his rush hardly seemed worth it. Marsh looked down at himself, the crumpled remains of his penis. He turned to the sink and washed his hands, then splashed his face. On the stainless steel shelf above the toilet, Norm's shaving kit lay zipped closed, a black leather pouch bearing a gold monogram. Marsh touched his stubble of beard, then opened the bathroom door a crack.

"Norm," he said softly. But he heard only the drone of Vickers' snore.

Marsh closed the door and locked it. He shaved, then doused his face with Norm's cologne. At the bottom of the leather kit he found Norm's toothbrush. He uncapped the toothpaste, then glanced to the mirror. He thought of the man lying in the bed outside. He gazed into the mirror thinking also of his mother—a woman shaking her finger at him throughout his childhood, her voice ordering, Don't touch, you can never tell where that thing has been. You could catch something.

"Yes," Marsh said to the mirror.

He brushed hard, aware only of Virginia now, and glad for the sharp peppermint taste, the foam filling his mouth and throat, gagging him close to tears, close to death. Go, she'd said. I'd like to know you can do it. And he would go gladly, anywhere at all. Just to be in proximity.

Norm was awake again when he stepped from the bathroom. The big man sat with his fingers hooked between the flimsy pages of the book as if holding his place. He nodded at Marsh, then struggled up on his elbows.

"In there," he said, pointing toward the nightstand beside his bed.

Marsh moved to the metal stand. There seemed something peculiar about Vickers' gaze, his tone of voice. Drugs, maybe. They were probably keeping him doped up day and night. Marsh slid open the stand's shallow drawer—Norm's wallet, one white business card, a pair of gold-plated dog tags.

Norm strained for the white card. "My father's address. If you would be so kind . . ."

"Yes," Marsh said. He slipped the card into his blazer pocket, feeling the no-code order folded there. For a minute he gazed across the room, the afternoon sunlight falling through open venetian blinds, his hand warm in his pocket, fingers groping along the form. He cleared his throat, turned back to Norm.

"I'll come by again tonight. And tomorrow. Just like last time."

"And this," Norm mumbled. He nudged his book toward Marsh. "You'll need this."

"Of course," Marsh said, just to be kind, if he would be so kind. He straightened the brittle, yellowed pages. *A Frontier Companion,* the title read. And in smaller letters: *The Way West.*

Marsh slipped the little book under his arm, then leaned over Norm's bed. He grasped Norm's big hand. He squeezed those long black fingers—so black yet all the combinations of blue—beneath the wide nails, pale violet moons. He pressed that extraordinary hand and felt nothing in return.

Vickers smiled, his head drooping into his chest. "And tell my father . . ."

Marsh turned away then, leaving on tiptoe. But at the door he heard Vickers speaking again. Marsh swung around and saw Norm squinting across the room, his words a whisper growing stronger—then his voice practically booming, big as the man himself. "Tell him I have seen the moon strike the Great Divide!"

Marsh jerked straight. He glanced to the corridor, worried Norm's outburst might bring a nurse running, a doctor. Any minute the whole hospital. And sure enough, he spotted a cart suddenly rolling his way, heard it clattering closer. He stepped into the hallway, about to speak to the two orderlies wheeling the cart at a canter—those two men a rush of white paying no attention, rubber soles squeaking up the corridor. The cart rumbling past him, all jiggling machinery—black hoses and stainless steel, one red light like an eye winking around a doorway and out of sight. Then a voice through the intercom paging Dr. Greenberg. And Marsh ran. He raced as though the voice was calling him—*his* name up and down the corridor. From the far end of the hallway he saw Alexandra rushing toward him. "Marsh," she cried as they met, but he flung her hands away, pushed past her. "Oh, Marsh!" His name truly called. His wife inside that doorway where the cart had rolled to a stop. All the machinery for her, and more than two men. Suddenly a crowd in her room—nurses, Dr. Greenberg from out of nowhere, Richard on his feet and clutching the handle of his open briefcase, papers sliding, falling everywhere around her bed.

Marsh pressed to see. He glanced between the barrier of white shoulders, then to the crash cart beside her. He saw the line across the monitor gone flat, no longer rising and falling with the mystery of mountains, but straight and relentless as the utter truth. From somewhere down the hall—no, right here—he heard a high-pitched beeping like the sound of his off-course alarm at sea. But the line across the screen stayed constant and steady ahead, as if all the men and machines in this room were in error, this new course beyond their reckoning.

Marsh himself comprehended nothing. Was this an emergency of seconds or hours—he didn't know what kind of time was passing here. He watched these people laboring over his wife, the machines brought to rescue her, pounding at her chest. He witnessed this, confused between horror and hope. He heard the quick terse instructions—language from some higher intelligence rendering his own whisperings Neanderthal.

Then all of a sudden, silence. Marsh pushed next to Dr. Greenberg. The doctor glanced over at him, startled. "Wait outside," he said, turning to Virginia again.

But Marsh stayed where he was, in the middle of everything now, leaning with the rest of them over his wife—her eyes still wide open, her chest naked and puckered with the old sorrowful scars, exposed for anyone to see, to press with a listening ear, to touch. Only he could not. He stood among these others, the book clutched under his arm. And he didn't so much as lay a hand. He simply looked on until at last they charged her chest with electricity. Once, twice, and each time he winced as if the powerful current seared through his own ribs, jolting his heart. The third time he could've sworn he saw her eyes open even wider with surprise, her mouth spring round in exclamation Oh!

He would have snatched the paper from his pocket here and now. Here and now he would've signed. But on the video screen he glimpsed the line still running straight and fixed, the shock unregistered. Even so, when he turned back to his wife—in that instant when everyone else began turning away and the doctor stood noting the exact time—just then, Marsh could've sworn he saw her body rise.

4

Services were held at 3:00 P.M. Wednesday in the courtyard of St. John's Episcopal. Alexandra put together a program titled A Celebration of Virginia. Alex insisted that people come away feeling somehow reassured, feeling better. The Los Altos Chamber Ensemble—a group Virginia always supported—played stirring selections from Mahler. Herb Redick, the cellist, gripped Marsh's hand and whispered, "You were a lucky man to have her."

Maybe it wasn't so odd that much of the afternoon reminded Marsh of his wedding day some thirty years before. He might still be that spectator bridegroom sipping champagne punch from the sidelines, watching what seemed the whole world take a turn round the dance floor with his flushed and extraordinary wife.

Petunias, snapdragons, and pansies blazed in beds lining the flagstone walks. Not a cloud in the sky, and no sign of a casket anywhere. Friends stood to pay tribute. Julia Oakes, mainstay of the local drama club, read "Do Not Go Gentle into That Good Night." And Norm Vickers sent balloons.

As the service ended, a nervous young man dressed in a ruffled shirt and tuxedo ducked between the rows of folding chairs. Two jumbo helium balloons—one black, one silver—tugged above his head. "Deepest regards from Norman Vickers," the delivery man blurted. Then he released the balloons and scrambled back to the street. At that moment,

46

the sound of taps drifted from a yellow van painted with the words UP AND AWAY—24 HR. DELIVERY.

Beside Marsh, Richard jumped to his feet. Alexandra, who'd been holding up so well, holding her positive thoughts, crumpled into Marsh's shoulder and heaved loud gulping sobs. Everyone else sat dumbfounded, gaping after the two balloons shimmying higher overhead. And when the two dots disappeared, leaving only blue sky which seemed nothing, then a murmur drifted up—Norm's name, a curious whisper along the rows.

But nobody looked to Marsh for an explanation that afternoon. The balloons weren't even mentioned the following week when almost everyone telephoned or stopped by the house. Marsh sensed a polite silence on the subject, a sort of deference to the bereaved. Only Richard muttered something about "that kook in the hospital," as they sat around the kitchen table one night. But even Richard let it go at that. He was busy with what he called "death taxes," over Alexandra's more gentle reference to "the estate."

Richard and Alex had been staying at the house, helping out until things settled down. That's what Marsh assumed, anyway. He was beginning to wonder if Alex ever intended to return to the condominium she and Richard owned in the suburb just north. Every day it seemed Alex found more to do. She answered phone calls, rushed at the sound of the front door chimes. So far she'd frozen sixteen of the twenty casseroles dropped off by friends and neighbors in the first week. The sudden appearance of these casseroles from people who'd long since moved on to watercress salads and poached salmon struck Marsh as curious. It seemed all the demands of death were regressive. But no matter. Alex had divided the casseroles into small foil trays and sealed them like TV dinners. She was still wondering about what to do with the three Jello Jubilee salads and five bundt cakes. Marsh worried this decision might take her another week.

One afternoon he found Alex in his den, his mahogany desk strewn with engraved thank you notes. Alex was laboriously adding a personal message to everyone who'd sent cards, flowers, or plants. Marsh wondered how she could work in the dim light. The blinds were shut at the window and over the sliding glass door, those pale designer blinds chosen by Virginia like everything else in the house. But it seemed Ginny had filled their rambling ranch-style mostly with herself. Now the rooms looked barren. So it didn't bother Marsh to see that Alex had taken over his den. He felt almost touched watching her from the doorway, her head resting on her arm like a schoolgirl while she struggled with yet another personal reply.

Finally she glanced up at him. She tapped the pen along her lower lip. "I'm writing Mr. Vickers, but nothing sounds right." She swept her slender arm across the desk, the scattered vellum cards. "What do you want me to say?"

Marsh frowned across the room, trying to think where he'd put that tattered book Norm had given him. He remembered the hospital room, Norm saying, You'll need this. Marsh shook his head. "Tell him—"

"Tell him the good news," Richard called from the hallway. He spoke in a voice too loud for a house that seemed suddenly overlarge and empty, an afternoon of such muted light. But then, Richard had spent most of the day at his office—out there in the world. Now he'd begun tackling the garage, sorting through a corner of dusty cardboard boxes bearing his name.

He nooded at Marsh, his smile held a secret amusement he might use in court, worrying the defense. "Your wife's made you a millionaire." He rested his hand, professional and sure at Marsh's shoulder. "Not that you weren't already close. But *she* did it for you. You're bona fide."

Marsh moved out from under his son's hand.

"Actually more than a million," Richard said. "She made two very smart investments. Plus she got herself an excellent lawyer—namely me. And I should add the Economic Recovery Tax Act. You can thank Congress for that."

Marsh looked over, about to say it wasn't possible. He had no idea of any investments, wasn't up on economic recovery.

Except Virginia hadn't recovered. Marsh believed he'd seen her body rise. He'd watched those balloons climbing side by side, heard Norm Vickers' whispered words: Virginia too. He glimpsed Norm's face—a dark speck high overhead, still visible after the silver balloon blended out of sight with the sky. These things Marsh understood. He turned to Richard. Wasn't this the real point here? But Richard was already moving away.

Marsh stepped into his den and opened the blinds at the sliding door. He stared into his backyard—the Johnny-jump-ups, flowers she loved, a wrought-iron table and chairs, white and dripping lace like the eaves of an old Victorian. He'd always intended to enclose the pool so she could swim year-round or maybe just float in that silly inflatable lounger she'd been so crazy about. Was it possible the woman he'd watched bobbing there with a wine cooler in her hand—that woman grinning from under a floppy canvas hat—had she been the one who'd made two very smart investments, turned him into a millionaire?

Behind him Alexandra nodded. "In that corner near the barbecue—the pot of double chrysanthemums the Eberlines sent. That's a good place for them. And maybe over there the emperor tulips from Julia Oakes." Alex touched his arm. "You know, a shade garden. I've been thinking how peaceful . . ." She gazed out, her voice almost a whisper. "There's a honeysuckle that holds its leaves in winter. I've seen a plant, *hosta grandiflora*. I was thinking of periwinkle. Or forget-me-nots, bleeding heart."

What had become of that book, Marsh wondered. And those leis he'd placed on her bed. It seemed everything had been lost in the frantic rush to save her—vanished like the pressure in his bladder. Or maybe Alex had snatched up the orchids, frozen them along with the silver-wrapped casseroles. Whatever might keep in the freezer, hold leaves in winter. Marsh frowned out to his sunny, summertime lawn. I am beside myself, he thought.

"Just an old-fashioned shade garden," Alex said softly.

Marsh started from the room, then glanced back at her. "Don't worry about Norm Vickers. I'll write him."

But he ignored the card Alex put aside for him that day—then a week passing into two, time he hardly noticed except for the sound of Richard revving the Volvo's engine each morning. And as always, like clockwork, Richard backing from the driveway, hollering to wake the whole neighborhood, "I mean it, Alex. Tonight we're sleeping in our own bed!"

From somewhere deep within the house—a room which seemed to be sinking deeper everyday—Marsh would hear this and slide lower under the blankets. He would turn his face into the pillows and think to himself, Our bed.

But then Alex suddenly refused to answer any more phone calls, forcing him to reach for the extension on the bedside table. She told Marsh contact with the real world would do him good. "It's time," she said. Everybody else must've thought so too. His friends hardly mentioned Virginia now, referring only to her "fine memorial service" as if she'd become that occasion, the space of an afternoon.

Instead they asked about him. "How're *you* doing?" "Getting along," Marsh would say, aware he'd used this same reply before, but about Virginia. "Under the circumstances doing the best possible . . ." Speaking from the bed, a comforter bunched around him, Marsh began to feel that the mantle of his wife's disease had been passed onto him—illness bequeathed with investments making him both a millionare and a shut-in. But then the callers rushed on. It seemed almost everybody had been thinking of those balloons. They wanted to talk about Norm Vickers.

"About this Norman Vickers," Jack Strawn said, phoning during Old Business at the Wednesday Rotary Meeting. "A bunch of us were just sitting around down here trying to remember who we had on that team in '78 when we blitzed San Jose Kiwanis. Seemed to me there was a Vickers playing shortstop—managed the Chevrolet agency out on El Camino."

Marsh pulled the blankets higher. "That wouldn't have been Norm."

"Oh," Jack said after a long pause. "Then who is he?"

Later that evening Julia Oakes called, inviting Marsh for the hundredth time to join Footlighters.

"I know I vowed never to ask again after last year, but we've got a new season coming up with three wonderful plays, really ambitious for us, and I thought—" Julia stopped for a quick breath, her voice dropped low. "A whole new season for you, too, Andrew."

Marsh clamped his chin over the blankets. I could make you a bet, Virginia had told him. Write their names and seal them in an envelope and later . . .

"It might be just the thing for you. I mean, getting involved."

Marsh covered the receiver, closed his eyes, and said, "My God."

"So if you're interested we're meeting tomorrow night at eight, my place. Except there's one condition."

He cleared his throat. "What condition?"

"Mr. Vickers," Julia said. "Bring him along. That man has such a feel for the dramatic moment. I mean, the utter simplicity of those two balloons . . ."

By Friday night, Julia had made at least a dozen calls. Marsh finally unplugged both phones. He wondered what Alex could've been thinking—encouraging contact with the real world. He sat down to dinner looking forward to an evening of peace. But beside him, Richard was already resuming what seemed a running argument with Alexandra.

"No ifs, ands, or buts," Richard said, glaring across the table. "Tomorrow we're going home."

"Honestly," Alex said. "Couldn't we talk about something that really matters for a change? I don't suppose either of you would care to hear the latest unemployment figures. Or how about inflation, cuts to the disabled . . ." She raked a fork through Marjorie Eberline's oriental hamburger casserole, then sighed. "All right, Richard. Tomorrow." She glanced at Marsh. "That is, if you think you can get along."

"Oh sure," he said. "I'll be fine, really." He refolded his napkin, unable to face another leftover casserole or the resurrected fruit salad with its whipped cream dressing separated and forming a watery pool around peeled green grapes. Never mind that Alex believed in recycling. She'd admit to anyone that cooking wasn't for her. She took pride in telling people this, as if she'd overcome something major, like drugs.

Marsh cleared his throat. It seemed pain had been his only meal for days. "Alex, I've been thinking. I'd like you to have some of Ginny's things. Her coat maybe—the sable."

He nodded across the table. Alex was just young, another generation. He'd been something of a rebel once himself. And Richard, too, sitting here in yet another three-piece suit, arms folded, eyes squared. Except Richard seemed a complete holdout. Against everything, Marsh thought. Against me.

"You know how I feel about wearing dead animals," Alex said. She polished off a glass of milk, then blotted her mouth with the back of her hand. A broken blister glistened on her palm. Her nails were ragged from transplanting tulips, chrysanthemums, dwarf roses. Today she'd made a start on the shade garden.

Richard reached for her hand. "Where's your ring?"

Alex studied her fingers a moment, then shrugged. "Seriously, Marsh, maybe you should think about going away for a while. It might help— you know, getting out in the world. We could stay on a little longer, look after things."

"Are you out of your flipping mind?" Richard shoved from the table, jerked a thumb at Marsh. "He just got home, for God's sake. In case you didn't notice, *he* wasn't here!"

Marsh stared as Richard grabbed up the dinner plates and tramped from the room. "Thanks anyway, Alex," he said. He heard Richard banging pans on a kitchen counter, the faucet running full force. He could feature Richard yelling, that anger seemed almost normal now. But it was hard to imagine his son in the kitchen. When had Richard started doing dishes?

Finally he turned to Alex. "I wish you'd take the coat. Just to remember her by."

Alex frowned toward the kitchen, Richard clattering silverware into the sink. "I've *got* something to remember her by. Really, I don't think I could handle any more."

"But Richard's not like her," Marsh said before he thought. "I mean, Ginny was . . ." He put his hand to his forehead, not knowing what he meant, or might be saying, what was happening here.

Alex leaned across the table and caught Marsh's hand. "Then who is he like?" she asked, tears suddenly filling her eyes. "Who is he?"

Marsh eased his hand away. He gazed past Alex to the beige wall with its sheen like raw silk and a large painting glowing pastel under soffit lights. If Virginia were here she could explain once more that the painting wasn't simply a nude seated on a white blur resembling a toilet. In the same breath she'd answer Alex's question and they would all feel a hundred percent better. Marsh realized this had been her talent—interpreting each to the other, to themselves. He saw it only now, though Virginia must've understood all along. Once she'd remarked, "Sometimes I think if everybody wasn't leaning so hard on me from different directions, I'd probably just fall over." Well, she'd been wrong. Without her, they were the ones toppling.

Alex poured him a cup of coffee. He hadn't even noticed she'd left the table, standing over him, looking troubled, the coffeepot trembling in her grip. He heard no sound from the kitchen. Richard would be in the garage again, rummaging through another box on which Virginia had long ago printed his name in the same careful hand she'd used labeling her jars of marmalade. A boyhood preserved.

Marsh shook his head as Alex settled across from him. "Alex, listen," he said. But that was all he could say. How could he explain anything about Richard, when he couldn't even begin to conceive of himself. Sitting here, it struck him that the man who would sooner or later move from this table—that man who must act in the future—was a stranger whose behavior he could not predict.

5

Marsh lay awake that night, relieved that Richard and Alex were finally going home. But stumbling into the garage the next morning, he didn't feel so sure. Richard had completely vacated his corner. Cardboard boxes that had lined the walls for years now sat wedged across the Volvo's backseat and jammed Alexandra's Econoline van.

It seemed Richard had spent the night among his boxes. His suit was crumpled, a red Stanford booster button dredged from some carton hung cockeyed in his lapel.

Marsh peered into the Volvo's open window, trying to think what Richard would want with a green sponge football, a tattered Batman's cape. He turned to Richard wanting to ask, You too? Going for good? Instead he said, "That was some year the Cardinals went to the Rose Bowl—you were a sophomore if I remember right. What a game."

"I was a senior," Richard said, sliding behind the wheel. "And we didn't see that game because *she* was in the hospital again."

Marsh glanced up, confused by Richard's anger—anger which had always been aimed at him, never Virginia. Somehow he'd come to count on it. He reached through the window, as if to hold on to that anger, hold on to something. Because there'd be time now to sort it all out. No work, no hospital keeping him away. He touched Richard's arm. No Virginia.

But Richard was leaning into the backseat for a small clay ashtray

53

lodged beside bronzed booties. "I think this belongs to you," he said, shoving the ashtray into Marsh's hand.

Strings of clay had been wound to form the ashtray's bowl. Richard's snake phase, Virginia called it, the serpent's yellow mouth open to hold a cigarette. Marsh turned the ashtray over, reading his son's initials, the year 1955. For a moment it seemed they could begin with that year, begin all over again. Marsh smiled at the ashtray. "You did a great job."

"I believe you've said that before," Richard muttered, starting the engine.

Then there seemed nothing at all to say. Marsh lingered beside the car, then stepped back, hearing Alexandra calling him.

Alex made a production of opening the big chest freezer, sweeping her hand over the foil packages inside. Her words clouded with the deep cold rising into her face. "According to my count, you've got enough food to last for at least three weeks."

Marsh looked down at the rows of silver crammed like shiny wrapped gifts under a Christmas tree, or the mouthful of adolescent braces Richard once wore. Then his eyes caught on a larger dark shape frozen solid in a clear plastic bag. That package would belong to Alexandra.

She followed his gaze, bending to touch the frosty plastic. "I'll have this rascal out of here soon as I locate a new taxidermist. Mr. Pagni retired." Alex sighed. "I don't need to tell you what a hassle it'll be finding somebody else. And who knows if I'll even get funded."

"I'm sure you will," Marsh said, aware that she always was.

He stared at the dark shape, but didn't ask what animal. He'd learned not to get Alex started. She could recite food chains by heart, rattle off order, genus, and species. It struck Marsh as strange that she'd object to wearing dead animals, then turn right around and tour the peninsula schools with a whole collection of them crowded into her van. But he guessed these creatures, stuffed and mounted, represented something different. Teaching aids, she called them. Like those casseroles—recycled.

From the Volvo Richard shouted, "Let's get this show on the road."

Alex paid no attention, giving Marsh a smile. She nudged him with an elbow. "Taxidermy is a dying art."

Marsh forced a chuckle, the best he could do. He followed Alex to her van, thinking how all the old combinations had been tossed out. It seemed he and Alex had been suddenly rearranged, somehow aligned.

Alex started up the van. Beside her, Richard revved the Volvo. The double garage roared with noise. It sounded like a whole convoy preparing to move out, leaving the scene of some battle with peace restored.

"Drive straight home," Richard yelled to Alex over the din.

Alex rolled her eyes, cranked down her window. She waved Marsh closer. "I almost forgot." She dropped a ring of keys into his hand. "Your extras."

Marsh gazed down at the key ring with its clunky gold initial, not just some extra set. He dangled the initial at Alex's window. "*V* for Virginia."

"For victory," Alex said, making that sign with her fingers. She shifted the van into gear. "I'll call in a few days to see how you're holding up."

"She'll call," Richard hollered as his car rolled forward.

Marsh watched the two of them pull away, their vehicles flashing sun as they cleared the garage. He didn't follow them out, but stopped at the edge of the concrete floor. When they swung onto the road he reached over and pushed the button to close the garage. The big overhead door vibrated above him, then rattled down, slicing the daylight to nothing but a thread at his feet. For a minute Marsh stood in the dark emptied garage, holding Richard's lump of an ashtray in one hand, Virginia's keys in the other. He weighed these in his palms like a juggler. Then he turned and walked inside the house.

He set the key ring and ashtray on the kitchen table, then glanced at the stove's clock. Not even ten yet. He poured himself a cup of coffee thinking, The whole day. Of course, he was used to being alone. A man couldn't sail an ocean single-handed without enjoying his own company. Besides, there were probably a dozen chores needing his attention. He could make a list. But for some reason all he could think was: Air the house. He guessed Virginia had put that notion into his head, though he couldn't recall her ever doing such a thing.

There was always her closet, her dresser drawers. How does a person go about disposing of everything, Marsh wondered. Where in the world would he begin? Still, Alex had told him it must be done. "Hah," Marsh said out loud. Alex who wouldn't so much as take Virginia's sable from the closet.

Marsh wandered down the hall to the bedroom and pushed open the closet's sliding door. He swayed back on his heels, staggered by a fragrance he knew—not by name but only as hers. He moved to shut the door, unable to face this now. He had days and days. On the closet floor, his duffel bag lay in a jumble of her shoes. Marsh grabbed it, thinking of weeks, months in front of him.

He sat on the edge of their bed and unzipped the bag. His blue blazer was still folded inside. A toothbrush, toothpaste, shaving cream. At the hospital, Alex had seen that he got everything he needed, everything in traveling sizes. The toothbrush folded into a compact case, the razor was disposable. Norm Vickers' book lay at the bottom of the bag.

Marsh opened the ragged little book in his lap. A faded inscription read, "Presented to me by Mr. George Grant, April 25, 1873." Marsh turned to the middle, a chapter titled Mules: *In crossing rivers the bell mare should pass first, after which the mules are easily induced to take to the water* . . . A square of white stationery had been folded between the book's brittle pages. In pencil, Norm had scribbled numbers—mileage from here to there, but no mention of where. He'd made a list headed To Do. 1. Wheel alignment. 2. Oil change . . .

"Right," Marsh said, because he'd been meaning to check the oil in their car. "*My* car," he added, making the effort for singular. Then he slapped the book shut and dashed from the bed.

He hurried up the hall and into the garage, knowing before he looked that the car wasn't there. A quick panic bumped in his chest. He glanced to Richard's corner stripped bare, the freezer where Alex had left him food. She'd told him, You have enough to last three weeks. Then she and Richard had roared away, stranding him there.

Marsh moved to the wall phone in the kitchen and dialed. Alex answered. She sounded out of breath, as if she'd just rushed through the door.

"I was wondering about my car," he said.

"Your car?"

"Yes, where is it?"

"Hang on," Alex said. Marsh waited, squinting at the clock. Richard and Alex were barely home, and he was already on the phone. They'd worry he wasn't holding up.

After a minute Alex was back. "Your car's around the side of the house. Richard parked it there so he could pack in the garage."

"Right," Marsh said, his voice rough from his foolishness.

"Listen," Alex said, "maybe I should come over. You sound a little down."

In the background Marsh heard his son groan.

"Thanks, but I'm fine," he said. "I just needed my car."

He hung up, then stepped outside. His red Chrysler sat parked on the patch of asphalt where Richard once played basketball. For a minute Marsh sat behind the wheel. He thought about taking a drive, tried to think where. Then he headed for the house.

He tramped down the hall, shaking his head over his momentary panic. But it seemed a relief just knowing the Chrysler was out there. At hand. He felt ready to get on with things. He'd start with the closet. "Hell," he mumbled, "I could get along without a car. People do survive." Then he frowned, recalling Richard's words. *You weren't here.*

He stood at her closet, thinking of the day miles out on the Pacific, the radio message: Call your home. And the afternoon in the hospital when Virginia's heart quit beating—at that instant he'd been somewhere else, shaving in a room down the opposite end of the ward.

Marsh reached into the closet, touched a yellow sleeve, then her white cashmere cardigan. And down the rack, the sable she'd considered an unforgivable extravagance on his part, but adored nevertheless. He brushed the deep collar that had circled her neck like a muff. "Sable is a heraldic color," she told him once. "How do you know?" he'd asked. These ideas of hers always made him smile. She'd shrugged. "Oh, just from somewhere."

He slid the coat off its wooden hanger, surprised by the sudden weight in his hand, the slippery coolness of the satin lining. He moved with Virginia's sable draped over his arm, the way he'd wandered looking for her at the end of a party. He stopped before her dresser, a small French clock—enameled porcelain and centuries old, or so she told him. The clock rocked away in the quiet, growing louder with every stroke as if Virginia herself were rowing time endlessly toward him. She'd wound that clock not long ago. The pressure of her hand was stored inside its spring. Marsh glanced around the room, thinking about Richard who'd left, taking every trace of himself. But people never completely vanished. Such familiar things in dressers and drawers . . . Yet even as Marsh stood there, the silver-backed hairbrush, a teardrop pearl earring—these things he'd known so well—suddenly entered the realm of the past and became forever mysterious.

Marsh sank onto the bed. He hauled the sable over his knees and turned to Norm's list. 3. Check battery. The phone rang. 4. Add anti-freeze to thirty below. Marsh thrust his arm into the sleeve of Virginia's coat and reached for the receiver.

"It just occurred to me," Julia Oakes said, as though they'd been speaking only a moment before.

Marsh glanced up as Julia's voice registered. Across the room, the hands of Virginia's little French clock had stopped, failed just minutes ago, but already behind time. Marsh stared at the Roman numerals. It seemed the large pain he believed came only with the worst would be lurking from now on out in small things.

"Oh, but never mind," Julia said. She gave a throaty laugh. "I'll be over in ten minutes and we can talk about it."

Marsh felt a shiver in his chest, his heart taking a dive to thirty below. Not Julia, he thought. Not so soon. He frowned at the receiver, his sable arm, his bare wrist exposed too far below the fur cuff. "This is a bad day," he said. "I'm feeling pretty rotten, must've picked up the flu or something."

"Then maybe I'd better stop by the pharmacy on my way."

"You mustn't," Marsh said. He heard his voice, too high and jumpy. "I mean, I'm just leaving."

He glanced down at Norm's list, trying to think where. Where in the world to begin. He saw a name, a telephone number. Then squiggling quotation marks wrapped around Norm's scrawl. *"In the beginning all the world was America."*

Marsh turned back to the phone. "I promised to go see Norm Vickers' father."

6

Marsh drove south and a little west through the Los Altos hills. The damp countryside with its tangle of redwood forest and underbrush didn't seem much of a place to locate a retirement community. There'd been a time when these hills lured only the young. Aspiring poets, organic gardeners. Once, Richard and Alex had even talked about making a move here. What they were talking about was dropping out.

In those first days of marriage and law school, Richard wasn't rooting for the Stanford Cardinals anymore, but marching for migrant workers, clean air, and a nuclear freeze. He was against war, yet always looked as if he'd just come back from one. His face turned thin and long in a beard, his blue jeans rode low on bony hips, and Alex adored him, keeping him forever on the march with her soldierly shoulders square beside him.

"Richard's radical phase," Virginia used to say. It had taken her a full year to admit that Richard's campus rallies weren't what she called pep assemblies. In the end, she'd been right to see that time as temporary. But Marsh had felt oddly disappointed. Not that Richard had let him down in any way. Marsh was caught by a feeling that he himself had somehow failed. The night Richard quit the American Civil Liberties Union, there was an argument with Alex. Richard had finally turned to Marsh. "You know how it is—a person just grows up. Right, Dad?"

A person just grows old, Marsh thought. He eased up on the gas, squinting to read numbers on mailboxes screened in sword ferns and gooseberry vines. Over the phone the director of Heather Hills Community for the Aged had told him to take the last right before the town of La Honda. Marsh had scribbled everything down on the list in Norm's book. "If you pass the City Limit sign, you've gone too far," the director said.

Marsh felt he'd already gone too far, driving here in the first place. He should've just told Julia Oakes he didn't want company. But then, he'd made Norm a promise, more or less. He'd kept the calling card Norm had given him, plus the hospital no-code order he could've signed. Except he'd escaped that responsibility. At least that was probably how Richard looked at it.

Marsh checked his directions, then swung down an overgrown lane. He supposed Alex might've been happy living in this place with a couple of kids. But she and Richard had tabled the subject of children—first the world wasn't good enough, and then Richard said he wasn't established enough. Still, Marsh could see Alex sinking roots under these dripping redwoods. Although it seemed almost criminal, sticking elderly people out here. Visitors must be getting lost all the time—that is, if anyone ever bothered trying. Marsh wondered just how often Norm Vickers had managed the trip.

Then Marsh spotted the golf course. It looked like a full eighteen holes, with fairways rolling off to either side of the road. He braked as a golf cart bumped across the lane. A stout, ruddy-faced woman beamed at him from the passenger seat, raising her putter like a salute, her other hand clamping a red tam on her head.

Marsh entered what seemed the official gateway to Heather Hills. Beyond the filigreed gate, a turreted building rose, flying an array of flags none of which Marsh recognized. He saw that he'd been wrong about visitors—the parking lot looked almost full. He grabbed Norm's book and slid outside. The stone building appeared to be headquarters. More than just headquarters, with those turrets and rearing granite stags lining the steps. The place resembled a castle. Marsh started up the walk, feeling he'd entered some fantasy on the order of a theme park.

People wandered the grounds, some with older stooped figures on their arms. Others plowed wheelchairs through flower gardens and down brick paths. Although the day didn't seem as dark and damp since he'd left the redwoods, most everyone was roaming around dressed for cold weather. Advanced age, Marsh thought. Poor circulation and thin blood. He stepped aside as a stocky tweed-bundled pair ambled past. Then he glanced across the lawn to a man waving a white handkerchief at him from a wooden bench.

Marsh started over the grass toward Norm's father. Though he'd seen

Reginald Vickers only once, he felt sure about the small man standing erect beside the bench, one hand resting over the slatted back as if posing for a formal portrait. Marsh couldn't imagine many blacks living out here. This old man wasn't even dressed like the rest, but wore a shiny black suit and a gray felt hat.

As Marsh approached, Reginald Vickers tucked the handkerchief into his pocket and adjusted his navy blue tie. He thrust out his hand, his fingers knurled as the big black oak behind him.

"Andrew Marsh," the old man said. "Mr. Macleod suggested I might look for you around two. I've just come from the brook." He released Marsh's hand, then turned with a shaky quickness and bent over a wicker creel on the bench. "Look here, I've caught a trout."

For a moment Marsh stared at his palm, warm from the old man's grasp, misted as if with a sneeze. "Nice catch," he mumbled. He squinted toward the parking lot, his car gleaming in the sun. What could've possessed him to come here? He hardly knew Norm Vickers. He might as well be speaking to the father of a complete stranger. Nodding over the pitiful small fish, he felt something close to the clumsiness of his first blind date. Even his smile felt jumpy and young. It's too soon, he thought. Too soon for new people.

"You understand these are the wrong clothes for fishing," the old man was saying. "The trout are skeptical, otherwise I would have more to give you." He removed his felt hat and stuffed it alongside the fish, then tucked the creel under his arm. His gaze wandered to the high branches of the oak. "As you can see, I am in mourning."

"I'm sorry," Marsh said. "I didn't know." But of course he'd known. He looked away, thinking he should've stopped by Norm's room one more time, he could've at least phoned.

The old man nodded. "I'm relieved that you thought to bring our little book with you. Of course, Norman assured me you would. You have no idea how much that boy counted on coming along."

Marsh glanced down at the battered book, Norm's scribbled mileage for a trip never taken. "I'm sorry," he said again, thinking he should leave. "Maybe this isn't the right time . . ."

"Please," the old man said. He latched his fingers at Marsh's elbow. "If you would call me Reg."

The old man nudged Marsh across the lawn. They walked slowly, the wicker basket creaking. Marsh could smell the fish, not an unpleasant odor, but one of fresh water, the damp grass. He felt the old man's hand steering him—the father's grasp much stronger than the son's had been that last time. Of course, Norm was very sick then. But Marsh was still surprised by Reg's grip. Toward the end it seemed Virginia's cancer had turned her suddenly old. Now he would need to sort out his confusion between illness and aging. "My wife died, too," he said. "It's been almost three weeks."

Reg nodded. "The director notified me. He's been quite good about giving me word from the hospital." Reg spoke as if he held some personal stake in all developments there. As they moved past the stone mansion he sighed. "So we walk in our sadness. A deforming garment, as my one friend would say." He clutched Marsh's arm tighter. "Watch out or it becomes the most interesting thing about you. A man can get anywhere with a sad smile, Mr. Marsh. Women are especially fascinated. I understand this because at the moment I am sad plus very old. I'm inclined to believe that makes me twice as interesting." He glanced up with eyes more yellow than brown. Then he winked. "Even so, you realize the trout refuse to bite."

Marsh started to ask how many years amounted to very old, then decided against it. After a minute he said, "Please call me Marsh."

"Suit yourself," Reg said. "But Andrew isn't such a bad name. There's the young British prince, remember." He chucked, a startling deep sound that could belong to a man much larger. "Of course, no one mentions the monarchy here. I should warn you that this place is teeming with Jacobites."

They'd ambled well behind the main building, down a path lined with sheared boxwoods. Every so often the hedges gave way, opening to narrow yards and numbered stone cottages. At number 19 Reginald Vickers turned and led Marsh to his front door.

As they entered the small, pine-paneled living room Marsh was reminded of miniature houses people sometimes built in their backyards for guests—minor versions of the real thing, maintained at a slight distance, unattached.

The old man closed the door behind them, still chuckling. "Do you know we have people here—poor souls—who actually believe they're living somewhere in northern Scotland? But then, you realize this is not the real world." He stuttered past Marsh and placed the wicker creel on a scuffed chest beneath a window. "Well, so life goes. First your money, then your clothes, as they say. Not that you and I need worry, wrapped as we are in our sadness. But please—" He waved a hand. "Sit anywhere. I'll just be a moment."

A slipcovered sofa and a leather armchair faced each other, cramping the room. Between them, a coffee table stood on a narrow throw rug. The wooden table looked flimsy—spool legs with a sheet of glass protecting its dark top. Under the glass, photographs had been arranged as if on the page of an album.

Marsh glanced to the worn chair, a mangy fur pelt bunched over its back. After a minute he settled into the sofa. He sat with Norm's book in his lap and squinted at the photographs, upside down from where he sat. The photographs were old and grainy with enlargement, difficult to make out on his side of the table.

In the other room he heard Reg clattering dishes and wondered if he should offer to help. He felt confused by such a very old man, as if he'd never seen one. But the elderly were out there. In the real world, Marsh thought.

For a minute he sat still, listening for noises from the kitchen. Finally he stepped around to the leather chair. He remembered years ago, his first partner in the firm telling about a rickety great aunt who'd come to visit, spent one night, then remained all next morning in the bathroom. When Jim finally went to investigate, he'd found this great aunt dead beside the bathtub. Jim had snapped his fingers in front of Marsh's nose. "They go just like that," he said.

Marsh scooted to the edge of the chair, avoiding the dark fur at his back and its musty smell. Coming here was probably the worst thing he could've done so soon after Virginia. Practically asking for it, he thought.

As Reg entered the room Marsh jumped up, the book slid to the floor. "Don't disturb yourself," the old man said, cups and spoons rattling on a metal tray in his hands.

"But I'm in your place." Marsh glanced to the photographs—every face turned toward the scuffed leather chair.

"So you do me an honor," Reg said. "And my father as well. You'll find his buffalo robe a considerable comfort." Reg lowered the painted tray to the table, then sat on the sofa opposite. "You may recall when that robe was presented to my father by the young Sioux, Hole In The Day, shortly after he fell ill."

Marsh frowned down at his feet, the book lying there, its faded inscription. *Presented to me by* . . . He wondered if Reginald Vickers really expected him to remember. Maybe Reg assumed that Norm had told him. Or maybe the old man was suffering some sort of mental lapse. He seemed a little winded from his efforts in the kitchen. His hands trembled as he hooked them over his knees.

Marsh reached for the china teapot. "Allow me," he said, smiling at his own formality. But there was something contagious in the way Reg spoke—a subtle lilt in his words—a gravelly resonance similar to Norm's, yet surprisingly clear.

"I'm sorry I have no real cream for you," the old man said, unscrewing the lid on a jar of Dairy Mate.

"I take it straight," Marsh said, but Reg was already spooning out the powder.

"My half and half expired yesterday." Reg set the spoon aside, fumbled into a box of sugar cubes and dropped four lumps, one by one, into Marsh's cup.

Marsh said nothing. He watched, unable to think why the sight of this old man stirring and stirring, now tapping along the cup—just someone fixing him a cup of tea—why this small gesture would put a tightness in his throat. But it felt like years—maybe never—since anyone had done such a thing for him.

"A person alone—just one like myself—should never stock perishables," Reg said. "The dates always run out. I dread the sight of those stamped numbers. I don't mind telling you that's the one curiosity of my age." The old man stopped stirring and slipped his hand inside his suit jacket. The black serge rose and fell as his fist thumped beneath it. "This is my heart when I look into the icebox and see how soon everything will go bad." He withdrew his hand, glanced at it, then shrugged. "But perhaps you will know, since no one here seems to remember . . . What did we do before they gave us all the dates?"

Marsh smiled. He gazed down at the glass-covered table to a young man in uniform saluting between the rim of a saucer and the metal tray. He studied the photo, then looked over, matching the soldier's flat nose, the wide curving mouth, to the person sitting here now.

Reg didn't notice, busy rummaging through his jacket pockets. He pulled out two cellophane packets of saltines, the kind found in restaurants. He opened these and placed them on the table, covering the soldier's face. Then he reached into his breast pocket, removed a pack of cigarettes and shook one out for Marsh.

"The last Chesterfields in the world," the old man said loudly as if making an announcement.

Marsh glanced at the cigarettes, wondering just how long since Reg had worn that suit. The crackers tasted like dust, so stale they could've been forgotten in the old man's pocket for years. "Thank you," he said, "but I quit smoking."

"Then I hope you won't object." Reg dug for matches. He clamped the Chesterfield between his teeth and squinted out through smoke.

For just an instant Marsh saw Norm sitting there, gazing from hospital pillows. Never mind that the old man was as small as his son had been large. Dangling from a Vickers mouth, the cigarette looked strongly genetic.

"Oh, I can tell what you're thinking," Reg said, catching Marsh's stare. He wagged the Chesterfield between his fingers. "This will ruin a man's health. Well, you may rest assured that I would certainly have taken care of myself if I'd known I was going to live so long. But enough about yours truly. I understand you're retired like myself. Free to make plans, that is." Reg brushed ashes from his lapel, then glanced up with a smile. His teeth glinted small as his eyes—everything in his face worn to the same little gleam, the same little size. "I'm speaking now of travel."

"I have no plans," Marsh said. He frowned across the table, disturbed that anyone—especially this old hazelnut of a man—might presume he'd come here for a regular conversation. Or that there could be any connection between them. Other than Norman.

Marsh pushed the saltines aside. He looked down at the photograph, keeping his eyes on the soldier frozen in salute. "Your son wanted me to see you. He told me to say that he remembered everything and it was a pleasure."

"My dear boy," Reg said, "the pleasure is entirely mine." He glanced down then, bending over the table, cocking his head at the photo. He leaned so close his wiry hair brushed Marsh's forehead. "Myself in the first war," he said in a voice that sounded like a secret. After a moment he slid his cup and saucer to the left, revealing another man in uniform—the shoulders and up. "Here is Norman in the second." Reg pulled on his cigarette, sighed a stream of smoke. Finally he lifted the teapot. He smiled at a faded yellow photograph underneath. "And now you see where everything began. My father, our beloved Algie, veteran trooper of the great Indian wars, and most courageous of us all."

Marsh studied the smaller photo. The man pictured there hardly looked like a soldier. His dark eyes crinkled as if with an amusing thought. He might've been smiling under his bushy black moustache. Unlike Reg in the first war and Norm in the second, this middle-aged black man wasn't snapped at attention, but just gazing out good-naturedly, cradling a bugle in the crook of his arm.

"A bugler," Marsh said. He sat back, relieved that they'd switched from the subject of his future to another man's past.

"His true instrument was the French horn," Reg said. "He was a musician through and through. *Principal* musician, Ninth Cavalry Regimental Band, Department of the Platte. And his own good person from start to finish."

The cigarette sizzled as Reg dropped it into his milky tea. The old man tapped his chest. "You are looking at what's left of a fine military tradition. Unworthy as I am it falls to me to make the journey back."

Reg sank against the sofa, shaking his head. "Of course, I'd depended on Norman coming with me. If I hadn't waited so long . . ."

"You couldn't have known," Marsh said.

Reg gave a little shrug, then looked up. "It seems I will have to close the circle by myself. That's not to say your company won't be appreciated." He leaned, tapping his finger over the photographs. "You mustn't be offended by my pointing out that you aren't exactly one of us."

"Not at all," Marsh said, just for the sake of it. He doubted Reg was talking about a real trip. The old man didn't look capable of going anywhere except out of this world. For a moment Marsh frowned off, remembering Norm in the hospital, those two balloons traveling up the sky together.

Reg waved a dark speckled hand toward the book lying at Marsh's feet. "If you please . . ."

Marsh placed the worn book on the table and Reg opened to a page. But it seemed the old man quoted entirely from memory. " 'Fortune,' " he began, " 'has always smiled upon those who ventured west. Abraham traveled west to the land of promise; Columbus went west and found a new world.' " Reg closed the book, nodded. "I'm speaking now of the Divine Direction."

"We're *in* the west," Marsh said. He crumpled his paper napkin and stuffed it into his empty cup.

The old man chuckled. "Although Abraham could not have known at the time that Canaan was far inferior to Nebraska."

"Nebraska," Marsh said. He moved from his chair, trying not to seem in too much of a rush. "I think maybe I should be leaving. There's my wife's estate, papers—you understand."

"Yes, indeed," Reg said. He fingered the book a moment, then pushed himself straight.

"Please don't bother getting up," Marsh said.

"Norman left me his house, the Establishment—all of it."

As the old man swayed from the sofa, Marsh reached, catching his elbow.

Reg looked up and smiled. "What did you get?"

Marsh stared into those glittering eyes. Reg sounded almost delighted, as if they'd both been lucky winners of door prizes. He felt the old man's weight, insubstantial, but bobbing beneath the black suit with the hidden energy of a jumping bean.

"My wife gave me everything," he said. "But without her—" Marsh gazed off, blinking in the small quiet. "Without her, I don't know."

"Naturally you don't know," Reg said, sounding suddenly agitated. "You've lost your wife and worse yet, your idea. Live to my age, and you'd understand it's your idea that keeps you going on. Once you lose it—" The old man stepped to the wooden chest, then glanced back at Marsh. "I feel I must tell you that you're doomed forever to small behavior."

"Now wait just a second," Marsh said.

"And so I'm offering you . . ." Reg bent over the wicker creel on the chest, shook open his napkin, and wrapped the trout inside. He turned to Marsh. "I'm offering you, number one my fish, and number two . . ."

Marsh grabbed the trout and stepped away, not about to hear any more.

But the old man was already nudging beside him, shoving another photograph under his eyes. Marsh saw Algie again—in black and white and upside down—bravest of them all.

"Number two, my idea," Reg said.

Marsh flicked at the snapshot, the beloved Algie standing on his head.

"You'll see the Great Continental Divide," Red said, thrusting the photograph closer. "Glimpse the snow-capped Sangre de Christos. And there beyond sight, the wide Missouri gathering up the Yellowstone. The Powder, the Tongue, Little Big Horn . . ."

Marsh looked away, ran a hand through his hair. "Your father is standing on his head."

"For luck, for love, for new beginnings." The old man's voice tumbled like a little song in Marsh's ear. "For this, a man stands on his head."

Marsh turned for the door.

"I give you my idea," Reg said.

Marsh stepped outside, then hesitated, aware of Reg moving after him.

"And of course I give you my sympathy, it goes without saying."

"And you have mine," Marsh said.

As they moved down the path he thought of Reg's loss, equal to his own, if not greater. You are looking at what's left, the old man had told him a minute ago. Marsh could at least depend on Richard for somebody—for family. That's how it was supposed to work, anyway. But just now he felt more comfort in Reg's arm sliding around his shoulders. He glanced down and noticed the old man springing practically on tiptoe to keep his hold. Marsh slumped a little, trying to make it easier.

At the hedges Reg stopped and shook his hand. "You should be aware that I'll be ending my stay here as of the first." Reg sounded pleased, gazing off as if this place had already become a memory. "I gave notice today, once I learned for certain you were coming. But you mustn't worry yourself—I'll be in touch soon." The old man gripped Marsh's shoulder again. "I'm a member of Triple A and hold a valid driver's license. I have American Express, Visa, Shell Oil, and Carte Blanche. Nothing remains except the Establishment. Once that is seen to . . ."

Marsh nodded. This had to be Norm's doing—some last-minute reassurance to a father left behind. *Someone will come, you will be taken.* Like a promise made to a child. *Anywhere you want to go.*

He moved out from under the old man's arm and started up the lane. As he walked, he kept nodding—nodding at the boxwoods, nodding to the tall black oaks. He'd been placed in the middle of something. An innocent bystander one minute, an accomplice the next. But still innocent, he could still get away. Then he heard Reg calling him.

Marsh turned back to the old man. From a little distance it looked as if Reg had no eyes, only a smile sunk deep in the dark folds of his face.

"I neglected to ask if you own a good heavy coat," Reg said, a little breathless, as if he'd been the one doing the walking.

Marsh blinked down at the old man. In his hand the worthless fish had gone stiff, sopping the napkin and his fingers. He wanted to say—this is California. Nobody walks around in wool overcoats. But the day had weakened him. If Reg pointed right now to the turreted, flag-flying castle and said Scotland, Marsh believed he'd have only enough strength to reply, Whatever. If the old man said, Stand on your head, Marsh might've answered, Yes.

"I suppose I have a coat," he said finally. He frowned off, trying to think. "Somewhere I do."

"Well, that's a relief." Reg clapped his hands together as if finished with important business. "You realize there may be snow."

"Right," Marsh said, already stepping away.

He hadn't walked far when he heard the old man clapping again, but like applause. Then the sound keeping time—a thin beat parading him up the lane. Before he took the corner he stopped and looked over his shoulder.

Reg quit clapping. He cupped his hands around his mouth and shouted, "We are going to need our warm coats!"

It was close to five by the time Marsh swung down his block, heading the Chrysler home. He'd sped out of the redwoods, surprised to find the sun still bright—something left of the day. Earlier, walking down the shaded path from Reg's cottage, he'd felt a sudden end of summer. Rain looked possible, the dense coast fog imminent. But that would be winter. There was a week of August yet, and then fall.

Not that the seasons came anywhere close to extreme on this peninsula. A man might find more interesting weather in the space of a brief ocean sail. He could spend a whole lifetime and never once consider a good heavy coat. So it was ridiculous to be thinking about one now. Still, Marsh drove down his street and through the accumulated heat of the afternoon, making a mental search beginning with the hall closet.

He pulled into his driveway, wondering if it was just grief. Everything he did these days—his most remote thought—seemed some sort of manifestation. A deforming garment, Reg had told him. Wrapped in our sadness.

Marsh gazed toward his front door. After sitting in Reg's cottage at

Heather Hills, his own house looked enormous. He left the Chrysler running, reluctant to go inside. He snapped on the radio, punched buttons. It seemed the cigarette lighter had never really worked. He checked the oil pressure, the rear defroster, then finally shut off the engine. He grabbed Reg's fish and headed for the house.

The phone was ringing as he stepped inside. He glanced to the coat closet, then dashed for the kitchen. He picked up the receiver, hearing Alexandra's voice crackling on the line. She was asking if he'd seen anything of Richard. It seemed Julia Oakes had stopped by hours ago and dragged Richard off to her grief therapist.

"And we all know how much good that's done in *Julia's* case," Alex huffed.

"Yes" Marsh said, because everybody knew about Julia's case. Although nobody could say exactly what Julia was mourning. He looked down at the fish, gummy in his hand. Alex rattled on, her words rising like a siren. Had to be another argument with Richard, he decided.

"Honest to God," Alex said. "Sometimes I wish I'd married into a family of complete nerds. I mean, it's the truth. Ever since Mom died . . ."

Marsh winced, hearing Alex falter. He waited for her to regain her anger, hang up, anything. For a moment he gazed out the kitchen window. He thought of dense trees standing cool across the lawns at Heather Hills. And boxwoods shadowing the damp lane he'd walked—Reg hollering, We are going to need our warm coats. Finally he turned back to the phone.

"I was wondering about the backyard—your idea. You remember, the shade garden."

Alex sniffed. "Nobody seemed interested."

"Well, I'd like you to keep working on it."

"All right," Alex answered after a minute. Her voice softened. "I'll do it before autumn comes."

Marsh hung up and dropped the fish into the sink. He rinsed his hands, letting the cold jet over him, like ice stinging his fingers—the chill of a winter day.

He wandered through the house, wishing he was still out there, sitting in Reg's dark cottage. They could be eating supper by now, eating something substantial like kippers and porridge, wearing their good heavy coats.

At his bedroom, he stopped and peered in at the mess—his bed still unmade, Virginia's sable bunched like some animal curled in the sun. Marsh moved to the bed, thinking he ought to get hold of himself. But there was still too much left of the day. Virginia's French clock had stopped, the sun would never go down. Richard would be sitting forever in grief therapy, when they should've been grieving together. How did that old line go? The family that prays together, stays together. Maybe that was the trouble. They'd never prayed, never said, Give us this day.

Marsh prayed for this day to end. He moved down the hall, dragging Virginia's sable by the scruff of its neck. He stepped through his den and stared out the sliding glass door. Finally he pushed open the door and sank into a chair on the patio.

The coat slid from his knees and he grabbed for it. He watched the low sun flashing the pool and prayed for Richard to come home and find him, just as he himself had come home after a long day. Day after day, home from the real world. But he'd never found Richard. Only Ginny. Through sickness and health. Then only sickness. And Richard taking it all to court—prosecuting, looking high and low, looking everywhere to place the blame.

"Look here," Marsh said. But he prayed to be anywhere except here. No father to be found.

He tucked the sable around him like a lap robe and squinted into the dusky air—finally an end to this day. But no answer to his prayers. And so he wished on the stars. He asked for a wide open sky curving to the limitless horizons at sea. He wished for a cold blowing wind, the shade garden before autumn. He yawned into the mild summertime of his backyard and asked the leaves on every tree to please come down—drift over him like soft falling snow.

Then Marsh shut his eyes. He dozed, wishing and dreaming a circle that closed with the wheel of seasons. He dreamed the distance of an old man's journey and saw that he stood somewhere far away from himself, bundled in a fine warm coat.

7

In the farthest corner of the back-
yard, Alexandra rocked a slab of rough slate into place, then pushed to
her feet. "Too hot to do any more," she called, ambling across the lawn.

Marsh watched her brushing at her jogging shorts, the ties to her halter
top dangling around her neck. Too hot for clothes, he thought. September finally here and still these warm days—still no word from Reginald
Vickers. Today like every day since that afternoon at Heather Hills,
Marsh caught himself waiting, never straying far from the phone, continually checking the mail. But the postman brought only the usual, plus
a growing stack of dinner invitations which Marsh declined. He couldn't
imagine going anywhere—except away.

Alex tossed her trowel onto the patio table. She shucked off the knee
pads she wore for working in the dirt, then headed for the house. "I've
been thinking," she said, glancing back at him. "Maybe you should just
call Mr. Vickers."

Marsh had considered phoning. Last night he'd lain awake, remembering soldiers snapped in salute and Reg talking about a military tradition. *You are not exactly one of us* . . . Marsh had turned for the phone,
wanting to tell the old man about Norm seeing the moon strike the Great
Divide. He'd say that locating a warm coat was absolutely no problem.
He would mention that he'd just missed being sent to the Korean War.

Alex sauntered back to the patio with a pitcher of iced tea in one
hand, her full glass in the other. She slid into a chair and pulled the

rubber band from her hair, letting it fall loose on her bare shoulders. She smelled of the heat and of dark humus soil.

"I guess I should go home," she said. But as always she made no move to leave.

These late afternoons had become something of a ritual to Marsh—his daughter-in-law lounging beside him, the phone at his feet reaching into the backyard as far as the cord would allow. Otherwise he'd be out there helping with the shade garden. But Alex also wanted him near the phone. She was waiting for a call, too—some last-minute word that her wildlife program had been funded even with school underway.

Besides, she insisted the garden was her job. Marsh should sit back and relax. The first rule of traveling, she'd told him the other night at dinner, was to start a trip feeling rested. Richard had glanced up from his barbecued chicken and sputtered, *What* trip?

Marsh reached for Alex's iced tea, sharing the glass—her idea to save on dishes, create less work for himself. But work was probably what he needed. If he'd kept busier these past two weeks he might've forgotten Reg Vickers. He looked over at Alex, her knees banded pale where those pads had blocked the sun. "I'm pretty sure this is only grief," he said.

"I don't know," Alex said. She tipped back, linking her hands behind her head. "There's just something about taking a trip. Maybe it comes from all those fairy tales—the ones where little children keep going off on long journeys. There's always that part—the part that used to grab me." Alex fell silent a moment, staring into her lap. Then she spoke as if by heart, "And they set out together to walk through the whole of the great wide world."

Marsh glanced up, hearing Alex's voice fading off, as if she'd already started walking. Except Alex would never walk through the world—she'd jog. Jogging for what, Marsh wondered. Was she racing as he'd raced, toward some uneasy survival? Racing just to sit in his early retirement backyard?

"Anyway, I'd go," Alex said.

She moved from her chair and shook out her slim arms and legs, like a track star finally ready for her big event. But she wasn't going anywhere, only leaving for home. Well, maybe something of an event. There was no telling what went on between Alex and Richard these days. Although Marsh didn't believe it could be good. He'd hardly seen his son, and whenever he asked Alex, she just shrugged and said, "Richard's busy." She'd used those words so often, Marsh began hearing them in his mind as the monotonous beeping on a telephone line.

Alex gathered her knee pads from the table, then glanced away. "I mean if I were you, that is—I'd go."

Marsh walked her around the house to the driveway where her van sat parked. As Alex slid behind the wheel he caught sight of her wildlife collection jammed into the back. Inside the sweltering van those animals seemed to be waiting for word about funding, too. Some reared, others crouched or simply stood—at the ready, stuffed and mounted. And all California natives. These animals deserved a phone call. At least the grizzly appeared to think so, looming over the rest with fangs bared, his polished claws shining, a fistful of switchblades. Marsh had seen the grizzly before. But it was still enough to give a person something of a shock. And Alex, too, brushing a quick kiss across his cheek, her knees striped with the markings of some rare creature.

"Same time tomorrow," she said.

Marsh shook his head. "Listen, Alex, maybe you should do something else tomorrow—have some fun for a change."

"Like what?" Alex asked, her voice climbing. She jammed the van into gear. "Don't you think I'm happy—I'm happy, for God's sake."

"Hang on," Marsh said.

But she was already backing down the drive, hollering, "Everybody's happy—just read the paper. The President gave us a mandate!"

Marsh stood at the curb, gazing after her. Across the street, his neighbor stared from her picture window. She raised her hand in a tentative greeting and Marsh nodded. Everybody was happy. All along this sun-dappled street, with this season's decorator colors and Neighborhood Watch. Everybody. Richard, Alex, even Julia Oakes—grieving but happy.

Marsh bent to pull a dandelion, then moved up his front walk. Somewhere down the block a horn was blaring. The horn sounded stuck and loud as a whole wedding party. But it was only a truck heading this way, the noise streaming closer. Not really a truck Marsh noticed, but one of those motor homes he hated on sight.

As he stepped into his house, the noise stopped. Marsh crossed to the living room window and gazed out at the abrupt quiet. His neighbor was still staring from across the street. And then Marsh was staring too.

The motor home sat in his driveway—not idling, but parked there, huge and cream-colored with an outsized front bumper that appeared capable of leveling buildings. Marsh saw no one behind the wheel. A satellite dish was strapped to the long roof, the license plate said California. Marsh squinted to make out the words printed above the grille. He read the name, then whispered, "I'll be damned," and rushed outside.

In the driveway he stopped, not sure whether to knock at the side door of this monstrosity or try the cab. But just then the side door swung open.

Reg Vickers smiled down from the narrow entry. "At last you're here," he said, as if this wasn't Marsh's own driveway. A metal step dropped like a drawbridge from the motor home's chassis. "As you see, we're entirely automatic." Reg moved out of the doorway, waving Marsh inside. "We have Norman to thank for all this. I tell you, when that boy was made, the mold was smashed with a hammer."

"Yes," Marsh said, but thinking No. Not this gas-guzzling road hog. He ducked inside, ducking from habit. But this wasn't the cramped cabin of the *Whither Thou*. A person could stand with headroom to spare, even somebody Norm's size. Marsh glanced up the orange shag aisle, picturing the big black man here. He could smell Norm's cigarettes, Norm commanding the plush driver's seat.

Across the aisle, Reg turned from the gas stove, a potholder in his hand, the cigarette in his mouth. Marsh noticed he'd come out of mourning. He wore a lime green polo shirt and pale gabardine trousers with white loafers. Maybe it was the change of clothes—or maybe just leaving Heather Hills—but the old man look livelier, suddenly prosperous.

Reg nodded at the built-in range, a coffeepot steaming. "Four burner," he said. The old man glanced up. "Eye-level oven. Not for my eyes, mind you. People are tall nowadays. We used to be much smaller you remember." Reg drew on his cigarette, then crushed it in a beanbag ashtray on the kitchen counter. "Take that old Minneconjou, Jump The Sun. Today he'd measure only average. However, Crazy Horse was always small, no matter when."

"Right," Marsh said, without the slightest idea. He watched Reg rummaging through a cupboard, taking out two plastic mugs. Like the sloop's galley, this kitchen had been made for travel. The birch cupboard doors were secured with positive catches so they couldn't fly open, the cupboards themselves lipped at the lower edge. These details Marsh understood. He knew each drawer would be notched, every dish unbreakable.

Reg motioned him to the dinette table, poured coffee into their mugs, then settled on the seat opposite. A smile pouched the old man's cheeks. "So," he said, his eyes gleaming, "How does all this luxury suit you?"

Marsh glanced down at the table, Norm's dog-eared little book lying beside a road atlas. He wanted to ask why in two weeks he'd had no phone call, no letter, nothing. He looked over at the plaid sofa that would double as a bed. At least Reg could've given him some warning. When the old man mentioned the Establishment, Marsh assumed he'd meant the refrigeration business—not the brand name of a motor home.

Marsh cleared his throat, trying to keep his voice casual. "Under these seats, I imagine there'd be stowage."

"Yes, storage," Reg said. "Plus this table drops down and the whole apparatus turns into a bed. We could sleep six in here if we had a mind to."

Marsh turned to the long side window. If it weren't for the familiar view down the street, they could be sitting in the dining car of a train. Or if he lifted a cushion and looked below he might discover the dark hold of a ship, smell the sea. He sat back thinking he ought to ask exactly where Reg planned on going. The Great Divide? Nebraska, that place far superior to Canaan?

"Believe me, we have everything we could ever desire," Reg said. He looked very pleased, his chin tipped, eyes half-closed. Sunlight slanted through the window, giving his skin the sheen of deep-rubbed burl. "You'll find hot and cold running water, flush toilet, shower. Our freezer crushes ice."

"Yes," Marsh said. He smiled across the table, smiling mostly at his own desire to get moving, no matter where.

"You realize we're completely self-contained. That makes all the difference, considering we're forced to cross the territory of Utah. Much as it pains me to admit, a detour would cost us too many miles."

"Utah," Marsh said. It was something of a start.

"I'm hoping we can reach Nicodemus by day five. That's providing the pace isn't too much for you."

Marsh glanced to the road atlas. *U.S.A. Completely Revised and Updated,* the cover read. "I'd have to look at the map."

Reg thumped his forehead with the shiny heel of his hand and chuckled. "Forgive me. Norman and I made this trip so many times—at least in our minds—I assumed everybody must have some notion. After supper we'll study our route, sit up all night if it comes to that. Although I should caution you—it may appear that we are traveling east, but our true direction is west." Reg gripped the table's edge, scooting himself from his seat. "Westward ho! as they say."

The old man poured more coffee, then bent near Marsh's face. "In a nutshell we are going after my father Algie. I understand this means nothing to you, unacquainted as you are. But I will do my utmost to prepare you." Reg nodded closer, his yellow-flecked eyes soft with kindness or perhaps only patience. "As a traveler I hold with the late Dr. Johnson who was so fond of quoting the Spanish . . . 'He who would bring home the wealth of the Indies must carry the wealth of the Indies with him.' "

"Very true," Marsh said, hearing the old man's quiet inflection in his own voice. It seemed they were speaking in secrets only they shared. Just the two of them, or maybe Norm could be included—and the beloved Algie. Family secrets, Marsh thought. He felt somehow counted in, as if he'd been taken under this long streamlined roof by a whole host of Vickers.

"That's not to say Dr. Johnson and I haven't had our differences. The gentleman was prejudiced, you know. Still, I believed we should make some allowance for him. A person can take his intelligence only so far past his own time."

Marsh glanced away, realizing that a large part of him would prefer not to notice Reg was black. He didn't even want to discuss it. "If you could just give me some idea of when you'd like to leave . . ."

Reg pursed his lips as though trying to think. Finally he said, "Would morning be convenient for you?"

"*Tomorrow* morning?" Marsh said, mostly for the sake of it. Packing his clothes wouldn't take long. He could stop by his bank on the way out of town. A moment's notice, and he was free to go.

"Tomorrow's fine," he said.

Then without warning, he thought of Ginny. He moved from the dinette, down the aisle. For a moment he gazed out at his house, aware of all the loneliness his freedom had brought him.

Reg stepped to the small, built-in refrigerator. "I expect you have a few things to do."

"I was supposed to sort through our bedroom," Marsh said, his eyes still on the house. "My wife's personal effects."

"Well, you certainly wouldn't want to do that. You want to remember things as they were. Isn't that correct?"

"I would like to remember," Marsh said.

"And well you should." Reg poked his head around the yellow refrigerator door. "I believe that's why the young Sioux Hole In The Day taught my father to walk backwards. You realized what an art—take a walk backwards, and you'll never forget where you've been. And what is behind you will always remain in front of you."

Marsh glanced over, trying to work his way through the old man's words. After a minute he turned for the door. "You could wait in my house—I won't be long."

"I'd prefer not," Reg said.

Marsh walked up his driveway, wishing Reg would come inside. He stopped at his mailbox, certain his neighbor was watching from behind her picture window. Marsh didn't look over. But he had a mind to wave and let her know, You are seeing the last of me. He sorted through his mail, another dinner invitation, more notes of condolence still arriving. The last of these. And at the bottom of the pile, a letter from the Northern California Racing Association. Results of the race, probably. The committee had taken long enough to send official word. But now it seemed too soon for place, win, or lose. The returns couldn't possibly be in yet. He and Reg hadn't even left the driveway. Marsh slid the letter back through the mailbox slot and stepped inside the house.

In the kitchen he dialed Richard's number, but it was Alex who answered. "Well, that's terrific—really wonderful," she said when he told her the news. But she sounded disappointed, her voice thin in his ear.

"Leaving in the morning. I mean, that soon. What *time* in the morning?"

Marsh glanced around the kitchen. Maybe a big place like this would seem sort of overwhelming to an elderly man used to small spaces. "We can't get away until after the bank opens."

"I'll come over, we'll have breakfast," Alex said. "Don't leave until I get there. I just wish I could tell you . . ." Her words faded out a moment. "Never mind," she said. "Anyway, Richard wants to say good-bye. Hold on—he's standing right here."

But it seemed quite a wait. Marsh leaned into the hallway; the walls rose cavernous in the dusky light. He wondered if he should sleep in his bedroom or outside in the motor home.

Finally Richard's voice broke onto the line, cheerful but too loud. "So you're taking off with Mr. Vickers."

"Tomorrow morning," Marsh said, deciding it might be better if he slept outside. "Only a short trip," he added. He frowned at the phone, trying to think why his conversations with Richard almost always took the form of apologies. "Reg—Mr. Vickers, that is—has some idea about his history. Finding his roots, I guess."

"Sounds great. Where're you going—Africa?"

Marsh switched on the ceiling light. "We'll be crossing Utah," he said. He eased onto a kitchen stool, then stood straight again. "Mr. Vickers owns one of those motor homes—sleeps six. You'd be surprised, Richard. It's self-contained."

"Oh God." Richard's voice trailed off. He sounded suddenly very tired. "Oh Dad."

For a moment Marsh couldn't answer, bewildered by the way Richard had spoken his name. Have I become a lost cause, he wondered. It seemed his son knew. Was there a reason here for pity?

He leaned, touching his forehead to the wall. "Listen, Richard—why don't you stop by with Alex in the morning. It's been a while."

"Can't," Richard said, his voice lifting sharp again. "I'm due in court first thing."

"When I get back then—we could have lunch maybe." Marsh slumped onto the stool. He might be speaking to an old business acquaintance, somebody you just bump into. "This won't be like sailing, you know. I can write letters."

"Send a postcard," Richard said. And then he was saying good-bye.

Marsh lingered in the kitchen, shutting windows, locking the door to the garage. He stepped outside for the pitcher of iced tea he'd left on the patio. He wondered if he should take the extension phone inside, too. Although maybe Alex would want it out here. Marsh gazed toward the shade garden. He thought of Richard whose anger he could not contain. And Alex on her knees to make a garden where there was no sun. Not to mention his own muddled mind from which he could not form one clear connection. For just an instant Marsh was struck by the feeling that he shouldn't be going away at all. It came over him like a sudden sickness. But he knew it would pass—this moment when all the reasons for leaving present themselves as every reason to stay.

He carried the lukewarm tea inside and poured it into the sink. Then he moved through his warm summerstill house. He took an empty garment bag from the front closet, slung it over his shoulder, and stepped down the hallway. He spread the garment bag open on his bed, rummaged through closets, dresser drawers. He crammed his duffel bag, then glanced around the room one last time. You want to remember things, Reg had said a while ago.

Marsh pulled Ginny's sable from its hanger. As he stuffed the coat into his garment bag, her scent billowed up from his hands, dizzying him. He took a deep breath and closed the zipper, being careful not to catch any fur.

Outside, lights shown from the motor home. They cast a soft glow, reminding Marsh of the *Whither Thou,* sailing with running lights. He almost wished they were leaving tonight—rolling away from this serene neighborhood of still backyard pools and mandated happiness. He turned to lock his front door, aware of Reg stepping up the walk behind him.

"You mustn't," he said as the old man stooped for his duffel bag. But Reg was already stumbling away, hauling the bag over the lawn like some feeble skycap.

For a minute Marsh lingered in his driveway, then he climbed into the motor home. The automatic step folded up behind him. He squeezed his garment bag into the narrow wardrobe closet and caught a dankness— the dark smell of everything that was old in the earth. Across the aisle, a pot simmered on the kitchenette stove, Norm's little book lay open under a kerosene lamp. The last Chesterfields in the world were on the dash. They would sit up late, studying their route. The old man would point the way. They'd be traveling east. But West was their destination.

"I want you to tell me everything," Marsh said.

Reg turned from the stove, a wooden spoon in his hand. "Everything," he said, touching the spoon to Marsh's nose, "in good time. But first, you must allow me to feed you."

The old man smiled, his glowing amber eyes large and nocturnal behind gold-rimmed glasses. And in that instant Marsh saw exactly how it could happen—how a man would follow a stranger, allow himself to be guided, even if it might be in the wrong direction.

Going After Algie

They leave flags, slogans, alphabets, numbers, tools, tales of flaming performances; they leave moths, manuscripts, memories.

—Carl Sandburg
"Good Morning, America"

8

"**M**y father entered this world on the slave ship *Suzanne* bound for Virginia Commonwealth in the spring of 1860. That slaver was captained by an Englishman named Jack Beef." Reg glanced over, then squinted back to the road. "I'm introducing the captain here because he later showed a kindness."

Marsh nodded, wondering about kindness and the slave trade, especially coming from this man. But Reg didn't seem to be talking about his own flesh and blood, just rattling off events of an old tale. He sat behind the wheel, perched on one of those springy webbed cushions Marsh associated with elderly drivers.

Outside of Reno they'd left the interstate for Highway 50. As they started across the long stretch of desert and salt flats, Reg switched the motor home into cruise control. The Establishment's speedometer remained at a steady fifty-five. Marsh had stopped checking it, bored with the monotonous speed and the straight road up ahead—straight as far as he could see.

"You should understand, Jack Beef had built a life supplying Africans to the cane colonies, and then the states. Never mind that the market for slaves had fallen. That business was all the captain knew. So on this particular passage his thoughts might've turned to the end." Reg nodded over. "Perhaps that accounts for the captain's rescue of my father. Algie came to hold this view. Of course, he'd also tell you that his parents were murdered by Jack Beef as surely as if the man had fired bullets through their heads."

"So your grandparents died at sea," Marsh said, trying to muster a little feeling for these people.

"Those two were hardly old enough to call grandparents. Remember, I never knew them. Not even Algie could tell you their names." Reg pulled the windshield visor against the sun, the day growing warmer with each desert mile. "Remind me to buy dark glasses when we stop for gasoline. I can scarcely see for the glare."

"Maybe you should take a break," Marsh said. They'd begun their second day on the road and Reg was still at the wheel. Earlier, Marsh had considered asking to drive, but the whole idea reminded him too much of Richard's pesky adolescence.

"Now, as I have it, the young woman who would be my grandmother gave birth not long into the middle passage. By then, the ship's hold was pestilential. You can imagine her labor—the galling chains, that hold like an oven. It's believed the young woman died in childbirth. The man thought to be Algie's father took his own life while being prepared for market. Or who knows—perhaps Jack Beef simply chose this event by way of ending his account."

Reg shook his head, clamping an unlit cigarette in the corner of his mouth. "But then, I'm only giving you another version of what the whole world has heard. I should be listening to your story. A person never learns anything new when his tongue is wagging."

"Right," Marsh said. Ever since they'd pulled out of the driveway, Reg had kept up a steady monologue. Marsh couldn't hear himself think—except to wonder exactly what he was doing here.

He pulled off his crew-neck sweater and tossed it into his bunk above the front seats. Reg called the motor home a cab-over, referring to the cushioned bunk that spanned the driver's well. Last night, climbing up to bed, Marsh thought of a phrase: sleeping loft. The words struck him as old-fashioned, a place existing in somebody's childhood. But maybe that was because he felt so much like a child now, restless and fidgeting at Reg's seat.

After a minute he moved down the aisle. He poured two lemonades, allowing for bumps in the road. His carefulness reminded him of working in the sloop's galley, braced against a counter, feet spread apart. Except the Establishment boasted a small version of a freezer with pebble-sized ice and a miniature silver scoop. While the motor home bullied the highway like some pituitary giant, almost everything inside it looked scaled-down for the use of midgets. The silver scoop seemed a toy in Marsh's hand.

"Maybe I should've been a stewardess," he said, moving up the aisle. He set their drinks on the wood-grained console between them. "Or steward, I should say."

Reg pressed the gas pedal, releasing the Establishment from cruise control. They'd started climbing. The highway wound through hills thick with rabbit brush and piñon pine. Dry prickly poppies fluttered in the motor home's wake.

Marsh opened the road atlas, glad for a little quiet. He figured they must be halfway across Nevada. No use trying to judge distance to the next city—there didn't seem to be one. He recognized nothing on the map except names shrouded in mysterious activity—the bases of land-to-sea missiles, nuclear test sites, ammunition depots—names hidden like secrets among wildlife refuges and small desert towns.

Reg swilled lemonade through his mouth, then smiled. He reached over and tapped Marsh's arm. "Stewards, porters, I knew the greatest of the greats. No doubt you're acquainted with the name A. Philip Randolph, founder of the Brotherhood of Sleeping Car Porters. Well, I met the man, shook his hand."

Marsh slumped in his seat. "That must've been something," he mumbled.

"That man was the New Deal—before Mr. Roosevelt."

Marsh nodded. "Before Roosevelt."

He glanced out as a Volkswagen drew alongside, then passed them. It seemed every car heading east had overtaken them. Of course, this wasn't a race. And he wasn't in charge. Reg sat behind the wheel like an emperor on his throne. He'd brought along the musty buffalo robe from Heather Hills, draping it in regal folds over the seat. Marsh looked over and shook his head. *Men,* Ginny used to say—her one-word explanation for all male behavior.

"You might not know," he said. "But I sailed the Pacific this summer—single-handed."

"Norman told me." Reg eased off the gas as another car zipped by. "That boy took a keen interest. Toward the end he allowed as how you were one of the finest friends a person could have. Coming from him, you understand what a tribute."

"Yes," Marsh said. Except it wasn't possible. He hadn't even attended the man's funeral, he'd been no one to Norm. Marsh glanced away, thinking of home and Richard, Alex—even Julia Oakes. He thought of all the days amounting to the distance he'd kept. Days like excuses—excused on account of work, on account of sickness. Excused on account of death. Finally he turned to Reg.

"The truth is—" But he couldn't tell the old man what he was starting to believe—that he might've been no one at all when it came right down to it. Not to anybody. He cleared his throat. "Truth is, I don't know yet where I finished in that race."

"Well, you mustn't imagine it would alter my opinion of you one iota if I learned you'd placed last. I only think it's a pity you couldn't find someone to go with you." The old man gave a little shrug. "Although nothing could've persuaded me to make that voyage. You can leave me on native soil, thank you. I've no desire to be cast onto another shore—unless, of course, we are speaking of this country's defense. In that case I am willing."

Marsh put a hand to his face, hiding a grin.

"And honored to step forward," Reg said. "If they'd asked me to write the book of Genesis, I would have started with John Locke's words: 'In the begining all the world was America.' "

Marsh nodded. He thought of the list stuck in Norm's little book, those words scrawled at the bottom.

"However, I would not be my father's son if I didn't tell you that by America I mean the great frontier."

"Yes," Marsh said. He reached for the atlas, deciding not to explain that the whole point of a single-handed race was doing it solo.

He checked the map as Reg slowed for a small town ahead. When he looked up, he saw three or four stone buildings, a few houses, then nothing but sagebrush. "Maybe we should've stopped for gas." He glanced back at the town, feeling the need to stretch his legs, the need to do something.

Reg chuckled. "You're forgetting our reserve tank. We can manage the distance to Ely, unless you'd prefer a stop now. You have only to say the word."

I'd like to drive, Marsh thought. He stepped into the aisle and rolled his shoulders, working the tightness from his back. Two days, and he already felt out of shape.

"Ely's okay," he said. At least that would put them close to the Utah border. He leaned around Reg's seat. "I'll fix us some lunch."

"Don't trouble yourself for me," Reg said. He wore a plaid madras shirt, unbuttoned at the neck so the turkey skin of his throat jiggled as he spoke. "When you reach my age you'll discover that your appetite wanes. It takes very little to stay alive. And I should add, precious little to send you to the last reveille."

"You know that's not true," Marsh said, thinking maybe so.

Reg smiled. "A precarious balance, but better than none at all. Why, sometimes just a sneeze . . ."

"I'm having lunch," Marsh said.

". . . the heart stops."

Marsh moved for the refrigerator, not about to listen. He filled his plate with leftovers, wondering how Reg stayed so thin on this food. But then it was true, the old man hardly ate, although so far he'd cooked all their meals.

"Tonight I cook," Marsh called up the aisle.

Reg didn't glance around. "The top speed of a sneeze is two hundred miles per hour. If you consider that force alone . . ."

Marsh made a grocery list in his head. Something healthy, something to keep body and soul together, to keep an old man alive. After a minute he leaned back in the dinette and gazed out the long side window. The highway seemed busier, full of trucks streaking past. Pickup country. Almost all the traffic was moving in the other direction, toward the mountains. Marsh noticed mostly men. He counted eight cowboy hats, then slid lower in the seat's corner and closed his eyes.

A light breeze from the louvered window above the sink swept his face. He heard the whoosh of trucks one after another. Then Reg singing some little song, the old man's voice drifting high and reedy. "And what they used, what they used was a great big number . . ." Marsh counted hats and fell asleep. In his dream he sat behind the wheel, driving two-hundred miles an hour.

A stillness settled. Marsh felt it—that absence of movement with only the engine's quiet ping. They couldn't have been stopped for long, but the motor home already sweltered in the late sun. Marsh's face was slick with sweat, his hair damp on that side where he'd slept. He blinked, glancing around, trying to come fully awake. Then he bolted straight.

Across the aisle Reg sat on the sofa with a rifle balanced over his knees and a cartridge box beside him. As Marsh started to speak, the old man pressed a finger to his lips. He motioned Marsh onto the sofa, then leaned close.

"I don't mean to alarm you, but I believe we may be in some danger."

"What is it?" Marsh said, his voice quick and loud. He glanced at the long-barreled rifle. The gun looked old and well-used, its walnut stock dark with wear.

"Please." Reg tapped his lips again. He nodded toward the window. "Out there."

Cautiously Marsh turned to look. He saw a gasoline pump and two pickup trucks parked side by side. Three men drank beer in a pickup bed, their legs dangling over the open tailgate. Another stood loading a shotgun. Marsh saw more guns racked in the rear windows of both trucks. As he sat staring, the man with the shotgun suddenly looked over, gazed directly at him. Marsh ducked.

"Hey you," the man hollered up to the window. "You planning to camp here or fill your tank?"

Marsh frowned at his hands locked in the cushions. Finally he lifted his head.

The lanky man pointed to the gas pump. "Got a sign here, says self-serve."

"Right," Marsh said, nodding behind the glass.

In the aisle Reg had dropped to one knee, rifle at the ready.

"Put that gun away," Marsh said, disgusted by his own jumpiness. He glanced to the window thinking, This is how things happen. "Those men are just hunters, dammit."

Reg gripped the sofa and pulled himself up. His voice sounded dazed, "I'd forgotten about hunters."

"So did I," Marsh said, softening at the sight of the old man.

Reg moved with a halting stiffness, as though his embarrassment was a disease of the joints. In the motor home's alcove, he propped his rifle against the mirrored wardrobe closet and stared at his reflection. He touched his chest, his face, then turned to Marsh.

"I thought they were armed men."

"Don't worry about it," Marsh said, stepping down to the gravel. He blinked in the bright sunshine, then reached to help Reg outside. But the old man brushed his hand away.

The lanky hunter ambled closer, shifting his shotgun to his other hand. "You got yourself quite a rig here."

Marsh glanced at the gun, then moved to fill the rear tank. Armed men, he said to himself, feeling light-headed with words, the smell of gasoline, the hot desert air. "This isn't my motor home." He nodded toward Reg. "It's his."

The hunter looked over. He rubbed his chin, then tilted his head, as if seeing the old man from another angle might make a difference.

"I apologize for the delay just now," Reg said. "I presume you and your colleagues are eager for the hunt."

The hunter stared, sliding his tongue around the inside of his mouth so his face turned lumpy. "Well, yes and no," he said after a minute. It seemed he was thinking of something else altogether. He let out a little cough, then stepped nearer Marsh. "I've been trying to get away all afternoon, but you know how these days go. It's just hurry up and wait."

Reg chuckled, pulling out his traveler's checks. "You're a patient man. I've known cultivated sportsmen who wouldn't tolerate the slightest interference. A child could be shot for occupying too much space in a grouse field."

"He doesn't mean that," Marsh said. But the hunter had moved off toward the men in the pickup bed. Marsh glanced past them to the service station's wood-frame building. Whitewashed boulders and sagebrush ringed the station. Above the garage a sign read: BUD'S RADIATOR RE-PAIR—THE BEST PLACE IN ELY TO TAKE A LEAK.

"Put your money away," Marsh ordered as Reg started for the pickups. He loped past the old man, pulled out two twenties and handed them to the tall hunter who seemed in charge.

"I assume you're Bud," Reg said, stepping alongside.

"Depends." The man looked to the others in the pickup, then leaned his shotgun against the tailgate. He nodded at Reg. "You boys with the newspapers or the F.B.I.?"

Marsh glanced around, catching the exchange of smiles. "I think maybe there's some mix-up."

A heavy set balding man eased himself from the tailgate. "Okay, let's get this straight. You're not agents and you're not from the *Chronicle* or the *Deseret News.* You aren't going to ask for the umpteenth time today where the Russians went after they bought the map, and you don't want to know how to get to Isobel's place. Now, do I have that right?"

"Right."

"You don't care to hear."

"We most certainly do," Reg said.

"I thought so."

"Listen," Marsh said. "We're not with anybody, we're just plain people."

The tall hunter named Bud shoved his hands into his pockets and shook his head. "Your partner here doesn't talk like any plain person I've ever heard of."

"He's an elderly man," Marsh said, nudging Reg to keep quiet.

"Doesn't mean diddly squat." The balding man leaned into the pickup and pulled another beer from an ice chest. "We've seen you government boys all ages, colors—" He glanced at Reg. "No offense, just your equal opportunity."

"Everybody comes in pairs," a younger man grumbled from the pickup. "You'd think we were running Noah's Ark through here." He wiped his forehead in the crook of his arm, then climbed off the truck. He stood a minute, frowning into the low sun. "Hell, I'm going to Isobel's."

"Of course, the sheriff's office will deny everything." Bud glanced over and winked at Marsh. "Far as they're concerned the Russians, F.B.I.—none of you boys were ever in town."

"Well, I doubt they'll convince a soul," Reg said. "Puts me in mind of that day when the confidential news of General Custer's gold discovery was carried from the Black Hills. A private was sent out on a horse shod backwards so as to confuse the trail." The old man chuckled. "Twenty-four hours later, all of America knew that secret."

The balding man gave a shrug. "Doesn't surprise me in the least. Nothing personal, but we've got complete nuts operating this country." He dug into his pocket and dropped a set of keys into Bud's hand. "Drive my truck out to Isobel's, and I'll ride with these boys." He turned to Reg. "We have these dirt lanes around here, all look alike. I'll see you don't get lost."

"That's very kind," Reg said.

Marsh grabbed the old man's arm. "Excuse us," he said. He led Reg behind the white-frame building. "I am not—I mean it—*not* going anywhere with those men."

"You're under no obligation," Reg said. He took out his pocket watch, snapped open the gold case. "It's now 5:15. I'll return for you no later than eight o'clock."

Marsh gazed off, trying to think. "Well, what about Utah," he said finally. "We were supposed to camp at Green River."

"You will not catch me crossing Utah after nightfall." Reg slid the watch into his pocket, then rested his hand at Marsh's shoulder. "We must try and remain flexible, otherwise our journey becomes only a burden. Now then, I'm driving with the gentlemen to Isobel's. I'm fascinated to learn what brought the Russians here and where they've gone since purchasing the map."

"Listen," Marsh said. He leaned into the old man's face. "You do know that you're not some member of the F.B.I."

Reg smiled. "Come, come," he said. Then he tilted back his head and laughed so his thin shoulders shook.

"All right," Marsh said. "I'll go with you."

9

The man named Walt sat in the passenger seat, directing Reg down the highway. Marsh had taken the sofa just behind, but he might as well have been sitting in some other room. As they drove through town he leaned closer to catch Walt's low, easy voice.

"The town's been a little depressed lately," Walt said, making it sound more like a mood than an economic problem. "We used to have the world's biggest copper pit and some turquoise mining. Of course, we've still got the airfield. As long as you people in Washington keep talking about putting the MX missile in here, I guess there's hope."

"Hope." Marsh laughed, nodding at Walt. "That's a good one."

"No joke," Walt said. He waved a hand, pointing out the three gambling casinos on Main Street. Then the county library where the Russians first turned up. The two men had introduced themselves as tourists attached to the Soviet Embassy.

"And they both went by Vladimir," Walt said.

"Hah!" Reg said, thumping the steering wheel.

Marsh didn't say anything, gazing out the side window as the short blocks of town gave way to irrigated fields. He was thinking about the MX, how Ginny and Alex had signed a protest. But that was California. Home, Marsh thought.

They turned down a narrow dirt road. Fields of alfalfa straggled off, looking tattered and less green. A few more miles, and the fields gave way altogether. The road quit, too, widening into a dusty parking lot.

"Isobel's," Walt announced, though a sign over the low-slung building said THE PLEASURE TROVE.

Marsh wasn't surprised to see they'd driven to some hideaway bar. He'd figured as much, although the place seemed a little too isolated. The pink building sprawled where the desert began, as if it had chosen that wild side, refusing civilization. As Walt and Reg climbed outside, Marsh ducked into the driver's well and rolled up the windows. He punched both locks, not taking any chances. Then he dashed across the parking lot, startling a jack rabbit from under a Subaru Brat.

He nodded at Reg, the old man's hair glinting like steel shavings in the fading sun. "Maybe we can order dinner here," he said. At least he might not need to cook.

"That could be a problem," Walt said, pushing the bar door open. "Isobel's gone vegetarian. But I'll see what I can do."

Marsh glanced to a sign posted beside the door: NO WOMEN ALLOWED. But he noticed a few inside. He followed Reg to a table, glad Alex wasn't here to see that sign. Not that he could imagine her setting foot in this dim place.

He slid into a chair beside Reg, then nodded around the table to the men he'd seen earlier at the gas station. It looked like they'd been here a while, empty beer bottles already collecting. Otherwise, business seemed slow. There were more cars in the parking lot than people in the bar. Only one couple swayed on the small square of dance floor. Across the way, a lone woman nursed a soft drink, looking depressed. But the men from Bud's Radiator Repair appeared happy just sitting here ticking off every detail of the Russians' day in town.

"They told Jeanette they only wanted to *browse*," the youngest man said, giving Marsh a look. "A minute later they come back with the state's study on nuclear sites. That book's on the reserve shelf, but hell if they care. To top it all off, they tell Jeanette they need to make a copy."

"What cheek," Reg said.

"Jeanette thinks it over, decides that's okay."

Walt squeezed into the chair at Marsh's other side. "I figured you'd probably want your beer light. That's what most of your buddies drink."

"Light's fine," Marsh said. He wondered if these men really cared who he was, F.B.I. or not. It seemed they just wanted to tell somebody— anybody who hadn't heard. He looked over at Walt. "I guess you come here pretty often."

"Naw," Walt said. "Only when we get you boys through the area. You're entitled same as the regular citizen—you've got your normal urges. As my ex likes to say, men will be men. Not that I could personally screw any of these ladies myself, being as I know them."

"Hold it," Marsh said. Beer sloshed down his hand as he swung around. The couple on the dance floor had disappeared. The lone woman had been joined by a man clutching a cowboy hat to his crotch.

Reg scooted to the edge of his chair. "I assume the feeble-minded Jeanette has since been relieved of her librarian duties."

"Christ no," the young man said. "Your advance agents had turned up first, showed her pictures of the two Vladimirs and told her, give these Russians whatever they want."

"Impossible," Red snorted.

Marsh elbowed him. "Finish your beer, we're leaving."

The young man shrugged. "Those advance agents had their orders, same as you. I'd say Washington wants the Communists knowing."

"That's your cold war," Bud said.

"America," the young man muttered.

Reg raised his glass. "May it ever flourish."

"Whores," Marsh said, leaning to Reg.

"I have eyes," the old man said, and for a moment it seemed his eyes were shining.

Marsh looked up as Walt slid a pitcher of beer in front of him. "No more for me—we've got to get going."

"Nonsense," Reg said. "In my father's words, we must take every opportunity to cut the dust from our throats. Evenings my father would ride into town and order two drinks at the bar—one for himself and one for his horse. Algie gave his mounts their due after the example set by Hole In The Day, that young Sioux who trusted only those visions seen in his pony's ears."

Across the table the man named DeRay who'd been sitting silent cleared his throat. "Is that so," he said.

The old man nodded, then gazed toward the bar—a blonde woman leaning there smiling at nothing, except maybe the music drifting over her. Or perhaps her own thoughts.

After a minute Reg turned back to the table. "I expect it's too much to ask," he said softly. "But I'm wondering if we would happen to have one dear woman among us whose skin bears the tincture of my own."

Marsh stared at Reg, then glanced over as Walt nudged him.

"Are you talking about a black woman?" Walt asked.

"I'm not talking about anybody," Marsh snapped. He took a gulp of beer, noticing that he and Reg were the only ones drinking from frosted mugs. For an instant he felt like an ingrate. Try and remain flexible, the old man had told him. Ginny had said, I'd truly like to know you can do it. Do what, Marsh wondered. Accept the misguided kindness of strangers, the wandering mind of an old man? Accept the worst?

He turned to Walt. "Sorry," he said. "It's just that my wife died in July."

Walt clicked his tongue. "That's rough," he said.

"Well, there's always Angel," DeRay suggested.

"Could be she's off tonight." Walt leaned to Marsh. "This is Angel's slow time, being as it's hunting season. You get a few deer hunters from out of town and your black military stays put at the airfield. The two don't mix, if you catch what I mean."

Marsh nodded. "My wife passed away after thirty-two years." For just a moment it seemed he'd confused Virginia's age with the length of their marriage. "In all that time I never slept with another woman."

Walt let out a low, amazed whistle. "Un-believable," he said. "You must've been in honest-to-God love."

"Well, yes," Marsh said. He looked off, frowning to think that it could've been just love.

Walt gathered up the empty bottles. "This man deserves another beer. While I'm at it, I'll check on Angel."

Reg slipped several bills from his wallet and stuffed them into Walt's hip pocket. "I'm in your debt," he said.

Without Walt the table turned quiet. Across from Marsh, Bud lit a cigarette. Reg pulled out his Chesterfields. Overhead, a wooden ceiling fan stirred the stale air. Marsh wondered if the blonde at the bar could be Isobel. It seemed no one was in charge here. Nobody'd approached their table, not even to serve drinks.

After a while the young man shoved back in his chair. "Well, how about it—what do you say to hunting up some Russians?"

"Oh Christ," Bud groaned.

Reg stabbed out his cigarette. "Perhaps we should begin by determining where these Russians can be located."

"You're not locating anybody." Marsh glanced toward the bar, relieved to see Walt headed their way with a short black woman in tow.

"Doesn't take much brain work finding those Russians," the young man said. "We sold them the map and gave them directions out to the reservation."

Bud sucked at his cheeks a moment, then nodded. "Seems your foreigners are crazy for Indians."

"They get it from reading," DeRay said.

Reg shut his eyes. "God help us if those Russians incite the savages."

"I promised these boys a little something," Walt said, setting a plate of carrots on the table. "Vegetables being the closest thing I could find to food."

Walt pulled out his chair, and the small dark woman slid next to Marsh. "So here's Angel," Walt said.

Marsh nudged Reg, then leaned back so the old man could see.

Reg paid no attention. "These Indians we're speaking of—are they friendlies or hostiles?"

"Try just plain drunk," the young man said.

"Come now," Reg said. "Would you have me believe all these Indians are drunkards?"

The young man grinned. "Right down to the last tomahawk."

Beside Marsh, the young woman named Angel yawned. She slid a carrot from the platter. Around her wrist, gold bracelets clinked, her frosted fingernails gleamed. "Carrots are supposed to be good for your eyes," she said vaguely, as if she didn't expect to be heard.

"Helps you see in the dark," Walt said, winking at Marsh.

Marsh turned to Reg. "I think you and I better switch chairs. *Now.*"

The old man didn't look around. He lit another cigarette and exhaled a quick, agitated puff. "This business between the Russians and the savages smacks of that conspiracy which took place only miles from you in the Utah territory. I ask you—if Mr. Brigham Young felt no qualms in swaying the Indian against free Americans, do you imagine these Communists will hesitate for a moment?"

"Hang on," Bud said, suddenly scowling at Reg. "Let's back up a little here. There's nobody more American than a Mormon, in case you're interested. Besides which, my mother happens to be one."

Reg clucked his tongue. "Your mother—"

"Time for us to shove off," Marsh said in a rush. He pushed from the table and clamped Reg's shoulder. "We've got a long day tomorrow."

"Well, I am truly pissed," Angel said, crossing her short, muscular legs. It seemed this time she intended on being heard.

Reg glanced over. He stared.

"This is Angel," Walt said, nodding at the old man.

Reg smiled. "An angel indeed." He shrugged Marsh's hand away, taking in the woman's thick black curls, her blue-shadowed eyes, the fine penciled arch of her brows. "You are the very embodiment of your name," he said. "Do you see how the famous Cleopatra pales in your presence? Her complexion turns to whey."

Angel shifted in her chair. She looked around the room, as if expecting to see this other woman withering before her eyes.

"I can only beg your forgiveness." Reg pressed his hand to his chest. "My heart thrills, but I'm afraid otherwise I must fail you. I'm speaking now of my male member."

Angel touched the carrot to her glossy lips. After a minute she murmured, "That's okay."

"However, I give you Andrew Marsh, a splendid man who has asked to be called by his patronymic. This gentleman has recently lost his wife. I've heard him sighing in the night. His cot heaves."

"My bed does not heave," Marsh said.

Reg turned, squinting over his chair back as if from some high fence. He nodded at Marsh. "Will you pay me the honor of standing in my stead?"

"Absolutely not."

"Come on," Walt said. "You'd be doing it for Reginald here. The old guy's practically begging you."

"I am begging," Reg whispered through a cloud of smoke.

"Hell, I'd do it," the young man grumbled.

"You already have," Angel said.

Marsh shook his head at Reg, the old man's fingers hooked around the chair's rungs, those dark knuckles large and misshapen with age. Finally he stepped beside Angel.

"Will you come outside with me, please?"

"Better take your vegetables." Bud grinned, shoving the plate across the table.

Walt thumped him on the back. "Play this one for The Gipper."

Marsh turned away, thinking any second he'd hear applause from the table. But at Walt's words the men had moved on to football, already arguing about whether or not the NFL really meant to strike. Reg will be out of his element in that discussion, Marsh thought, following Angel across the planked floor. She led him into the rear of the building, through what seemed a sitting room. The room was empty except for a pale red-headed woman reading on a sofa. The woman said nothing as they walked by, didn't even look up.

Outside, they moved between folding plastic lawn chairs and chaise longues. Japanese lanterns were strung around the dusty yard, their colors shedding a soft glow in the desert night. Beyond the yard, lanterns dotted a row of teardrop trailers overgrown with sagebrush.

Angel nodded, the top of her head no higher than his shoulder. "My place is last—number six."

Marsh took a step backward, bumping into a plastic chair. "I was thinking maybe we could just go for a walk or something."

"Rate's the same," Angel said. "Walking, talking, screwing—you can have thirty minutes or an hour."

"I could use a walk." Marsh looked past her, unable to meet her gaze.

Angel shrugged. "You're the one buying the ticket."

"I appreciate this," Marsh said. "You see, my friend—"

"Lead on," she ordered. "But I can't go off the premises or into any unlit areas. This is for my own protection, understand."

Marsh clutched the vegetable plate as they started across the yard. With his free hand he steered Angel from one lantern to another, trying to stay inside the light. He moved carefully, thinking of old movies with prison yards illuminated bright as day—machine guns raining bullets from four deadly corners. It occurred to him that he probably deserved this. As they rounded the corner of the pink building he felt finished, sick of himself. He hoped the bullets would catch him. But at his side Angel was shaking her head no.

"No way am I strolling onto that parking lot in my baby dolls. Isobel's got rules."

Marsh stopped walking. He turned, staring down at her. He hadn't even noticed, the bar had been so dark. Years had passed since he'd seen those filmy ruffles. He might've gone the rest of his life—died just now—without ever remembering. For a moment he frowned into the brilliant night sky, baffled by a world which could restore a memory at such random.

He glanced at Angel, the warm desert breeze lifting the ruffles over her small shoulders. "I wouldn't worry about being seen." He waved toward the few pickups, the Subaru Brat still there. Across the parking lot the motor home loomed pale in moonlight. "It's a slow night," he said.

"You're telling me," Angel muttered. She grabbed Marsh's hand and yanked him onto the dusty lot. "Whatever works for you," she said, bobbing beside him on her satin sling-back heels. "But I'm only going once around."

As they circled the lot Marsh said, "I'm sorry about the hunters. Walt mentioned they hurt your business."

"Well, it's a free country." Angel reached over his arm for a carrot. "They've got the right to hunt on federal land, and in this state that's practically every acre. I'm talking according to Isobel. She says Nevada's just one big company town, except the company's the U.S. government. Since I depend on the military you don't hear me complaining."

Marsh stopped at the motor home. He leaned against the big front fender and gazed at Angel. "I don't know," he said after a minute. "I mean, doesn't it ever bother you?"

"Nope," Angel said. "Seems like I've been living in the company town my whole life. All my brothers joined the marines—every last one—the day they turned eighteen. Before them there was my daddy, signed on for the complete tour. Except he died in Korea."

"I'm sorry," Marsh said, ashamed of his curiosity, shamed by her innocence as to the question he'd really asked. He looked down at Angel's black satin shoes. He thought of Reg, the old man's photographs under glass. "I was almost sent to Korea," he said quietly.

"I guess you got lucky," Angel said. She sighed and combed her fingers through her hair, swept the curls behind one ear. "Anyway, after Korea the government mailed my mamma a check and it's still coming to her every month, for life. Money from Uncle Sam, she used to say. Got to where I believed it was a real person sending those checks."

She moved next to Marsh, swaying against the Establishment's fender. Her hair gave off a faint musky odor. "You know how you do when you're a kid—dream things up like rich uncles. Sometimes a mood gets on you and you're thinking you must have an extra relative somewhere who cares about you for your own true self. So I'd look into my mirror and say, one of these days your Uncle Sam is going to walk right through the door. Be ready, Angeline, I'd say. He's coming to see you and he's bringing you a Hula-Hoop." She turned, touching Marsh's arm. "Angeline is my true given name."

"Yes," Marsh said. He looked around, hunting for somewhere to set the plate. He reached for the passenger door, then realized he'd locked it. He tried the driver's side, then scrambled for the side entrance. The handle turned. Silently the metal step dropped down. Marsh touched his forehead to the open door as if some profound mercy had been extended.

"Have you gone nuts?" Angel called from the fender. She took a few steps toward him, then stopped and put her hands on her hips.

Marsh shoved the plate onto the carpeted alcove floor, then poked his head out, waving for her to come.

But she didn't budge. She ran her fingers along the gold chain at her neck and dipped into the scoop of ruffles riding her breasts. She squinted at her mother-of-pearl locket watch. "You want the other half hour?"

"Will you come on!" Marsh jumped the metal step, landing in the dust beside her. He touched her slender arm, her face. Somewhere far away he could see Cleopatra turning pale and Julia Oakes grieving, crying for salmon pink baby dolls.

"Uh-uh," Angel said. She pointed to the motor home. "I'm not allowed to do business off the premises."

Marsh jiggled her hand. "We're *on* the premises."

"And this rig belongs to you."

"My friend, Mr. Vickers. Reg." I'm standing in his place, Marsh thought, deciding to believe this even as his body raced to tell him otherwise.

She stepped around him and peered into the alcove. "You got any large animals in here?"

"None," Marsh said, squeezing past her. He switched on a ceiling light, then pulled her inside.

She bent for the carrots, but he drew her straight and led her beneath the light.

"No unlit areas," he said, using her own words. He wrapped his arms around her, kissed the crown of her head, her quick mouth. Then he plunged his face into sheer ruffles and called her by her own true name, "Angeline."

10

"So you choose not to tell me," Reg grumbled.

"Nothing happened," Marsh said, opening the atlas in his lap.

"Deny me the kindness of a small detail—the dusky angel's breasts, her nipples like amethysts . . ."

Beneath the atlas, Marsh felt a stirring. He leaned to the dash, fiddling with the radio as Reg rambled up and down Angeline's body.

Utah was just ahead. An announcer read the weather forecast, warning of strong winds gusting north to south throughout Millard County, possible thunderstorms in the Wasatch. Marsh looked down at the map, welcoming Utah despite the weather prediction. Across that border he'd meet civilization again. He'd shave and shower, change out of the crumpled clothes he'd slept in. Last night he hadn't been himself. He'd landed on Angeline like the whole air force. Her Uncle Sam.

He blamed Nevada, wide-open country with teardrop trailers and sleek-barreled rifles glinting in pickup windows—all the talk about Russians, savages, and men will be men. In the end, he would've taken any woman. Anyone at all. He glanced across the map to California where people spoke of meaningful relationships. At least those men tried. But in Nevada . . . No civilians, he decided.

Reg nodded from behind the wheel. "I expect you're filled with remorse, tortured by the infidelity to your departed wife's memory."

Marsh looked away, reading the sign: WELCOME TO UTAH.

"Another woman," Reg said.

"We're in Utah," Marsh mumbled.

"And the fallen black angel, besides." Reg sighed, pulling off the highway. "Well, no matter. I'm depending on you to deliver us through this peculiar territory and Mr. Brigham Young's armies of Nauvoo."

Armies, Marsh thought, closing his eyes. "There are no armies."

"Legions," the old man said. He slid his buffalo robe from the driver's seat, then pressed his shaky hand at Marsh's shoulder. "Take care how the wind blows. Their troops will set fire to the grass on our windward and otherwise annoy us in every possible way."

Marsh blinked out to the highway. The two-lane road had dropped onto a wide desert plain, more desolate-looking than the Nevada land they'd left. In the distance, a dust devil funneled among sagebrush. To the north the Deseret Test Center stretched toward Interstate 80. Proving Grounds, the map said. No public access. Ahead lay the low, soot-gray hills called Confusion Range. I should stop studying the map, Marsh thought. Stop listening to Reg, a man so old he'd forgotten the present.

"For your information, Utah isn't a territory. It's a state." Marsh tucked in his shirt, catching a cheesy odor in his clothes. Sex-soaked, and not just any woman—the fallen black angel. But Reg was wrong, last night had nothing to do with Virginia. He'd chosen sex at a far remove.

He slid behind the wheel, glad the old man had taken the buffalo robe with him. Reg sat in the passenger seat, the mangy fur clutched in his lap.

"I'd appreciate it if you'd quit living in the past," Marsh said, steering onto the highway. He felt much better with his hands finally at the wheel, his foot on the gas.

Reg drew the buffalo robe higher over his chest. "You'll find that I do not live in the past," he said softly. "I live with it."

Marsh nodded, distracted by the radio and a local broadcaster announcing items for sale. *Plastic figurines . . . records . . . slightly used learning machine . . .*

"Mormon cretins," Reg said, rolling his eyes at the radio. "Inbred, imbecilic half-wits."

That winds up this morning's edition of Tradio. Next, regional news. But first a reminder . . .

Marsh speeded up, figuring the broadcast must be coming from Delta, a town he'd spotted on the atlas. Not long and they'd be past this empty, blowing stretch.

So come out today, fellows, and let those lovely young Rainbow girls wash your filthy car . . .

"Oh God," Marsh said. From black whores to thin-legged girls laboring in pastel dresses over dirty cars. It seemed his desire had crossed the border, oozing a silver thread across the map like some nocturnal slug in his backyard. He glanced at Reg, thinking if he could just make contact, talk to somebody who really knew him. "I've got to call home."

Reg frowned off, not listening. His fingers pulled at the matted fur. " 'And He caused a sore cursing to come upon them because of their iniquity . . . the Lord God did cause a skin of blackness to come upon them.' " The old man let out a shaky breath, then turned to Marsh. "Book of Mormon. Nephi, you remember—chapter five."

"Craziness," Marsh said, feeling the wind pick up.

And of regional interest—Utah Republican Dan Marriot has urged consideration of splitting MX bases, reducing to half the missile bunkers proposed in Nevada and four Utah counties . . .

"And yet we believe," Reg sighed. "Credo quia absurdum est—we believe because it is absurd."

"Well, I don't, Marsh said, catching the tremor in Reg's voice. It had to be this place—just being here. Unfortunately we must cross the territory of Utah, the old man had said.

However, Texas senator Lloyd Bentsen told reporters that before he'd support basing in his state, the Air Force would need to find a location where there weren't any people . . .

"Put the whole damned thing in Utah," Marsh muttered before he thought. But he was glad he'd said it. He looked over, hoping his words had stirred the old man. Reg appeared to be cowering against his door, sliding farther beneath the buffalo robe with every mile.

They were entering the town now, passing under a cloud cover so definite it seemed they'd rolled into the shade of an awning. At the first stoplight a raindrop splatted the windshield. Then another. The highway broadened into a four-lane avenue that looked too big for such a small town.

Marsh nodded at the old man. "They have very wide streets here—regular gas a dollar eighteen."

The old man didn't budge. "The way is wide," he whispered, "but narrow is the gate."

"A dollar sixteen point nine," Marsh said as they passed another gas station. Across the street the city park took up one block of the five he'd counted. He saw nobody in the park, although he thought maybe the young girls might be there, rain or no.

He swung into a convenience market with gas pumps out front, then turned to Reg. "Come on, I'll buy you a cup of coffee. It'll do you good to get outside for a minute."

"I don't think that would be wise," Reg said, not looking over.

"I'll bring you a cup." Marsh stepped around the motor home, smiling at the rain which seemed to be falling as if from a leaky faucet, one fat drop at a time. He glanced toward the market and a woman inside. She cleared the gas pump, then waved. Marsh rapped at Reg's window. "Regular gas," he called. "Regular people, regular everything."

Behind the glass, Reg shook his head, his eyes closed.

Marsh filled both tanks, glad they wouldn't need to make another stop in Utah. He figured the sooner he got the old man out of this state, the better. It seemed Reg had fallen into some low spell—the gray clouds casting more than a shadow. A sore cursing, Marsh thought as he hurried inside the market. He felt a vague urgency, as if this crossing might be truly dangerous, the fire racing hot on their windward.

Then he heard the rain let loose outside. It drummed the market's flat roof, splashed in the open doorway.

"Would you mind?" the young woman said from behind the counter. She gestured toward the entrance.

Marsh closed the door, then moved to the cash register and signed two traveler's checks. He glanced at the woman. She was barely an adult—early twenties maybe—and so beautiful he couldn't look at her for long. If he'd seen her face on a movie screen, he would've stared. But over the counter . . . He could hardly speak. It was his impression that such extraordinary beauties weren't what a man would call friendly. Not the smiley ones from whom you might buy weak coffee-to-go in a Styrofoam cup.

As she placed his change on the counter, he cleared his throat, asking anyway, for Reg. "I don't suppose you have coffee."

"Only decaffeinated," she said, pointing toward the end of the counter.

"Right," Marsh said. He saw that the young woman's face held an apostolic radiance, consecrated by angels and Latter Day Saints. It seemed the sun had never touched her fair skin, no clouds skiffed her blue eyes.

He poured two jumbo cups, added powdered cream and sugar to one, then stepped back beside the cash register.

She pressed plastic lids onto the cups. "The rain," she said, tapping a lid.

"Yes," Marsh said. He turned to leave, then hesitated, wanting to ask if she'd ever read about a sore cursing in the Book of Mormon. He would've asked her to step outside, assure Reg no one really believed anymore. Tell the old man nothing personal, just history. But because she was so beautiful, he couldn't ask. Instead he mumbled, "Rotten day for a car wash."

She nodded as he turned for the door. "They called it off."

He hurried around the motor home, ducking the weather. But Reg had locked the driver's side. He juggled the Styrofoam cups in one hand and knocked at the rain-streaked window. "Open up!"

The old man leaned, a small dark form blurred behind the glass. "Forgive me," he said, pushing open the door. "There's been a party requesting assistance. I took precautions."

Marsh set the coffee on the console between them, then looked out at the empty street. It seemed the weather had sent everybody indoors. Home, Marsh thought.

"I don't see anybody," he said.

"I believe they've taken shelter in the phone booth." Reg wiped fog from the windshield and pointed to the opposite corner. "Yes, that would be them—the child is standing in the puddle again."

"You took precautions against a *child?*" Marsh pulled away from the pumps, then stopped at the corner. "Honestly," he said, digging change from his pants pocket.

Reg pressed farther into his seat. He'd wrapped the buffalo robe around him so the fur spiked at his bumpy chin. "I wouldn't use that telephone."

"Drink your coffee," Marsh said. "I was supposed to call home last night, in case you've forgotten."

He dashed for the phone booth thinking, last night. Now there was a time and a place where a man would want to look out for himself. But not Reg. The old man chose today—this caffein-free state and a little girl stomping in a mud puddle, dangling red sandals over her sopping head. He nodded at the child, then turned to the phone booth. Inside the booth, a stocky dark-haired woman glanced out and held up one finger as if she wouldn't be long.

"Take your time," Marsh said loudly, stepping back.

The woman blew her nose in a wad of Kleenex, then pushed the door open. "Did you want to use the phone?"

"After you," Marsh said. He looked back to the motor home, deciding to wait in the rain. It was something of a relief coming across this plump ordinary woman, as if her presence canceled out the sainted beauty he'd seen a minute ago.

"Oh, I'm not calling anybody," the woman said, sidling out of the booth. She gave a breathy laugh that sounded more like a sigh. "I was just in there having a major nervous breakdown . . . falling to complete pieces." She shoved the strap of her cloth purse higher on her shoulder. "A cosmic crack-up, if you can relate to that."

Marsh nodded at her, making a correction—not overweight, but pregnant. "Well, it certainly isn't much of a day."

"Not to mention the weather," the woman said. She glanced past him to the soaked little girl. "Tiffany, get your bod out of that hole before you drown." She pushed the dripping hair from her cheeks, then looked at him. "Kids."

"I can find another phone," Marsh said, thinking a woman in her condition should be inside. "I'm in no rush—just wanted to check in at home." He glanced over his shoulder to where Reg sat waiting, probably behind locked doors again. The old man ought to be ashamed.

The woman shook her head and moved away from the booth, her sandals squelching rain. "I'd call now if I were you. Wait too long and there might not be anybody on the other end. I'm talking not a single person thinking about you, wondering how you're doing." She stepped nearer the child, then looked back at him, her eyes wide, her full face suddenly tight. She clamped one hand around her purse strap. Rain clung like gauze on her fringed wool poncho. "Oh, maybe once in a while somebody'll say, Whatever became of what's her name—you remember, good old grab 'em by the balls Sharon. Well, I can tell you exactly what happened—"

"I'll only be a minute," Marsh said, stepping into the booth, not about to hear.

He gave the operator his credit card number, then dialed Richard's office. While he waited for the secretary to put Richard on the line, he glanced out and saw the woman brushing at her long navy poncho, her hands moving over her belly as if rearranging everything inside. Good old Sharon—but young enough to have that wading child and another on the way. Old before her time, Marsh thought. Then he heard his son's voice.

"You almost missed me," Richard said. "I was just leaving for lunch."

Marsh frowned as the woman pulled out her tattered Kleenex and dabbed at her wet face. "I forgot the time difference. We're an hour later here."

"Mountain time," Richard said.

"Yes," Marsh said, bothered by this small talk. While they discussed the time, that drenched woman stood pressing the Kleenex to her eyes. Probably in tears. "We're crossing Utah," he said. "It's raining."

"I figured you'd be in Colorado. Alex left me a copy of your itinerary. She had you down for Pueblo tonight."

"We were delayed in Nevada." Marsh glanced down to his soaked deck shoes, unable to explain why Nevada had taken so long. The way things were going, he didn't even feel entitled to write a postcard. "How is Alex?"

"Don't ask me," Richard said. "Haven't you called home?"

Marsh squinted to see outside, the glass misted with rain and his breath. "I'm calling you, Richard."

For a moment there was silence. Marsh cleared a circle on the pane with his elbow. The little girl had left the puddle, standing beside her mother—the two of them hand-in-hand, gazing his way. "There are some people waiting. It's coming down cats and dogs."

"We're split," Richard said.

Marsh turned, blinking at the phone. "What do you mean, split."

"Alex and I."

Marsh fisted his hand in his pocket. He wanted to remind his son— we're talking about the time, the weather here. I'm only checking in. "Richard—" He coughed, feeling the day now, his cotton shirt clinging, the change damp and sticky in his pocket.

"I figured you'd already called your place, spoken to Alex. She stayed there last night. At least I thought she did." Richard breezed along, his voice so casual they really might've been discussing the weather. "Be honest, Dad. You saw this coming."

Marsh shook his head. "Just a problem, is all."

"A divorce," Richard said. "I wasn't going to tell you till you got back, but I need to start somewhere. Start over," he said.

Marsh pressed his forehead to the glass, took a deep breath. "Maybe if you and Alex could talk a little more, hold off." He gazed out and the woman gave him a weak wave. The gray ball of Kleenex rolled from her open fingers, fell to her feet. "If I was there, maybe. I don't know, Richard—it seems like everything happens while I'm gone."

"And I suppose you think that's some kind of accident," Richard snapped. "The fact is—" His voice faltered, lost ground. After a moment he said, "It's just how things are, Dad. You know—life."

"Yes," Marsh said. But it struck him that whatever his son and daughter-in-law were doing couldn't be chalked up simply to living. Ginny, Marsh thought. He felt a sudden anger, as if she'd done this—jumped teams, taken her winning ways to the other side.

"Speak up," Richard said. "I can't hear you."

Marsh looked away, stunned by his thoughts. "Listen, Richard, I'd better get off the phone. There's a woman waiting."

Richard's voice dropped, a brand-new man-to-man sound. "Anybody I know?"

"Besides, Mr. Vickers isn't feeling well." Marsh rushed on, refusing to take this turn in the conversation. He heard secrets in Richard's words, the implicit partnership of single males. If he wasn't careful, his son would be wanting to know if he'd got laid yet.

"Well, I hope the old man isn't seriously sick," Richard said, his tone shifting, countering. "I sure wouldn't want to see anybody pull out on you."

"I've got to hang up," Marsh said.

He placed the receiver in its cradle and stood for a moment, feeling numbed, as if he and Richard had been on the line for hours. Then he dialed his house. He let the phone ring, thinking Alex might be outside. He pictured her in the shade garden, her firm shoulders caped by the golden willow, her knees massed in daylilies. Or maybe she'd finally been funded—on the job, her arm slung around the stuffed grizzly while kindergarteners lined up to count those razor teeth.

He stepped from the phone booth, deciding to try again later. The soaked little girl hopped toward him. He glanced down at her, then nodded to the woman. "Sorry to make you wait, but there was a problem at home."

"Then it's lucky you called," the woman said. She trudged beside him, all belly, her hand at her forehead, a visor against the rain. "Is there anything I can do?"

Marsh stared, trying to imagine why a stranger, especially this down at the heels woman . . . "Thanks, but no," he said. Then seeing her eyes dim, her hand drop to her side, he added, "I don't think anybody could help now, except maybe a good marriage counselor."

As he turned to leave, the woman stepped after him. "Get home fast," she said, dragging the child behind her. "I've been this route. If your old lady's going to dump you, then *you* be there. Don't make it easy." She caught his arm. "People want out—you and I can understand that. But I'm talking about the ones who wait till you've fallen asleep. The lowlife who takes the car. The long-distance cowards . . ."

Marsh stopped beside the motor home and swung around, the woman a blur in his eyes and his voice flooded, too, so even he couldn't hear. "My wife's dead."

". . . the thing is, you need to be told. You need the kiss good-bye."

"I'm not going home!" He heard himself suddenly hollering, his voice slamming in her face. "My wife's gone."

She nodded, her mouth open and working, the strap of her cloth bag slipping down her arm. "I need a ride."

Marsh jerked straight. He turned, ran a hand through his sopping hair. Rain dinned the Establishment's hood, splashed the grille. He trailed a finger over the fender. Finally he looked back at the woman. "Okay."

She hustled to the side door, pushing the child ahead. Marsh heard the little girl's breath, thick and rattling as she struggled inside. So far there hadn't been a word out of her, though Marsh believed she must be old enough to talk—he guessed maybe three. But then, he felt a little rusty when it came to children. They were a subject he'd let slide.

The girl flopped into the alcove, her knobby legs bound by the dripping folds of her sundress. Marsh bent to help her up, but she'd already shoved to her hands and knees, the red sundress hiked over her pale bottom. Marsh looked away, wondering what kind of mother would take her child onto the streets minus underpants.

The woman pressed behind him, her belly nudging. "You won't regret this," she said as he turned to let her through.

Marsh stepped into the bathroom and grabbed towels from a cupboard, then moved up the aisle. He glanced toward the driver's well, but he couldn't see Reg—not even the top of the old man's head above the high-backed seat. Maybe rain drumming the roof had put Reg to sleep. It might be a good thing. With any luck the old man could skip the rest of Utah.

"You have no idea what this means," the woman said, sinking onto the sofa across the aisle. Her voice faded, a muffled sound. "Until you came along this was the third worst day of my life."

Marsh glanced over. The woman's head had disappeared under the roomy poncho. In the aisle, the child stood looking worried, as if afraid she might never see her mother again. Finally the heavy, soaked poncho fell to the floor.

The woman grinned and shook open a towel. "It sort of restores a person's faith in the world. Not to mention the cosmos."

Marsh stared. Beneath the poncho there was no belly—no pregnant woman to rescue, but a lumpy canvas bag stifling an infant's squawl. For a moment it seemed she'd done this on purpose—tricked him. "You aren't pregnant," he said, surprised by the tone of his voice.

"You should've caught me a couple of weeks ago." She flapped her hand at him, then puffed out her cheeks. "Multiply what you see now by five, then double that. You couldn't feel a bone on me. Everything swelled up—hands, feet, even my tongue." She patted the green canvas sack strapped over her chest. The bag moved at her touch, bottom heavy. "This kid swam in an ocean. Fortunately I was taking a bath when my water broke."

"I thought you were pregnant."

She sat back against the sofa and cocked her head. "Is this some kind of issue with you, or what? I asked you for a ride, not a shotgun wedding." She sighed, rolling her eyes at the little girl. "Talk about overreacting."

Marsh tossed a towel onto the table, tried to calm himself.

"So your old lady walks out on you. That doesn't give you the right to start grinding on me. I mean, think about it. I'm on your side."

He turned, deciding not to repeat what he'd attempted to tell her outside. "If you could keep your voice down. There's an elderly man trying to sleep." He glanced up the aisle. "A gentleman."

She nodded at the little girl. "Did you catch that? A gentleman."

"Now, where is it you're going?"

She shrugged. "On Welfare, I guess. Government services."

"Just tell me how to get there," Marsh said, stepping up the aisle to the driver's seat.

She moved along the sofa until she sat behind him. "My name's Sharon. You already know Tiffany—and the baby, of course."

He started the engine, switched on the windshield wipers. "Andrew Marsh," he said. "You'll need to direct me."

"Has to be the next county," she said. "I got dropped from the Rolls here. Which way are you going?"

"East." The sound drained from his voice. How far to the next county, he wondered. He glanced to the passenger seat, Reg stirring under the buffalo robe.

"East's okay," she said. She poked her head into the driver's well. "Is this the gentleman?"

Marsh nodded as he pulled onto the street. He hit the gas, anxious for open road, the next county.

Sharon leaned closer. "I don't see him." She stroked the fur hanging over the seat. "This gentleman wears *mink?*"

Marsh looked over, wishing she'd keep still. "It's a buffalo robe."

"Far out," Sharon said. She sat back and cradled the green bag higher on her chest. Then she began toweling the girl's damp hair. She spoke softly to the child, her voice a hushing singsong. " 'As I was going to Saint Ives . . .' "

Marsh listened, relaxing a little at the wheel. He nodded at the woman's jingle, the slap of windshield wipers, the pelting rain—everything beating quick time. It couldn't be much of a distance to Welfare. He'd deliver this family and reach Colorado before nightfall. Maybe he'd drive until Pueblo. He thought of Alex typing up their route like a travel agent, keeping track. She'd even left Richard a copy.

" '. . . every sack had seven cats, every cat had seven kits.' "

"Split," Marsh said under his breath. He'd better call Alex at the next county, before things went any farther. It occurred to him that he should never have encouraged her to make the shade garden, that lush green stillness he himself had longed for. Now Alex had escaped there—maybe even spent the night curled among coral bells and maidenhair fern where the moon didn't shine and the phone never reached.

" 'Kits, cats, sacks, and wives. How many were going to Saint Ives?' "

Marsh glanced into the rearview mirror. A family more or less—that nursery rhyme surviving still. He reached for the coffee he'd left on the console, then looked down, startled by a touch. Reg's spidery fingers brushed his hand.

The old man nodded up from the blanket. "The Saints traveled north," he whispered.

"Only in your sleep," Marsh said. Behind him, the woman fell silent. The little girl stared. "There are people here," he said. "The ones from the phone booth. We're giving them a ride."

Reg paid no attention, coughing into his robe. After a minute he looked up at Marsh again. "The Saints carried The Book with them. At the river they met the young Sioux Hole In The Day and greeted him in his native tongue. They promised him eternal life and a white and delightsome skin. Then the Saints led Hole In The Day into the river. They prayed that his scales of darkness would be washed away. And when at last they opened their eyes to see . . ."

Marsh jiggled Reg's hand. "People here," he said loudly.

"Sharon and Tiffany," the woman said. She nudged the child forward.

The old man shifted, drawing the fur higher, hooding his dark wrinkled face. He blinked around the seat.

"We haven't named the baby yet." Sharon said, fingering the flannel-lined bag. "I've been depressed."

In the aisle the little girl's eyes widened on Reg. She took a step back. The corners of her lips drooped. She whispered, "Monkey."

Marsh frowned over his shoulder. "Mr. Vickers isn't feeling very well himself," he put in quickly.

"So that makes two of us," Sharon said, as if she was trying for a quorum.

"Monkey!" the child cried, lurching from the aisle, flinging her arms around her mother's neck.

Sharon yanked herself free, grabbed the girl's clutching hands. "Cut it out, Tiffany. There's *no* monkey. They all flew away—every last one."

"Mama!" the girl shrieked, struggling to be held.

Marsh gripped the steering wheel and glanced at Reg. "They're only going as far as the next county."

The old man nodded. He looked over, his eyes rimmed red, his mouth drawn to nothing but a slit. He appeared even smaller—ancient and fur-shrouded, the deep shine of his face checked with a hundred lines.

Behind them, the little girl howled, gulping for breath. The rain pelted harder. Marsh turned the windshield wipers high. He punched the defrost button. Deep within its sack, the baby hiccupped, then let out a cry.

Sharon dug into her cloth purse and pulled out a disposable diaper. Marsh watched her in the rearview mirror, reminded of a magician—a one-woman road show, whipping surprises from every pocket. Now the infant's lolling head appeared, a fringe of straight black hair worn bald at the back. Sharon unbuckled the canvas bag. She tugged up her white jersey and plopped her left breast into the baby's face.

"I would like a cigarette," Reg said. But he made no move, his hands hidden under the robe.

At the sound of his voice, Tiffany wailed louder, climbing Sharon's arm.

Marsh slowed as they started into the Wasatch. Hardly a mountain range—at least not here between soft blurred hills and the sky sifting down green gullies. Still, he couldn't very well leave these people stranded beside the wet road. The baby might drown in its sack. Sharon's milk would turn to rain. Tiffany had no underpants. Marsh reached for Reg's cigarettes, then glanced into the rearview. "Maybe I should drop you off here."

Sharon slapped her hand over the little girl's mouth. "There won't be another sound out of her. Look—she's almost asleep. Any minute." She pushed the child's face into her lap. At her breast, the baby startled, then resumed sucking. Sharon's voice raced. "It's those monkeys from the *Wizard of Oz*—the ones that flew out of the castle wearing those little fur capes. I think the buffalo threw her. She doesn't know her animals."

Marsh pulled a Chesterfield from Reg's pack. He lit it, feeling an instant dizziness, his head clouding with smoke. He thrust the cigarette toward Reg. I've lost my resistance, he thought.

"You'd think she'd forget," Sharon said.

"I have never forgotten," Reg whispered, gazing out the flooded windshield.

Marsh glanced at the clock. It was only a little past two, but the day had grown steadily darker, the storm's twilight lifted only by lightning. For an instant the hills blanched. Marsh's hands turned pale at the wheel, his face washed albino. And then the jolting thunder. Marsh winced, felt the Establishment slammed by wind, the rain battering. He drove faster.

Sharon wound a damp strand of the girl's hair around her finger. "A whole year since we saw that movie and she's still freaked."

Reg nodded. "I am terrified."

"Not much longer and we'll be through this storm," Marsh said. He strained to see beyond the next bend, hoping. He turned on the headlights, then grabbed the atlas and shoved it toward Sharon. "Take a look. We should be getting close to the border."

"But what about Welfare?" Sharon opened the atlas, covering the baby's bare waxen feet and the girl snuffling in her lap. "I was sort of planning on Green River."

"You'll have to wait. I'm not stopping until Colorado." Marsh hunched over the wheel, as if his eyes could move them faster. Everyone would have to wait—this woman, Richard, Alex—all of them.

"Maybe I don't want to go to Colorado, did you ever think of that?" Sharon let the map slide into the aisle. "I mean, what if someone was trying to find me . . ."

"I'm getting Mr. Vickers out of this state." This territory, Marsh thought. The other side of the world wouldn't be far enough.

Sharon frowned out the side window, then gave a sigh. "Well, I guess if a certain person was really looking for me, he might go one state over. He *did* take the truck, after all." She pulled the baby from her breast, then eased out from under both children. The little girl shuddered, cramming against the baby. Sharon moved into the aisle. She sat on the orange shag carpet, her back resting against the console. "Wherever he is, it could just come to him all of a sudden, what he needs to do. You know— the right thing."

"Only authorized individuals are empowered to receive revelations," Reg whispered. He opened his window a crack, letting the rain snuff his cigarette.

Marsh shifted into second as they started down the grade. He ducked at the glare of lightning, thunder crashing. He reached over, grabbed Reg's fur shoulder. "*Nobody's* cursed you."

"Sometimes it takes a separation like this to finally bring two people together," Sharon said. "Right now he might be realizing how much he actually cares."

Reg turned. The robe slipped from his shoulders. He gazed at Marsh, his eyes dull yellow, a faint pulse ticking in the hollow of his collarbone. "And this is loving our neighbor as ourselves . . . If a man shall desire salvation and it is necessary to spill his blood, spill it. That is the way to love mankind."

"Don't," Marsh said. He shook his head at Reg. "Don't do this."

Sharon drew her knees up, locking her arms around her legs. "The thing is, I would've done whatever it was he wanted." Her voice caught and she fell silent a minute, nodding, rocking herself in the aisle. Finally she dropped her hands, her legs slid straight. "All I ever needed was a word."

Marsh glanced over his shoulder, saw her bending low, her jersey seared beyond white in the storm's flash. He switched on the radio, hearing only a crackle. He snapped it off, then grabbed for the cigarettes again. He wished the baby would wake up wailing. Tiffany, too. Let them cry Monkey for miles. Anything but this—a woman down to nothing, scalded by tears. And Reg sinking deeper into the bleaching rivers where Saints waited hailing prayers and God spoke thunder to the authorized individual.

The cigarette trembled in Marsh's lips. Smoke wreathed his head, crowned him. He felt authorized, empowered by all the power vested in him. Men will be men and No Women Allowed. Down every highway it seemed he'd nailed up the signs. Over mountains and rivers, the Man's book under his arm. He'd shattered the bottle against the ship's bow. I baptize thee in the name of the Authorized Individual.

He jammed the Chesterfield between Reg's fingers, then cleared his throat. "Her nipples were like amethysts." Marsh heard his voice loud above the storm. Words formed all at once in his mind, words streaming with the highway, his silver trail revealed.

"She had a Hula-Hoop around her waist and it glowed in the dark. I watched her take off her baby dolls." He nodded at Reg. "I guarantee— she was something of a revelation."

Reg looked over, drawing on his cigarette.

"She said this Hula-Hoop was from her Uncle Sam. She said we'd better stand inside the light. They have rules."

Sharon lifted her chin, wiped her eyes with the hem of her jersey. "What rules?" she sniffed.

"It's a company town," Marsh said.

They sped off the flooded slopes, tandem tires showering a wake of rain, the thunder grumbling after them. Ahead the sky looked clearer. Marsh hugged the wheel like a truck driver—shifted down, let her drift. He glanced at Reg, watching from the corner of his eye.

"There was something about her—for a minute I lost my tongue. She had a religious beauty."

"She was an angel," Reg whispered.

"I asked myself—what was she doing behind that counter? In California she would've been a star. I could've told her, but her looks made me nervous." He reached over, touched the old man's arm. "I worried I might come too fast, or maybe not at all. I mean, it'd been a long time."

"Years and years ago," Reg said. "I remember."

"But she told me she couldn't complain. She depended on the military. So I took the other half hour."

Marsh turned the windshield wipers to low as they started across the San Rafael Swell—plateau land he'd memorized from the passenger seat, his eyes scouring the map for civilization. To the south, Temple Mountain, and farther still, Cataract Canyon. Looking north beyond sandstone pinnacles, he might see the dark Coal Cliffs. Outside his window, a sign announced the turnoff: VISIT CASTLE COUNTRY WHERE BLACK IS OUR FAVORITE COLOR.

"Angeline," he said. "She gave me her real name. She pulled a carrot stick out of my hand and ran it up between her legs. Then she slipped the carrot inside her."

Behind him, Sharon snapped straight.

"The whole time her Hula-Hoop glowed around my shoulders and I got a little shaky trying to be careful. But I ate the carrot."

"Oh brother," Sharon said. "Now you've gone too far. I mean, even for me—that's sick."

Reg shifted in his seat. His eyes rested on Sharon as if he just now realized she was here. "You may be gratified to learn that I myself once tasted the sweet dates. Dates yes, but never a carrot."

Sharon stared. She tucked in her jersey, smoothed her straggling brown hair. "Well, I guess maybe dates . . ."

For a minute they drove without speaking. The rain had eased, and the land glistened with sunlight streaming through clouds. Sandstone slabs pitched like ships climbing the high side of an ocean trough. It seemed all the pale banded rocks angled east, a pastel fleet bobbing across the swelling land. And the Establishment sailed with them.

Sharon stretched in the aisle, then peered over Reg's shoulder. "Looks like it could turn out to be a nice day."

"I believe we are having a female rain," Reg said. "You'll recall how Hole In The Day walked smiling into such a rain and rejoiced at great length."

Sharon moved onto the sofa and gazed out. "A female rain. That might be the most beautiful thing anybody's ever said to me." She tapped Marsh on the back. "Did you hear?"

"Yes," Marsh said. He gazed out at the highway, the soft falling rain. Maybe it was only him—just his own thoughts hauled state to state. Or his words trailing women pulling down all the No Trespassing signs. Or maybe Sharon, the one here now. That mother whose breasts bloomed so full of milk to make his own nipples ache, until it seemed the whole dripping world was suddenly Female. Kits, cats, sacks, and wives milling the highway. But no man. For a moment Marsh didn't feel like anybody at all. Hardly human, just the authorized individual.

He looked over at Reg, unable to help himself. He couldn't quit now. Maybe never. "You might not believe me, but that carrot was like a torch. My blood practically exploded."

"I believe you," Reg said.

"I could've done it with anyone."

"Oh please," Sharon said, drawing Tiffany onto her lap.

"I guarantee I could've done it with a hundred young girls."

Sharon shook her head. "All right, so we believe you. There isn't a doubt in our minds." She tapped a finger along Tiffany's flushed cheek. "He could do it with sheep in the meadow and cows in the corn."

Reg leaned into the aisle. "He did it for me, remember."

"I'll just bet," Sharon said.

Marsh was quiet. He kept his eyes on the road. He saw the land beginning to level out—the banded rocks tacking south toward the Grand

Canyon. Not far ahead, they'd meet the Green River, that waterway also in a rush to go south. Somewhere along the highway they might take the turn themselves—drive the scenic route, follow migrating birds down the sky to Arizona sunshine.

But that first night Reg had pointed on the map. He'd said, There may be snow. We will wear our good heavy coats. We'll march into the long linen fields and you'll glimpse my father astride a gray horse. All the men you see riding in those fields will be black men, cavalry men, men of the Ninth. Then you'll hear the regimental band sound the call. And the song will be America from sea to shining sea, though you mustn't expect a shore—only the plains frontier.

Marsh slipped the Establishment into cruise control, set the course due east. He nodded into the rearview. "The gentleman is right," he said. "I did it for him."

11

From the sleeping loft Marsh smelled coffee. Last night he'd pulled the drapes over the windows and closed the vinyl divider, sealing the loft from everything below—Reg snoring on the sofa, Sharon jammed between her children in the dinette's convertible bed. He'd driven late, stopped only by the Rockies. It seemed safer to take the summit by daylight. The past two days had turned him cautious.

Out west, Marsh thought, shoving open the divider. California was beginning to feel like a whole different region. Living there, he would've sworn the frontier had ended at his doorstep, that the west had made him the man he was. But today he felt only coastal, like some swamp creature struggling onto real land.

He grabbed his wadded clothes and slipped into the aisle. The dinette's bed was empty, sheets stripped and heaped on the cushions. Across the aisle, sunlight flooded the sofa. Reg's buffalo robe draped a pillow.

The stove's clock said only a little past nine, but it seemed everyone had been up and gone for hours. Coffee mugs sat unwashed on the counter. The bathroom held a dampness, the mirror misted. Soapy gray water stood in the sink and shower stall—backed up.

Marsh lit a burner under the coffeepot, realizing he knew nothing about this vehicle. He glanced down at the empty cups, a square of paper folded between them. He'd planned to shower, change into clean clothes. Maybe the problem was in the holding tanks. He'd need to start staying on top of things—aboard the *Whither Thou* he wouldn't have let a day pass without checking the bilge.

He reached for the folded paper and spread it open, reading Sharon's penciled note: *Andy, Gone to find Welfare. I left the kids next door. Be back soon.*

Marsh moved into the bathroom and combed his hair. He risked flushing the toilet, then stepped outside. He saw it had been a mistake pulling in here after dark. By daylight the campground looked more like a crowded trailer park. The gravel drive was crammed with trailers, campers, and motor homes. A strip of crabgrass just large enough for a picnic table and a spindly sapling separated each space. Numbered signposts lined the gravel like street addresses.

"Next door," Marsh grumbled. From the sound of Sharon's breezy note, you would've thought they'd known each other for years. Andy . . . Be back soon, as if he was supposed to understand exactly what she meant by that. Not to mention dumping her children with complete strangers.

He trudged across the patchy lawn to a maroon and tan motor home bearing the name Southwind along its side. The vehicle looked brand-new, long as a bus. Beside the door, three little dogs yipped in a portable pen. A rubber doormat spread over the gravel read WELCOME TO THE VALDIVIAS!

Marsh glanced up, catching sight of Reg seated at the motor home's side window. The old man seemed in deep conversation, nodding, now pulling on a cigarette. Marsh ducked away, not in the mood for more new people—these Valdivias with an exclamation point. He imagined loud strangers, too friendly.

As he stepped around the motor home, the girl Tiffany stared out at him from the rear window. She curled her fingers in a small wave. He waved back, surprised by her smile. She seemed glad to see him. A familiar face, Marsh thought, hurrying down the lane to the campground office.

A bell chimed as he stepped through the office door. In the far corner, four men looked up from a card game. A woman behind a counter sipped at her coffee, then glanced his way. Marsh moved to the counter, feeling so tired of strangers—this continual effort.

"I wanted to pay for last night. We pulled in late, you were closed."

The woman handed him a printed form and a ballpoint. "You'll need to register. Ten dollars for two, add another dollar for the extra person."

Marsh studied the form, trying to recall the Establishment's license plate number. "Three extras," he said. But standing here he felt more like the extra person, waking up alone, too late to use the shower. "One's a baby," he added.

"Well, for heaven's sake," the woman said. She tapped a finger to her chest as if this little conversation was a joke on her. "I had you pictured as one of the singles. We've got the SOARS staying here." She leaned closer, sounding friendlier since the mention of children. "Singles On American Roads. You know—one of those clubs, except on wheels."

"Oh, I'm not with any club," Marsh said, thinking of Rotary. From this distance, he couldn't imagine ever belonging to that professional group lunching at banquet tables, talking stock market.

"How about hookups?" the woman said. "There's a charge for the water hookup, electricity, sewer . . ."

Marsh slid a twenty from his wallet. "I'll take the works." He glanced around the office, feeling better at the mention of these connections—anchors to the permanent world.

Across the room one of the card players swept his finger over his tongue, then began dealing another round. Maybe the four men were part of the singles club. But they looked more like senior citizens. Probably local retirees who enjoyed sitting in this office—a travelers' way station offering groceries in miniature sizes, racks of bumper stickers and postcards, toilet paper sold by the single roll.

"I'm totaling," the woman said, her fingers poised at the cash register.

"Add an orange juice," Marsh said. He doubted Sharon had bothered to fix Tiffany a decent breakfast. He grabbed a candy bar from a rack, then moved for the cooler.

"I'm throwing in the baby no charge," the woman said when he returned with the orange juice. She handed him a courtesy garbage bag, then spread a pamphlet open on the counter.

Welcome to Big Hermo's Colorado Camper Court
Your Hosts—Herm and Vivian Callahan
***
Enjoy Your Stay in Grand Junction
Proud Home of the Atomic Energy Commission

The woman gave Marsh a wink. "The stork paid Herm and me a late visit, too."

"That's nice," Marsh said, refusing to explain about Sharon—his family of extra persons.

"You'll find you're never too old," the woman said. She flipped the pamphlet to a detailed map and clicked her ballpoint pen. "Now then, we're standing here. Out this door you'll come to the laundry. Above it the recreation room. Tonight we're showing *Ben Hur,* free to all campers. At the rear of the building, the Ladies and Gents—showers, etc."

"Showers," Marsh said, too loud.

The woman looked up. She touched the ballpoint to her lips. After a moment she said, "We rent towels."

In the corner the men fell silent, staring over their cards.

Marsh glanced their way, then dug into his pocket. He nudged a fistful of change across the counter. "I'd like to rent one towel."

Richard was spending the day in court, the secretary said. Marsh tried Alex. He leaned at the pay phone, wishing he and Reg were on the road, already over the Rockies. Or maybe heading home. There was nothing stopping them from turning around—no spot on the map declaring Point of No Return. He let the phone ring a little longer, then finally gave up.

On his way back through the campground, he inspected the long rows of motor homes. All the hookups. Heavy-duty electric cords ran from paneled sides to outlets bordering the lane. Hoses snaked to faucets and large-mouthed pipes sunk into the grass. Marsh looked away, reminded of life lines—the blazing white room where Virginia had lain surrounded by machines, wires plugged at her scarred chest, a plastic tube taped to her wrist.

Get home fast, Sharon had hollered at him yesterday. Marsh ducked into the Establishment and pulled on clean clothes. Wait too long and there might not be anybody on the other end. He toweled his hair, still damp from the shower. He shaved at the clogged sink, wondering if he'd already waited too long.

Split, Marsh thought, stepping out the side door and across the grass. As he passed the wire pen, the three fussy dogs yipped louder. Taken together, they wouldn't even amount to a toy poodle. He knocked at the Southwind, frowning at its giant size, the traveling doormat pretending neighborhood.

A tall, big-boned woman held open the side door and waved him up the step. "We were beginning to think you'd sleep all day." She grinned, then called over her shoulder, "Pour another cup—Andy's here."

As he moved inside, the woman pressed his hand. "Any friend of Sharon's, God love her." She tapped a plastic badge pinned to her blouse. "I'm Evelyn—Evie for short."

Marsh nodded, seeing the woman's name repeated on her yellow badge. HI, I'M EVIE. COME SOAR WITH ME! He moved up the aisle, wondering who the man at the dinette table could be. He'd imagined a married couple.

"My brother Frank," the woman said. She pulled a tray of cinnamon rolls from a microwave. "Older brother, I should add. *Much* older."

"Hah!" the man named Frank said. He elbowed Reg, beside him in the black leatherette seat. "Tell her to go blow-dry her face."

At the sound of the man's loud voice, Marsh heard another noise starting up—a baby's squawl. He glanced down the Southwind's long aisle to a vinyl divider drawn shut across the rear. Tiffany's head poked around the vinyl. The little girl spotted him and tore up the aisle, legs chugging beneath her red sundress. It seemed she leapt the distance into Marsh's arms—his hands startled around her bare bottom.

"Looks like you've got a fan," Frank chuckled.

Evie moved past and set the rolls on the dinette table. She pointed to the seat opposite Reg where an elderly woman slumped so small in the corner, Marsh might never have noticed.

"Sit yourself next to Jewel here," Evie said.

Marsh let go of the little girl and slid onto the dinette cushion. Across the table, Reg looked surprisingly rested considering his bad spell in Utah.

Marsh leaned over, keeping his voice low. "How are you feeling?"

"I'm fit as a flea, thank you. Perfectly *compos mentis*."

"What a kick," Evie said, pouring more coffee. "I can't get over the way this man talks."

Marsh gazed out the window, thinking maybe he should ask about the hookups. Four days on the road and he had no idea how to connect the Establishment. Finally he said, "We've got a little plumbing problem."

Beside him, the old woman named Jewel nodded. She turned to him as if plumbing was a subject leading up to her. She tapped his arm, the touch of a butterfly. "Two weeks from today," she said, "I can be seen on national television."

"Not long now," Frank said, grinning at Marsh. "It's been a tough climb to the top, but she's almost there."

She's almost dead, Marsh thought. He stared at the badge fastened to the ruffles of the old woman's pink blouse. COME SOAR WITH ME! But it seemed every part of her was feeling a pull in the opposite direction. She might've been sitting in her own field of gravity, scented with violets, bent by a strong down draft.

"Jewel made the final cut," Evie said, rocking back in her swivel chair. She opened a *TV Guide* and spoke like an announcer. "Get set for another round of 'Simon Says,' the game show where a little bit of knowledge goes a long way."

"All the way," Frank said.

In the aisle, the girl Tiffany leaned closer, avoiding Reg's side of the table. She inched a finger along Marsh's knee.

He ignored her, glancing at the microwave, an air-conditioning unit set into the ceiling. "I see you have all the hookups," he said.

"I myself admire a competitive individual." Reg nodded across the table to Jewel. "I'm reminded of those high-spirited females who tamed our frontier. Consider the beautiful Saro, that temptress who would be my own mother. Or the pitifully plain Annie Oakley, so gifted with a firearm." Reg smiled at the elderly woman. "Of course you recall the name bestowed upon Miss Oakley by the savage Sitting Bull . . ."

Jewel glanced up, her eyes quick in her pink powder face. "That would be Little Sure Shot."

"What'd I tell you," Frank said. "Mind like a steel trap."

"And the name of Miss Oakley's dog?"

The old woman frowned, looked to Frank.

"That's not in our Famous Animals category," Frank said. "The network sent study sheets. Nothing crooked, just a guide. We've been drilling Jewel up one side and down the other. I've figured it so she'll peak right around air time."

Evie shoved the *TV Guide* between the cushions of her chair. "The network doesn't want contestants coming in cold. Audiences like winners, especially in the over-sixty-five division. It makes people feel better—you know, about old age and all."

"You've got to understand how to train for these things," Frank said.

"I couldn't agree more." Reg winked at Jewel. "Perhaps you can tell me—what two heroic cavalry regiments gained fame throughout our great frontier as the Buffalo Soldiers?"

Frank glanced over. "No offense, but I think it would be better for everybody if I ask the questions."

"There's just something about getting old," Evie said, her voice trailing off. After a minute she turned to Marsh. "I hear you're a single."

"My wife died in July," Marsh said. He gazed down at the table, a U.S. map set into the formica. Not much farther and they could start up the orange rectangle of Kansas.

Beside him the elderly woman fidgeted. "Regiments," she mumbled. "I don't suppose it would be the Rough Riders."

Evie tapped Marsh's arm. "You qualify for SOARS."

"Excuse me," Marsh said, sliding out of the dinette. Tiffany grabbed his hand, as if to the rescue. "If you'll tell me where to find the baby."

"Claire's got him in the back," Evie said. "We've been having a ball passing that baby around."

"A ball," Marsh said as Tiffany tugged him down the aisle. He saw the baby high in the air, being lobbed from one stranger to the next.

"Claire's one of our charter members," Evie called after him.

But there was no baby, no charter member behind the vinyl divider. The rear of the Southwind was dim, drapes drawn over the windows. It seemed Marsh no longer moved within the confines of a motor home, but had entered a spacious master bedroom. Off to one side he glimpsed a mirrored dressing room, a pastel bath opposite.

Tiffany broke away, racing to a queen-sized bed. She glanced over her shoulder at him, let out a giggle, then dove into the down comforter.

Marsh moved to stop her, but she bounced free laughing, her red dress flapping above her waist. He shook his head as the little girl rolled to a stop. She smiled up at him from a pink pillow edged with lace. Marsh grabbed her sandaled feet.

"Tiffany—" He paused, surprised by his voice, the sound of her name. For a moment it seemed this child wasn't homeless or poor—could never be. Not on her way to Welfare with that lace framing her head and red-ribboned shoulders.

After a minute he leaned to pull Tiffany up. Then he stood straight, hearing the baby howl. He stepped toward the sound. As he passed the dressing room, Tiffany bumped by him and dashed inside. Marsh turned, poking his head into the doorway. He saw a pale, bony woman sitting in a blue wing chair. She cradled the baby in her arms. Her head was bent over the infant, her print dress unbuttoned to the waist. A yellowed bra strap hung down her arm. Marsh swayed back, seeing the baby at her slack breast.

The woman glanced up. The baby's head fell away, his face bright red from sucking, his forehead misted with the effort. He let out a cry, sounding enraged at all his hard work for nothing.

Tiffany clucked at the baby, then looked over at Marsh and plugged her ears.

Finally the baby found its fist and quieted.

"Please," the woman whispered. She nodded toward Marsh, her hand clamping her dress closed. "If you'll just take him a moment."

Marsh stepped to the chair and gathered a blue flannel blanket from the carpet. He wrapped the baby, trying not to breathe the sour smell, the dingy blanket stiff with dried milk. Or maybe worse.

"I must ask you to avert your eyes," the woman said.

Marsh held the baby to his shoulder and turned away. But as he started out the door, the woman spoke again.

"Isn't it sad," she said.

He glanced back. The woman's dress was buttoned all the way to her ropy neck. Beside her, Tiffany fiddled with the yellow SOARS button sagging at her chest.

"I settled on names for my babies before they were ever born," the woman said. "Used to be that's the way we did things." She sighed, nodded toward the bundle at Marsh's shoulder. "Now here's a little one, already in the world over two weeks and still no name. I'd like to know what's sad if that isn't."

Marsh propped the baby higher, feeling suddenly defensive, as if this infant's honor was at stake. "I think the mother's been depressed."

"That's no excuse," the woman said. "We're all depressed. Take a look in the mirror if you don't believe me."

Marsh stared at her, seeing how very old she was. A charter member. And her eyes watery like the eyes of so many old people, always looking full of tears. "I've got to get going," he said. "We have a lot of miles to cover."

"Not yet." She crooked a finger for him to come closer. "Terrible things are happening—terrible. Last month somebody stuffed a newborn into a Kentucky Fried Chicken box, left it on a picnic table, then drove away in broad daylight."

Marsh shook his head, holding Sharon's baby tighter.

"It's a fact," the woman said. "I saw the whole thing on TV." Her chin bobbed up at him, hands fumbling in her lap. On one knobby wrist she wore a plastic medical bracelet, as if she'd just been released from some hospital. She raised that hand—a bird's banded claw. She clutched his arm.

"If you could tell me what's come over people, if I just knew . . ." She looked away then, put her hand to her face. "I used to have so much milk," she whispered. "I did."

"Yes," Marsh said.

"My breasts were always full and I'll say it myself, they were beautiful. There was a famous man—this is the truth—offered me a hundred dollars if I'd open my blouse so he could look for himself." She sniffed at him. "I don't suppose it would do for me to tell you who that man was."

Beyond the divider Marsh heard a door slam. The woman looked up at the sound, shook her head.

"Jewel's going to be a TV star. Me—I'm just Claire and nobody cares."

"That's not true," Marsh said, glancing away. It seemed Reg should be here. Reg and his way with words.

Under the flannel blanket Sharon's baby wriggled, his tiny mouth smacking, drawing nothing but air. Marsh lifted the blanket from the baby's face.

Finally he mumbled, "Maybe if you tried again."

"I don't think so," Claire said. But she opened her arms.

"Remember you're never too old." Marsh frowned at the phrase—a slogan for fools. Then he settled the baby into Claire's lap. He felt the angle of bones beneath her print dress, her body like a winter tree, reduced to simple geometry.

Claire sat back, gazing at him. For a moment she smiled—smiled as if with a fond memory.

"I nearly died young," she said.

12

In a corner of the laundry room a dryer ticked into its Fluff cycle. Upstairs trumpets sounded, muted through the room's high-gloss ceiling. Marsh heard the rumble of chariot wheels, horses' hooves thundering. He bent over the postcard balanced on his knee, "Dear Richard," as far as he'd got. Above him the music swelled and a crowd roared. In the audience Tiffany would be cheering, too, watching *Ben Hur* from her mother's lap.

Sharon had returned from Welfare late that afternoon, so exhausted she'd slept through dinner. "Burned out," she claimed by the Mesa County bureaucracy. A Methodist church around the corner had finally come through. The Women's Society gave Sharon a hundred dollars from their emergency fund and a shopping bag stuffed with clothes intended for a rummage sale. Marsh insisted on washing the castoffs with his laundry. He'd picked through the paper bag, wishing somebody had thought to donate underwear along with the faded blue jeans and corduroy jumper. He also wished he had some idea of what Sharon planned to do now. When he tried asking, she just shook her head as if too depressed to think about it. She'd perked up only after Evie mentioned the campground's free *Ben Hur*. She plopped the baby into Claire's arms again, then dashed for the movie like somebody without a care in the world.

Marsh slid lower in the orange plastic chair. He guessed Sharon was entitled to a little pleasure. But her sudden lift in spirits bothered him.

He felt almost cheated, as if Sharon had failed to stick to her end of some mutual agreement as the needy party.

The dryer clicked off. Marsh piled his laundry on a long table near the door and began folding. The hand-me-down blue jeans were still warm—the whole room, warm from the day and the row of dryers, quiet now. It was late, close to ten, and he felt relieved to be alone in this utility room with its white machines and peach-colored walls, the cement floor canted toward a large metal drain. He should probably thank Sharon for taking so long to get back from Welfare. It seemed he'd needed some time—a break from traveling to catch up with things, with himself.

"Spending the day in camp," Evie called it. She told him home is where you park it. Maybe she was right. As the day progressed, he'd felt less frantic about getting in touch with Richard and Alex. After dinner he decided not to even try phoning. A call to California might ruin his mood.

He felt better about the whole trip, somehow grounded in the midst of movement. With Frank's help the Establishment had been connected to water, electricity, sewer. And everything worked. At the Dump Station near the campground office, Frank demonstrated how to empty the holding tanks. Marsh watched, reminded of his first outings on the *Whither Thou* when every task was new. It seemed he was learning the ropes, getting his sea legs.

He stacked the folded laundry in his arms and walked up the gravel lane, glad for the fresh air, mild as a summer evening. Maybe there was such a thing as the Point of No Return, even on a trip like this. Because he felt it now, his course fixed and irrevocable—inland.

Marsh set the laundry on a picnic table outside the Establishment, then slid onto the wooden bench. Not long and he'd spot Sharon and Tiffany coming back from the movie. He leaned at the table, lighting a citronella candle Evie had given him, guaranteed to keep bugs away. Who'd played the original part of Ben Hur, he wondered. Hard telling how old that movie was. The music whining through the laundry room had sounded warped, trumpets dragging like bagpipes.

He guessed Jewel would know—Jewel with her mind like a steel trap. Except Reg claimed she was weak in one area. "Her Achilles' heel," Reg sighed at lunch, shaking his head over the game show's study sheet, that category titled Wild West. Frank had groaned as the old man crumpled the sheet in his fist. But Reg paid no attention, turning to Jewel. "Now we must erase everything and begin again."

Marsh gazed off toward an open area of the campground where the SOARS had gathered after dinner. Their campfire blazed, as if they intended to stay up all hours. Reg was probably out there, too. At the

SOARS Happy Hour he'd mingled with a gin and tonic in his hand, looking thrilled to be invited.

Tiffany broke away from her mother, calling to Marsh from the gravel lane. He waved despite the sound of that back-slapping name he'd always avoided. Andy. He could blame Sharon for this—her irritating presumption. He claimed no connection to the good old Andys of the world. Never mind that all the SOARS seemed to think so. But no matter. Tomorrow the SOARS would be gone, heading down the highway to their next weekend meet. It seemed a person could drive year-round attending these rendezvous—somebody with a name like Andy.

The little girl climbed onto the bench beside him. She placed a small paper bag on the table, propping it up with both hands. "Popcorn," she said. She opened the bag, removed four kernels and dropped them one by one into Marsh's hand.

"Thank you," he said, smiling at the child's face—all business. He was glad to see somebody paying attention to details, even the most trivial. It seemed Reg had set out in the motor home without ever looking at the owner's manual. Now the old man couldn't be bothered with holding tanks and hookups, too busy revising Wild West history.

Marsh glanced up as Sharon flopped down across the table. And here was another case—this hitchhiking, mother-of-two, moviegoer. She sat oblivious to everything, dividing up the laundry, arranging the rummage sale clothes in a separate stack.

Marsh followed Sharon's hands moving across a faded red T-shirt, a thin silver ring on her index finger, her nails bitten so close to the quick it hurt to look. He stared down at the table, unable to ask point blank what she planned to do. Finally he said, "So how was the movie?"

Sharon looked up, shrugged one shoulder. "There was a problem with the projector. They couldn't get it into focus."

"That's too bad," Marsh said, wondering how anyone could bear to sit through two hours of blurred action.

"Otherwise it was okay." Sharon folded the T-shirt and placed it on top of her pile. "We need to get the baby from Claire." She moved off the lawn, then stopped, waiting for Tiffany.

The girl turned to Marsh and handed him the greasy popcorn bag as if she was presenting him with a fortune.

"I'll come along," he said. He bent to blow out the candle, then caught Tiffany's elbow. "You do it."

Tiffany leaned, her face golden in the light. She took a deep important breath.

"Make a wish," Marsh said, reminded of a birthday. But the little girl blew while he spoke.

Sharon shook her head as they stepped onto the gravel lane. "Tiffany doesn't know about wishing yet."

They walked past the big Southwind, dark except for a dim light burning above the door. Frank and Evie would be down at the campfire. Frank was planning to tell a ghost story, one he claimed had made him famous.

Sharon kicked at the gravel, shoving her hands into her jeans pockets. "My mother used to say, if wishes were horses. Least little thing I asked for, I'd get that as an answer."

Marsh nodded. "Beggars would ride," he said, hardly aware of the words, this shabby woman beside him.

"I honestly think it warped me. My ex-mental health worker told me I was riding a downward cycle."

Sharon stepped alongside a small motor home. She opened the side door, still talking. "And do you know what came into my mind when she said that? I saw merry-go-round horses, up and down and round and round."

"Merry-go-round," Tiffany whispered.

"Freaked me out," Sharon said. Then she was gone, leaving the motor home's door ajar. Inside Marsh glimpsed straw flowers on a kitchen counter, a refrigerator dotted with magnets holding torn squares from milk cartons. A gallery of missing children like coupons redeemable.

He clutched the popcorn bag tighter and led the little girl around the motor home, inspecting the scaled-down outfit built on a Toyota truck chassis. Frank called the small rigs Micro-Minis, easy handling for somebody like Claire. Still, Marsh couldn't picture the elderly woman seated behind the wheel, tooling along some highway.

"Claire's asleep," Sharon said, stepping out the side door. She tucked the blue flannel blanket around the baby and flapped one corner over his face. "She dozed off with this kid wide awake in her lap and the TV blasting."

As they started down the lane, Sharon nodded back to the Micro-Mini. Her voice dropped, sounding confidential. "You know she gives him her breast."

"I know," Marsh said.

"Not that I really care. They say even old men have produced milk in emergencies. I think it's sort of an instinct—like in tribes."

"Yes," Marsh said, wishing Sharon would move onto another subject. He squared his shoulders, aware of his own middle-aged chest, his knit shirt putting an itch into his nipples.

"I mean, it does happen," Sharon said as they stepped onto the lawn.

Marsh gazed past the Establishment to the SOARS campfire. "There's a get-together out there." He turned, seeing Sharon settling at the picnic table as if she planned to stay put all night.

"After *Ben Hur* I don't think I could take anymore." She shook her head, plopping the baby across her knees. "Doesn't it ever get to you—hanging out with so many old people?"

"I'm not hanging out with anybody."

"Oh please," Sharon said. "What about your gentleman friend? Don't tell me he isn't a walking page from history, on top of being a complete wacko."

Marsh dug into his pocket for matches and lit the citronella candle. "There's nothing wrong with Mr. Vickers' mind."

"Well, he had me snowed. I'm not saying I don't like him, but think about it—you've got an old guy wrapped up in a buffalo robe, raving about Indians and saints. Now wouldn't you agree that's just a little bit weird?"

"That robe belonged to Mr. Vickers' father."

Marsh sank down beside Sharon on the bench. He almost smiled at the sight of her round scrappy face, her shoulders set, the baby's feet thrashing in her lap. For some reason he wished his son could meet this woman. He imagined Richard wearing his prosecuting attorney's suit, his briefcase under his arm, locked alone inside a small room with Sharon.

Across the table Tiffany giggled, as if she was picturing this, too. Then she reached into her popcorn bag and placed one kernel before Marsh.

"The robe was a gift from a young Sioux Indian named Hole In The Day," Marsh said, fingering the popcorn. "Mr. Vickers' father—Algie—was a hero of the Indian Wars. He played in the Ninth Cavalry band. All the men of that regiment were black." He smiled at Tiffany. "They were called Buffalo Soldiers."

"And you believe this hero stuff," Sharon said.

"I believe Mr. Vickers has an excellent memory."

"And I thought *I* was desperate." Sharon glanced down at the squirming baby and tugged up her jersey. "Anyway," she said, shrugging her breast into the baby's face, "I've been thinking."

Marsh nodded. It was about time.

"Evie's offered to take Tiffany for a few days. I don't think I'd need more than a week at the most to get myself together." Sharon ran a finger across the baby's flushed cheek. "Or maybe Rolf will show up. I put in a call. They said he was out looking for me."

Marsh turned, staring at her.

She leaned away from his gaze. "I could use a break from the kids. I'd leave the baby if I wasn't nursing . . ."

"With total strangers," Marsh said. He looked across the table at Tiffany. The little girl was paying no attention. Too young to understand—so young she didn't even know how to wish. She sat dumping all the popcorn from the bag, scattering kernels everywhere. It seemed she'd suddenly decided to give up on neatness.

"You ought to be in bed," Sharon said. She turned to Marsh. "I can always tell when Tiffany's out of it. Her eyes go bright like that. People think she's wide awake, but I know. It starts with her eyes, then—"

"As if you care," Marsh snapped.

"I *need* a break," Sharon said, her voice rising. "Get a doctor over here if you don't believe me. Any moron can see I'm a wreck. I spend all day at Welfare taking nothing but abuse and they say come back tomorrow. They ask have I applied for a job. They want documents, signatures, proof." She grabbed his arm. "You tell me how I'm supposed to do everything and drag two kids around. I've just been through child-birth, for God's sake."

Sharon slapped the drowsy baby onto her shoulder, pointed to her lap. "Down here I'm a mess. This kid tore me to complete shreds. I've got seventeen stitches, every single one infected. I should be in a sitz bath this minute. Instead I'm sitting all the way in another state just because you refused to stop at Green River."

"Well, if you'd told me . . ." Marsh looked off, avoiding Sharon's lap. "Maybe you should try calling the father again. Let him take Tiffany. He's got some responsibility here."

Sharon shook her head. "If you're referring to Rolf, the answer is no. The baby, yes. But not Tiffany. He isn't her father."

"Then phone whoever is!" Marsh shoved from the bench, disgusted by this woman, the sleeping baby with its sour blue blanket, disgusted by himself.

"I wouldn't know who to call," Sharon said, moving to stand beside him. Her voice sounded smaller, directed into the night air. "I used to believe in free love."

Marsh frowned across the lawn to the Southwind. "Your girl has no father, your son has no name, and *you* don't care." He looked down at her, then turned away. "Some mother you are—that baby's lucky he didn't wind up in a Kentucky Fried Chicken box."

"I'd like to know exactly what that's supposed to mean."

"Never mind," Marsh grumbled. "I'm going down to the campfire."

"Well, okay," Sharon said, as if he'd issued an invitation. "Give me a minute. I'll just put the kids in bed."

She moved to the picnic table, leaning into the glow of the citronella candle. She spoke softly to the little girl. Marsh saw that Sharon was right—Tiffany stumbled for the Establishment like a sleepwalker.

After a moment a light went on inside. Sharon's head poked out the doorway.

"The popcorn," she whispered.

Marsh gathered up the scattered kernels and dropped them into the paper bag.

"She likes to have something to sleep with," Sharon said as he handed her the popcorn.

He nodded, then turned to put out the candle. For a moment he leaned over the flame, feeling suddenly tired—not from the day or his exertions, but from the world. He gazed across the campground, vehicles lined row after row, and beyond this place, all the highways never-ending.

Behind him, Sharon pulled the side door closed. He blew out the candle, his breath weak from his thoughts. What kept people going on, he wondered. What kept a small girl sleeping when a nightmare came and all the monkeys flew out of the castle and she had no wishes to make and nothing beside her but a crumpled bag of popcorn.

As they walked down the lane, Sharon glanced back to the Establishment. "I left the kitchen light on. What she really needs is one of those little night-lights."

Marsh fisted his hands in his pockets and stared straight ahead. "What she needs is a home."

Sharon looked up at him, then shrugged. She'd pulled on her heavy fringed poncho so her shoulders looked even rounder. Her hair straggled across her eyes as she walked, but she made no move to brush it away, her arms hidden under the navy wool. She squinted through a wispy brown strand. "There's not much of a moon tonight."

Marsh said nothing. He coughed to clear his throat, then spit onto the gravel. For a moment he stopped short, realizing he'd never done this before, at least not in public. It had to be Sharon's company.

She stepped ahead, then turned, waiting for him to catch up. As he moved beside her, Marsh saw her face go tight. She dodged in front of him and jabbed him in the ribs. "Let's get this straight—I love my kids."

He moved to push past her. "Like hell you do."

"Hold on!" Sharon hollered. She folded her arms under the poncho, blocking his way. "Where do you get off telling me how I feel about my kids." She leaned close, butted him with her shoulder. "No wonder your old lady dumped you!"

Marsh tried to shove around her. "My wife's dead!"

"Oh, sure." Sharon nodded, her eyes narrowing. She bobbed in front of him like a prizefighter. "The lady doesn't want you, so she just doesn't exist, right?"

He reached to brace his hand on her shoulder, but she pushed him away, bullied him backward. His eyes burned from the sight of her. She was too close, so close he smelled the baby's foul blanket on her skin, saw the wool fringe snapping around her knees. He heard himself grunting, "Watch it," felt his mouth suddenly twitching. Her knee hammered up and then his left hand flew, swelling in the air, smacking hard against her ear. She reeled as if with a gust of wind. For a moment she stood stock still. Then she turned once more. She faced him.

It seemed he had no breath at all. He looked at her, her hands still lost inside the long poncho. He tried to breathe, to swallow. He blinked down at his deck shoes, then up at her again. "I didn't hit you."

She tipped her chin. "Don't tell me I don't love my kids."

He shut his eyes. His hand throbbed. "I'm going to the campfire."

"Don't ever," she said.

She stepped beside him. It seemed he hadn't struck her. Nothing had happened. She frowned into his face. "I think you'd better sit down."

"No," he said.

Sharon freed her arms from the poncho and took his aching hand. She led him off the gravel to a picnic table. She pushed him onto the bench, then sank beside him. For a minute she didn't speak. She felt along her face, pressing the heel of her hand against her cheek. Finally she looked over. "Your wife really died, didn't she."

He turned his head away as Sharon leaned toward him. She touched his arm. Her fingers fumbled at his shirt pocket.

"Okay," she whispered. She pulled out his book of matches. "You want a campfire. I'll give you a campfire."

Marsh hunched on the bench, feeling suddenly cold. "This isn't our table."

"You ask for a campfire story. Listen—I'll tell you a story." Sharon struck a match and held it between them. She gazed at the small bright flame, as if trying to think. Finally she nodded. "This is the story of my high school graduation banquet and my Chinese fortune."

"We shouldn't," Marsh said. He trailed a shaky finger over the plastic lace covering the table, a Parchesi board open before them. "We shouldn't be sitting here."

"To begin with, I'd never eaten Chinese food. I don't think anybody had, except maybe Skylor VanSickle." Sharon screwed her lips as if the mention of this person had put a sour taste in her mouth. She dropped the burning match, then lit another. "Anyway, we all voted for the House of Jade."

Marsh looked up as a light blazed on in the rear of a camper parked next to them. He ducked at the table, lowered his head. Had somebody seen him struggling on the gravel with Sharon? Only a minute ago—had he hit her?

Sharon reached over and closed the Parchesi board. "Well, I don't have to tell you, that banquet was a real scene, not just owing to the fact that a few of us had decided to come stoned." She tapped his shoulder. "I assume you know about the proven connection between pot and food."

Marsh raised his head. "Tell me if you're okay," he said. "I need to know if you're all right."

For a moment she cocked her chin. Then she laughed, a soft remembering sound. "I've never eaten so much with a plain fork, let alone trying to use those crazy chopsticks. I finally put them in my hair. I wore my hair up that night. I used to do different little things like that. You might not know it, but I'm very good with hair."

At the rear of the camper, the light still burned. Marsh saw no one behind the door's square window. The window was bordered with decals, a silent monologue of miles traveled, sights seen. An orange sticker on the bumper read Tiltin' Hilton.

"Then they brought out our fortunes. We couldn't choose our own." Sharon stopped, struck another match. "Only one to a person, they said. And it was special—I guess because we were graduating and getting our fortunes in those cookies you have to break open. And then you see the little pink strip of paper inside and you can't help it. You get this feeling like it's New Year's—all those streamers they throw. Or wedding confetti. That's how I felt, anyway." She nodded at Marsh. "It was the best night of my life so far."

"Yes," he said. He watched the match burn down, setting a glow into Sharon's fingertips, the skin ragged around her torn nails.

"Except I didn't understand my fortune. Other people got things like, 'Your sunny disposition will win you many friends,' or 'You are about to embark on a journey that will bring you great happiness.' "

But there was no happiness. Only the worst, Marsh thought. Terrible things happening—that's what the old woman Claire had told him. He blew out the match. "You're going to burn your fingers."

"My fortune said, 'There is someone . . .' " Sharon looked off, tapping the matchbook against her lips as if to remember the exact words. " 'There is someone who loves you as much as he can, but he cannot love you very much.' " She turned and straddled the bench. "So that was it—my Chinese fortune."

"Terrible," Marsh said.

"That's what I thought. But then, I was only eighteen. It seemed to me love was love—period. If you cared, you cared."

Marsh moved from the bench, feeling a weakness in his legs. Across the way, the SOARS campfire still blazed. He stepped onto the gravel toward that light.

Sharon trudged after him. She caught his arm and dropped the matchbook into his pocket. "Well, I care."

"I hit you," he said. He reached to touch her face, but she walked on.

"It's just that there are things you never expected. Circumstances."
Sharon sighed, tucking her arms under the poncho again. "A day comes
along and you're standing on the street giving the fortune to your own
kids. You're in a condition. Nowhere. You haven't got anyone left to
trust, so you trust everybody. That's how it works. You're walking
around telling your deep secrets to strangers, your worst troubles to the
authorities. You're asking people you don't even know. You ask them
like they were your best friends, your relatives. And you get tough. But
you still care." She glanced up at him. "You just care as much as you
can."

They moved past the last picnic table, across a dirt path marked Dog
Walk. Marsh squinted into the smoke from the campfire streaming their
way. He thought of Chinese fortunes, of Richard. There is someone who
loves you as much as he can, but he cannot love you very much. Yet
for a moment Marsh believed any love at all might be enough.

He felt for Sharon's arm through the wool poncho. "You care," he
said finally.

"Even if it kills you," Sharon said.

Marsh steered her around the campfire. It looked like almost all the
SOARS had turned in for the night. The fire snapped, a man's voice
rose and fell, not Frank but somebody else. Across the circle, Evie
spotted them and waved.

Marsh bent close to Sharon's ear. "You should never have got that
fortune. I shouldn't have hit you. I don't know what came over me—
I've never touched a woman."

Sharon clicked her tongue. "Well, you learn."

Evie smiled up at them, making room. Beside her, Reg lifted one
finger, acknowledging their arrival. Frank passed a thermos their way.

Marsh looked down at the dusty space next to Evie's lawn chair. He
thought of the camp stools stored under the Establishment's sofa.

"We can make do," Sharon said. She pulled off her poncho, spread
it over the dirt and plopped down. She turned in the direction of the
man's voice, three chairs away.

Marsh settled beside her, wondering how long he could sit like this
with his legs jackknifed, his back already aching. The man was talking
about Napoleon—or rather, the dead Napoleon—and a mysterious au-
topsy performed by the exiled emperor's physician. But Marsh wasn't
really listening. He gazed beyond the crackling fire and thought of children without homes and mothers without hope. He thought of men giving
milk in emergencies—all the wizened tribal men gathered around the
flames. And he sat with them, Sharon's baby clutched to his chest.

After a minute Evie leaned from her chair and handed him the thermos. "Napoleon is Lester's hobby. I wish you could see his library."

"I think we can survive without it," Sharon said. She nudged Marsh. "I can't believe you dragged me out here to listen to this."

Marsh took a long swallow from the thermos, glad to taste more alcohol than coffee.

A silence fell over the circle. The Napoleon storyteller folded his chair, nodded to the group, and stepped away.

Two chairs over, Reg coughed and threw his cigarette into the fire. He smiled, scooting forward in his seat. "I imagine you're all wondering what became of the newborn Algie after his rescue on board the slave ship *Suzanne*."

Around the circle, heads turned. Marsh saw the old woman Jewel teetering on her chair at full attention. In her thin lap she held a pen and notebook, as if ready to write everything down. For a minute it seemed these die-hards around the campfire really had been wondering—had waited through every story just to hear. Everybody except Sharon. She sat with her arms folded over her knees, her head drooping into the crook of her elbow.

"Now then, you remember that Jack Beef was the slave captain's name—an Englishman of substantial wealth and connections. He dropped anchor outside Norfolk, Commonwealth of Virginia. It was late in the spring of 1860 . . ."

Marsh capped the thermos, then leaned toward Sharon. "Listen—" He paused, waiting for her eyes to open.

"No more," she whispered.

"I'll take Tiffany for awhile—until you get things worked out."

But Sharon only shut her eyes tighter and buried her head.

"Tiffany knows me." He tapped Sharon's shoulder. "You know me. Right now I'm probably the closest thing to a relative you've got."

"Two weeks later Jack Beef sailed for England with Algie installed in the cabin of the ship's surgeon. When Captain Beef arrived at Falmouth, he sent for his carriage and traveled straightaway to the Somerset estate of one Squire Ditsun."

Sharon lifted her head. "You hit me."

"I care," Marsh said. Starting tomorrow he'd buy Tiffany everything new. He'd feed her popcorn by candlelight, teach her to wish, then make all her wishes come true. He'd be her closest relative, her favorite uncle walking through the door.

"And here, if you will, is my father's story . . ."

Marsh jiggled Sharon's arm. "So, what do you say?"

Sharon pulled herself straight and gazed at him. It seemed she sat staring for a long time while Reg's voice fell over them. Finally she looked away. "It kills me," she said.

13

Reg sat back while Frank placed an-
other log on the fire. For a minute the flames leapt high, casting shadows
up the old man's thin dark arms, setting a gleam into his eye. His voice
held the quality of memory, a sound coming close and clear:

"There was a stream, flowed past the front gate on its way to join the
Parret River. The river, in turn, wandered a short distance to empty
into the Bristol Channel. When the night was mild you could see the
lights of Cardiff twinkling on the other side.

All the land rolled gentle and green. After the heavy rains of spring,
the meadows ran wild with bluebells, primroses, and sweet clover. On
the hillsides you couldn't tell sheep from the daisies. Every fruit tree
burst into blossom. You would hear the singing of tens of thousands of
birds building their nests in the brambles and hedgerows.

It was on just such a day that the slave captain Jack Beef arrived at
Squire Ditsun's Somerset estate. A heavenly day—perhaps that alone
accounts for the Squire's excellent mood. And so when his wife took the
orphaned black infant from Jack Beef's arms . . . Well, I expect the
Squire felt more or less disposed to allowing her the child.

This is how it happened that my father came to live at Bridgewater
Grange with Charles and Elizabeth Ditsun and the young Charles who
was then nearly eight years old.

Elizabeth Ditsun arranged at once for the infant to be christened. She
aimed to make an Anglican of her 'sooty little stranger,' as she delighted

calling him. I'm sorry to say Mrs. Ditsun was a woman besotted by both motherhood and religious fervor. Also, it seems even then young Charles had begun to disappoint her.

She chose to name my father for a favorite parish priest—one Algernon Grundy, then retired. Of course, Squire Ditsun approved. He was prepared to offer the child every privilege except the one afforded by his name. I don't doubt but what a few villagers harbored the random suspicion over Algie's arrival at Bridgewater Grange. The Squire, you remember, journeyed to London twice a year for the purpose of business. However, one could never be sure about those trips. As word had it, every other street in that great city was Negro Row.

But in Fiddington Village amid the green Somerset hills, the townspeople saw only our Algie who they took to calling the Vicar's Boy. Before long, Algie had only to open his mouth to speak and villagers marveled. But you understand that hearing a small black boy using the King's English must've been an entertainment something on the order of a pet parrot who's been taught to recite a few words.

Algie himself spent those first years at Bridgewater Grange scarcely aware of his novelty. Every morning after prayers he took his lessons in the old oak study, seated next to young Charles. He learned a page a day from *Magnal's Historical Questions* and finished that duty before Charles was even halfway through. In the afternoon he received instruction on the piano and French horn, both instruments Charles had given up forever.

Now, you may be wondering if young Ditsun took exception to Algie's presence. He was the only child, remember, and to be surpassed by a boy eight years his junior . . . Well, Charles couldn't have been happier. You see, even then he aspired to the life of a sporting gentleman. While Mrs. Ditsun sat in the parlor's window seat, sighing at Algie's recitation of 'The Buried Flower,' Charles could steal from the house, throw a bridle over his sorrel jumper, and be off tearing across the fields.

You recall that Charles rode hatless and in his shirtsleeves and was given to nosebleeds. In the sunlight his hair shone so fair as to appear silver. His eyes were such a dark blue that outside his presence you might have difficulty remembering their color. He woke every morning with such a fierce energy, it seemed the world had crept next to his bed during the night and offered him an irresistible dare. I don't need to tell you that Charles accepted every challenge or that he nearly always won.

Perhaps it was the frequent sight of his own blood that made young Ditsun so reckless. Why, even a wide grin could start his nose to flowing. But generally the blood would start with the kick of his rifle against his cheek or his sorrel taking a fall after a slick rain. There was an old woman in the Ditsun employ—one Mrs. Rupp who supervised the kitchen. Mrs.

Rupp kept Charles supplied with bits of rags he stuffed into his nose before going out for a ride. But it was Algie who waited at the stables for his return, who grasped the reins while Charles yanked the rags free. And then to see those sopping strips red as banners—perhaps that alone could've put the fear into Algie's mind.

Of course it's true, we are all of us endangered if we agree that by living we also invite death. But there are among us those few who will appear in a rare moment to be not just endangered, but positively imperiled. And this is what Algie saw in young Charles Ditsun, though he'd say it had nothing to do with the bloody rags. Algie will tell you it all began on the night Charles shot the wretched galenes.

At the time I'm speaking of, Charles would be seventeen and Algie nine. Now, if you aren't acquainted with a galene, you cannot know the terror a child might feel at its unholy sound. The galenes roosted in the uppermost branches of the elms that lined the carriage drive—some fifty of them more or less, big as turkeys with gaunt naked heads and sharp black eyes. It's been said that these birds were once sacrificed to the madman emperor Caligula because he so prized them. And this may tell you a little something about Squire Ditsun who is the only person I can name, outside of Caligula, to ever think highly of a galene. The squire kept a pack of them as you or I would keep watchdogs. But the galene will sound its alarm at the rustle of a falling leaf. Their ignorance has no limits. Regardless, Squire Ditsun claimed he slept better knowing the galenes were on patrol. In some ways I suppose this was true, since no one at Bridgewater Grange even bothered to look out a window when the birds commenced their ruckus.

Except on one particular summer night when Algie could not, for the life of him, fall asleep. Our boy lay upstairs in bed, holding himself perfectly still under the sheets. The hall clock tolled its deepest hour. Algie heard a creak on the winding stair. Then all of a sudden, such a racket from outside—up and down the carriage drive, the galenes began to screech—not a warning, but the terrible voice of danger itself.

Algie sat straight up. Across the room, coals in the grate still held a weak glow. His saucer bath sat before the fire—that shallow tub, gleaming and pitch black as any galene ever was. Algie held his breath. He waited for the wicked bird to move. Then slowly, very slowly, he swung his legs from the bed. At last his bare feet touched the floor. He crept, feeling his way along the wall. Any instant, the galene might sink its alarming claws into his ankles. In a flash his feet would turn white . . .

Algie raced the length of the long, long upstairs hall. And all the while, those galenes screamed terror in his ears. When he reached Charles' bedroom, he flung open the door and dashed inside.

Charles rolled over. He blinked into the darkness and asked, 'What is it?'

But Algie couldn't speak. He could only look to the window, with his eyes wide from fear.

Charles sat up on his elbows, listening. 'The galenes,' he said.

Algie nodded. And then the tears streamed down his cheeks, so he couldn't have spoken even if he'd wanted to.

Charles reached up for his nightshirt hung on the bedpost. He stepped to the window and shook his head. 'I swear,' he said. 'Those birds are tarnal mean.'

'Yes,' Algie whispered. He felt a good deal better just hearing the irritation in Charles' voice. After all, there is nothing so heartening as to hurl a little anger into the face of fear. Algie moved next to Charles and stared out the window. 'Those birds are without a redeeming feature.'

'Right you are,' Charles answered. You can imagine he smiled at Algie's words which seemed too big for a boy so small—a boy, small and bright as a button.

Charles walked to his dresser and lit the candle nub in its brass cup. Then he slid his pistol from the dresser's top drawer. He tucked the silver shot box under his arm. 'I will catch the worst for this,' he said.

'Well, I am with you,' Algie whispered. And it was a vow he made as they tiptoed down the hall and descended the winding stairs. The big front door closed with a hush behind them. It whispered, With you. The pebbles on the carriage drive pinched their bare feet, made a sloshing sound, said With you, With you.

Over their heads the elms arched into the damp night sky. There was no moon and the stars flickered far, far away. That is the sky you will find in England. It is a narrow roof, that firmament, and very high.

Algie and Charles stood in the utter darkness with only the candle nub, no brighter than a firefly. The galenes, true to their contrary natures, had quieted their racket upon hearing Charles and Algie approach. In the lofty branches of the elms they sat conferring among themselves. They warbled and clucked. They flapped on their roosts. Twigs snapped. But in the darkness those monstrous birds could not be seen. And then suddenly the galenes made no sound at all.

Algie stared up, his face turned full to the night sky. Right then he will tell you he felt a hundred cruel and glittering eyes.

Without a word, Charles gave the candle to Algie. Then he cocked his pistol and raised it. He squinted as if to take aim, but of course he could see nothing, not even the tall branches twisting over his head. And so he shot blind and straight into the air.

In an instant the night cracked and slammed open with noise. Algie pressed close beside Charles. He cupped a hand round the candle as they moved along the carriage drive. The deeper they walked, the more deafening the noise grew until it seemed a great storm blew around them. Branches splintered. Leafy twigs fell as if from a blasting wind. The galenes screamed and Charles kept shooting. In the dim candlelight he loaded and reloaded. He wiped his bloody nose on his shirtsleeve and howled into the sky—howled for the birds he couldn't see. And Algie cried. The candle flickered out. Far away, dogs were barking, but who could hear? Now light blazed from the windows of Bridgewater Grange, and Charles was going to catch hell for this, indeed. But Algie will tell you hell was dropping from the sky and all that noise was the din you'll hear at the end of the world. Until there isn't a sound left.

The galenes lay black as stones up and down the carriage drive. It was a terrible time Algie had to step over them while trying to keep hold of Charles' hand on the way home. Charles had lost the most blood ever from a nosebleed. That is what Mrs. Ditsun said when she saw him. The Squire had nothing to say. But the next morning he sat at breakfast with a green willow switch across his knees. Being the gentleman even then, Algie offered to bend first for the switch. The Squire and Mrs. Ditsun wouldn't hear of it. You see, while Charles had returned from the carriage drive drenched in his own blood, Algie had come home still crying. The Ditsuns were touched by the sight of the boy who stood sobbing in the great hallway. Now there is a curiosity for you—how tears will almost always make the stronger impression over blood.

I don't doubt but what Charles' nose erupted again from the magnitude of that whipping. He looked peaked for weeks, but you realize it had nothing to do with his health. It seemed the events of that night on the carriage drive had crowned his summer. After that he became literally pale with his manhood. Old Mrs. Rupp, who'd long since run out of patience with Charles, claimed that the answer was wedlock, and the sooner the better. It seems Mrs. Rupp had fallen under the influence of Mr. Percy Shelley, who claimed that 'When a man marries, dies, or turns Hindu, no more is heard of him.' Of the three alternatives, I expect Mrs. Rupp felt marriage was the most immediate solution for Charles. But even the village beauty, one Jessamyn Bagshaw, couldn't keep young Ditsun from his arduous hunts. Mention Miss Bagshaw's flowing auburn hair, and Charles would go into raptures describing the fox and its dung— dung which he said was gray and pointed at both ends, making the animal so very simple to track.

Of course, Charles had always been the restless sort. But now he took to roaming the house, nervous as a prowler. In every room he appeared to be looking for something. He rode the meadows with his blue eyes fixed firmly on the far horizon. And so Algie shouldn't have been surprised when Charles finally spoke about going away.

One evening as dusk settled, Algie and Charles sat on the sloping back lawn of Bridgewater Grange. Neither of them was given to speaking at that hour when the first faint stars appeared and the cuckoo was liable to call. So for a while they sat silent, with only the sound of Charles flicking his braided riding crop through the still air. At last Charles lay back on the lawn.

'One day I'll be leaving here,' he said. He looked at Algie and nodded. 'I'm bound to go.'

Hearing this, Algie frowned out to the kitchen garden. He watched the darkness gathering under the long rows of turnip tops and he glimpsed in that darkness the very worst of his fears. He turned to Charles, unable to speak. But he will tell you there is an instant when the last light shines through a person and you see them gone—not anywhere in the world.

Mind you, I'm not suggesting that Charles was to suffer an unusual end. Though some might argue otherwise, all true men know that to fall in battle is to die a natural death.

Nevertheless, Algie could not put the fear from his mind. And so on that evening, with Charles lying pale against the grass and his white shirt open at the throat, Algie could do nothing but clutch at young Ditsun's sleeve. Naturally Algie was clinging there to all dear life. He may have been clinging to his own childhood as well—a childhood that was even then beginning to slip away. It's possible he already had an inkling of the truth about himself. And here I must tell you what that truth is . . .

When you are a black child among white individuals, you can remain mostly a child. And when you are old as I am old, you are almost always more elderly than black. But to be a young black-skinned man . . . Well, then you are indeed black from your head to your toes. Your breed is black, and the very name of your sex is black, and there will be trouble for you. It is no accident that you are twelve when this happens. You've grown lean and strong, but your hands are still small. These hands of yours are so small and agile that you are the only one in all of Somerset County who can reach into the thrashing cow and deliver the calf born backwards. You are the only one with brains to mount the chicken house on wheels and tow it out to the harvested fields where there is a feast for every fowl. But when the villagers look at you, they no longer remember your brains or your cunning hands or the fine King's English you speak. They see that you are the only one. And you lay awake on your natal day, having turned thirteen, and you wonder whatever will become of you. Just what in the world are you going to do?"

Reg sat a moment, shaking his head. He gazed around the circle. In the silence the fire made a ticking sound. Blue flames licked among the embers. Stars blazed across the wide Colorado sky, but over the campfire the night hung dark and close. For a minute it seemed a dew had fallen as if after a brief rain. The branches of the elms still creaked in the soft fading fire.

Beside Marsh, Sharon let out a sigh. "I really don't know what to do. First they love you, then they don't. I mean, what's the use of trying? Why go anywhere?"

Evie leaned out of her chair and touched Sharon's shoulder. "You wouldn't be saying that if you were young."

"I'm young," Sharon snapped. "My God, you think I'm not young?"

"Well, I wouldn't stay in the village, that's for damn sure." Frank stared at his hands a moment, then glanced down the circle to Reg. "For darned sure," he said.

The old woman Jewel slid her pen into the crack of her notebook. "I believe the answer is London."

"I don't think so," Reg said. He dug into his pocket for matches and lit the cigarette he'd held all this time between his fingers. "What you will do is go to Kansas."

"Kansas," Evie said. "I can't see how a boy barely thirteen years old is supposed to get himself all the way over there."

Reg lifted the crease in his trousers so as not to lose it, then crossed his thin legs. "You forget Charles will be going."

"You can take the Queen along for all I care," Frank said. "But I wouldn't get into any boat headed for this country until I knew what year we're talking about. There was a Civil War, in case you don't remember. No way would I go near that."

"You're not black," Sharon said.

Frank shrugged. "I'm just telling you what I would or wouldn't do."

"In America you'd be free," Reg said. "The war is over."

Down the circle a man chuckled. "All over but the shooting," he said softly.

Reg nodded at Frank. "You would be thirteen and Charles almost twenty-one." The old man tossed his cigarette into the embers, then smiled. "You see, that previous winter there was a gentleman, traveled down to Bridgewater Grange from London . . ."

Sharon poked Marsh with her elbow. "I think you'd better put another log on the fire. God only knows how long it's going to take to ship these people to Kansas."

"The man's name was George Grant. There was some talk around the village that Mr. Grant had been knighted by Her Majesty Victoria, but no one knew this for a certain fact."

"It won't take that long," Marsh said, turning to Sharon. "We'll be in Kansas tomorrow." For a moment he frowned at his own confusion with time and this distant story. It seemed he'd entered Reg's muddled mind, wandering between events as if there were no boundaries left. He winced at the stiffness in his knees as he moved to the campfire. He chose the smallest log and hoped it would burn down fast. Then he stepped outside the circle. He stood behind Evie's chair, refusing to sit again. Tomorrow he'd get some exercise, go for a long run. "Kansas," he mumbled.

"Now, this man George Grant was an individual of considerable wealth. He'd amassed his fortune as a silk merchant. At the Paris Exposition he'd set up a great textile display that had the Japanese dignitaries in bits. It was their silk, remember. But that was how Mr. Grant proceeded in business. He bought low and sold high, as they say. And he was shrewd. When word was finally allowed out that Prince Albert had fallen ill, Mr. Grant set his personal feelings aside and banked on the consort's death. He purchased all the available black crepe in England and France, right down to the last scrap. And when in fact Albert died and the whole nation mourned . . . Well, there you have the story of another fortune.

It can be said that George Grant cut an imposing figure. He stood not more than five foot, eight inches in his stocking feet, but his shoulders were broad and his face bore the rugged features of a Scottish chieftain. Here I should tell you that more than anything in the world, this man loved the Aberdeen Angus cow. He might trade his own mother to turn a profit, but the liquid gaze of an Aberdeen would put the tear into his eye.

Of course, the larger part of Mr. Grant's sentiment for the Aberdeen was lost on Squire Ditsun. No such breed ever grazed the fields at Bridgewater Grange. What's more, the Squire had never heard of Kansas. But George Grant assured him there was no finer spot in all of Christendom to establish an English colony and raise the Aberdeen than on those fertile plains. He'd once journeyed there for his health and could vouch for that sunset land, as rich as any in the tight little isle called England.

Now, you may wonder over the establishment of an English colony at such a late date. Or that a man would travel to Kansas for his health. But this will tell you something about Mr. Grant. . . . He was an original thinker. Nor was his mention of the tight little isle just chitchat. With those words, you could see Squire Ditsun looking cramped and most uncomfortable in his deep leather chair.

'In the New World,' said Mr. Grant, 'there is the rare opportunity to develop that son of yours and build up a rich enterprise which will be an honor to the British Empire and a credit to your noble family.'

You realize Mr. Grant had acquired some 70,000 acres of prairie belonging to the Kansas Pacific Railroad. He'd offered eighty-eight cents an acre, to which the railroad agreed. Naturally they were anxious to see that country settled so as to create business for the road.

And so with the bargain struck, Mr. Grant returned to England and was proceeding round the countryside promoting his colony. He sought Englishmen of wealth—men whose sons were dowered with both fortune and good blood. In these travels of his, Mr. Grant discovered that the more wayward the sons, the more the sires were willing to invest. Many of these noble gentlemen stood prepared to pay up to fifteen dollars an acre. Even Squire Ditsun considered that price reasonable. But he wasn't thinking only of Charles. Seated in his library with a fire blazing up the chimney, Squire Ditsun was already seeing himself as the lord of his own empire—an empire far-flung as the British domain itself.

You can imagine young Charles was as agreeable as his father to the prospect of Kansas. Some months had passed since he'd first spoken of leaving Bridgewater Grange. And in that time Charles had come into his full manhood. A youngblood, as Mr. Grant liked to say.

Of course, Charles didn't envision his father's empire in Kansas. He saw wild women. He saw the vast prairie, never vexed by a plow—a paradise for the hunter and his hounds. There, antelope and wolves abounded. He might track the great jack rabbit, far better sport than the English hare. He would ride for the fox and bring down the buffalo.

Right here I should tell you that Charles' view of Kansas had something to do with a long walk he and Mr. Grant took on that January day. You see, Mr. Grant did truly know how to appeal to a person.

Algie remained the only one without an idea of Kansas. But he determined to accompany Charles regardless. He'd made the vow, remember. And he'd discovered the truth about himself. It seemed safe to assume that if there were Indians in Kansas, there might also be black people. Old Mrs. Rupp had spent several nights in her kitchen expounding on this subject. She counted among her relatives a second cousin who'd journeyed to America as a missionary. This fellow had written back that it was a colorful country. Mrs. Rupp told Algie she felt no objection whatsoever to Kansas because of John Brown's body. But she fretted no end over Algie's name. She said it was one thing to be called the Vicar's Boy in Fiddington where a person lived with good Christians—quite another when you were entering questionable territory.

Algie felt satisfied with the proper name of Grundy, seeing as that had been Mrs. Ditsun's choice. But Mrs. Rupp wouldn't hear of such a name, and to that woman I owe my everlasting gratitude. Were it not for her, I'd be sitting among you—an old man Grundy.

One evening Mrs. Rupp dug through her letters from the missionary cousin. Then she sent Algie to fetch a pencil. On the back of one letter she instructed him to make a list of names. Mind you, Mrs. Rupp could neither read or write, but she so enjoyed Algie's hand. He wrote Vicars, and Mrs. Rupp shook her head and said, 'Too close to the Anglican.' As for the singular Vicar, she objected likewise. But when Algie put down Vickers, Mrs. Rupp smiled and poured them each an inch of whiskey.

And so when Algie stepped on board the *Alabama*—that sturdy ship docked in Glasgow harbor—he gave his name as Algernon Vickers. However, the ship's captain wasn't entirely satisfied. He was a man well-acquainted with stowaways. There seemed something suspicious about one black boy among thirty-eight youngbloods setting out to establish an English colony in America. The captain scowled at Algie and demanded his rank. 'I have no rank,' Algie said. The captain tried again. 'Your capacity!' Then the captain gave up altogether. He looked past Algie to Charles who stood close behind. He asked, 'Who is this person?' And Charles replied, 'He is my body servant.'

Now, Mrs. Ditsun had come on board with the Squire to see Charles and Algie off. When she heard these words—He is my body servant—she burst into tears. She flung her arms around Algie's neck and cried, 'Not so!' You see, she did love Algie with all her heart. She loved the look of him on that morning. He wore his best wool suit and a tweed cap on his shining head. He carried his French horn in a black leather case, so he could not return Mrs. Ditsun's sobbing embrace. But the tear was in his own eye, and he called her Mother. He led her to the ship's rail and turned her so she could look past the harbor to open sea. It was April first of 1873, and the ocean was gray as it will be at that time of year. All thirty-eight youngbloods had come on board, and a band was playing a popular sad song called 'The Fair Young Bride.'

As Algie pointed out to sea, he could hear the shrill squeal of Charles' sorrel jumper. It was quite a job loading those spirited hunters into the hold. And of course the hounds weren't helping. Next came the bleating sheep. There were thirty of the long-haired variety herded below that day. And then the cattle—all great muscled bulls—one red shorthorn and four black polled Aberdeen. Those bulls shambled on board. They bowed their enormous blowing heads and bawled. You realize they were in no big hurry.

And all the while, Algie was telling Mrs. Ditsun about Kansas. He said he would build her a house beside a river and this house would have a gilded piano. By next year she'd come to visit. She'd sit in a rose garden and in the evening the whippoorwills would sing. But Mrs. Ditsun only shook her head harder. 'I have no son,' she wailed, 'if that one would make you his boy. No, you will never see me in Kansas.'

Then suddenly the band struck up 'God Save the Queen,' and Mrs.

Ditsun was turning to leave. Everywhere around them, people were smiling and weeping and holding fast to the sons—those youngbloods, pale youths, those men. And at that moment Algie caught Mrs. Ditsun's hand. He gave her the one solitary fact he knew. He told her Kansas lay at the very center of America. He said from Kansas every direction was the same. He said it was the heart. And Mrs. Ditsun took comfort. She brushed away her tears and kissed Algie's forehead. 'If that is the case,' she said, 'perhaps one day I will come to Kansas.' "

Reg clapped his hands over his knees and smiled around the circle. Then he swayed to his feet.

Frank looked up as Reg folded his chair. "Wait a minute—are you one-hundred percent positive you've got your facts straight here?"

"I've told you the story precisely as it happened," Reg said. He propped the lawn chair under his arm, then gave Marsh a look. "I believe Mr. Valdivia has been spending too much time with his television particulars."

"I'm talking about the geographical center," Frank said. "Seems to me you've got the wrong state for that."

Sharon pulled her poncho over her head. "I don't think it makes any difference one way or the other. The center's a moot point, far as I'm concerned."

"Well, it would certainly make a difference to that boy." Evie slammed her chair closed and let it fall toward Frank. "There's the poor thing sailing off with only that one little idea. A person needs something to hold on to, just to start out with."

"Otherwise you woudn't go," Jewel said.

"Of course you wouldn't," Evie said. "Then where would this country be—somebody tell me that!"

Frank rubbed his eyes, kneaded his wide forehead. "Okay . . . You've got all these Englishmen, not one of them knows where he's going. So I'll give them the center. Right or wrong—I'll give it to them."

Evie waved a hand toward the sky. "Well, praise God. Old thunder throat has spoken."

"Anyway, I'll go," Frank said. "If it'll make you happy, I'll drive over there myself." He turned to Reg. "Where is it exactly?"

Jewel trembled up from the circle. "If it doesn't interfere with my appearance on national TV, I'll go, too." She knotted her head scarf under her chin. "That's two weeks from today, I can be seen."

"Head 'em up and move 'em out," somebody called across the way. "Kansas or bust."

Frank laughed, rising from his lawn chair. "Now you're talking—in God we trusted, in Kansas we busted!"

Then suddenly everybody was laughing and chattering and clapping

Reg on the back. Marsh moved to kick dirt onto the dying fire. Behind him, he heard the clack of chairs folding as if all the tents were being struck—the cavalry moving on.

Sharon nudged beside him. "I think what we're seeing here is something my ex-mental health worker used to call the spontaneous moment."

"Well, I don't believe it," Marsh said. He turned from the cold smoking fire and saw Evie, Frank, Jewel—everybody—walking Reg to the gravel lane.

"Believe it," Sharon said. "They're all on the boat with the chickens and goats. Frank doesn't know if he's white or black. Try and tell me the world isn't weird."

"Maybe by morning they won't want to go," Marsh said as they crossed the sandy Dog Walk. "You know, in the light of day."

"Uh-uh," Sharon said. "They'll probably have more comers signed up by then. This is a club—overnight recruiting. These people are into it. Besides which they've got nothing better to do than drive all over the country, like a certain somebody else I could name." She grinned over at him. "You know what they say—after a point it's just turn left and go downhill."

Marsh nodded, too tired to feel insulted. Anyway, he thought Sharon was probably right. After a minute he said, "Tell me . . ."

"Tell you what," Sharon said.

"Well, nothing," he said. "I was just wondering about myself, is all." He hesitated a moment, then walked on. "I mean, take last night. Last night—or was it the night before—I slept with this woman. A prostitute. Then tonight I hit you."

They started up the lane, past rows of motor homes, fluorescent bumper stickers glowing one after another like highway stripes. Marsh saw a long caravan laboring up the Rockies, crossing the Continental Divide. *I have seen the moon strike the Great Divide,* Norm had hollered in the hospital. Evie'd said, A person needs something to hold on to. And so I'm offering you number one, my fish, and number two, my idea. Reg had said that. Now everybody was going to Kansas. And what did they expect to find? Algie would be gone—Charles dead in some battle. Exactly where was the geographical center?

"It's just that I used to know something." Marsh felt for Sharon's arm beneath the poncho. "I mean, about myself."

"We're communicating now, right?" Sharon turned, staring straight into his face. "You're asking me for the painful truth, and I say relax. Your only trouble is you've led a very sheltered life. I'm talking sheltered here, as in Tax Shelter."

Marsh shook his head, paying no attention. "I'm fifty-three years old, for God's sake. I used to have some idea."

"Forget it," Sharon said. "You never had a clue." She pulled her hand from the poncho and tapped his arm. "Anyway, I've made a decision—I'm naming the baby after you."

"Will you listen to me? I'm saying I—" He stared down at her, took a step back.

"You said it yourself. Right now you're the closest thing to a relative I've got. Tomorrow that kid's going to wake up with your name."

"Wait a minute—my name?"

"Resign yourself," Sharon said.

Marsh ran a hand through his hair and frowned into the sky. For a moment it seemed the stars blazed brighter, scrambling to scrawl his signature.

"I mean it. After what you've done for me, taking Tiffany and all." Sharon paused, let out a little gasp. "Oh my God, it just hit me. Tiffany's going to *Kansas?*"

"Say the baby's name." Marsh touched her chin. He thought about the baby with its fringe of black hair. He'd held the baby in its blue blanket. The baby hadn't cried, not even a peep in his arms. And that child would be bright. Sharon was intelligent, and he wasn't any fool himself—not when you came right down to it. He grinned at her. "I want to hear his name from you."

"You've got it," Sharon said. She turned a full circle and reeled up the gravel, just spinning and smiling as if it was—all of it—only a dance. Finally she stopped to look back. "Here goes," she hollered. Then she cupped her hands around her mouth. She shouted to wake the campground, shouted to all the brilliant stars in the sky . . .

"Aaandy!"

14

Marsh leaned around the passenger seat, checking on Tiffany. The girl lay sleeping in the orange shag aisle, her popcorn bag clutched to her chest. A while ago when Marsh tried shifting her to the sofa, she opened her eyes and let out a howl. Otherwise she hadn't uttered a word since they'd left Big Hermo's Campground. It seemed the instant they turned onto the highway, Tiffany was asleep. Or maybe playing possum. Marsh gazed out the windshield, thinking of those small animals feigning death when they sensed danger.

"Maybe I shouldn't have offered to take her," he said, turning to Reg. "She'd probably be better off riding with Evie."

The old man shook his head over the steering wheel. "If you'd had the courtesy to consult me, I might've given you my opinion. As it is, I have nothing to say about this—this person."

"She's got a name, in case you've forgotten." And the baby, too, Marsh thought.

He opened the atlas, tracing Highway 50 across the Rockies—Evie'd said something about lunch at the pass. But he and Reg had got a late start. Marsh had lingered over a last cup of coffee with Sharon. While she copied their itinerary, he held the baby. His namesake—Andy. But he couldn't say the name, not even as Sharon wagged the baby's limp arm in a wave goodbye. Instead he said, "I wish you were coming." And he honestly did, though the idea that he should miss this difficult woman before they'd even driven a mile struck him as impossible. But

146

Sharon had nodded as though it was completely understandable. "If wishes were horses," she said, bending to kiss Tiffany. And Tiffany hadn't cried, only clamped her arms tighter around Sharon's blue-jeaned leg.

Marsh slid the atlas onto the dash. "At least she isn't any trouble."

"That remains to be seen," Reg said.

The old man let up on the gas as they passed the Gunnison City Limit sign. Along the highway, billboards announced The Mountain Air Lodge, Stagestop Market, Crested Butte Antiques and Good Junque.

Of course, Reg had more or less invited the SOARS along—not just one little girl, but a whole club. That morning, Evie had tried to pin Marsh with one of her yellow badges. She handed him an announcement. The SOARS would be celebrating Thanksgiving at the Fountain of Youth R.V. Resort. "Anyone who can, bring large electric roasters," the invitation read. Evie had mentioned a married daughter, two grandchildren. Marsh figured she'd prefer spending Thanksgiving with them. But when he brought it up, Evie just smiled and told him a joke: "Once there were three men of faith . . ."

Marsh looked into the aisle, hoping the slow drive through Gunnison might finally wake Tiffany. But the child didn't stir, except for her tight curls jiggling with the bumps.

"Maybe we should make a stop," he said. "She might need to stretch her legs."

Reg reached for his Chesterfields. "If I may make a suggestion . . ." He punched the cigarette lighter. "I advise that we let sleeping dogs lie."

"She isn't a dog."

"And I am not a monkey."

Marsh glanced to the old man. "That was only a nightmare she had. Not you, but the movie—a bad dream."

"Of course, you realize . . ." Reg nodded, braking at an intersection. "We have always been your bad dream."

"That's not true," Marsh said. He looked away, worried that today could be a repeat of Utah—the old man sinking into another low spell.

Across a frontage road, the Gunnison River followed the highway. The river headed pell-mell in the opposite direction to join the mighty Colorado. Well, maybe not so mighty. "They say the Colorado is a bankrupt river." Marsh smiled, steering the conversation past bad dreams. "One of these days we might have to foreclose."

Reg gave him a quick look, then scooted forward, pressing the gas pedal as they left the town.

Almost instantly they began to climb. The sunlight turned sharper. To the north, timber grew thick, becoming whole forests marching up mountainsides. The sky rose, as if giving the towering peaks room. Out

Marsh's window the river tumbled more like a creek. Just this side of the river, a man stood in a small meadow baling hay with a pitchfork. Marsh looked for the man's pickup, or maybe his house hidden in scruffy cottonwoods. But he saw only a lone man working in a bright green meadow. For some reason, the sight filled him with a strange melancholy. He gazed out as if groping toward something that was both new and vaguely old—old as a first memory.

After a while the river veered north, away from the road. Trees dwindled, giving ground to bald granite and scraggly Rocky Mountain juniper. Now and then the highway widened into dirt turnouts for vehicles needing a breather from the climb. They passed a silver Grand Prix parked with its doors hanging open, a couple eating sandwiches in the front seat. Behind them, a logging truck strained up the grade.

Marsh checked the Establishment's temperature gauge. The orange needle quivered safe in the middle. After a minute he sat back and cranked down his window. Air streamed cool through his hair. He saw deep ravines plunging below, granite cliffs rising on Reg's side. Tall land, Marsh thought. He smiled at the words, reminded of Hole In The Day who'd talked about a female rain.

He nodded at Reg. "This is tall land."

Reg frowned over, as if a complete imbecile had just spoken.

But in the aisle, Tiffany opened her eyes. She whispered, "Tall."

The child struggled to her hands and feet and slung the crumpled popcorn bag onto the console beside Marsh. She craned at the windshield, pushing a finger to the glass.

"Tall," she said.

Marsh looked out. "Yes, the mountains."

Her finger moved, pressed white on the windshield. "Tall."

"And the sky," Marsh said.

"Tall."

"The trees."

Tiffany turned, her face still flushed from sleeping. She pointed at Marsh.

"No, not me," he said. "I'm not that tall."

"Andy," the little girl said. Then she frowned at Reg. Her finger moved his way, hesitated.

"Your bad dream," the old man said.

Marsh reached over and pulled Tiffany into his lap. "Didn't your mother tell you it isn't polite to point at people?" He glanced to Reg. "I don't think her mother ever told her."

Reg nodded, shifting down to second. "You'll recall Mr. Booker T. Washington and his abiding faith in personal hygiene. I doubt you'll find another man to equal Mr. Washington's enthusiasm for the toothbrush."

"Is that so," Marsh said, wondering at this turn in the conversation. He noticed the speedometer dropping below twenty, now hovering at fifteen. As they started up a steep grade, a plastic bowl slid, rattled in the sink. Marsh thought he felt the engine miss, losing power for an instant. But maybe it was only Reg's driving. The old man seemed especially tired, worn out from last night's campfire and the long story he'd told. But this morning he insisted on taking the wheel. Now his thoughts seemed to be stuttering along with the Establishment's engine.

Reg gave Tiffany's knee a tap. "You understand it was only a notion. But I expect Mr. Washington did truly believe you'd find less to fear from a people who were conscientious about brushing their teeth."

Marsh felt the little girl flinch at the old man's touch. For a moment it seemed she'd stopped breathing. Marsh grabbed for the atlas—anything to distract her and the howl he worried was coming. He flung the map open like a storybook and zipped his finger across the state of Maine. "Once there were three men of faith . . ."

Reg winked at him. "Look closely and you'll find that I have only one minor bridge in my mouth, plus two silver crowns. Otherwise these teeth are my own. There is, after all, some compensation for our efforts."

Marsh paid no attention, holding the atlas close to Tiffany's face. She stared at the page so it seemed she was reading along.

"Now, each of these three men were asked the same question."

Reg dropped the Establishment into first as they labored up another hill. "Our engine is lagging."

"This question was: When does life begin?"

Tiffany looked up at Marsh, her mouth pursed as if deliberating.

"Of course, the first man didn't even need to think. Without batting an eye, he answered, 'At the moment of conception, life absolutely begins.' "

"That would be the Roman Catholic," Reg said. He looked over, raising a finger. "There—did you feel the hesitation?"

Marsh tipped his chin, concentrating. After a minute he said, "Try letting up on the gas a little."

Tiffany touched his wrist. "Tinkle," she whispered.

"Perhaps we should pull over," Reg said.

Marsh smoothed Tiffany's tangled curls and glanced at the temperature gauge. The needle was still holding its own. He figured the pass couldn't be much farther. "We've only got a few miles to go," he said.

Reg nodded, easing back in the driver's seat. "You're correct, of course. Once the charge commences, we must not falter. 'Audacity, always audacity,' in the words of General Forsythe."

"Tinkle," Tiffany said, jiggling Marsh's hand.

Marsh looked down at the atlas and propped it a little higher. He listened a moment for the engine's stutter, but heard only a steady whine. He cleared his throat. "Now, the second man wasn't quite so sure about this question. He thought and thought. Then finally he answered, 'The people of my faith have different opinions. Some say life begins after four months in the womb. Others say it doesn't actually start until birth.' "

Reg chuckled, reaching for his cigarettes. "There's the befuddled Protestants for you. Those people will never in this world be of one mind."

"Never," Marsh said, glad to see the old man finally smiling. Even Tiffany was enjoying his little story. She sat very still in his lap, her eyes intent on the atlas. And they'd almost reached the crest of the hill. The pass was at hand, only the punchline remaining.

"Well, the third man just shook his head when he heard those other answers. 'You couldn't be more wrong,' he told them. The man lit up his pipe and propped his feet on the porch rail. He said, 'I'll give you the simple truth. When all your children grow up and move away and your dog finally dies—that's when life really begins.' "

Marsh closed the atlas. He nodded at Reg, waiting for the words to register, and then the old man's soft laughter.

But Reg only bunched his shiny brow, looking puzzled. "I believe I heard you say these were men of faith."

"That's not the point," Marsh said. "It's a joke." He forced a chuckle, then glanced out the windshield. The road stretched into a wide curve. Not far ahead, he spotted another turnout. Two vehicles sat parked in the rust-colored dirt, steam billowing above a van's raised hood.

"Forgive me," Reg said, "but I fail to comprehend the faith of the third man."

"Just a joke," Marsh said. "Evie told me. I thought it was funny at the time." He pulled Tiffany straighter in his lap and gave her a tickle below the ribs. "Only a little joke."

"Well, there's no denying the third man possessed a sense of humor," Reg said.

Tiffany giggled, squirming under Marsh's fingers. Then she turned suddenly limp, as if from laughter. She seemed to sink into his knees. Marsh looked down, feeling an odd warmth spreading in his lap, now seeping over his legs.

Reg shook his head. "Even so, I'm wondering—what was the third man's faith?"

Tiffany slid to the floor at Marsh's feet. She gazed up at him from below the dash. The corners of her mouth drooped, as if she was about to burst into tears. She wound her fingers in her sopping red skirt. "Tinkle," she whispered. And then she was crying, pressing her face against the passenger door.

"Pull over," Marsh said. He waved toward the turnout, then reached to drag Tiffany off the floor.

Reg shifted into second. "Once the charge commences . . .''

"Can't you see she's wet her pants!" Marsh looked away thinking, No underpants.

In the turnout a man and woman leaned at the van, their heads hidden under its hood. A Ford Mustang sat nearby. The woman's long legs looked very dark against the white van. She stretched over the engine, her shorts riding high.

Tiffany buried her face in Marsh's shoulder as they bumped off the road and stopped behind the van. Marsh patted the child's head. He picked at her dress, trying to smooth the sopping folds.

"It isn't your fault," he said. "I made you laugh."

Reg shut off the motor and clucked his tongue at the girl. "You ought to be ashamed."

"She already is, dammit." Marsh looked over, shaking his head. "Don't you know anything about children?"

Reg smiled, moving into the Establishment's aisle. "I know better than to let a child urinate in my lap."

"The word is tinkle, for your information."

"Tinkle?" Reg rolled his lips to hold back a laugh.

Marsh frowned out the windshield, wondering what kind of mother would teach her child such a word. Sharon could've at least told him.

Outside, the man stepped back from the steaming van and moved their way. Tiffany scrambled into the aisle as Marsh leaned out his window.

"Engine overheated," the man said. He flicked a shock of blond hair off his forehead. "Would you have some water?"

Marsh nodded. Down the aisle he heard Reg cackling, a sound new to him. As the young man turned from the window, Marsh called, "I'll be right with you."

But for a minute he couldn't bring himself to move. His tan summer slacks clung damp at his thighs. Between his legs, the upholstered seat had turned a darker plaid. He gazed out, thinking Sharon would never in a million years get herself together.

The van's doors hung open. The woman had disappeared into the front seat, her legs dangling from the driver's side. At this altitude the air finally felt like autumn. Along the turnout a thin stand of aspen stirred, dry leaves clacking like tongues. A blue jay shrieked. And just inside the van, a grizzly loomed, flashing its claws at the back window.

Marsh rammed straight. He stared into the van's window—the bear's glittering glass eyes, the sharp snout thrust high as if to catch a scent on the wind . . . *The very last wild grizzly in all of California is believed to have been killed on May 22, 1951.* When Alexandra spoke, kindergartners wrung their hands with regret. They stepped closer to touch those polished claws.

Marsh looked away, let his hands fall to his lap. "Not here," he said. "Alex." He sat a moment, dizzy with the idea. Then he stumbled down the aisle.

At the kitchen counter Reg stood spooning instant coffee into mugs. Tiffany had pulled off her sundress. She leaned at the wardrobe closet, wearing only her red sandals. But somehow she still looked completely dressed. Marsh slid a plastic pitcher from an overhead cupboard and turned on the faucet.

"Somebody with car trouble," he said. He heard his voice, thin with omission, unable to say daughter-in-law. He felt guilty of coincidence—his guilt a perverse vanity refusing chance.

Reg smiled as the teakettle let out a shrill whistle. "You see, our water's already boiling. The rarified air will do that. However, you must allow more time for the three-minute egg."

The pitcher shook in Marsh's grip. "I won't be long."

"Of course, Norman always told me you were a kind man."

Marsh moved from the sink, carrying the pitcher with both hands. "I was never kind." He stepped past Tiffany, then glanced back. "Right now—put on some clothes."

"You realize we'll be late for lunch," Reg said, following him into the entryway.

Marsh pushed open the side door. At the van's rear window, the grizzly still aimed its razor claws.

The old man caught his arm. "Must you help this person?"

For an instant Marsh hesitated. It seemed possible they could just pull away. He hadn't glimpsed the bear behind the window, never seen Alex's long legs stretching from the front seat. So far from home, who would expect him to notice? Marsh shut his eyes. Somewhere close by, the cranky blue jay squawked louder. He glanced back at Reg. "I'll only be a minute."

As he took the metal step, water spilled over the pitcher, sloshed between his hands. He walked toward the van, preparing himself—what to say. Alex, how did *you* get here? Alex, why aren't you home? Alex, what in the hell . . .

But she was already scrambling from the front seat, taking all his words, his breath, hollering, "Marsh!"

He blinked into her face, her arms fierce around him as if it had been years. For a moment she clung to him, he clung to the pitcher. Then he ducked under the hood. The owner of the yellow Mustang looked up, puzzled. "Do you two know each other or something?"

"Stand back," Marsh said.

The cold water sizzled and popped over the radiator.

Alex pressed behind him. "I had to get away, Marsh." She touched his elbow. "You were the only place I could think of."

"I'm not a place," Marsh said, frowning at the radiator. After a minute he turned to her. He stared at her navy T-shirt—a white slogan across her chest, No Nukes Is Good Nukes. A button at her shoulder, Stop Violence To Women. For a moment it seemed she'd arrived here, not as a person, but as a collection of messages.

He thumped the pitcher along his pant leg. "You're just damn lucky you didn't crack your block."

Alex jammed her hands on her hips and glared at him. "I thought you were supposed to be in Kansas today."

"Forgive the interruption," Reg said, squeezing between them. He smiled at Marsh, the coffee cup steaming in his hand. "But it's finally come to me—the upshot of your little story."

"Not now," Marsh said. "You remember my daughter-in-law."

Alex shook her head. "We're no longer related."

The young man leaned past Marsh to shut the van's hood. "Well, it's a small world," he said.

Reg nodded at the man. "And who would you be?"

"Oh, I'm not anybody." The young man grinned, as if pleased to be no one in particular—no relatives here whatsoever. He hitched up his faded Levi's, then looked over, winking at Alex. "Next time this buggy starts getting hot, turn on your heater—it'll help. Your heater's just another little radiator." He smiled at Marsh. "Not many people think to do that."

As he moved for his car, Marsh stepped after him. "Thanks for stopping."

"Any time," the man said, sliding behind the wheel. "My number one rule of the road—always brake for a beautiful woman in trouble." He sat a moment, revving the Mustang, grinning out his open window at Alex. He touched his forehead so it seemed he was tipping a hat. "So long, Miss California." Then the Mustang bolted forward, stirring the red dust along the turnout.

"I hope you thought to ask him about our flagging engine," Reg said as Marsh moved back to the van. He nodded at Alex. "I don't need to tell you, that fellow was an automotive genius."

"There's nothing wrong with our engine." Marsh glanced toward the Establishment, Tiffany standing naked, waving out the side door. He looked down to his crotch. His pants had dried, leaving a dark ring. He held the pitcher over the stain and turned to Alex. "You could've at least told Richard where you were—I've been phoning for days. And here you are, broken down with a total stranger. I'd like to know what would've happened to you if we hadn't pulled over."

"Careful," Alex said, shooting him a look. Then she shrugged. "I would've found you."

"A resourceful woman," Reg said. "You'll recall Hole In The Day claiming that a people is never defeated until the hearts of their women are turned to dust."

"That's enough," Marsh snapped.

Reg chuckled, nodding at Alex. "Pay no attention to this gentleman. I believe he's in a temper because the child urinated in his lap."

"What child?" Alex said.

Marsh frowned to the motor home, Tiffany still not dressed. "Never mind," he said. As he stepped toward the Establishment he heard the patient lilt of Reg's voice. The old man would be explaining, giving Alex an update of everything she'd missed. Marsh glanced back, wondering where anybody would even begin.

Tiffany stepped aside as he pushed through the door. He tossed the plastic pitcher into the sink, then yanked open the wardrobe closet. Maybe the old man would start here—Algie's shaggy campaign coat taking up half the space. Algie's carbine rifle, his saddlebag, a threadbare haversack holding Norm's battered book from the hospital. For a moment Marsh stopped at his garment bag, Ginny's sable zipped inside. *And now you see where it all began . . .*

Marsh hunted through Tiffany's rummage-sale pile. He grabbed a pair of patched blue jeans and the red T-shirt—hand-me-downs he'd vowed the little girl would never need to wear again. "Next stop," he said, tugging the shirt over her head, "we'll buy you new clothes."

He snapped the blue jeans at Tiffany's waist, then stared out the side door. Reg stood nodding close to Alex's face, his hand resting along her arm. Or maybe the old man had started with this trip. *In Ely he slept with the fallen black angel. He said a carrot blazed between her legs . . .*

"Leave Angeline out of this," Marsh said, as if the old man could hear.

Then the fire swept our windward, and we fled from the armies of Nauvoo . . . Marsh glanced to the wet dress Tiffany had left lying in the aisle. "We'll do another laundry," he said.

But there hadn't been any fire, no armies. He kicked off his stained trousers and pulled a clean pair of shorts from his duffel bag. A lot of nerve Alex had asking him, what child. If anybody owed anybody an explanation, it was his daughter-in-law showing up like some runaway, her grizzly in tow. Marsh turned, shaking his head at Tiffany.

"Has she lost her mind?"

The little girl shrugged, reminding him of Sharon for a moment, making him smile. He looked at the blue jeans, too long in the legs—so long they fell in folds over Tiffany's sandals. He bent, rolling up the jeans, trying to make both legs even. "You must be hungry." He checked his watch—Frank and the others would be at the pass, probably eating lunch.

He grabbed Tiffany's hand and hurried her out the door. "If they don't wait lunch, we'll buy ice cream," he said. For some reason he felt better with Tiffany beside him, as if they'd shared years, reached a mutual understanding of the world. "Maybe chocolate cookies, potato chips."

"Ice cream," Tiffany said.

"Or maybe we'll just stand on our heads."

She glanced up at him.

"That's what some people do when they get to the Divide." Marsh thought of the faded photograph—the middle-aged Algie upside down against mountain peaks, his loose-trousered legs aimed at the sky. *For luck, for love, for new beginnings.* Even now, Reg might be telling Alex that story.

"We'd better get on the road," Marsh said, moving alongside.

Reg didn't look over, his eyes on Alex. "Remember, the third gentleman possessed a sense of humor. That should tell you something."

Alex let out a sigh, slumped against the van.

"It doesn't matter," Marsh said, thinking of all possible stories—this one. He turned to Alex, finally taking a good look. It seemed she'd lost weight since those afternoons in the shade garden. Her eyes were shadowed and pinched at the corners. He touched her shoulder, the hard knob of bone under her T-shirt. "I think we'd better start feeding you."

Reg flapped his hand in Marsh's direction. "Naturally, finding the third man's faith doesn't matter to you, seeing as you already know it."

"Ice cream," Tiffany whispered, looking up at Alex.

Alex stared at the girl a moment, then shoved her sunglasses higher on top of her head. "Don't worry about me. It's just that I've been driving nonstop. Plus, I couldn't eat in Utah." She nodded at Marsh. "I had to fast. You know—because of Sonia Johnson."

"Yes," Marsh said, without the slightest idea.

"Now, here is the upshot as I see it," Reg said. "Our third man kept his belief rooted firmly on Earth. You understand that the man's sense of humor is a kind of faith. Otherwise, he cannot go on with the world."

"It's getting late," Marsh said. He gazed toward the stand of aspen, a breeze whispering through yellow leaves— Who is Sonia Johnson? What was the third man's faith?

Alex pulled her keys from her pocket and climbed into the van. "I'll follow you."

"We're having lunch at the pass," Marsh said. He leaned to her open window and felt suddenly glad to see her, as if he'd been homesick all this time and hadn't known.

Reg tapped him on the back. "Of course, I could be wrong about all this."

"You're absolutely right," Marsh said, just to make Reg happy. He touched the button at Alex's shoulder, then stepped away. He'd say anything, do anything. Stop violence to women, skip lunch for the unknown Sonia Johnson.

Tiffany dashed ahead as he steered Reg toward the motor home. "It's almost two," he said. "They might've gone on without us."

"They'll wait," Reg said.

Marsh nodded. He wanted to say, They'll wait because you're the one with the story nobody else can tell. Instead he said, "I'd like you to do me a favor."

Reg climbed into the driver's well. "Whatever you ask."

"I want you to take my picture." He shut Reg's door, then reached through the window and punched the lock. "When we get to the Divide, I'm going to stand on my head. I mean it—no arguments, no questions asked."

"Very well," Reg said. He gazed out at Marsh, his amber eyes steady, unblinking.

But by the time Marsh slid into the passenger seat, Reg's mouth had begun to twitch. His narrow shoulders shook as he leaned to turn on the ignition. And by the time they pulled onto the highway with Alex close behind, the old man was laughing full out.

It seemed Reg laughed for miles—until the laugher spilled from his eyes and ran down the cracks of his cheeks. Until Tiffany plugged her ears. And they saw the summit—the caravan of campers, trailers, motor homes. Everybody bound for Kansas. Here, only the rivers parted company.

And here Marsh lifted himself up, his wobbly legs propped high against a monument which read, Elevation 11,312. His feet in the clouds, blood rushing to his brain, rivers plunging off to either side, to east and west, to every ocean he might've sailed. Just to be standing here on his head, while an old man snapped his photograph and exclaimed:

"Ah, faith!"

15

"**A**gain," Tiffany hollered, splashing at the shallow end of the campground pool. "Again!"

"This is the last time," Marsh called. Then with a grin for Alex sitting at the pool's edge, he dove to the bottom and shoved his legs into the air.

Ever since the Divide, Tiffany had been demanding repeat performances of his shaky head stand. But Alex wasn't impressed. She combed her fingers through the water, then slid into the pool.

"More!" Tiffany shouted. She sounded put out, confined at the shallow end while Alex breaststroked toward Marsh.

"Not now," he said. It seemed standing on his head had somehow loosened Tiffany's tongue, increased her vocabulary. He smiled at the little girl wading back and forth, her rummage-sale T-shirt wet and clinging around her knees. Later when the afternoon cooled off he'd take her into town and buy her a bathing suit along with the promised new clothes.

Alex bobbed beside him, water lapping her chin. "You're starting to remind me of an uncle who used to turn up every summer when I was a kid—drove us crazy with card tricks."

Marsh glanced at her. Yesterday, standing in the dusty turnout, it had felt like autumn and Alex's voice sounded cool as the air. *We are no longer related.*

"Listen Alex—" He gave a little cough. "Did you phone Richard?"

As if he had any right to ask, considering he hadn't talked to Richard since Utah. But then, it seemed he had so much on his mind, what with Sharon and Tiffany, now Alex . . .

"Richard was still in court when I called," Alex said. "I forgot we're two hours different."

"Well, try again," Marsh said. He felt a little better hearing the stern sound of his voice. "I mean it, Alex. You have to get ahold of him today."

Alex nodded, then ducked under the water and surfaced at the deep end. Marsh watched her floating clear of the diving board. She wore her lavender bikini, the one he remembered from home. But that had been California, over a thousand miles away and more than two hours different—so different the bikini now looked indecent. Alex drifted practically naked, exposed by an enormous wide sky and yellow fields mowed flat to the horizon. Here, the world wasn't round. From this place every direction was the same. Only the wind moved, free to blow anywhere. At the shallow end its heat crackled through Tiffany's wet hair, frizzing her curls tinder dry. Marsh waded over and grabbed the little girl's hands. He swept her across the water.

"Say Kansas."

But Tiffany just sputtered and kicked her feet harder, as if her life depended on it.

Beyond the cement strip edging the pool, Evie struggled with a metal gate. She banged it open, clamping beach towels and a folding lounger she'd dragged from camp. A stocky energetic-looking woman trudged behind. Marsh didn't recognize her, but the phrase pigeon-breasted came to mind. He figured she must be another of the SOARS Frank had enlisted in Grand Junction.

The new woman lugged a plastic webbed chair, plus a canvas bag stamped with the words When the Going Gets Tough, the Tough Go Shopping. But it seemed this motto hardly applied to Muriel. As Marsh helped the women unfold their chairs on the hot cement, Muriel explained away the tote bag—a gift from a pet niece forever lecturing her to start living now that she was retired.

"As if you'd been dead all those years before," Evie quipped, rolling up two pink washcloths. She tucked a washcloth under each armpit and gazed off. "If the wind's got to blow this way, at least it could be cool."

Tiffany ran dripping to the foot of the lounger and plopped down. She pressed her hands on the cement, then smiled at the dark, wet prints.

Marsh hoped Alex would stay in the pool. With the arrival of these other women, Alex's bikini looked even smaller. She seemed all sleek-shining skin, coursing like a seal, fanning the water with her expert turns.

At the foot of the lounger, Tiffany was staring at the concrete. Each splayed finger had disappeared. Then both palms vanished. The child held her hands up to Marsh and shook her head. "All gone."

"I'll tell you what makes the wind blow like this," Muriel said. "I don't believe there's a single thing standing between us and the North Pole except maybe one little cedar tree this side of Winnepeg."

Marsh chuckled, hitching up his brown cotton trunks. He snapped the elastic, aware of the paunch at his waist. Now that they'd reached Kansas he'd need to start exercising. Standing on his head wasn't enough.

"Well, it's unseasonably warm for this time of year," he said.

That's what the woman at the campground office told him when he registered this morning. Because of the heat she'd decided to keep the pool open for late campers. People from surrounding farms came by to swim, too. Had the woman said farms or ranches? Marsh wasn't sure which it was. But whatever, he didn't see much else a person could do here. Even the campground seemed a sideline for agriculture.

"I just hope Frank doesn't get blown off the road trying to find that crazy center," Evie said. She frowned toward the pool, speaking loudly to be heard above Alex's fierce butterfly stroke. "Last night we passed the sign. So there, I told him—Welcome to Kansas, Midway U.S.A. But no, he's got to see the exact spot before he'll believe it."

Marsh squinted toward the new brick house across the way. Definitely farmers. The pool sat closer to their house than it did the campsites. A farm pool—no umbrella tables arranged on the cement, the water chlorinated but not without a pale murkiness and a taste of sulfur. No flashy water slide, only a low wooden diving board. Farm machinery clogged yard and driveway. The campground office consisted of a single counter just off an open kitchen.

While he'd registered, two gangly adolescent boys bumped past, hurrying for a school bus. A heavy solid-shouldered man sat eating coffee cake, leaving his wife in charge of campers. She handed Marsh his change along with a campground information sheet and a tourist's guide titled "Kansas—Land of Ahs." Then the woman motioned for him to wait. She cut a piece of coffee cake and brought it to him on a paper towel. "Mulberry *Kuchen*," she said. She smiled, not at him but toward her husband. "The mulberries grow wild by the creek." Marsh turned to leave, the cake warm in his hand. At the door he glanced back. *"Kuchen?"* The woman had nodded. "We're all German here, you know."

Muriel pulled a newspaper from her tote bag. "I can't imagine there really is a center anymore. Now that we've added Alaska and Hawaii . . ." She opened the paper, giving it a snap over her legs.

Marsh moved to the pool's edge and dipped his hand in the water, raking up the feathery tag of some weed. They couldn't all be German.

There was Algie, the English youngbloods. According to Reg, George Grant grazed his blue-blooded Angus on this very ground. Reg had sounded awed—the Establishment camped at the actual place. Then the old man had climbed into the Southwind with Jewel and Frank, off to find the center. "I want to be there when he sees it," Reg said, with a wink for Marsh as the Southwind pulled away.

"Steelers 36, Cowboys 28." Muriel grinned up from her newspaper. "Terry Bradshaw completed three touchdown passes last night." She ran her thumb across her tongue, then turned the page, scanning the paper back to front.

Alex heaved an elbow over the side of the pool. "They're going to strike. Two weeks at the most and the whole NFL will walk out."

"I don't think so," Evie said. She spoke reluctantly, as if it pained her to allow that Alex was even here. "They're athletes first, after all."

"They're men who've been reduced to nothing but chattels of the rich." Alex pinched water from her nose, then waved a hand. "Men depreciated every year like cars, simple tax write-offs . . ."

Muriel whacked the newspaper straight. " 'Princess Grace of Monaco suffered fractures and her seventeen-year-old daughter was injured slightly yesterday when their vintage Land-Rover plunged off a winding mountain road. A spokesman for the royal palace reported that both princesses were in good condition.' " Muriel paused, skimming down the column. " 'It is not known how long they will be hospitalized.' "

"Princess Grace," Alex snorted. She looked up, rolling her eyes at Marsh, then dove away.

"It says here that Grace sustained a fractured right thigh bone, a broken rib, and a shattered collarbone."

"Thank goodness it wasn't her face." As Evie sat up, the pink washcloths fell away. Tiffany snatched them off the cement. But Evie never noticed. She frowned down at herself, disturbed by the NFL, Princess Grace—Marsh couldn't tell which. Or maybe it was Alex looking so young in their midst.

"It's awful," Evie said. She turned to Muriel, tapping a spot just above her knee. "My scar always comes up when I'm in the sun."

"That's only because you know where to look. Anybody else would need a magnifying glass." Muriel closed the *Wichita Times,* folding it like somebody once involved with paper routes. She thumped her newspaper on the questionable knee. "Over."

Marsh watched the two women as if witnessing a ritual. He pictured poolsides all across America—Evie rolling onto her stomach, arms folded under her head, her eyes closed, trusting to Muriel who knew what to do when the going got tough.

Alex splashed from the pool and stood dripping beside him. He eased

a washcloth from Tiffany's fist and handed it to his daughter-in-law.
"Have a towel."

Evie never opened her eyes to see how near naked. Muriel didn't look
around either, her fingers kneading up and down every bump in Evie's
spine.

Marsh scooped Tiffany in his arms, speaking quietly, as if the two
women had dropped suddenly asleep. "We're going into Victoria and
buy you new clothes."

Alex trailed him across the concrete, blotting her arms, her neck with
the washcloth. "They hate me," she whispered.

"They're crazy about you," Marsh said. He stopped at the metal gate
and gazed out a moment, bouncing Tiffany at his chest.

The youngbloods had named their town for Her Majesty The Queen.
They grazed their noble bulls on these golden fields. They filled their
goblets, sang Britannia Rule the Waves . . .

Marsh gathered the two pink washcloths in his hand. He spread one
on Alex's sopping head, the other over Tiffany's curls. They smiled
without understanding. They had been crowned. Then Marsh swung
open the gate.

Behind him, Muriel slap-slapped the length of Evie's loose, flushed
body. The sound came to Marsh like applause, a tremendous ovation.
The youngbloods raised their goblets to the sky. The princesses were in
good condition.

From Fort Fletcher Campground the gravel road ran flat and utterly
straight, intersected by dirt lanes that squared the land mile after mile.
Alex might've been driving up a sheet of graph paper, her van plotting
dust true north.

"Sections," she explained, nodding at Marsh. "Of course, most of the
homesteaders farmed only a quarter section. It's no wonder so many
failed."

"You don't know that," Marsh said. He stared out his open window,
unwilling to believe Alex could possess any knowledge he hadn't already
credited her with. Six years Alex and Richard had been married—long
enough for him to have some idea about her. Although it seemed now
that Alex had gone back to where she and Richard first began, taking
up causes right and left—the unknown woman in Utah, nuclear weapons,
football players. She sported wordy T-shirts and buttons the way she
might wear a string around her finger. Anything to remind her of who
she'd once been.

Marsh slid lower in his seat as Alex chattered on about sections and
the plight of American farmers. She'd offered to drive into Victoria,
insisting her van got better mileage than the Establishment. Marsh

couldn't argue on that score. Besides, he was starting to like the passenger seat—the road atlas open on his knees, or Tiffany in his lap. The little girl dozed against his chest, worn out from the swimming pool. Plus this heat.

The afternoon hadn't cooled off. If anything, it felt warmer. Outside his window, black-eyed Susans bent with the wind. Fields were hemmed with barbed wire strung along stone fence posts. The land had yielded more rock than timber. Marsh thought of the youngbloods—saw them raising the limestone posts like Stonehenge on the New World plains.

But there were trees now—cottonwoods shading farmhouses, breaking the wind. Cedars, boxelder, ash . . . others Marsh didn't know.

"Write down western meadowlark," Alex said. She reached beside her on the seat and handed him a small hard-bound book and a ballpoint pen.

The little book reminded Marsh of a diary—the kind young girls keep—imitation leather stamped in gold. The cover read *Explorer's Notebook, Western Edition*. Alex had already made several entries in a sliding, uneven scrawl. She must've been trying to write while she drove.

He propped the book on Tiffany's knees. "You saw *five* coyotes outside Ely, Nevada?"

"Well, three of them had been hit by cars. I noted that—three dead."

He scanned down the page, saw the word *accidental*. "Too bad you didn't have your taxidermist along."

She scowled at him. "Put the date first, then the time and place."

Marsh flipped to a blank page and checked his watch. He began writing, glad the bumpy gravel road had turned to asphalt. He shouldn't have mentioned the taxidermist. Alex's California Wildlife project was a touchy subject—it turned out she hadn't been funded. She sounded more upset giving him this news than when he asked about Richard. She told him Richard was still working. And that's all she'd say. "He's working," as if that took care of the subject of their marriage. She herself had spent every day since Marsh left puttering in the shade garden, trying to think. At least that's what Marsh gathered. "Just wandering around your garden," was how Alex put it. "Thinking and snipping off deadheads."

It occurred to Marsh that if Alex hadn't lost her job she probably wouldn't have left home. She'd be pulling into the parking lot of some school, her star-attraction grizzly still on native ground. Instead the bear had crossed the borders of four states. It stood at the van's rear window as if patrolling for enemies on their trail. Back in California children might've lined up to touch its polished claws. But Tiffany had taken one look and refused to budge from the front seat.

Marsh wrote down meadlowlark and closed the book. Every so often they passed a field with wheat rippling knee-high. *Section,* Marsh told himself. It seemed he could see a full mile, and in the far corner of a section, an oil rig. At the next field he spotted another one.

"Maybe we should include oil rigs." He smiled, tapping the book's cover. There was something laughable about this record Alex was keeping. *Explorer's Notebook,* as if she was the first person ever to spot a meadowlark. And Frank, Jewel, Reg—the three of them off to find the geographical center like a party of surveyors mapping unknown territory.

Finally the road curved. The van neared an underpass bridging railroad tracks. Across the cement bridge, Marsh read MOOSE LOVES YOU in rough red letters. He turned to Alex wanting to say, Look—somebody's been here before us. We aren't the first.

And then he saw the town—just ahead—Victoria, the youngbloods. Houses lined the road: wood frame, new brick, clipped lawns, no sidewalks. Marsh looked for a face behind living-room windows. In one backyard he glimpsed a stone grotto, the Virgin Mary clasping her hands. At the next corner a plastic blue-robed Madonna stood beside front steps as if to escort him inside. The blessed little woman wouldn't have reached to his knees.

They drove on. Marsh looked up, spotted a street sign: Cathedral Avenue. And then the cathedral itself.

"My God," Alex said. She slowed, staring out. "I had no idea *that* was here."

The cathedral filled the window on Marsh's side. Limestone towers thrust into pale blank sky.

"I think they call this Romanesque," Alex said.

"I know about buildings," Marsh answered, his voice gruff, but not on her account. He frowned at the towers, figuring the depth of a foundation that would support such weight. And the concrete footings themselves—they'd need to be sunk at least four feet and probably twice that wide.

He glanced to a limestone statue across the street—a family kneeling at a cross. Their carved stone bodies looked stolid, long suffering. A dog cowered at their feet. That dog would never run braying for the hunt.

"Pull over," Marsh said.

He slid from the van, leaving Tiffany rubbing her eyes in the front seat. Here, there was a sidewalk. He leapt it, then up the wide cathedral steps.

He pushed through the tall double doors and felt a sudden stillness—the wind gone, only the heat. Becalmed. A woman stepped toward him, across the tiled vestibule. She spoke in a hushed voice.

"There are eighteen different types of dressed stone in the cathedral.

The pillars supporting the walls and vaulted ceiling are Vermont granite beneath which—"

"Tell me," Marsh said. He leaned nearer the woman, her blue eyes pale and serious behind gold-rimmed glasses. "Are you all German?"

The woman placed a hand to her throat. "So touched was William Jennings Bryant upon seeing this structure that he proclaimed it Cathedral of the Plains. The church has since been declared . . ." She paused, blinking into his face. "Everyone," she said. "German Catholic."

Marsh turned for the double doors, then stopped. He stared up at a stained-glass window, colors falling like rainbows. He dug into his pants pocket and left some change on a table beside the doors.

"I'm looking for a clothing store," he said.

"For that you'll need to drive into Hays. We're only a small town." The woman's voice rose louder, more abrupt, as if the secular world required another language altogether.

Marsh moved outside, thinking he should've asked point blank about the Englishmen. A youngblood given to nosebleeds and a black boy age thirteen. The two of them last seen in the company of Mr. George Grant, some say knighted, some not . . .

"We need to go to Hays," Marsh said, climbing into the van. "There's no clothing store here." He turned to his window. No Englishmen.

As Alex pulled away from the curb, he gazed back. Tiffany stared from his lap. Only a very small town and one very big church, followed by a whole block of cemetery crammed with Catholics. Then a sign, just before the interstate: WELCOME TO VICTORIA, HOME OF THE KNIGHTS, 1981 DOUBLE A STATE CHAMPS.

"Home of the Knights," Marsh whispered into Tiffany's ear.

The wind took his words, scattering Germans across the plains. Wide receivers ran their Stations of the Cross, the Knights charged from the line of scrimmage. Then a flag on the field and the Germans were down, one linebacker called Moose, grumbling his thick-tongued,

"Fe fi fo fum."

Tiffany nodded. "Again."

"Fe fi fo fum." Marsh laughed, jamming a finger into the little girl's belly.

Alex shook her head. "I'd like to know what's so funny."

"Back there." He jerked his thumb out the window. "The youngbloods just won."

"California," the sales clerk said, copying Marsh's driver's license number along the bottom of a Visa charge slip. "I've never been to California." She looked off, a softness coming into her eyes as if she was picturing herself in that state. "Do you have a phone number there?"

Marsh leaned over the pile of Tiffany's new clothes and recited his number. Then he glanced up, hearing Tiffany in tears again. She wailed from the back of the shop, lost behind racks bunched with mix-and-match playwear, sleepwear, snow suits so thick-padded they could've stood on their own. Marsh had picked one in navy trimmed with red. Forget this hot spell—it was unseasonable. Any day they'd need their good heavy coats. He'd chosen T-shirts with the word Jayhawker, denim overalls from OshKosh, underwear—a hundred percent cotton and Fruit of the Loom. He grabbed up flannel nightgowns and on second thought, ruffled seersucker baby dolls. Alex had picked the child's bathing suit, a tank model called Speedo, so modest Marsh thought about suggesting something similar for his daughter-in-law.

And where was Tiffany these past forty-five minutes—the whole time he and Alex spent debating color, size, and wash-and-wear? Had the child cared one way or the other? No. She'd chugged between them and the rear of the shop, to a corner billowing dresses white as cumulus clouds, dresses frilled like white carnations, lacy dresses in a row—all the little white lambs following Mary—sure to go. This girl Tiffany wasn't interested in underwear. She'd walk around in hand-me-downs forever, no complaints. She wanted only one white dress.

"I give up," Alex said, pushing beside Marsh. "You'll have to drag her screaming from that . . ." She stopped, pressed both hands on Tiffany's brand new pile. "I almost hit her and I *like* children. I mean, I really do." Alex shook her head, then frowned at a small yellow stretch suit Marsh had added to the stack. She lifted the pair of yellow legs, no bigger than fingers on a glove.

"They're for the baby," Marsh said.

Alex snapped straight, stared at him. "Baby?"

Marsh smiled, thinking of his namesake, a fringe of spiky dark hair. Wearing this yellow suit, the baby would look something like a dwarfed Kansas sunflower.

He signed his charge slip, then stepped away, aware of the sudden quiet—only tissue paper rustling in the young sales clerk's hands.

Deep in the white corner, Tiffany stood gazing up at a crowded rack. Her tears had turned into hiccups. She glanced to Marsh—a pitiful flushed face—then crooked her finger at the white dresses, as if she believed one might float down to her of its own accord.

"You don't want anything like this," Marsh said.

Tiffany's breath jumped with a hiccup. She nodded, kept her finger going, imploring, just one white vision: Descend.

"These are for older girls." He placed his hand on the child's shaky shoulder. "There's a religious significance here."

"Andy." Her mouth strained hard, too wide for such a small sound.

"It's no good working yourself up this way." He stepped to the dresses lined one after another. He imagined all the smiling girls. They filed between granite pillars, moving down the cathedral aisle like the young brides they were and would someday be. Twice married for life.

Marsh hunted through the rack, pulled a dress from its hanger and shook it before Tiffany. "Look—even the smallest one is way too big for you."

Tiffany stared. Her finger stopped in mid-air. For a moment it seemed she might burst into more tears. She rolled her lips, her eyes holding tight.

He shook the dress again, then gave up and shoved it into her arms. The cotton lace buckled below her feet, hid her face. Tiffany sputtered as if he'd just doused her with feathers. Finally her chin emerged over the edge of a puffed sleeve. But she had no smile, no hug for him. She gathered up the dress, bunching it into a mammoth ball. Then she held the whole stiff wad to her chest, placed one hand on top, and stumbled up the aisle.

Marsh moved after her, still looking for a smile. But Tiffany never glanced back. She'd reached the counter, stretched on her toes, delivering her wrinkled load to the sales clerk.

As the child opened her hands, the white lace sprang out like a Jack-in-the-box. Marsh laughed and Tiffany turned. He saw her bright eyes, her radiant face.

"My dress was a lot like this one," the sales clerk said, reaching for more tissue paper.

Alex shook her head at him. "How could you do this, you of all people?"

Marsh shrugged, keeping his eyes on the young sales clerk. He reached into his back pocket for his wallet. "She just likes the dress—that's all there is to it."

"All there is to it baloney." Alex stabbed a finger into the dress. "This is where everything begins—this young. And you wonder why we can't pass the Equal Rights Amendment."

"My mother never voted for it." The sales clerk looked pleased, as if these were the words Alex wanted to hear.

Marsh leaned at the counter, watching the young woman fold the dress into a white box. He cleared his throat. "I don't suppose you'd know—" He paused as she slid the box his way. "We're camping outside of town, near Victoria . . ."

"Old Fort Fletcher," the sales clerk said. "Sylvia Wessel's my aunt. You probably saw her at the house."

Marsh smiled. He would've bet on those pale blue-gray eyes, a combination that seemed to require glasses. Except in this case. He heard the abruptness in her voice—an accent softened by generations, but still there in the new brick farmhouse, inside that Cathedral of the Plains.

"Actually, Sylvia's my double aunt."

Marsh folded his arms on the counter. "Your double aunt—that's something."

"Not around here it isn't." The young woman laughed. "We're all related somehow or other."

Marsh slid the white box from the counter and propped it beside Tiffany. Standing on end, the box looked almost as tall as the little girl. She wrapped her arms around the flimsy cardboard as if she'd just been reunited with an old friend.

"You'll probably catch my brothers at the swimming pool," the young woman said. "Before you come to the campground—you remember those three granaries? Well, one section after the granaries you'll see our land. That's our homeplace."

Marsh gazed past the sales clerk, trying to recall: three granaries. Beside him, Alex crackled giant paper sacks—Tiffany's new wardrobe—two bags in each hand.

"I could've commuted to Hays State this year," the sales clerk was saying, "but it seemed like a good idea to be on my own, at least a little. I wanted the dormitory experience."

Alex nudged his shoulder. "We'd better get going. It's almost time for the stores to close."

He never heard. He thought of Charles and Algie, pictured them standing in a field—the two of them standing there with wheat up to their knees. He noticed they wore their best wool suits, even though the day sweltered. He saw the sun shining everywhere through the wheat and six meadowlarks wheeling. He should write that in the book while he remembered. Six meadowlarks: time, date . . . Because it seemed a true memory as if he'd been there, too, and had always stood there in his mind's eye, recalling each little detail the way you will do—without exception—whenever someone mentions your homeplace.

He reached across the counter, touched the young woman's hand. "Do you know the Englishmen—the ones in Victoria."

"Them," she said, easing her hand away. "We studied them in school, our local history."

"Listen, Marsh." It was Alex at his ear. "I'm going outside to call Richard. There's a phone booth." Alex paused, as if waiting for her words to penetrate. Finally she turned away. At the shop's door she hollered, "I'm taking Tiffany with me."

"I did the English for my project," the clerk said. She glanced around as if looking for customers, then leaned against the cash register. "There was this clock they put into the steeple of a barn—a clock just like Big Ben. That's the way they were. They had this idea about everything being exactly like England."

"Yes," Marsh said.

"And lazy—those people were terrible farmers. They were aways standing around watching their big clock, just waiting to quit work."

Marsh looked away, feeling like a failure. Only a while ago. He'd been out there standing in that field.

"Well, anybody can tell you, a farmer works from sunup to sundown. And so the do-nothing English lost everything they had." The sales clerk fished under the counter and came up with a set of keys. "Then we got here—we took up where the English left off. But of course, they didn't have one single thing to leave off."

She locked the register and covered it with a black plastic hood, then glanced at Marsh and made a face. "I should've closed fifteen minutes ago."

"Sunup to sundown," Marsh mumbled, following her from the counter.

The sales clerk stepped outside and turned a key in the bolt lock.

"If you could help me . . ." Marsh leaned over her shoulder. "I mean, it's important. I'd like to find someone—you know, an Englishman."

She shook her head, and for just an instant he caught the glint of her contact lenses. "I told you. In Victoria we're all German."

"Yes I know that." Down the block he heard Tiffany calling him. He waved, not looking around. "I'm asking about Englishmen, young-bloods—"

"Please," the girl said. She was just a girl now, Marsh could see that. "How am I supposed to help you if you won't let me think."

"Please think," Marsh said. He rocked up and down on his toes, glanced toward the phone booth, waved again to Tiffany. The child leaned against the booth, holding her big white box with both hands.

"Here in Hays you could try Randall Tharp at the hardware store. I think his people came over to be foremen. But they're Scotch. I don't know if they'd count."

"They count," Marsh said.

"Tharp's Hardware is down there." The girl pointed in the direction of the phone booth. "On the next corner."

He grabbed her hand, shook it hard. "You'll never know what a help—"

"And there's Mrs. Houseright. Try her."

"I will, absolutely."

"And tell my Aunt Sylvia that Trish says hi."

"Right," Marsh said, turning in a rush for the corner. "Trish says hi . . ." He took a few steps, then stopped as the words caught up to him. He swung around grinning at the girl named Trish. "I hope you make it to California one of these days."

"Oh, I don't think so." She spoke louder, as if already putting the distance between them—a thousand miles of highway and more. Then she nodded, the softness coming into her eyes again. "Well, maybe on my honeymoon."

"Now you're talking," Marsh said. He started down the sidewalk, wondering why on Earth, California. Hadn't Trish ever heard of Hawaii?

Alex was finally off the phone, holding Tiffany by the hand. As Marsh dashed toward the hardware store, a man rounded the corner, hailed Alex and stepped beside her. Marsh frowned, seeing it was one of the SOARS—that man named Lester who knew so much about Napoleon.

"Andy," Tiffany shouted as Marsh tried to dodge past. The little girl scrambled, dragging her white box onto the sidewalk like a barrier.

He stopped, turned Tiffany toward the phone booth. "I'll only be a minute." Across the street, a customer stepped out of the weathered limestone building. The store hadn't closed, he could still catch Randall Tharp. But Alex had grabbed his elbow.

"You know Mr. Harmon," she said, smiling at Lester. "Mr. Harmon's been in the library all day."

Lester squeezed next to Marsh. "The library has quite a bit of information, especially when you consider the settlement's brief existence." His voice dropped low at Marsh's ear. "I think you should know the British colony was a complete joke—an absolute nothing. They might never have been here for all the difference they made."

Marsh turned, staring into the man's lean gray face. "I thought your hobby was Napoleon."

"Hobbies are for people with free time." Lester gazed into the wind, his crewcut stiff as a steel brush, his blink like an eagle. "You'll find I'm not a man of leisure."

But Marsh wasn't listening. A young man stood locking the hardware store. Marsh shoved past Lester, then stopped, watching the man move away in the other direction.

"Randall!" Marsh hollered.

The man halted. He looked up the sidewalk, puzzled.

It didn't matter. Marsh would've known Randall Tharp anywhere. He recognized the shock of ruddy hair, those eyes nowhere near pale German blue.

The young man hesitated, then raised his broad-knuckled hand and waved. "Hello," he called.

Marsh grinned at the sound. It was Randall Tharp's voice. Then the young man hurried away. Marsh stepped off the curb, about to follow. But somehow just hearing Randall's hello seemed enough. He stood a moment, then turned and raced back to the phone booth.

"Who was that?" Alex asked, frowning after the man. She glanced to Lester as if he would know.

Marsh banged open the phone booth. He grabbed the directory, flipped to *H,* ran his finger down a page, then rummaged for change. He dialed. A woman answered, he recognized her voice. It was Mrs. William Marcus Houseright. He stuck his arm out the booth, made a fist like a cheerleader.

"Honestly," Alex said, giving Lester a look.

"Hello, Mrs. Houseright—"

"No, this is her nurse. Mrs. Houseright can't come to the phone. She isn't well."

"Please," Marsh said. "I don't have much time. I'm looking for some-one—" He faltered, closed his eyes. "Someone in my family. This would be years ago—the English colony. Could you ask Mrs. Houseright if she's ever heard of Algernon Vickers?"

"Algernon Vickers. Well, I'm not sure." The nurse spoke as if the inquiry had been made of her.

"He's black," Marsh said.

There was a pause.

"It's very important."

Marsh waited a moment, then realized the nurse wasn't there. He leaned from the booth, keeping the receiver to his ear. "She's gone to ask."

"I could care less," Alex said. She waved a hand toward Lester. "Mr. Harmon's been at the library all day long. Ask him, for God's sake."

Marsh glanced at Lester. Ask Lester, hah! That gray-eyed man poring over books, memorizing failure on the tip of his tongue. Marsh shot a finger Lester's way. "If you so much as mention one word about the library to Reg—"

"Hello?"

"I'm here," Marsh said.

"Mrs. Houseright says if it's the colored school teacher you're looking for—that one her father had. Well, if he's the one, she says to tell you he was a fine boy."

"That's him," Marsh said, nodding fast at the receiver. "You probably don't know how smart he was, good in history and music—way above average. He had this way with words, he—"

"Yes," the nurse said. "I understand."

The sun was beginning to set as Alex turned off on the narrow asphalt road. But it would be a while before dark. In this sky, the sun needed to travel a long way. Clouds generated another light, which was their own, and gold. The fields had forgotten their complicated division, stretching one into one as far as the horizon. Wheat gave off a burnished dust that gilded the stone fenceposts beside the lane. Birds didn't have to raise their voices. The evening settled their arguments, settled the wind, became all settling light.

Tiffany had agreed to the back of the van, but only because she now possessed the big white box—her talisman against the menacing bear. After today she'd never sleep with her crumpled popcorn bag again. And good riddance. Marsh couldn't wait to throw the greasy bag away. If for no other reason, he was glad he'd bought Tiffany the dress.

He smiled out his open window, thinking of the young sales clerk who'd once worn something similar. When they hit the gravel part of the road he'd look for those granaries. And beyond them, her homeplace.

He turned to Alex, shaking his head. "You'll never guess where Trish wants to spend her honeymoon."

"Trish who," Alex said. She sounded fed-up with strangers, and with Marsh, too—hollering at unknown men on the street, calling up a bedridden woman from a name he found in the phone book. "Never mind who, I don't really care."

"California," Marsh said. He gazed out the windshield, chuckling. "That's where she wants to go."

"Trish can go to hell!"

For a moment Marsh stared, then sat straight. "Listen, Alex, I know how you feel. You drove so hard to get here, probably didn't sleep, never even ate in Utah . . ." He frowned at the dashboard. How many years since he and Reg had crossed that barren territory? It seemed a decade, maybe more. "And then having to meet all these different people—I mean the SOARS. I felt like that before." He tried to think back: Before what? "Anyway, it's just too much."

"You're too much. *You.*" Alex fisted her hands around the steering wheel. "Or rather the all-new you. You standing on your head like an idiot, you putting little girls into white dresses, then serving up your own brand of first communion. You telling me, Reg said this. Algie did that, and then—oh yes—you tell me the youngbloods won."

Marsh put his hand to his forehead, looked away.

"Well, I'll tell you something—this isn't the Land of Oz we've come to—this is *Kansas* and that sun out there is setting on the real world, except you're not in it!" Alex opened her fist, slammed her palm on the wheel, took a big breath. "But in case you're interested, I'll give you the news from here and now. They're killing each other in Beirut, over ten million Americans are out of work, the President's polluting the Clean Water Act . . ."

"The NFL is going to strike," Marsh whispered.

"And your son—remember him?" Alex tramped the gas and the van leapt forward. "Last night your son Richard slept with Julia Oakes."

Marsh jerked around in his seat.

"A woman old enough to be—"

"Alex, please," he said. "Please. Don't tell me this."

He braced his hand on the dash as they hit the bumpy gravel stretch, going way too fast. The van bounced hard—rattling, tires spinning. Gravel pinged hubcaps, pelted the windshield.

Suddenly the still air boiled with dust. It poured into Marsh's window and rolled through the van. He glanced back, hearing Tiffany cough, then cry his name. Behind the little girl, he saw the grizzly teetering, rearing. And then he couldn't see the bear at all. He grabbed for Tiffany and caught her just in time, holding on as the dust swung them round and round and the three granaries whirled past his window and the grizzly soared by on its way down. Tiffany hollered, slipping from his grasp. He lunged for her—too late. His hands clutched nothing but the careening air. Then Alex flew into his lap. The bear's claws raked the dashboard, and that was the last sound.

The dust stopped rolling. It fell like the softest rain. Marsh opened his eyes and saw that it was only dust everywhere—dust filming Alex's hair, his knees, Tiffany's red sandals. He stared at her sandals wiggling beneath the collapsed bear. Then he heard the little girl sneeze. He slid out from under Alex and shoved the grizzly toward the steering wheel.

Tiffany pushed to her hands and feet, gave Marsh a quick look, then struggled over him, searching for her white box.

Finally Alex moved. She wiped her dusty face in the crook of her arm. "We spun out," she said in a choked voice. "We turned completely around." She leaned to the windshield. "It's true. We're still pointed in the right direction."

Marsh sat a minute, marveling that any animal the size of a grizzly could pack so little weight. Then he opened his door and climbed outside. The van looked okay, though it had come to a halt just inches from a massive stone fencepost. The fencepost rose like a gravestone—a spot where they all might've been killed. Because it could've happened, quick as that.

As Marsh walked around to the rear of the van it came to him, how near miracles were to disasters. Those two events breathed on each other—they stood that close together with the whole world crammed in between. And so it seemed the Earth must truly be flat just as he'd thought, and narrow as a surveyor's line, a line so thin there could be no two sides—only one.

Then Marsh gave up thinking. His head hurt and he believed he must've bumped it in the spin. He opened the van's back door and crawled inside. Tiffany scooted out of his way, clutching her white box. She looked perfectly calm, as if nothing had happened. But even so . . . Marsh touched her face. "I should never have let go of you."

He leaned into the front, working to haul the giant grizzly back. He shoved the bear one way, then the other. The grizzly's fur smelled like dust. And as if realizing what a tight squeeze over the front seat, it seemed to hold itself smaller, helping out.

Marsh set the bear in place, then stepped down to the gravel and shut the Econoline's rear door. As he moved for the passenger side, Alex walked toward him, shaking her head.

For a minute she leaned against the van. "So," she said, "maybe you'd better drive."

He nodded, gazing past her. Through everything the evening had kept such a quiet. Up the road a meadowlark lit on a yellow fencepost and sounded its clear flute melody. He would write this one in the book, plus the six he'd seen earlier in his mind's eye. That made seven, and two sections over—three granaries still rooted secure in a field. Marsh faced that direction and let the warm golden air fall over him. He squinted to see beyond those granaries to the homeplace.

Finally he turned to Alex. He felt a strong desire to tell her all he knew about the real world—how flat it actually was, a line so thin as to have only one side. Instead he said, "When you get a scare like this, they say it's a good idea to climb right behind the wheel again. You drive."

He slid into the passenger seat and glanced back at Tiffany. She lay with her arms wrapped around the box—not sleeping, her eyes open, just gazing off. She wasn't smiling, but she looked infinitely happy.

"I'm calling your mother tonight," he said.

As Alex started the engine, Marsh tried to think what kind of happiness that was, to be so quiet and restful. But he couldn't find any one word.

Alex looked over. She drove extra slow, her seat belt fastened. "I don't want you to believe this happened because I was upset. You know—the spinout."

Marsh reached down for the ballpoint near his shoe, then took the explorer's notebook off the dash. Somehow the small book had remained

there during the spin, almost exactly where he'd put it. He opened to
the next free page and wrote Time, Date, and Place.

Seven meadowlarks.

"I mean, I wasn't that upset."

Three granaries—inanimate.

Though the sun still lingered, Marsh could see lights coming on, not
far up the road. He saw the darkening trees that marked the creek
bordering Fort Fletcher Campground. In a little while Reg would sit
telling his story. It would be a story about life to which there was only
one side. Marsh looked down at the page again.

One Scotsman—young Randall Tharp.

"You were upset," he said.

One Englishwoman—Mrs. William Marcus Houseright. (Not well.)

He closed the book and turned to Alex. "You have every right to be
worked up after what happened. Not the spinout, I'm talking about
Richard."

But he didn't want to talk about Richard. It seemed he and Richard
might never stop foundering. Because he could've been the one with
Julia. As it was, he'd taken the black whore, taken her miles from home
as if she wouldn't count—counted for nothing.

Alex leaned to the windshield. She concentrated on her driving, the
tip of her tongue curled along her lip. "Although I admit I have been
sort of beside myself."

In the back of the van Tiffany had begun to hum, not a real song but
little disjointed notes. The child sounded simply happy.

"The truth is I've got my share of problems."

As they took the turn into the campground, Marsh reached over his
seat for Tiffany. He eased the big box from the girl's hands and pulled
her into his lap.

"But this hasn't got a thing to do with Richard."

Alex braked, rounding the dirt road past the swimming pool. "Well,
I guess it does and it doesn't. Have to do with Richard, I mean. It's just
that—" She shook her head. For a moment her shoulders sagged at the
wheel.

"What?" Marsh said.

But it seemed Alex would never be able to say. Her eyes veered around
the van, as if to find something, anything else to come up with. Finally
she sighed, "Just nothing." Then her gaze came to rest on him.

"It's you," she said.

16

Marsh entered his credit card number, then dialed Big Hermo's Campground in Grand Junction. He let the phone ring, folding the brochure the campground hostess had given him last week: Proud Home of the Atomic Energy Commission. You'll find you're never too old, Vivian Callahan had told him. She'd included the baby no charge and invited him to the original *Ben Hur*. But it was Sharon's voice he heard coming onto the line.

"I gave Vivian the night off," Sharon said, as if she'd somehow become boss in that short time since he left her. "It's a total madhouse—booked so full I had to put three big outfits in the tenters' sites, no hookups, no nothing. And complain—you'd think we were running the Waldorf-Astoria for these people.

"It's empty here," Marsh said.

"You couldn't prove it by all the noise. What's going on there?"

Marsh glanced out to an oil rig rising from a field across the dusky road. Earlier, when they'd driven off to buy Tiffany's new clothes, the rig hadn't been there. Only a few hours and it had gone up, lights strung top to bottom and an engine grating the air.

"I think they're drilling for oil," he said. He wondered if the field might be part of Trish's section—on her homeplace. Sometime during the night maybe the young sales clerk would strike it rich, turn into a millionaire. It could happen while she slumbered in the town next door, enjoying her dormitory experience, dreaming of California.

"Put Tiffany on the phone," Sharon said. "Tell her to talk loud."

"She's already asleep. We had a big day—" Marsh caught himself before he mentioned the spinout. "We went swimming, bought new clothes. You should see this dress."

But nobody'd glimpsed the lacy outfit since the clothing store. Tiffany wouldn't give up her big white box. She slept with it now, arms wrapped tight.

"How's the baby?" he asked. "I got something for him, too."

"Andy's sitting right here on the counter. Vivian loaned me an infant seat."

"Well, tell him I said hello."

"Tell him yourself," Sharon said.

There was a pause, but not a real silence, so split by memory—a long time ago—Virginia holding the receiver against Richard's ear before he'd learned to talk. And Marsh sat in his downtown office smiling at the silence on the other end, saying Hello this is Daddy. Hi Richard, hello. Then Ginny had come back on the line. You scared him to death, she said. But Marsh could hardly hear her over Richard's shrieking cries.

So he waited, afraid to speak to Sharon's baby. He glanced out the phone booth, then stared. Alex leaned against the swimming pool fence, dressed for jogging, cocking one knee, then the other. Marsh turned back to the phone wondering if she'd followed him. Had she raced from the campsite to tell him another time—it's you.

Sharon broke onto the line, laughing. "Andy says hi, too."

"Listen, Sharon—" He pushed his chin to the receiver, talking in a rush. "I need you to come. Right away. Something's happened . . ."

"Tiffany," Sharon said, the child's name leaping high.

"I mean, nothing's really happened."

"Oh thank God."

"Maybe it isn't anything." For a moment he shut his eyes, blaming Virginia all over again. She'd been the one who made that imaginary list. She'd sealed the names in an envelope and said, *Are you in for a shock.*

Sharon sighed into the phone. "Well, if it's the old gentleman you're worried about . . ."

"My daughter-in-law," Marsh said. "She left Richard—you know, my son. And now she's here." He stopped, took a breath, lowered his voice. "With me."

And then Alex was really there. She opened the booth a crack and wagged an envelope inside. She whispered as if she didn't want to interrupt. "I meant to give you this first thing. It came the day you left home." She slipped the envelope into his hand, then loped away.

"Hold it," Sharon said. "Are you talking with you as in the Bible? Is that what you're telling me?"

Marsh glanced at the envelope. He pictured a square of his wife's blue stationery, names listed inside.

"The thing is, Alex says it's me, but I don't think it really is, I think there's something—"

"Calm down," Sharon said, "I'm not making any judgments. You're not related, after all. Her voice softened. "Whatever you've got going, I'm on your side. Remember that."

Marsh turned the envelope over. He read his typed name, his street number, zip code, then the return address: Northern California Racing Association.

"It's only the results," he said.

"There are always results," Sharon answered. "But if you start worrying about every single thing you do, you might as well quit living period."

He folded the envelope and stuffed it into his pocket. "I still wish you'd come here."

"Listen, have you got that book of matches on you?"

Marsh felt at his shirt.

"Well, strike another match and keep going. That's my advice from this end."

"Will you come?"

"I'll think it over," Sharon said. "Rolf should be showing up soon. I put in that call, remember."

Marsh frowned at the receiver. How could a person smart as Sharon turn out so ignorant on the subject of men? "Look," he said, dropping his voice, trying to go easy. "I know something about this. You won't be seeing Rolf."

But she paid no attention. "Plus there's bus fare. Besides which, you were supposed to bring Tiffany back on your way home."

"I'll send you the fare." He glanced toward the field, listening to the big engine driving its bit deep, drilling into the very quick of the earth. "Maybe you already know this, Sharon, but the fact is . . . Well, I'm sort of a millionaire."

She let out a snort. "Oh brother."

"It wasn't all just me," he added, as if this news required an apology.

"I need to get off the phone now," she said. "Almost time for the movie. I'm running the projector tonight."

"Just think it over," he said. "You've got our itinerary."

"And next time bring Tiffany when you call. Give her a kiss."

Marsh nodded, reluctant to hang up. "What movie are you showing?"

"Charles Laughton," Sharon said, her voice fading away. "The original *Down to the Sea in Ships*."

Marsh stepped from the phone booth and gazed beyond the gravel road. He tried to spot Alex jogging the section, her dark silhouette leaning for turns as she took the square mile, then streaking through trees—black locusts in single file to break the wind. But there wasn't even a whisper of a breeze. The night deepened, ranged to the distant four corners of this flat world. Marsh walked toward the campsites, moving through a darkness as wide as the Kansas sky.

Before he joined the SOARS' campfire, he stopped at the restroom. A single yardlight shed a gleam over the building's pink cinder blocks. The door to the men's half read GENERAL CUSTER. Inside there was no light at all, only a glow from the yard.

Marsh started across the cement floor, then ducked, hearing a flap of wings above his head, the air rushing. He bolted for the urinal, then sprang back as a man chuckled.

Lester turned, showing his pale gray face in the dim light. He zipped his coveralls. "That wasn't a bat. Just a swallow—must've made its nest in here."

Marsh stood at the urinal, aware of his knees, a slight tremble. He washed his hands and groped for a paper towel, hoping Lester would leave. But when he stepped to the door, the quiet-spoken man was waiting.

Lester aimed the beam of a pen-sized flashlight across the name on the flaking restroom door. "He was here at Fort Fletcher, you know—not long before your Englishmen."

"I thought Custer was supposed to be in Montana." Marsh heard his voice gruff and loud, as if he could force Lester's words from that irritating half-whisper. He turned away, barely able to see Lester beside him. "Anyway, they're not *my* Englishmen."

"Custer rode in with four companies of the Seventh. Your friend Mr. Vickers might be interested to hear that the General flatly refused a commission with the black Ninth Cavalry." Lester raised his little flashlight into Marsh's eyes. "I'd say the Ninth came out lucky, wouldn't you?"

Marsh frowned off, the campsites quiet with almost everybody gone to the campfire. He thought about checking on Tiffany. As usual, Claire had volunteered to babysit. Marsh glanced past her Micro-Mini, past Muriel's silver-bullet Airstream. Lester's rig sat last in line—not much of a rig, just a converted stepvan with a crooked shingle roof and rusted stovepipe.

As Marsh turned for the creek, Lester nudged beside him. "Custer's young wife waited at Fort Riley. Elizabeth C. was fuming over new recruits—a hundred darkies turning cartwheels on her sacred parade ground. Libby never forgot that blasphemy."

"Maybe not, but I think you'd better," Marsh said. He tramped through high weeds separating ruts in the sandy road. "I mean it, Lester—forget your damned books. This is Reg's story."

Lester looked over, shaking his head. "I'm not such a bad man." For a moment it seemed his voice rose from some loud sorrow, though he spoke even softer now. "I'd like you to know that in my later years I've made every effort to find the where, when, and why. I've never quit trying."

But Marsh wasn't listening. They'd crossed a planked bridge to a clearing where the fort had once stood. At the edge of the clearing, citronella torches glowed from metal stakes. SOARS wandered over the grass toward a picnic shelter. Marsh was reminded of a slow-moving herd ambling home from pasture.

"Of course before your Englishmen arrived, this fort was abandoned and the garrison relocated." Lester nodded, kept talking as they stepped through a straggle of SOARS. "You must've visited Fort Hays when you were in town today."

"I did not," Marsh said, wishing Lester would shut up. But then he heard Reg's gravelly voice beside him, so close the old man seemed to be speaking in his ear.

"Yes, it was a time then—such a time," Reg said.

The old man gripped Marsh's elbow as they moved into the picnic shelter. Behind them, Marsh caught the elderly Jewel leaning for Reg's every word. She was still cramming for her upcoming appearance on TV, the spiral notebook wedged in the crook of her arm.

"In those early years you would've found Mr. Bill Cody trotting around this prairie, attempting to make his mark from the rump of a little mouse-colored mule." Reg chuckled, waved a hand. "Biased? Well, I may be. But my father will tell you that in his own mind, the title Buffalo Bill rightly belongs to a daring young lad named Will Comstock."

Jewel eased onto a picnic bench, flipped a page in her notebook and kept scribbling. For a moment Marsh felt like crossing out all those words. He wanted to tell her, facts are facts. But Frank Valdivia had rushed over.

Frank grinned and slapped an arm around Reg's shoulder. "Your fans are waiting." He escorted the old man to a card table, then tapped a microphone.

Marsh winced as the sound crackled, bouncing against the shelter's low metal roof. He guessed Frank was responsible for setting up the sound system, plus making Reg a star. Marsh moved to a picnic table up front, wishing it was just the two of them again. And Algie, of course.

They should be standing in that field he'd pictured in his mind's eye. Instead they'd arrived at this fort turned into a campground. The cavalry had been relieved from duty by campers.

Frank dropped another log into a blazing barbecue pit, then unfolded a lawn chair. Slowly, almost cautiously, Reg lowered himself into the chair. But before the old man could start speaking, Frank leaned to the microphone.

"I just want to remind you that plans for our Annual Anti-Freeze Dance are in the works—time and place to be announced. After last year's big success I think we're damn lucky to have Muriel heading up the committee again. And now—" Frank grinned, waiting out the applause for Muriel.

Marsh glanced around at the crowd—there seemed more SOARS than he'd counted yesterday at the pass, maybe twenty-five, thirty. All of them clapping and calling Muriel to her feet. The stocky woman bounced up at the rear of the shelter and waved a white golf cap. Marsh spotted Alex standing behind her. He couldn't make out Alex's face, but something about the way she stood—head cocked, shoulders antsy—gave him the idea she might bolt away any second.

"And now," Frank said as the applause straggled off. "Now I'm going to turn the mike over to Mr. Reg Vickers who's got the program for tonight, maybe even tomorrow night . . ." Frank laughed, thumping Reg on the back. "Hell, for anytime he wants."

Frank stepped away, settling onto the bench beside Marsh. "How do you like that sound system—I put it together for our regional meet. Two hundred SOARS, half of them hard of hearing, and not one missed a word."

Marsh didn't look over. Behind him, the SOARS waited in such quiet he could hear the fire snapping in the barbecue pit.

For a minute Reg just sat there squinting out at the crowd. He wore a pink shirt Marsh hadn't seen before. His dark face looked even more wrinkled, reamed deeper by the humming mike. Near his feet a fluorescent insect trap flickered blue-white. The crackling bug zapper flashed its warning up the old man's legs. He cleared his throat—in that pink shirt, only a candy imitation of himself. He didn't even sound like himself.

"Perhaps I should begin by telling you—" Reg fumbled at his shirt pocket, ran a shaky finger inside, then blinked down at the card table.

Marsh felt Frank's elbow. "What'd he forget—is it his glasses?"

"His cigarettes," Marsh said, watching Reg dig into his trousers. He glanced at Frank, tried to think. "Where are they?"

"Hell if I know."

"Never mind," Marsh said, already hauling himself from the bench.

He worked the crowd, one table to the next. At the end of the rows he gave up. What had happened to people, anyway? Wasn't there one addicted soul still smoking? For a moment he wished he'd never sworn off. Then he saw Alex moving his way, sauntering like the loose-limbed athlete she was. She loped the last few steps, then fished into her baggy sweats and pulled out Chesterfields.

"I went by to check on Tiffany." She dropped the pack into his hand. "These were in the dinette. I thought maybe—"

"But you hate cigarettes." Marsh touched his pocket, the book of matches inside.

Alex flicked her hair behind her ears. "You don't know me, Marsh." Then she turned away, but not before he heard her grumble, "I absolutely hate cigarettes."

Marsh shook out a Chesterfield, rolled it over the table to Reg, then reached for his matches. Just strike another match and keep going, Sharon had told him on the phone.

"My advice is to start where you left off and keep going." Marsh lit the old man's cigarette, then grabbed the fluorescent bug trap and lugged it across the cement to Frank.

"Turn this thing off," he said.

He sank onto the bench and spread his hands flat on the table. Tomorrow he'd pick up another book of matches. He'd send Sharon bus fare just in case. And Alex . . . Marsh gazed at the old man, unable to think about Alex. Not with Reg finally finding his voice.

"It was April first of 1873, the *Alabama* set sail from Glasgow Harbor. And here I must tell you, that was a very rough crossing, indeed. There was young Charles, so ill as to lie groaning in his bunk, white as salt and gimlet-eyed for the duration. Only Algie seemed spared by the green tossing ocean. Of course, he'd made those sea voyages before—had, in fact, entered the world in the dark hold of that other ship."

Marsh nodded as the old man's words rang full from loudspeakers. At the card table Reg himself looked stronger, restored by a cigarette, or maybe the story coming back to him, home on the heels of a father.

"Well, you can imagine poor Algie's situation with Charles out of commission and the rest of the youngbloods virtual strangers. Not long into the voyage, and that miserable excuse for a captain ordered Algie to his cabin. 'So, nigger boy,' he bellowed, and a smile wormed across his lips. 'They say you are a body servant!'

I don't need to tell you how Algie suffered from Captain Clarkson's cruelty, or how he labored day and night through that stormy passage. But I can say this to you . . . There is another kind of passage. It is the one a heart makes, beating with such a pain. For the first time ever, a boy will wish for his real mother. He may try to find her face in his dreams, but his fitful dreams are black—black as her skin, black as the deep hold of a ship.

And so it shouldn't surprise you that one night toward the end of that passage, Algie finally crawled below, into the dark belly of the *Alabama*. Did he think to find her there, a girl in chains? Well, no matter. In the ship's hold he stood like a blind man groping to see. There was no light, only the sound of the ocean surging past the hull and under his feet. And then a great moaning and a clatter of such force as to split the cross-timbers. For a moment it seemed the whole ocean might come crashing down, and a boy's short life would close under one green swell.

But then Algie stumbled against the shattered stalls. He jumped at the sound of a voice. A quick hand clapped his shoulder.

'Where is the lantern?' the voice said.

Algie stood dead still beneath that urgent hand. A man's face hung at his ear, an alarming breath fell on his shirt collar.

'Where's MacDonald? By God, man—answer up!'

And the answer came loud from the darkness, 'Sick, sir. The collies as well.'

A man lurched through the hold, a lantern in his hand—that yellow light swaying with the list of the sea, casting shadows over the creaking timbers. Algie ducked. Did he fear discovery in the lantern's glow? Well, regardless . . . The hand tightened at his shoulder, pulled him inside the splintered stalls.

There, Algie saw the great bulls bound for Kansas. Only the moaning shorthorn remained on its feet, still charging the collapsed boards—but weak now. The shorthorn's eyes rolled in bony sockets. A green bile dripped from its nostrils. Not long and that shorthorn would be down, too. Down like the big black Angus—those mighty bulls on their knees, their massive heads bowed low, and so sick as to be past caring.

And here I must tell you—what a pathetic sight when an animal of that size and strength goes down. And grave, too. In no time the beast will scarcely make a struggle to stand. Never mind that he may still possess the power. Once on his knees, the sick animal loses hope. Leave him down and he will die. There's a fact for you, simple and true. But the persuasion to live is not so simple. Three men in the hold—and that is the number if you count Algie. All three of them tugging together could not haul an Angus bull to its feet.

Algie understood this. He'd tell you there is only one thing to try. And this he learned in the milk barn at Bridgewater Grange. Of course, Mr. MacDonald the stock man would've known, but he'd fallen ill along with most everyone else. This left only our Algie, plus the two well-dressed strangers, neither of whom had the slightest idea.

And so Algie squeezed among the black lowing bulls. From the corner of the stalls the red shorthorn dipped his head and pawed loose planks, eyeing the boy. The two men watched, taking turns holding the lantern high. The ship heaved and Algie braced himself against an enormous black rump. His good leather shoes slipped in runny manure. He nearly stopped breathing for the stench. And then he was down with the bulls—on his knees, on a bed of straw turned sour. Dark mountainous hides rose around him, shutting out the light. Do you wonder that for a moment Algie believed he'd entered the very blackness of his dream?

With all caution he worked his fingers up a matted tail, then clasped it high, almost to the deep crack of buttocks. He gave that tail a turn. The big bull shuddered and craned its thick muscled neck. Algie cranked the tail again, kept cranking. He could've been pumping water from a well. But you and I know otherwise. He was giving those animals a little encouragement. And all the while he sang to the bulls. He sang them a song about a bed of red roses.

Algie cranked with both hands. He felt a jolt like an earthquake—a rumbling through the great beast, all the way to its tail. Then a scramble of hooves, the hind legs first. And Algie rose with the bull.

Well, how the two onlookers cheered. They hung the lantern on a hay hook and went to work, tailing up the remaining Angus. It seemed those two believed a song was part of the business. And they were not without a sense of humor, cranking like wild men and chorusing at the top of their lungs—*Stand up, stand up for Jesus!* Until at last, each black Aberdeen did precisely that.

Perhaps you've already guessed that the man singing loudest—the one who'd clapped Algie's shoulder in the dark—that gentleman was none other than Mr. George Grant himself. Of course, Algie didn't realize this at the time. However, you and I would've known by the tear in the older man's eyes—just to see his fine Aberdeen saved.

Yes, you'll be glad to hear, those blue-blooded bulls lived to graze these Kansas plains. But not before the *Alabama* ran aground on a Mississippi sandbar. Was there ever a sea captain so inept as that vile, pea-brained Clarkson? I think not. But then, you may claim I'm prejudiced. Nevertheless, there was no one more relieved to abandon ship for a Mississippi stern wheeler than my father Algie.

Up that wide river the *Great Republic* churned. Seasick youngbloods regained their health from the pure fragrance of magnolias. Standing at the rail, Algie could see cotton fields stretching away on either side of the river. He saw the cane brakes, as well. And in these places he glimpsed bands of people wearing the strangest assortment of clothes, their heads bound in turbans. From his station on the high deck, our boy thought those individuals must be gypsies, like the ones who'd come wandering through Fiddington Village juggling fire and silver balls. Shall

I tell you now . . . Will you believe? After such a distance and an ocean of visions when he'd imagined the happiest moment, and that moment finally here before his eyes, then slipping by without his ever knowing— well, there you have the truth of it. Algie had not recognized his own people.

And of course she was there, too. Her name, you recall, was Saro. Somewhere along the Mississippi, she'd looked up at the sound of the paddlewheeler's hoot. She stood shielding her amber eyes from the sun, and she whispered, 'North.'

But then, Algie would see his people again, and up so close there could be no doubt. In St. Louis, clutching Charles' coatsleeve on a dash to catch the westbound locomotive, he tried to keep count of a milling black blur.

Never once in all his imaginings had it occurred to my father that there could be so many like himself. Boarding the train he felt overcome by a peculiar sadness. Perhaps it had something to do with the unexpected shabbiness of those people. But at the station on that particular afternoon, you would've found a host of white citizens looking nearly as frayed. This was America, remember, and the great financial panic of '73.

Just then, Algie may have been sitting in St. Louis wondering whatever possessed him to leave Bridgewater Grange. But he'd made that vow on the night Charles killed the wicked galenes. He'd whispered, I am with you. Not that Charles appeared any too eager himself. It seems the Kansas Pacific had provided each and every youngblood with a gratis ticket west. You would've thought Charles might feel honored by such a compliment, but no. The free pass seemed to trouble him in a way Algie couldn't divine.

Now Charles, as we all know, was trusting to a fault. You can be sure if a Borgia sent him an invitation to tea, young Ditsun would straightaway accept. Nevertheless, he could not stop fidgeting with that ticket, worrying it between his pale fingers.

I expect Mr. Grant had anticipated some minor lapse in morale along about St. Louis, because at that moment he stepped into the day car, with a smile all around. He opened a book. You remember he'd packed up his library—a whole roomful—every volume bound in Moroccan leather. Mr. Grant read in a booming voice those words from *Beyond the Missouri* which begin: 'I wonder if the Almighty has ever made a more beautiful country than Kansas . . .'

Well, this reading seemed to cheer the youngbloods one-hundred percent. You realize the printed word will sometimes do that. Except Charles hadn't heard a syllable. He'd been sitting glassy-eyed, staring out his window.

Just below him on the platform, a magnificent gray staghound leapt at the end of a silver chain. A rather prosperous-looking gentleman in a serge suit appeared to be having a difficult time trying to keep the quick, high-strung animal in check. With one hand he held on to his hat. He glanced around, as if seeking help.

Charles leaned in a rush to open the window. 'Here!' he called, and the man looked up. 'How much will you take for your animal?'

Charles was fairly shouting. Not even the presence of a beautiful woman could've inspired such eagerness in his voice. But then, you must appreciate the fleet staghound who never stoops to track with his aristocratic nose, but hunts entirely by sight. Bring the staghound into a field, and you will witness something close to a miracle.

But the gentleman on the platform just smiled and shook his head. 'If he were mine, I'd offer him for nothing. I only thank God I'm rid of him today. A half hour more, and this nuisance is bound for Dakota Territory where the wolves may have him for all I care.' With that, the man reached into his breast pocket and removed a folded yellow paper. He handed this scrap up to Charles.

Here I give you the message precisely as it was written . . . *Dear Ernest, Please send Ruggles at once. I leave for the Yellowstone and intend to bag my first grizzly or know the reason why. Your sincere friend, G.A.C. P.S. Libby sends fond regards.*

Of course, this note made absolutely no impression on Charles, what with his keen disappointment over the staghound. But the man outside the window insisted otherwise.

'You cannot have lived in this country long,' the man said with a laugh. 'Keep that letter—I have a packet of them, each one worth more than a whole kennel of hounds.' "

For a moment Reg smiled out at the crowd.

Marsh nudged Frank. "That letter's from Custer."

"Shut up," Frank said, keeping his gaze on the old man.

Reg lit another cigarette and leaned back to the microphone. "Well, poor Charles—he could only frown at the note still in his hand, that free pass to Kansas in the other. Young Ditsun stretched even farther out the window.

'We have purchased land in Kansas,' he said, and an urgency crept into his voice. It seemed his words had formed a question upon which the entire world depended.

But at that moment the gentleman on the platform appeared to have been seized by a knee-slapping joke only he knew. He wagged a finger toward the yellow paper. 'Remember that name,' he said. 'You may very well need it.' "

Marsh glanced over at Frank. "What'd I tell you?" He nodded to the table of SOARS behind him. "Custer."

"Sshhh," a woman breathed.

"Cut it out," Frank said.

"Just then the train gave a jerk. It was all young Ditsun could do to keep from flying out the window as the cars bolted forward. Algie grabbed him by the coattails and held on for dear life. Then suddenly the prancing staghound took it upon himself to sound a call. And Charles shouted, 'What is the name?' He waved the letter worth more than a kennel. 'The name, sir!'

Now, do not ask me why at that particular instant Mr. George Grant chose to present our Algie with one of his leather-bound books. I can only suggest that successful men—and Mr. Grant was surely in that category—such men have no appreciation whatsoever of chaos. I should also say that Mr. Grant was simply grateful to Algie, owing to the boy's triumph with those bulls. In the years that followed—though there wouldn't be many for George Grant—our boy's presence never ceased to give the utmost pleasure. But I'm rambling ahead of myself . . .

Somehow Charles had managed to catch the name hollered after him from the platform. Of course, this information only mystified young Ditsun all the more. Having lived his twenty-one years in Fiddington Village, you could scarcely expect him to recognize that name. Even in the great city of London, you'd be hard put to find a man who knew it. Mention America's Civil War, and four out of five Englishmen would chime: Harriet Beecher Stowe. And do you think that woman ever so much as lifted a carbine?

Well, it isn't any wonder Charles dropped into a mood that lasted clear across Missouri. However, the rest of the youngbloods seemed to be rising to the occasion, which you realize was the very last leg of this journey. A silver flask had made the rounds more times than Algie could count. But then, Mr. Grant's book was commanding most of his attention.

Though he was violating the strictest rule of manners, Algie brought his book to the dining car. But he needn't have given a moment's pause. Every American aboard seemed thoroughly addicted to reading. You must disregard all you've ever heard about the unenlightened frontier. It seemed the farther west that train penetrated, the more obsessed those people became with anything that might be occurring elsewhere.

The majority suffered from what you might call newspaper-absorption. Illiteracy presented only a minor complication to a man clutched in the throes of a gazette. He'd find a way. And in the months ahead even Charles would become engrossed, an event his mother might celebrate at long last. Poor Mrs. Ditsun . . . How was she to know that the multitude of words which had opened her life, would suddenly arrange themselves in a trail that ran off the page. Those words would string Charles along to a hillside where Death stood waiting to print the end of that story in blood. Even now the first few sentences had formed, scribbled across a yellow page crackling in young Ditsun's pocket.

Naturally, Algie paid no attention as Charles frowned over the brief message again. He thought it was only the staghound causing such a mood, or perhaps some lingering suspicion of the free pass to Kansas. And so he never glanced up when Charles smoothed the crumpled note flat on the dining table and said,

'This person George Custer is going to the Yellowstone to shoot a grizzly.'

Now right here, you would've heard such a galling envy. Charles pointed a finger and cocked his thumb. He took aim, then let his hand fall. He leaned across the starched tablecloth, his blue eyes flashing. He asked, 'Where is the Yellowstone?'

'I believe it is in Kansas,' Algie said.

You understand the boy was speaking from the tip-top of his head. He'd directed his full attention to the passing landscape. Outside his window, Algie saw nothing but a sickly dwarfed grass growing clear to the horizon. He sensed an icy stillness. This would be a silence of the whole universe, before a sound was ever made. In truth, this was Kansas where the season called spring is a terrible laggard. I am not exaggerating when I say that Charles and Algie might've frozen precisely where they sat if the train hadn't come equipped with a potbellied stove blazing in every car.

Not that Charles was given to sitting still for long. When Algie turned from the window, he saw that Charles—indeed every youngblood—had vanished from the train's dining car. And then Algie heard a sudden volley of shots. You can be sure he ducked at the quick cracking sound. However, none of the Americans seemed the least disturbed. They scarcely glanced up from their newspapers.

And so, after a moment Algie lifted his head. He pressed to the window, then blinked. It appeared that in the brief space when he'd taken his eyes away, the whole prairie had sprung to life. In every direction the pale grass lay trampled. The land fairly teemed with creatures, the likes of which our boy had never seen. But he knew the names . . . Great American bison, for one, and such a wonder those beasts seemed. The very ground rumbled with them, rumbled with the train. And that silence as large as the universe was broken.

Here and there, the buffalo fell. One of that lot struggled to its feet, enraged and dripping blood, now charging the train. Algie shrank from the window as the beast came careening. For a moment the glass misted with that animal's last sore breath. And then the big buffalo toppled, pitching onto its knees.

Algie leaned to gaze after the bison. Then he opened his window and stared out. From the day car up the line, the youngbloods were firing without so much as taking a sight. Their rifles gleamed under the sun, gleamed all in a row so it appeared this was not a train, but a carnival gallery with everything moving—the hunters, their targets, the prairie rolling by . . .

Then Algie caught a glimpse of Charles, a shock of shining blond hair. Young Ditsun stretched from a window, cheeking his rifle like a man in love, his nose bleeding onto the weapon's walnut stock, bleeding down the gray lapels of his worsted frock coat. Beyond the rails, the land itself seemed to be losing blood, turning ever more pale beneath dark carcasses and a few white-tailed antelope. Yes, those pronghorns had come running, curious to discover what all the commotion was about. They leapt beside the windows, and out of sheer devilment, they flirted their tails. You can be sure that in the days ahead—indeed, for his whole life—my father would never hear the phrase Bleeding Kansas without recalling this afternoon.

And so it went for miles and miles. Algie opened his book, determined not to look out again. By dusk, he'd read the little volume twice through. Until at last the booming rifles fell silent and the train came to a rattling stop. But regardless, Algie refused to budge. I expect he might be sitting there still, if Charles hadn't finally burst into the car to fetch him.

Now picture, if you will, a station house. This would be a two-story building, which Mr. Grant preferred to call Victoria Manor. It stood not far from this spot—a single solitary structure in the middle of a vast plain, in the middle of a cold blowing wind.

Well, I don't need to tell you what despair my father felt when he stepped off that train. He saw no river beside which to build Mrs. Ditsun a house. It seemed roses could never bloom and the whippoorwills wouldn't sing. There was no tree whatsoever.

However, Mr. Grant set about at once, making every effort. Not long, and a Mr. Edis of the Royal Society of Architects arrived. That monocled gentleman could be seen for months on end, dashing across the prairie with a sheaf of blueprints under his arm.

Mrs. Ditsun had furthermore packed up all the fixtures of gracious living. It appeared that Charles and Algie would want for nothing, what with a house full of furnishings and a postal order arriving every month from the Squire. However, Algie continued to worry about their wardrobes. According to the little book he'd been reading, their clothes would never do. You realize that Mr. Grant's gift, aptly titled *A Frontier Companion,* was at once a tourist's handbook and a how-to manual of the variety so popular today. Algie turned to that volume time and again, fretting no end over his lack of a red flannel shirt, not to mention a gutta-percha poncho. It seems Squire Ditsun had squelched the notion of such a wardrobe. I expect the Squire held with that soft thinker Thoreau who'd warned, 'Beware of all enterprises that require new clothes . . .'

Not that Charles gave any of this a moment's concern, living as he did in his scarlet hunting jacket and jodhpurs. Of course, he'd never featured himself as the freehold master of an estate numbering 640 acres. Two years later, and that land still lay in its virginal state, save for the few acres Algie had planted to kafir corn.

But perhaps it was just as well Charles didn't spend his days hacking at the stunted grass which held the earth in such a strangle grip. Let the great fires raze the prairie, let locusts touch down disguised as a south-easterly cloud. For all of it, Charles suffered no more than a nosebleed. He soared above the ground on the back of his sorrel jumper and found his mark below the bison's left shoulder. Oh, he was a crack shot, young Ditsun, and he fired and he fired and he fired.

Which brings me to the unexpected appearance of a magazine left lying at Victoria Station. I don't need to tell you it was a sportsman's journal, which explains why Charles snatched it up in the first place and immediately thereafter posted a subscriber's fee.

Now, among that journal's contributors you would've come across an author writing adventurous tales under the pseudonym 'Nomad.' But turning to the editor's notes—which is exactly what Charles proceeded to do—you would find the man's identity revealed. And at that point, you can be sure the name George Custer fully registered in Charles' head. What's in a name? Torment. A torment not unlike the mention of a lover who has spurned you. So here he is again. George Custer, regaling his reader—in this case Charles—with scores of hunting triumphs on rivers, hillsides, and valleys. Never on farms, mind you, though Algie continued to entertain a hope.

Charles would open that magazine, his eyes darting down a list of Nomad's most recent successes . . . forty-one antelope, four elk, three buffalo, and two white wolves. All in the space of a single outing.

Of course, there was some comfort in learning that George Custer hadn't bagged his grizzly on the Yellowstone, after all. That accomplishment wouldn't come until the next expedition—a blissful foray into the Black Hills. From a Sibley tent situated in a leafy glade, Nomad would lean at his little desk and write, 'I have reached the hunter's highest round of fame . . . I have killed my first grizzly.'

Well, do you wonder that Charles was sitting in Kansas believing these grand expeditions set out each summer for the primary purpose of bringing down wild game? 'I have given you my score,' Nomad wrote in *Turf, Farm, and Field*. 'Now then, I want to hear from the next. Can it be beaten by the correspondent of any other paper or by any other man? If so, hold up your right hand.'

Naturally, Charles did just that. In the days ahead nothing troubled Algie more than the sight of Charles grinning up from that magazine, with his hand raised straight above his head. My father knew it wouldn't be long before Charles truly took up the challenge.

And so we come to one New Year's Eve—a brilliant night, after a grand Hunt Ball and the whole prairie celebrating. But you would've seen a sad-hearted Algie accompanying Charles to the station house. As they reached the station, the great clock on Mr. Battell's estate began striking the hour. Perhaps a portent of war, Algie might tell you now. A deep tolling heard for miles, heralding the year 1876. And Charles loading his spirited jumper into a packet train bound for Fort Abraham Lincoln.

But that is hindsight speaking—a privilege young Ditsun was never to have. He galloped into Regimental Headquarters of the Seventh Cavalry, still attired in his scarlet hunting coat. He raised his right hand. And while his fellow recruits stood pledging their very lives in the service of their country, Charles took an oath to better his boasting commander's score.

Here I should say that even Algie found it hard to believe there could be any great number of Indians still on the loose. Those depredating Kiowas had long since left Kansas for the Indian Territory of Oklahoma. Down in Texas, old Chief Satanta had flung himself headfirst from a prison's second story. Now there was the death of a savage Algie almost regretted. It seems Mr. Grant had once mentioned that Chief Satanta possessed a French horn. I don't need to tell you how that piece of information excited our boy. Never mind that some question arose as to whether the old sneak could actually play the instrument . . . Algie had turned straightaway to his frontier manual. He committed to memory that chapter titled Meeting Indians. You realize he wanted to be prepared, just in case Satanta should ever come galloping across these plains blowing his French horn.

Algie practiced to the letter those instructions laid out in his little handbook. Every afternoon for one week he'd stood in the middle of a field and directed Charles to ride toward him as a true savage might— not that young Ditsun knew or felt the slightest interest. However, Charles had made an obliging attempt. He approached Algie at a trot, a canter, a wild dash, and finally with such laughter as to have him reeling in his saddle. Well, I expect Algie did look a sight, with his serious hands sweeping the air in one sign after another while his mouth remained clamped shut. But it was just conceivable that a redskin would understand something of those gestures.

Which is why on the first evening in May, Algie wrote to Charles: 'The sign for Sioux is cutthroat.' It had been a day still too cold for spring planting and rumors suddenly flying everywhere of General Custer's Seventh Cavalry mounted for war. 'In the event you should meet a savage . . .' Algie opened his little manual and copied out the words. 'The Sioux will identify himself by drawing his hand across his throat . . . Two hands clasped above the head can be deemed as friendly . . . Two fingers firmly locked, also friendly . . .'

Then, so as not to appear overly alarmed, Algie mentioned that he was still teaching Mr. Grant's niece piano. He wrote, 'I am sending you the two dollars which I hope will make enough for a flask of Dumfrey's Golden Wedding.' Finally he added, 'There is no one here who does not think of you every day. I am praying hard and will continue to pray to my utmost that you will shoot your grizzly.'

And then Algie left his silent house. He often did this of an evening, crossing the field to Victoria Manor where he would post his letters to Charles and sit for a time with the stationmaster.

Now I expect it's inconceivable that anyone would voluntarily remain in a room with a stationmaster such as the one employed at Victoria Manor. Here was a man privy to all current events—a teletype clattering on his desk, a train from the west and one from the east, both pulling in for a water stop each day. That stationmaster heard everything first. But do you think his fortunate position made the slightest difference? It did not. Dewey Prescott was a man preternaturally disposed to the boring detail. He could utter a single sentence and those within earshot were apt to remember a pressing engagement elsewhere.

Perhaps this will give you some notion of how forsaken a boy can feel. Because on those cold evenings, Algie would sit for hours. I expect this was when my father became such a wizard at the one-sided conversation. He listened well, and in doing so, he warmed the cockles of Dewey Prescott's heart.

If it grew very late—as regularly happened when Dewey commenced talking about proper fencing of the castor bean or some similar subject before the Kansas legislature—well, then the stationmaster would open his desk drawer and take out a key to an upstairs sleeping room. 'No sense walking all the way home,' he'd say.

And so Algie would climb the stairs. More often than not, he'd find a one-eared dog asleep on the landing. This dog, Brin, had taken up residence in the station house some months prior. The animal held quite a high opinion of himself, and rarely mixed with those he considered of a lower order. But over the winter he'd developed something of an interest in Algie. The big brindle would rouse himself and follow Algie down the upstairs hall to a sleeping room door. However, at that threshold Brin drew the line. He ignored every invitation to enter the room, though there were nights so lonely Algie offered him all the world and a brisket of beef in exchange for his company.

Well, you can imagine how stuffy that second story became when summer finally drew round. Even with every window open and the blankets turned back, Algie scarcely slept. He would lie awake for hours— just thinking and listening to the clack of the teletype below.

He'll tell you that's what he was doing on one particular June night. He was thinking that he might make a good crop. He'd planted his corn in check rows and believed he was seeing some improvement. Mr. Grant's niece Margaret had ridden over in the afternoon, and he'd tethered her gray gelding so they could walk through the promising green stalks.

In his boy's mind, Algie wondered—did he love Margaret Grant deep down like the good dark earth? Coming back from the field, Margaret had caught his arm and held a buttercup under his chin. She'd tried to see a little glow of yellow reflected there. But of course she would never find it on his skin—and Algie understood. Margaret Grant was looking for a blue-eyed man.

These were Algie's thoughts as the whistle of the eastbound sounded. The locomotive steamed into the station, exactly on schedule, two hours behind. On the platform below, Dewey would be collaring the brakeman. My father listened for the stationmaster's droning voice. That locomotive could gain an extra fifteen minutes' delay if Dewey had anything to say about it. But all of a sudden the train was pulling out, and Dewey already up the stairs and banging at Algie's door, then rushing into the close warm room and leaning out the window as if to be sick.

'They're all dead,' he panted. Dewey stamped the floor—was he stamping in anger, or perhaps for breath . . . He swung round, his face wild and astonished. 'General Custer and every last man with him, wiped out on the Little Bighorn River.'

Algie snapped straight. He whispered, 'Charles.' He grabbed the blankets in his fists, and Dewey rammed the floor again. Now, can you tell me—why should this man Dewey Prescott, a man who has kept such faith with the least of words, who's respected even the trivial and placed it important on his tongue—why should he be chosen by God and the teletype he despises and a brakeman who refuses to allow him the slightest sentence edgewise. Why must he speak these words? And where in all the world could there be a river so impossible as to be called both big and little?

'There is no such place!' Algie cried. 'I have never heard!'

'And I should not be saying this,' Dewey whispered. He stepped to light the lamp beside Algie's bed. There, in that instant with the flame flickering up, you might've seen the very heart going out of the station-master. 'Come downstairs,' he said to Algie. 'I'll give you a brandy or tea—some black tea.'

Algie let the blankets slide to the floor. He looked to a chair, his clothes still neatly folded, as if no chaos had ever happened. 'I must go home,' he said.

'Wait,' Dewey said. 'You are in a bad way just now. Have something to eat first.'

'I will never eat,' Algie answered. He flung on his shirt, his summer jacket, and then the trousers almost forgotten.

The big brindle dog scrambled up from the doorway as Algie rushed past.

'Come back,' Dewey called out the upstairs window.

'I will never drink, never sleep,' Algie said. All the way home he filled the night with his tearful vows, one after another. 'I will never think. I will never look at a tree, or walk anywhere, or say hello to a single person.'

When he reached his front door, Algie dashed inside and lit the mantel lamp. But he could not sit down, could not stand still. He thought of a river, though he'd sworn never to think again. The river was both little and big. Wild animals roamed beside that nighttime water.

Algie stepped back to the doorway. He saw the dog Brin coming through the fields at a swift, sure-footed trot.

But perhaps Charles had remembered—the sign for Sioux is cutthroat. The Indian will identify himself by drawing his hand across his throat in this manner . . .

At Algie's feet, the brindle dog drew himself to a halt, then settled on the doorstep.

Algie shook his head at the dog and at his tears—the stars all run together in the sky. 'I would not ask,' he said to the darkness, 'but just now I am in a bad way.'

On the doorstep, Brin lifted his ear.

'If there are wolves at the river,' Algie whispered. 'If his nose should be bleeding, or his clothes torn . . .'

Slowly the big dog rose.

'If he is dead, and any man still lives . . .'

The dog stepped across the threshold. Brin stood in the middle of the room as though waiting to be told—what should be done if there are wolves and one man left alive.

Algie tried to think. He closed the door and at that moment he'll tell you he became the last man. He saw himself stumbling through the smoky haze of a battlefield. He saw an army of squaws grunting over corpses—men flung everywhere like so much scattered corn. The blood was still dripping from Charles' nose. Wolves waited in the cover of darkness.

Algie moved to the fireplace and called the big dog. 'Quick,' he said. 'Come quick, we must build a fire.'

And in the swelter of a June night, Algie fed a blaze that would keep the cruelest winter at bay and all ravaging wolves vanquished forever on the other side of a river. Had you galloped to his house with Mr. Grant. . . Well, then you would've seen. Smoke rolling from a chimney. Smoke to fill the sky like dawn itself. The heat of an inferno in the front parlor. A boy chattering as if with fever. That boy drenched blacker than a boy ever was. And beside him, a brindle dog standing guard at the hearth."

17

Reg leaned to grind a cigarette on the cement, then nodded to the audience of SOARS. "I thank you for your kind attention."

"Well, that's a hell of a note," Frank muttered, turning to Marsh. "Winding up a story with Custer's Last Stand. No way are we stopping there. We've got our older members to think of—they don't need somebody handing them the taste of defeat. They've already got it, for Christ's sake."

Frank trudged to the microphone. "So, how about it, fun lovers—do I hear a motion for more?"

"You certainly do," Evie called from the rear of the shelter.

Marsh glanced back, noticing that Alex hadn't left after all. Sometime during Reg's story, the old woman Claire had also turned up. It was sort of a shock seeing Claire out in the open. Marsh had begun to think of her as a traveling shut-in. She appeared to have come straight from bed, and Tiffany too, standing there in her baby dolls, yawning over her big white box.

"I'd like to know what's going to happen to Algie," Evie said, moving between picnic tables. "Especially with poor Charles dead."

Evie stepped past Marsh and headed for the card table. Then all of a sudden Claire lurched forward. The old woman stopped beside Marsh, then turned to face the crowd. Her chenille robe hung open, a belt dangling around her terry-cloth slippers. But under the robe she looked completely dressed.

"I'll tell you who's dead," Claire said in a dry, rattling voice. Her hands jerked up and down her blouse buttons. "Princess Grace, that's who!" The old woman nodded to Evie at the front of the shelter, then to Jewel closing her notebook, and to all the SOARS shifting on benches. "Just now—it was on TV."

Marsh stared at her, hardly aware of Alex slipping onto the bench beside him, or Tiffany climbing into his lap.

"Listen, Claire . . ." Marsh tugged at her belt. She glanced down, looking half-crazed—a mad woman delivering her lunatic message in a bathrobe. "Are you sure about this?"

She pulled the belt from his hand. "We interrupt this program to bring you a special bulletin," she whispered. Then she gathered the robe around her, belted it with a double knot, straightened her small shoulders, and scuffed away.

Beside him, Alex shook her head. "I don't see how anyone could die of fractures—isn't that what the paper said?"

"There was something about her collarbone," Marsh mumbled, sliding out from under Tiffany.

He moved to the barbecue pit where Reg stood. "Maybe you should tell some more of your story."

"Under the circumstances I wonder if that's wise," Reg said.

Marsh glanced to the SOARS. "I think it's just sort of a shock. You know, the news."

"Well, I feel terrible," Evie said, squeezing between them. "First Charles, now Princess Grace."

Frank tapped the microphone. "Stick around, folks—remember, life goes on."

"Listen to him!" Evie said. "Meanwhile, I haven't felt this bad since Elvis went."

Frank shoved a cup of coffee into Reg's hands. "Maybe something just a little more upbeat," he said, steering the old man back to the table. "Send 'em out with a smile."

"Well, of course the whole country was outraged," Reg said.

Marsh leaned over the card table. "Listen, try to go easy."

"Two hundred and fifty cavalrymen dead on that hillside, left naked and white as marble stone. Their throats were slashed, arms and legs torn to bloody stumps . . ."

Marsh lifted Tiffany onto his lap. The bench had become more crowded with Evie and Frank on the other end, then Alex, plus Tiffany's big box.

"Not to mention their private parts," Reg said, nodding into the microphone.

"Oh God," Frank groaned.

Across the way, Jewel looked up from her notebook. "Was that two hundred and fifty naked men?"

"That is the number," Reg said. "News kept arriving as to what actually happened on that hillside. Naturally my father spared poor Mrs. Ditsun those heinous details."

"Naturally," Frank muttered.

"Hush up," Marsh said. He nodded toward the front of the shelter, Reg folding his hands around the microphone.

"Within the week, four youngbloods rode north to enlist. While up on Hat Creek, that theatrical gentleman, Mr. Bill Cody, made a production of taking the first scalp for General Custer. Algie himself reported to Fort Hays. Well, it's a curiosity—how even the best of us will sometimes feel that niggling little shame attached to simply remaining alive. Of course, Algie was turned away from duty. Some years had passed since a black regiment served at that fort, and it can be said— nobody'd missed their presence.

Now, this would also be the summer when the buffalo failed, for the first time ever, to make their migration through Kansas. But the grieving Algie never noticed how the prairie changed that season. He didn't see the endless trail of bawling longhorns, or dusty cowmen riding off the dead-line for a cold drink at Hays City.

After Charles fell, there was absolutely nothing consoled our boy. However, Mr. Grant did try. He set a place at his dinner table more often than not and organized musical evenings with his niece providing accompaniment to Algie's French horn. It was after one of these occasions, when the last duet had been played and the other guests departed, that Mr. Grant took out his Lebrecht cigars and another bottle of whiskey. On that night, he offered Algie his next-born black bull and the fruit of its increase for seven years.

I expect word might've reached Mr. Grant as to how Algie was selling off certain household articles for the purpose of paying debts. It seems that Charles had joined the cavalry leaving a pile of accounts payable. Or perhaps Mr. Grant's heart simply went out to the boy, moved by a good cigar and whiskey in considerable amounts. Which is not to say the gentleman acted under the influence. Mr. Grant could consume more than most, holding to his theory that liquor would never harm the man who strictly avoided drinking water for one half hour before and after indulgence.

And this practice appeared successful. The next morning dawned with

George Grant up earlier than usual and looking exceedingly chipper as he rode out to Algie's house. Mr. Grant found Algie sitting half-hidden between shriveled stalks of corn—the August drought, remember. That cornfield, so promising in June, had represented some small last hope. But by summer's end, my father could've carried his crop to market in one pocket. Little wonder that he simply sat and sifted dust while George Grant spoke.

First, Mr. Grant repeated his offer of the previous evening. And then he said, 'Mr. Edis has delivered to me the plans for a schoolhouse. I'm deeding land for both this school and our chapel. I don't mean to pry— but if God has called you, then I will give you the Church of England with a rectory for all your days.'

To which Algie replied, 'God does not speak to me.'

'Then I'd feel pleased if you would consider the school,' Mr. Grant said. 'Meantime, Mr. Prescott is requiring help at the station. Although it goes without saying . . . Mr. Prescott and I do understand that such a position is unworthy for a person of your education.'

'I am in need of work,' Algie whispered.

'A person of your elevated mind,' said Mr. Grant. Then he nodded down from the high polished saddle of his thoroughbred stallion and tipped his soft tweed cap. 'Victoria Station will be honored to have your assistance.'

And so Algie spent the months thereafter, putting up the mail, washing sooty window glass—and in the afternoon, sweeping great clouds of dust from the station platform. However, two trains arriving daily are scarcely enough to keep a person occupied. Those days dragged by, especially with Dewey stretching out long doleful silences between words.

You realize the stationmaster had given up almost all conversation since that woeful June night. Algie could see how it pained the man to speak, so he kept his own mouth closed. By the following summer, the whole idea of language seemed to have escaped him altogether. If you'd stepped off a train on any given day in that summer of 1877, you would've observed a thin black figure stooped low over his broom handle, silently sweeping his way up and down the platform. You might've said to yourself, what a very old man, because you would not have looked twice.

However, life will have its way—a moment here and there to which death cannot hold a candle. I'm thinking now of one afternoon, an afternoon hot enough for all ordinary purposes of cooking. And Dewey Prescott hurrying across the platform to deliver the news. You realize this was something of a miracle in itself, what with news being the absolute item Dewey had sworn never to deliver again.

'Any day now.' That's what the stationmaster told Algie. And just then you would've felt such excitement, Dewey giving the boy a little

shake and his voice rising as if to lift Algie clear off the platform . . . 'There are colored people coming.'

Algie stared up from his broom. At his feet, Brin cocked his one ear,
catching Dewey's every word.

It seems there were men—'boomers,' Dewey called them—men traveling all over the southern United States selling land in Kansas. Now
this may put you in mind of Mr. Grant who'd journeyed the English
countryside. But these boomers didn't seek out the wealthy. You
would've found them reclined on sagging cabin porches in Tennessee
and shouting from pulpits in Kentucky . . . 'Colored citizens elevate
yourselves! Ho for sunny Kansas the Promised Land!'

Well, no man of God has ever seemed more inspiring than those
boomers, preaching a quarter section homestead right alongside the Holy
Word. Never mind that the great war for freedom had been fought and
the South redeemed. You realize the Lord wasn't in charge of that
redemption.

Now among the boomers was a man named W. R. Hill. This Mr. Hill
had recruited an ambitious black fellow to assist him with selling town
lots in Graham County—that would be one county over and north from
where we're sitting. The Kansas Pacific was to bring the first group of
black immigrants to a stopping place at Logan Road. You understand
no train conductor with an iota of conscience would allow those people
to be dropped off in Hays City. It was a raucous place, that rail town.
And hell to pay for a black individual caught tarrying past sunset.

But no matter. My father could scarcely contain his excitement at
Dewey's news. And he gave the stationmaster no rest from his badgering.
Until finally Dewey sat Algie down in the station house. Dewey pointed
to a map fixed to his office wall.

'You'll find the Exodusters getting off there,' he said. 'Pray they have
wagons waiting to ride them up that road, else there'll be a long hot
walk in store.' Dewey ran his finger north. 'They're going here, to the
Solomon Valley, God help them.'

'And the town?' Algie asked.

Dewey shook his head. 'There is no town, only a name—Nicodemus.
The Solomon River is real, though it will be down to bottom now. We
must ask the Lord for a good soaking rain.'

'Yes,' Algie said, knowing full well he hadn't spoken a word in that
direction for something over a year.

Dewey stood frowning at the map, then gave a sigh and turned to
Algie. 'When you meet those people at Logan Road,' he said, 'tell them
Kansas cast the first stone at slavery. That could be a comfort. Say to
them, Kansas has opened her doors.'

'I will,' Algie said.

And so my father prepared himself. However, there remained some question as to exactly when the colored people would be arriving. Day after day, Algie waited. Every morning he dressed for the occasion, because there was just no telling.

Well, I doubt you've ever seen a railroad employee sweeping a platform in such fine attire. But then, Algie had been reduced to wearing Charles' clothes. I say reduced, when the truth is, our boy had actually grown out of his own wardrobe. And scarcely a boy anymore, but tall as Charles had been and even a little broader through the shoulders. And still slim, though I feel I should tell you—I've reason to believe there were women in a majority eyeing Algie with the secret conviction that beneath his elegant frock coat they'd find the muscled sheen of a panther's chest.

Of course, no one was more surprised than my father at this sudden change in his person. You understand that for a full year, his grief had been keeping him at a distance. We can only wonder how long it might've taken Algie to return to himself if that westbound locomotive hadn't pulled in a month later. And he finally saw them—face after face blurred behind sooty windows of a day car. His own people, arrived at last.

But my father didn't stand gaping for long. He dashed straight for the rear of the station and leapt onto Dewey's shavetail mule. He tore off with old Brin scrambling behind. You realize Brin had no intention of missing that wild race to Logan Road. But then, it wasn't much of a contest, what with Dewey's mule gaining such a head start on the train.

And how to tell you what a barren sight when Algie finally reached that stopping place. Well, this wasn't a regular railstop, remember. And Logan Road seemed nothing more than an old rutted path stretching through the endless prairie.

Pray they have wagons waiting—that's what Dewey had said. Algie gazed up the hot narrow road and saw no sign whatsoever. He recalled the day some four years earlier when he and Charles arrived at Victoria. He couldn't have imagined a more desolate sight—until now. No one waited here with a meal all prepared or drinks to cut the traveling dust.

Only Algie stood beside the rails with his top hat in his hands and the tails of his frock coat flapping in the breeze. Naturally, he wished he'd brought something to give those people upon their arrival. Perhaps he could've played a welcome on his French horn if he'd just thought . . . And he would need to say a few words of greeting—well, somebody should.

'Kansas has opened her doors.' Algie paced the tracks, practicing, flinging his arms wide as a gate. 'Welcome, colored people,' he said in his deepest loud voice. And then he stopped, remembering that other name Dewey had used. 'Exodusters,' Algie whispered. He spoke the curious word again, and then, again, again—a hundred times until that sound became the very rumbling of the train. Those wheels clacked down the rails singing Exodusters-Exodusters.

Algie leapt away from the tracks. He watched the locomotive's big black face rolling closer, shimmering through the heat, now drawing right up beside him. Steam hissed around his legs, and he dashed in a sudden fright to his shavetail mule. He clutched the reins, tempted to bound into the saddle and ride away quick before anyone ever saw he'd been there.

But a few people were already climbing from the train. They straggled out of one car toward the rear—how many, Algie couldn't say. It seemed his mind had stopped working and he'd lost his voice as well. However, I can give you the approximate number of those milling alongside that packet train. There would be 30 on this July day, and in September, 375 more. And after that they'd just keep coming, their numbers growing into the thousands. You can imagine within a few short years, Kansas would begin to worry about this special destiny she'd claimed. Had God truly appointed her prairie land as home for the whole Negro race?

Algie will tell you it certainly appeared to be so. No sooner did that band of people step off the train than they commenced to thank the Lord. Algie ducked in the grass, watching from a little distance as a tall thin man wearing a stovepipe hat and tails raised his voice above the others. This was Reverend Roundtree, looking pitch black from head to toe—and as Algie later discovered—those preacher's clothes all the man owned.

Reverend Roundtree removed his hat. As he spoke, tears streamed down his cheeks. But his jubilant face bore no relation whatsoever to a man in tears. 'The Lord Almighty has surely been through this place,' he hollered. 'Just look round you, childrens. Every mountain and hill has been laid low.' The Reverend spread his gangling arms into the wind. 'Oh yes,' he shouted. 'We did come to the free promised land. Look down and say, This here free ground. Look up—let the good Lord hear you. Them free and beautiful heavens. And you and me—we all *free* people. The Lord has delivered us at last, safe through Jordan's tide!'

And then everyone began to make such a racket—singing and wailing so they nearly drowned out the noise of the locomotive steaming slowly away. Well, Algie had never seen a sight like this one. He watched those people touching the hot, dry ground, then raising their arms to the cloudless sky. Until finally Algie looked up, too. He kept his face raised to those free and beautiful heavens and he asked for a good soaking rain.

When he looked down again, my father saw as how those wagons had finally arrived—two of them with a double span of mules pulled up just across the railroad tracks. Algie crept closer to the crowd. He crossed the tracks, holding to the rear while a man stood speaking from one of the wagons. This would be John Niles—that black businessman who'd been selling town lots for Mr. Hill.

John Niles commenced reading off names from a list, without so much as one word of welcome or a common hello. His gold watch chain glittered across his fine tailored vest, and something flashed gold in his mouth, too. Right here I should tell you—this man was a scoundrel. My father could see it even then. He caught John Niles' slippery smile and the way those quick eyes skipped over the crowd, lingering on a pretty face. Of course, you wouldn't have spotted many in that category. This throng of people looked mostly tired—the women worn out with children and sweating from faded mother hubbards and cotton shawls over big leg-of-mutton sleeves, not to mention bandanas wound tight around their heads. They seemed to be wearing entire wardrobes on their backs, carrying what little else they owned in pillow slips.

But you would have found one—just one face among that ragged band to which John Niles' gaze kept returning. And there's a curiosity for you, because Mr. Niles preferred his women no darker than the color of a paper bag. A high-toned female—that's the one he'd choose. However, this particular young woman he smiled on would fail that paper bag test by shades and shades. She stood directly in front of Algie, so he couldn't see her face. But he'd felt her presence, how she held her small shoulders and tossed her red-bandana'd head with sheer impatience.

Of course, you and I already know this woman as the beautiful Saro. And here I must ask you to indulge my feeble version of her speech. Remember, I had so little time with my mother. In matters pertaining to the grand science of linguistics, I am entirely my father's son."

Reg stopped a moment, nodding out to the SOARS. Then he cleared his throat, took a deep breath, and leaned to the microphone. "I thought we was gon north," he said in a startling melodious voice.

"Well, this is what Saro was saying as she stood with that throng at Logan Road. She cradled a baby in her arms and spoke to a broad-backed man beside her. And I feel I should tell you . . . This young man had no hands. My father couldn't keep his eyes from the dark bare arms hanging lank with white cotton socks sheathing the nubs of the man's wrists. But then Algie glanced up, realizing the fidgety woman had turned, speaking to him.

'North,' she said, and her voice fell in a whisper. She looked no more than a girl, and to be holding that child in her arms . . . She nodded at Algie. 'We was sposed to be gon north.'

Of course, my father couldn't speak for the very sight of her. He felt a tremendous ache flowing into his body, and blood rushing everywhere to make him wonder if he might've reached the very end of his life. Well, I expect between passion and death there will always be this confusion. Finally Algie regained himself. And then it came to him—this slender slip of a woman believed him to be one of them, an Exoduster waiting for his name to be called.

Algie buttoned up his frock coat and shook his head. 'This is the American frontier,' he said. 'You are in The West.'

Well, you can guess it was Saro's turn to be struck speechless, what with hearing Algie's perfect King's English. She stared as though he'd dropped straight out of the sky. For a moment her whole face trembled, jiggling a dusty black curl fallen from her red bandana.

'Nosah,' she declared. 'You saying west, when ain't noboby paid to ride there.'

With that she thrust the sleeping baby into Algie's arms. She dug into a pocket of her long cotton skirt and unfolded a slick, colored circular. She slapped the paper before Algie's eyes.

Algie saw a cottage trellised with roses. A beautiful black woman sat knitting on a front porch. In the distance, a black man returned from hunting with a deer draping his shoulders and a string of turkeys dangling from his hand. Across the top of the picture, Algie read in golden letters: *A Home in Kansas.*

Algie propped the baby at his chest and slid the circular from Saro's fingers. But just then, a large scowling woman leaned and yanked the baby away. Well, this would be Iwilla stepping in, a woman of such bulk as to rival the behemoth of Holy Writ. And they were all a family— these four standing near Algie, though he couldn't have known that yet. The strong-looking man without hands—well, he was Saro's husband. A man named Cease. And Cease's brother—he was there, too. Then Iwilla who'd born and raised these two grown sons. And of course, Saro herself who stood gazing at Algie, looking on the near side of tears.

'God hearing ever word you say,' she whispered. 'He ast you to speak the truth all times to all people. Now you come telling us west when we gon north.'

For a moment Algie could do nothing but stare at her, not knowing how to comfort her, or how to explain about this impossible place to which she'd traveled.

Finally he said, 'Wherever you go . . .' and then, scarcely aware of what he was doing, he turned the young woman round. Yet the instant he felt her firm shoulders beneath his hand, my father knew beyond all doubt that he loved her. He knew this before he ever heard her name or realized even the smallest fact about her or what she thought of President Hayes or the Democrats or citric acid lemonade. And some of you will be shaking your heads right now, grumbling Nonsense. There is no true love such as that. But think for a minute—think back to what you've forgotten. This love exists, showing itself to perfect strangers, passing all understanding. A heart can do nothing but bow down in its presence.

Algie drew Saro's hand from her side. He stretched out her arm, aiming her fingers into the low sun. Then he looked in that direction and said, 'Everything you see at your fingertips is west. Where you stand—on this spot—this is where The West begins.' Then Algie turned her again until her outstretched arm pointed toward the east. 'However far you travel,' he said, 'all the way to this place, just here where you've stopped—this is where The West ends.'

Well, you mustn't wonder that Saro stared at Algie as if thoroughly vexed. Finally she dropped her arm. 'There was three babies lost just to come here—took by the black measles,' she said. 'Three babies gone to Jesus, all the time thinking they was bound north.' She shook her head at the man named Cease. 'Now I'm thinking ever one a us is lost. Ever lost soul got to be their own Moses.'

'But you'll see the river,' Algie said, searching for one hopeful word. 'Remember when you reach the Solomon Valley—that river is real.'

The big woman Iwilla shot Algie a look. Oh, she had the electric eye, that woman. She shoved Saro close beside the man who had no hands. And then Algie watched that family walk to the wagons—their names called at last.

'Town lot number 25 registered in the name of I Will Arise Jones. Lot 26 to Pray Without Ceasing Jones and wife Saro. Lot 27—Tatum Jones . . .'

For a while Algie stood there, as if waiting for his own name to be called. He watched until all the colored people had squeezed themselves into the rough-planked wagons. Then the mules sidestepped round, turning from the rails.

Algie saw the man called Pray Without Ceasing crammed at the back of one wagon. Pray Without Ceasing sat weeping over the white cotton socks in his lap. His long legs dragged the dusty road. Then he suddenly looked up, his dark face ran even blacker with tears. He cried out—was he asking Algie or the whole world?

'How can I be my own Moses when I got no more hands for the working?'

Algie stopped still in the road. He tried to answer over all the noise—

pots and pans clattering against wagon slats, Reverend Roundtree shouting up another prayer, and then someone singing, only one, but a voice so deep and loud as to set the air thrumming.

And so Pray Without Ceasing never heard my father standing back in the road hollering after him:

'Keep waiting—help will arrive. Kansas has opened her doors!' "

18

Sometime before dawn, Marsh woke. Or maybe he hadn't really slept, because he remembered a bird singing. He lay in the motor home's loft, wondering what might cause a bird to sing in the darkness. The sound had come from the trees along the creek—a low melodious song breaking the deep silence of night, breaking over him.

He lifted the curtain at the side window. Across the way, the little glow of Reg's cigarette sparked the dusky light. Marsh slipped a shirt over his boxer shorts and stepped outside. He decided maybe it hadn't been a sound at all, but grief still catching him, putting this ache in his chest. Or maybe Reg's story—A Home In Kansas, like a page torn from a magazine. It seemed all of America had been sold with slick advertising, was still being sold. And he'd bought the works, sight unseen.

He moved over the grass and leaned at Reg's chair. "You shouldn't be out here." He kept his voice low, aware of the big Southwind in the space next door. "Come back to bed."

Reg nodded up from his pale blue pajamas and sighed a stream of smoke. "Perhaps if he hadn't been such an impressionable soul . . . well, then perhaps he wouldn't have met such a tragic end."

"Charles," Marsh said. He glanced to the dark trees lining the creek. Just a while ago, was it a bird he'd heard singing?

The old man touched Marsh's hand, his crabbed black fingers warm as the air. "Hole In The Day," he whispered. "You recall the night Hole

206

In The Day saw the cork fly from a champagne bottle and believed he'd witnessed a miracle."

"Save yourself," Marsh said. Soon enough it would be daylight and all the SOARS ready to hear more.

"He believed too much," Reg said, smoothing his roomy pajama legs. "He believed his people had crossed over from Persia and that he once possessed the knowledge of building large ships. But, of course, he'd entirely lost it."

"Well, he should've stayed there," Marsh said. "In Persia, I mean." He gazed down the row of campsites, the pale sky lifting with dawn. No use trying to sleep anymore. Reg wouldn't leave the story alone. It was a story Marsh believed could only turn sadder from now on.

"There was a little song my father sang him." Reg tipped his chin, humming a moment. "To the day he died, Hole In The Day never forgot that song."

Next door, a light switched on inside the Southwind.

"Listen to me." Marsh gripped the old man's shoulder. "You've got to ease up, think about yourself for a change."

Evie appeared at the door of the Southwind, belting a furry orange robe.

"Right now," Marsh said. "Tell me one thing about yourself."

"Well, there's the difficulty," Reg said. He tapped his fingers across his forehead. "When you reach my age you sometimes fail to remember where one person ends and you begin."

"Just try," Marsh said.

Evie stepped outside with a dog under each arm. She dropped the quivering miniatures into their wire pen and called, "Frank's making pancakes."

"Quick—remember one thing, that's all."

"I'm thinking," Reg said. He flicked ashes into his smooth palm, then smiled. "I distinctly recall my first wife's eyes. And of course, I'll never forget the great controversy over oleomargarine."

Marsh ran a hand through his sleep-tangled hair. "I'll put on some coffee," he mumbled. He started for the Establishment, then glanced back. "There must be more."

"I expect so," Reg said. "Always more to the story."

Marsh opened the louvered window above the sink and waited for the teakettle to boil. He watched the day beginning—Lester with a towel hung over one shoulder, heading for the restroom, that pink peeling door marked General Custer.

Then Alex was awake, poking her head out the flap of her one-man tent. A true camper, she refused to sleep in her Econoline. She ducked from the tent on her hands and knees, then stood to snap her cutoff jeans. Marsh looked away. Even when Alex and Richard had stayed at his house, he'd never seen his daughter-in-law straight out of bed—her hair so loose and tousled, her face still flushed from sleep. But then, this was camping with half the women wandering over the grass in bathrobes.

Beside Marsh the teakettle whistled, steaming the warm morning air. He hardly heard it. Alex was tying her sneakers, bracing one foot then the other on the van's bumper. She started across the field, sleek tan legs and long strides. But halfway to the restroom, she stopped and looked back. For a moment it seemed she'd felt his eyes.

Marsh turned to the stove and measured coffee into the pot. He'd need to call Sharon again—that's all there was to it. He pulled on yesterday's slacks, the results of the race still crackling in his pocket. For a minute he stood in the dinette, envying Tiffany's sound sleep. When he glanced out again, he saw Lester and Alex returning from the cinder block restroom, their chummy towels trailing from their hands. Marsh hunted up the camp stools, grabbed the coffeepot and hustled outside.

Frank lumbered over. It seemed he and Reg were having some sort of disagreement as to who'd actually taken the first scalp for Custer. Frank muttered something, then shoved a plate of pancakes topped with a fried egg into Marsh's hand.

"I slept just terrible," Evie said. "Between poor Charles and Princess Grace . . ."

Alex dragged a camp stool next to Marsh. "I shouldn't be eating this," she said as he set his full plate into her lap. "Soft fiber and high cholesterol."

Marsh glanced down to Reg's feet, the old man's breakfast sitting there untouched. He turned to Alex. "How long can he go on like this?"

Alex shook her head. "He smokes too much. Maybe you should talk to him."

"I can't talk to him," Marsh said, hearing the old man's voice rising at his other side.

"Given Mr. William Cody's bent for dramatics, I'm surprised you'd have any doubt he was the one to take Yellow Hand's scalp."

"Not according to Hollywood," Frank said. "It was Wild Bill Hickok with Gary Cooper playing the part."

Evie smiled, stroking her orange fur sleeve. *"High Noon,"* she murmured.

"I believe I can add something." Lester pulled his chair into the circle. "Eyewitnesses agree—Buffalo Bill took the scalp at Hat Creek. But the young Cheyenne known as Yellow Hand was actually named Yellow Hair. Although some Indians referred to General Custer as Yellow Hair, or Woman's Hair." For a moment Lester picked at bits of grass clinging to his gray coveralls. "I don't know how we'll ever unravel it." He looked up, his eyes gone to nothing in his ashen face. "I mean our whole tangle."

"You mustn't distress yourself," Reg said. "I'd like you to correct me if I should make such a mistake again. It seems my whole life I've been practicing up for this—" The old man flung out his arm, as if taking in the breeze, the wide prairie—all the frontier. "I don't believe my father ever knew that Yellow Hand was really Yellow Hair. Well, there's the sadness, because you realize—this is his story."

Evie patted Reg's arm, then moved to the Southwind. "I won't have you worrying one minute about your father. Never mind the little mix-ups," she said loudly, disappearing inside.

Reg smiled and sat back in his lawn chair. He rested his elbows on the chair's arms, his slippered foot bobbing.

Marsh glanced over, wondering why the old man would wear such big pajamas. He squinted to make out the monogram on the pocket. Then he realized Reg was humming again. Ragged little snatches drifted from the old man's breath. It seemed he was humming only to himself—just sitting out here on the grass as if still alone with his thoughts and the day had never dawned.

Marsh gulped at his coffee, uneasy with the quiet, only the stuttering sound of Reg's voice. A slight breeze had started to stir and soon it would be blowing across the fields, and hot again today.

Beside him, Alex leaned to set her plate in the grass. She'd eaten everything, high cholesterol and soft fiber.

"And another thing," Evie called, poking her head out the South-wind's window. "Wherever Algie goes next, I'll be there. You can count on that!"

Marsh caught the grin on Reg's face. Then it seemed everybody else was grinning, too. And the old man started clapping his hands, the sound cracking the air with Reg's foot tapping and Evie's little dogs leaping like dancers at their portable pen.

And then Reg was singing, his hands still slapping loud. It didn't sound like him, but somebody bigger, stronger. And somehow a relief—the old man clapping on and on like this, his blue pajama sleeves sliding to his elbows.

Marsh tried to stop grinning. He looked at Alex and she reached over and jiggled his hand. She laughed as if he was just too silly. But this song couldn't go forever, and except for the bouncing tempo, nothing silly about it.

> *And they found poor Lazarus, found him up*
> *between two mountains*
> *And they blowed him down—oh my Lord—And they*
> *blowed him down*

And what they used was a great big number
A number forty-four—oh my Lord—A number
forty-four . . .

Reg's words trailed off, but for a minute his hands kept going. Then suddenly he stopped. He clamped his fingers over his knees and leaned forward in his chair.

"Well, who's to say? Perhaps my father should've followed those wagons up to Nicodemus that first afternoon. But then, you realize what a heartache to recognize such love in one instant and in the next discover you can never say the words. Well, so be it. Algie determined to ride to Nicodemus and offer his services to the weeping husband who had no hands."

Marsh poured more coffee as Reg moved the story on. The old man was talking about the plight of the Exodusters, about how it had finally rained, bursting the banks of the Solomon River. And Algie had set out for Nicodemus.

Reg flicked a sandbur off his slipper, then squinted up. "But my father never reached Nicodemus that day, and perhaps just as well. At Logan Road he'd hollered to Pray Without Ceasing—Keep waiting. How could Algie have known that the man had been waiting all his life. All his life, praying for the free promised ground and himself a freedman. So now you will ask why—after these prayers were finally answered—why did Pray Without Ceasing steal from his bed in the middle of the night, in the middle of a soaking rain. When he walked into the Solomon River, did he believe those swollen waters would part for him as they'd leapt aside for Moses? Shall I tell you how he prayed and never stopped praying while the river swept him downstream and under? No, he did not ask for deliverance. It seems Pray Without Ceasing had already lost his life back in Scott County, Kentucky. On a warm spring evening, two night-riders had caught up with him. They found Pray Without Ceasing hiding deep in a sycamore woods and they cut off his hands. They tossed his bloody hands into his lap, then they whispered, 'Now go work in Kansas.' And they left him good as dead.

That is the story my father would hear, but not on this day. He would not see the scoundrel John Niles paying respects to a beautiful grieving widow. Nor glimpse the tears in Reverend Roundtree's eyes, hear him saying, 'This day in the land of Israel, a great prince has fallen.'

Not more than a mile outside of Hays City, Algie had reined Dewey's mule to a halt, his journey already interrupted. Close by, old Brin stood absolutely still, holding his perfect point. And then suddenly the shavetail mule was commencing to make such a ruction—flattening its long ears and braying to be heard for miles.

Well, they claim a mule can always smell a savage no matter which way the wind is blowing. Give that contrary animal the slightest opportunity, and it will announce your presence to an Indian every time. Not that my father appeared overly concerned. I expect he was feeling far too excited, his mind clicking into a rapid review of that little guidebook with its chapter titled Meeting Indians. Of course, Algie could recall the text almost word for word, having spent so many evenings with the book in his lap. Allow me to quote from that informative beginning:

> On approaching strangers the Indians put their horses at full speed, and persons not familiar with their peculiarities and habits may interpret this as an act of hostility; however, it is their custom with friends as well as enemies, and should not occasion groundless alarm . . .

But this savage was not riding toward Algie at a reckless gallop. The Indian approached on foot, and with such a wearisome pace, it seemed he'd been walking the prairie for days. He looked to be somewhat under the influence, but perhaps it was only the sweltering weight of his buffalo robe dizzying him on such a hot day.

Regardless, Algie dismounted so as to meet the Indian on equal terms. As the savage staggered closer, Algie raised his right hand. He pushed his hand forward, then back, giving the sign to halt.

But the savage kept coming. Quickly Algie swept his hand through the air—first right, then left. You understand this to signify 'I do not know you. Who are you?' And you also realize that by this time the savage stood directly before my father. Well, you've never seen such signals as Algie performed, his arms whizzing whole conversations. It's highly possible he may have added several new words to the body of that language.

Even so, this peculiar young savage did not appear impressed. He simply watched, unmoved except for his eyes flashing as if on fire. But after a moment he leaned very near—so near the sharp point of his sweat-dripping nose came within a fraction of Algie's face.

Then suddenly the Indian drew his right hand from beneath his buffalo robe. It was all Algie could do to keep from leaping back in such a fright. But he felt only a touch—a finger trembling on his lower lip, now tapping at his left ear. Then the Indian's hand came to rest on Algie's shoulder. And here I must ask you to believe . . . That savage shook his shining head and commenced to say:

'My poor sign-talker. I see you have no sound in your ear and the voice that never moves. Do not be afraid, my brother. I speak with the tongue that lives in my heart. My heart tells me the Great Spirit has put you in my path so I may set my foot upon the Jesus Road before I die.'

Well, do you wonder that Algie stood utterly speechless, looking for all the world like the deaf and dumb sign-talker that Indian believed him to be? For a moment he could only frown at the savage. He saw a person who might be near his own age and perhaps half an inch taller, but so thin in the face he could make out every bone—deep dark sockets around the eyes and hollow cheeks high as cliffs.

Algie deliberated whether to open his mouth at all. The savage appeared fairly overjoyed at the idea of coming upon a deaf-mute. And so my father finally offered his hand without a word. But as he did so, he recalled a passage from his little manual.

Extending the hand to an Indian is permissible. However, be aware that these people consider the gentleman's handshake one of the most amusing sights on Earth. If laughter should be indicated, it is suggested that all parties join in the jovial mood.

Algie nodded and smiled, in the event the Indian might be feeling a good howl coming on. But instead the savage let out a cough. The sound issued from deep within the Indian's chest. His face shone even brighter, washed with sweat. The great hawking cough exploded again and again, doubling him almost in two, while he clung to Algie's hand. And such a terrifying noise. A person does not need to have heard that dreadful sound before to know instantly what it means.

Algie pulled out his handkerchief. He thrust it toward the savage, but you understand that poor fellow was by now too weak, even for holding a handkerchief. And so my father held the white cloth to the Indian's mouth. He helped the savage to sit and there they remained with the prairie stretching for miles around them and no help to be found.

At this point, Algie must have asked himself why he should be sitting there at all, offering aid to a murderous cutthroat. But then the fearful hacking finally ceased. Algie drew the handkerchief away, feeling nearly faint from the sickness he held in his hand—his handkerchief heavy and painting blood onto his palm.

'I must find Father Sommereisen,' the savage whispered. You realize he spoke to himself, still thinking Algie deaf and dumb. In fact, he scarcely looked at Algie as he gathered up his buffalo robe and prepared to walk on.

Algie dropped the bloody handkerchief into a clump of grass and watched the savage start away. The young Indian dragged his buffalo robe behind him, weaving slowly in the direction of Hays City. Algie noticed that the Indian's hair was cut short round his neck. He wore a black suit of the kind Mrs. Ditsun would label working-class. The suit hung limp on his thin shoulders, casting a profound humility over his person. That is how Algie saw him as he walked through the prairie. He wore no hat. And no moccasins, only crude cobbled shoes. It appeared he owned neither horse nor mule, not even a French horn. And Algie wondered, what could this person be if not a savage. I expect for this reason he finally shouted:

'Who are you?'

Of course, that poor unfortunate scarcely understood for himself who he was, given his frightful condition. In truth, he was a Praying Indian of which there were so many in those years. He was also the young Sioux we know as Hole In The Day. And perhaps I should add the Christian name Ezra Holiday in light of his baptism by Latter Day Saints, Methodists, Baptists, and Episcopalians. Not all at once, mind you. Can you imagine the mix-up merely in the laying on of hands? And now this young Sioux had traveled all the way down from Yankton to seek Father Sommereisen and yet another brand of holy water.

The fact is, Hole In The Day believed in miracles, which will give you some idea of native ignorance or intelligence, whatever the case may be. And so he didn't find it surprising when he heard the previous mute Algie speak. Nor was he the least bit startled to wake up the next morning and find himself occupying an isolated bed at one end of the Fort Hays hospital. He accepted these developments as further wonders of Heaven and Earth, though it's doubtful he ranked them anywhere near the northern lights. And there's a shame when you consider what a time Algie had just to push that fellow into the saddle, not to mention leading Dewey's hysterical mule all the way to the fort.

Of course, precious little could be done for consumption, or phthisis, as the post surgeon insisted on calling it. But never mind—we all know how physicians love the odd word.

Naturally, everyone excepting Algie assumed Hole In The Day would surely die. However, that does not excuse what occurred on the Wednesday next. Those two bumbling hospital stewards will tell you it was an understandable mistake. But I ask you—can you find a particle of sense in two men preparing to toss an individual into the fort's Dead House, when that person is by no means expired? Yet this is precisely the scene Algie came upon when he rushed up the long corridor of beds with the Reverend Sommereisen right behind him.

Just as Algie reached the pile of quarantined sheets, he saw the two stewards about to chuck Hole In The Day through a trapdoor in the corner. 'Wait!' Algie cried. But even as he spoke, his heart fell, believing the worst. To think that after three frantic days spent locating the Father, and then arriving too late . . .

Algie dashed to the trapdoor. Instantly his eyes burned with the dust of lye rising from that chamber below. He glanced to the frowning stewards and Hole In The Day limp in their hands. Then he shoved the trapdoor closed. He looked up at the big rugged priest.

'If you could say your prayer before he goes,' Algie whispered. 'He has walked a great distance to hear your words.'

Father Sommereisen's mild face sagged into his collar as he gazed down at the Indian. Some years before, this priest had ministered to Hole In The Day's father. One night Chief Iron Members had said to him, 'Since we pray, we see that all of our people are carried away by death.' And ever after, Father Sommereisen felt a troubling doubt when he clasped his wide hands in prayer. Nevertheless, he knelt with his little black catechism book and his string of rosary beads. But for a moment it seemed he did not know where to begin. And in that brief silence, the two pudding-faced stewards caught a sound. Then Algie heard, the good Father heard . . . a faint clotted breath.

And how those stewards snapped to! Up came Hole In The Day and shoved back into bed before the post surgeon discovered that empty mattress. Algie couldn't contain his relief at discovering Hole In the Day with a breath remaining. He'll tell you that in his joy, he felt something like the post commander. But I suspect the Almighty made manifest might be nearer the truth. He ordered the stewards to fetch hot soup on the double. And not just any soup, but essence of beef. Naturally, those stewards were in shock. Why else would they have rushed off at a black civilian's command?

But no matter—by the time they returned with a steaming tureen, Hole In The Day had been baptized a Roman Catholic. And by the time the last rites were completed, Algie pronounced Hole In The Day positively cured. However, no one else seemed convinced, particularly Hole In The Day himself. Having become a Catholic, he now appeared more than ready for that final miracle which would waft him up the Holy Road to Heaven.

As Algie tried spooning a little soup between his slack lips, Hole In The Day whispered, 'My ancestors are taking an interest in me.' You understand this to mean that the departed relatives were up there, just waiting—every single one crooking a finger at him.

Algie forced a brimming spoonful into Hole In The Day's mouth. 'You are on the road to recovery,' he said. But he could see that Hole In The Day felt opposed to this. The Indian's face was drenched. His dark eyes blazed even brighter with the lung fever.

'I know where I am going,' Hole In The Day rasped. You realize how difficult for that Indian to talk, what with clots choking his throat and Algie shoving the spoon in and out between words. But regardless, Hole In The Day shook his weak head and said in the loudest voice he could muster, 'This is a good day to die.'

Well, you'll always hear that from an Indian. Show those people a calendar, and they're liable to tell you next Tuesday looks fine. So of course Algie paid no attention to that remark. Instead, he turned to Father Sommereisen.

'I would ask you to be my witness,' he said. Then Algie held the soup spoon in front of Hole In The Day's burning face. He leaned close to the Indian's ear. 'If you were not cured—if indeed you are going to die . . . Do you believe I would dare . . .'

And with that, Algie slid the spoon into his own mouth. He ducked from Father Sommereisen's hand reaching to snatch the spoon away. He stood a full minute. He nodded at Hole In The Day—the spoon bobbing between his lips, and the Father taking out his string of rosary beads for a second go round.

Well, why? That's what Father Sommereisen wanted to know. 'Why on Earth?' he asked when Algie finally removed the spoon. And we can only wonder ourselves. What possessed Algie to take such a risk? He was scarcely acquainted with Hole In The Day—and only a common Praying Indian besides. We're all aware that my father professed no faith except in the Republican Party. It was the young Sioux who believed, lying there in the pillows, looking full of another miracle. He'd be the one whispering 'This Jesus Road gets bigger and bigger all the way, but I will follow on.'

Is it enough to say that Algie had developed a keen interest in this Indian's case, or that he felt so tired of death? He drew the sheets around Hole In The Day's bony shoulders and said, 'Sleep.' Then he felt the Indian's finger touching his arm, and more words coming.

'My brother Wasicum Sapa,' Hole In The Day said in his faint voice. 'You told me to throw away my bad road, and I listened and am trying to follow on.'

'I never said any such thing—that is all in your head,' Algie whispered. But as he spoke he felt an overwhelming curiosity as to the meaning of those words: Wasicum Sapa.

After a moment Father Sommereisen glanced up with a nod. 'It's just possible he is going to live.'

'Sometimes I become discouraged . . .'

Yes, that would be Hole In The Day again, mumbling from his pillow. You understand he was not one of those silent Indians you've read about. In the times ahead—oh what stories he had for Algie.

'I get very weak,' he whispered, holding tighter to Algie's arm. 'But if you look for me, you will still see me following on.' "

19

Reg sat back, lit a cigarette, and sat smoking a minute. Finally he said, "Wasicum Sapa." His voice held a strange softness, as if he was distancing himself from the words. He turned to Marsh. "Ask me what this means."

"Tell me," Marsh said.

Reg tapped Marsh's hand. "You are the white man, wasichu. And I am black, or sapa. So there it is—Black White Man. That was the name given to Algie by Hole In The Day. The Indian gazed upon my father and saw an individual who appeared for all the world to be white, but whose skin happened to be black."

Marsh pulled his hand away, wondering if Reg had any idea what he was saying. Because it seemed the old man might be talking about himself. Or maybe Marsh only wanted it to be true. Hadn't they all—every one of them sitting in this circle—hadn't they wished for such a man? A black white man.

Reg smiled. "Well, I suppose the name truly was something of an honor, considering it came from Hole In The Day who'd done just about everything in his power to turn himself white."

"Maybe we should take a break," Marsh said. He gazed off across the fields and felt the story coming too close, coming to this.

Frank checked his watch. "We've got till noon."

"Let him go on," Alex whispered. She rested her hand on Marsh's arm, as if she sensed his thoughts.

"Allow me to tell you," Reg said. "What a mix-up. There was Hole In The Day willing to die for a change of color, while up in Nebraska the peculiar savage Crazy Horse was about to lay down his life in order to remain red. As for Algie . . . One month earlier he might've felt pleased to hear himself called Black White Man. But ever since he'd seen that crowd at Logan Road, he'd been tossing awake nights wanting only to be one of them—a true colored person.

So now you may ask, where does a person go to claim his own black skin? Could he return to Bridgewater Grange and Mrs. Ditsun in tears, still mourning her fair lost son? Could he ask Mr. Grant who'd once seemed so like a father? No, he could not. In any case, Mr. Grant was beset by problems enough, what with his great cattle enterprise floundering, plus work on the chapel and schoolhouse proceeding at the slowest pace.

Throughout those long troubling days, Algie approached Mr. Grant only once. He inquired as to the surefire remedy for a case of lingering consumption. To which Mr. Grant absently replied, 'Travel to the eucalyptus forests and breathe deeply.'

As if Algie could follow that advice, let alone transport a Praying Indian such a distance. Instead, Algie brought Hole In The Day to Victoria. And what an instant attraction. On any given afternoon you would've discovered a few youngbloods or Margaret Grant's reading club gathered at Algie's house to gape at that poor ailing Indian.

Of course, it was Algie's bed those sightseers stared at. Algie himself had been obliged to take Charles' room. Having donned young Ditsun's clothes, he now found himself squirming between Charles' white percale sheets. This new development only distressed my father all the more. He could not lay his head on Charles' goose down pillow, or begin to close his eyes, but what he remembered Hole In The Day whispering— Wasicum Sapa.

Now, I don't mean to hurt your feelings. But Algie spent most of August despairing over those words. It seemed he'd never be able to show his face in Nicodemus. How could he go among the colored people as a black white man? Then, toward the end of the month something happened. You understand that in time, something generally does.

It began with a simple errand to buy Chief Red Jacket bitters. Never mind that no Indian, including Chief Red Jacket himself, had ever heard of such a concoction. Two tablespoons would nevertheless snap Hole In The Day straight up in bed.

Algie was standing in the chemist's shop, when he caught a word directed at his back. He turned to see a surly gentleman loitering behind him. 'I beg your pardon,' Algie said. At which point the gentleman hitched up his chamois britches and sneered, 'You heard me—I said,

Nigger.' 'So you did,' Algie answered. And with that, he tore from the shop entirely forgetting what had brought him to Hays City in the first place.

Well, shall I tell you that Algie rode the distance to Nicodemus on the strength of that one word? Dewey's mule and the dog Brin, they accompanied him. But it was the word that carried him. It seemed those sore syllables were what my father most needed to hear. Perhaps he believed this could be the true password for membership in his race. Through all of an afternoon and a night, Algie rode as if in a dream. He rode with A Home In Kansas folded in his pocket. And a black man returning with a deer and turkeys on a string."

Reg looked up as Evie stepped from the Southwind. She carried a plate of cinnamon rolls in one hand, a fresh pot of coffee in the other. The old woman Jewel stumbled behind, dragging a lawn chair. Down the row of campsites, late-rising SOARS began ambling over.

"What'd I miss?" Evie asked.

"Algie's finally going to see the colored people," Frank said.

Marsh helped Jewel unfold her chair, then he reached for a cinnamon roll. He wolfed it, feeling the tightness in his chest he'd woken with. He thought of Reg's story, and of Norm lying in the hospital, his wasted dark skin glistening like an oil slick. He thought of Ely—the prostitute Angeline giving him her real name as if it made a difference.

"I didn't think we called them colored anymore," Evie said. It seemed she didn't see Reg sitting there—only white people for miles. "Isn't everybody saying black now?"

Jewel opened her spiral notebook. She looked ready to enter the correct answer to this question—some final up-to-date word.

Marsh glanced away, watching Alex rummaging in the back of her van. She opened a carton of orange juice and ripped the foil from vacuum-wrapped granola bars, then moved back to the circle. She ate with a vengeance, as if this food might cancel out the soggy pancakes.

After a minute she turned to Marsh, catching his frown. "What?"

He blinked into her face, wanting to tell her about Ely and the black woman dressed in sheer baby dolls. Because it seemed to him now that he couldn't have slept with just anyone, only Angeline. And there'd been a difference, after all—a difference giving him the go-ahead for anything. Not in a name—but her color.

"When Reg and I were in Ely—" Marsh hesitated, hearing the old man's words still pressing on, still trusting to the story.

"When you were in Ely what?" Alex set the orange juice carton at her feet and retied a shoelace.

"Dammit, Alex—look at me." Marsh reached over and grabbed her arm. "Maybe she was a prostitute, but that's not the point."

Reg's voice straggled off. Marsh glanced up, aware he'd been talking too loud. He saw Frank staring, Evie shifting his way. He remembered Reg saying, *We have always been your bad dream.*

"What prostitute?" Alex said. "What are you talking about?"

Marsh frowned at his hands clamping the coffee mug. "I'm talking about—" He dashed the steaming coffee onto the grass, kept his eyes down. "I don't know—it's just that I think I must be prejudiced, maybe worse."

Jewel dropped her pen into her notebook. "Oh, I'm not so sure. I can't imagine there's anything much worse."

"Well, this is just great," Frank muttered. He glared across the circle at Marsh. "Right when we've got the colored people in the picture, you decide to tell the whole world you're prejudiced, as if that makes you somebody special." Frank bit into his cinnamon roll, then shook his head. "How do you think the rest of us feel when you say a thing like that?"

Marsh looked up, seeing Alex kicking softly at the grass, Lester hiding his face in his hands.

"You're being way too hard on yourself," Evie said, pouring him another cup of coffee. "It hasn't been that long since your wife passed on. After my Jeffrey went I got the free-floating guilties, too. Almost everybody does."

Jewel closed her notebook. "Have you ever thought of prayer?"

"Will you stop with this," Frank groaned. "We're not holding some kind of group therapy here. That's the trouble with you Californians— all the time sitting around in your hot tubs trying to figure yourselves out. Then you give us your big announcement like nobody's ever heard before." Frank waved a hand toward Reg. "Do you think this man hasn't got any idea about the real world? Ask him—he knows the score."

The old man turned to Marsh. "There's nothing you need to tell me. I know the score, as Mr. Valdivia has put it. Contrary to what you might believe, I did not come down with the last snow."

For a minute Reg shifted in his chair, listening to the sharp tap of a woodpecker drilling somewhere along the creek. Then he crooked a finger for Marsh to move closer. "Do you think I don't remember the miles we've put behind us? Now give me your hand and I'll tell you what Algie found when he reached Nicodemus."

But Marsh didn't want to hear. It seemed he couldn't go any farther. Then he felt Reg's warm grip and the wind picking up, blowing over the fields like a breeze off the ocean. They might've been sitting side by side on the deck of a ship. Far out at sea—just the two of them—sailing all the way to A Home in Kansas with the wind sweeping their faces and the story never-ending, falling and rising from waves. Moving him by turns to laughter, to shame.

"It was along about dawn, my father crossed the muddy shallows of the Solomon River. But when he crested that bank, he saw no house whatsoever. Not a trace of a town, only wisps of smoke curling here and there. And prairie grass swelling for miles—grass covering everything as if out of pity.

Algie moved between the Exodusters' smoking dugouts until he came upon a woman gathering sunflower stalks for her fire. He inquired as to where he might find Mr. Pray Without Ceasing Jones.

And so it fell to that poor woman to explain what had happened on the night Pray Without Ceasing walked into the flooded Solomon. The woman wept as she gave my father that news. Then she pointed toward a dugout set into a hummock of grass. But when Algie turned in that direction, the weeping woman suddenly clutched his coatsleeve.

'I thought you was come from the Freedman Relief,' she said. She stared off across the prairie and shook her tearful head. 'We been waiting for Brother Niles to bring us the relief.'

Well, you can imagine what shame my father felt, having set out once again without thinking to bring these people even the slightest item. 'I have nothing,' he said.

And with that, the woman began to cry all the harder, wringing her string apron in her hands and wailing as Algie walked on. 'You got them shoes on your feet,' she cried, 'that mule fat as a pig. You come high riding to this burned-up country, while we near to dying for the relief.'

Now you see what a sad state of affairs for those Exodusters. Nevertheless, Algie spoke to no one on that day—nor any day thereafter—who appeared ready to board a train returning south.

Not even Saro would consider going back. On the very morning Algie arrived, she'd sent her brother-in-law off to file a homestead claim on a quarter section. She'd hurried that man away saying, 'The Lord give us this land, and we got only to file the papers, then prove up. And before long you gon see corn growing so green and tall. Big stalks—stalks wide around as old Iwilla's mother hubbard.'

Well, there was a joke, and Saro laughed even as she repeated those words for Algie. It seemed she hadn't stopped talking since Algie appeared at her dugout. You would've thought my father had simply stepped across the road to offer neighborly condolences. Not that Saro looked to be grieving just then. Her face shone in the rising sun, and she clucked like a little hen as she scooped her crawling baby from the low doorway.

But before you rush to judge a woman so gay in the wake of death, let me tell you this . . . For three days nobody in that shabby dugout had eaten more than a nibble from the last slice of a molasses cake. And after the cake there would be nothing. So there was cause for rejoicing when Reverend Roundtree came round that morning and presented Saro with two stems of green rhubarb.

Saro knelt on the dirt floor of the dugout and pulled her baby into her lap. She fed the baby the way a mother bird would, chewing the stringy rhubarb into bits for the child's mouth. Do you wonder that my father was standing there falling to bits himself, just seeing Saro take the food from her own lips? It could've been hours Algie watched her, whole days might've passed. Until there seemed only one thing left to do.

Algie pulled out the circular he'd carried in his pocket ever since Logan Road. He thrust the paper into Saro's hand and said, 'You can look for me no later than sunset. I am going to bring you supper.'

Now, we all know what possessed my father to make such a promise. But why didn't he stop to think—if wild game was abundant in that place, would all those Exodusters be going hungry, praying for the miscreant John Niles to bring them relief? Would the sight of rhubarb inspire such joy?

Well, too late for questions. Algie unstrapped the Creedmore rifle Dewey kept behind the mule's saddle. Then he called old Brin. Naturally, Brin recognized this hunt as an emergency. I expect that's why the dog tried so hard to appear optimistic, bounding through the tall grass and scrambling under painful bull nettles. Brin searched absolutely everywhere, for hours on end, testing the wind when there was no wind, then snapping into a point just to keep some little hope going. Even as the hot sun struck low in the sky, and Algie sat to catch his breath on the shaded banks of the Solomon, old Brin waded across that river, still hunting.

By this time Algie was feeling utterly used up and footsore from racing Brin all over the prairie. He wiped his sweating face with his shirttail and stared into the cottonwoods. He squinted to see a wild turkey cocking its eye. Or perhaps a deer would come down to drink from the river. Surely it was late enough in the afternoon for a deer. And growing even later as Algie kept hoping—watching and listening for a sound.

But when he looked toward the river, he saw only Brin showering muddy water over the grass. The big dog tried the still air one last time. Then he lay down. And here I must ask you to believe . . . Algie raised his rifle. He found Brin in his sight, and he whispered for the dog to stand. But Brin didn't move, except to let out a long settling breath.

Finally Algie rose to his feet. 'Brin,' he called. But old Brin stayed in the yellow grass. The dog lay flat on his belly, with his big scarred head resting between his paws. He did not even lift his ear when Algie cocked

that rifle. Shall I tell you now . . . Brin never knew. This dog who per-
ceived the slightest shift in a breeze, who anticipated all manner of
events—this dog failed to see his own end coming.

Well, there's the sadness, don't you know. If Brin had only scrambled
up from the grass, or simply looked at Algie as though to say he understood. Instead, my father took the dog's life. He was the one, tearing
dry grass and snapping twigs from trees until he'd gathered enough for
a fire. He singed every hair on that sleek mottled coat. And then he
took out his pen knife and dressed what was left of old Brin.

On his way back through the falling dusk, Algie determined to tell no
one about this grievous afternoon, not even Hole In The Day who'd
become such a steadfast friend. Never mind that the young Sioux claimed
to have eaten stewed pup on numerous occasions. But then, it was a
custom among Indians, with the best beloved animal chosen and tributes
paid and tears shed even as the meal commenced. So perhaps it wasn't
so unthinkable—taking this life for a family having nothing to eat but
two pieces of rhubarb.

All the same, Algie stepped into Saro's dugout, and before anyone
could ask, he said: 'Badger.'

Well, such excitement as went into fixing that supper, I doubt you've
ever witnessed. There was Saro, rushing to boil a pot of rainwater for
stew. And Saro's mother-in-law singing with happiness—or so Algie
assumed. Never in all his life had my father heard tunes like those. Old
Iwilla sat in the dugout, singing underground as it were. But no matter—
the big woman's voice issued like Gabriel's own trumpet. Until every
hungry man, woman, and child straggled from their dugouts to hover
within the aroma of that simmering stew. Of course, more water needed
to be added, owing to these extra guests. And all the while, Iwilla sang
on, clapping her mighty hands and shaking her head over someone named
Lazarus, shot dead from between two mountains.

It was on this note that everyone sat down to supper. The Exodusters
ringed a snapping fire while overhead the first faint stars appeared and
Reverend Roundtree shouted up eternal gratitude to God. He spoke of
that miracle which had fed a multitude—seven loaves, three
fishes . . . Then the Reverend hollered, 'One badger, Lord. And oh we
thank you Jesus!' To which those hungry people replied, 'Amen.'

And Algie whispered, 'I thank you, Brin.'

Well, I don't need to tell you what a shudder crossed Algie's shoulders
as he took up his spoon. It was all he could do to swallow that stringy
meat. And should you be wondering . . . I have it on my father's authority, that stew tasted like nothing unless you're prepared to call Tough
a taste.

But Saro's eyes were shining, and for no reason except the very luxury of a meal. 'I believe this badger taste just like a dolphin,' she said. She leaned over her shallow lap and nodded at Algie. 'Ain't one thing in the world better than dolphin any day.'

Naturally Algie nodded agreement, though he'd scarcely heard of such a dish. He stared at Saro, ignoring his manners in his desire to learn— Who were these people, really? Exactly what had they endured that would inspire such singing as he'd heard on this night? Could it be that all these Exodusters once dined on dolphin?

Well, just then you would've seen a despairing Algie giving up on ever becoming a colored person. How could he have known that Saro had glimpsed only a picture in a book, a dolphin sounding the bright blue sea—that picture every bit as beautiful as A Home In Kansas with roses trellising a porch. And these were the visions she kept in her mind's eye—visions you might call Faith, forever instructing my mother's life.

Of course, we could never say the same for Algie. One minute he was sitting there like a true colored person and in the next bolting off to Dewey's mule with no hope whatsoever. But then Saro came running after him. She breezed beside him, wanting to know, did he have a name. As if there was some possibility he might not.

And so that is what my father told her. 'I have no name,' he said, feeling altogether spent as he climbed into his saddle.

But you remember how irritated Saro could become by a defeated attitude. She reached up and gave Algie a sharp pinch on the leg. She said, 'Either you gon to say your name, or I got to beat you bloody.'

Algie looked down and saw Saro scowling, her arms clamped stiff at her sides. He thought of all the names—a baffling list from which he could not claim his own person. He nodded at Saro and said, 'Long ago . . .' Well, I expect my father wanted to appear somewhat older just then. He turned in his saddle and gazed off across the prairie. He remembered being the Vicar's Boy, and Mrs. Ditsun murmuring Sooty Stranger. Then kind Mrs. Rupp pouring him an inch of whiskey in salute to Algernon Vickers. And Hole In The Day whispering Wasicum Sapa.

He frowned toward the fire, the colored people taking up their songs. Finally he said to Saro, '*You* tell me a name.'

For a moment Saro looked straight into Algie's eyes. Then she said, 'West,' and her voice dropped in a whisper. 'I get off that steam train, and sinking low in my directions. Then you come long telling me whatever direction I go I still gon be right here.'

So on that night, with Exodusters singing on and on, Saro whispered a name to my father. She called him Man Of The West. She smiled, looking altogether pleased with herself. Then she gave Dewey's mule a satisfied slap on the rump. And wouldn't you know . . . That mule who never could keep orders straight suddenly experienced a mental breakthrough. He tore off across the prairie—lit out would be the phrase. His shaved tail snapped into the horizontal, that's how fast he flew, and poor Algie caught sitting sideways with the reins trailing lickety-split through the grass.

Of course, Algie could still see Saro, owing to his arrangement in the saddle. She stood waving after him, growing smaller even as he watched. But we all realize by now—my father never did grasp the difference between enough and too much. So that would be him, bouncing high as the prairie moon and hollering at the top of his voice:

'I'll be back . . . Tell the people I'm bringing the relief!'

Well, there he goes, promising those Exodusters relief while it's all he can do to sit his saddle. Another few miles and he'll be calling old Brin, when he knows for a fact that dog won't ever catch up with him again.

But never mind. He'd take the Exodusters' plight straight to Mr. Grant. Then the Man Of The West would ride, ride, ride, carrying with him the relief. He'd bring the relief to Saro's door. He'd call for her to come out—rise from the ground. He'd shout, 'Black beauty come on . . .' Algie grabbed the reins and pulled Dewey's mule to a halt. He gazed into the night, shaking his head at such old words—words memorized years and miles away.

'Long ago,' he whispered. And what a curiosity that those lines, returned to him now, could be traced to an English childhood and himself a small boy frowning over his lessons at a big oak desk, his finger helping him across the page as he mouthed the words—as he stood in his stirrups, shouting to be heard all over Kansas:

> *Black beauty come on!*
> *I must love thee or none*
> *You see my face black . . ."*

20

A little before noon, Marsh pulled out of Fort Fletcher Campground, hearing Frank's voice still crackling from a loudspeaker. "Okay, folks—propane. Who needs that propane?"

"Not me," Marsh said. He spoke to himself and felt glad of it. He turned the Establishment up the gravel road toward Victoria. Not that he wouldn't have wanted Reg with him. But it seemed the old man had been placed on the SOARS program of events, like some popular after-dinner speaker permanently held over. Even Alex opted to stay behind, promising Tiffany another swim in the campground pool.

Marsh took the curve under the railroad bridge, wondering if the SOARS would make it to Nicodemus by nightfall. He'd found the town on his road atlas, and under its name the words Colored Colony in small red letters. Coming across that phrase in the updated and revised atlas struck Marsh as antiquated as the chapters in Algie's frontier handbook. It seemed nothing had changed, the whole country still divided up into colonies and territories.

Judging from the map, Marsh figured about an hour's drive. But the SOARS had organized a tour of the Englishmen's cemetery. "In the heart of downtown Victoria," Frank announced. And then a trek out to George Grant's estate.

Before he hit the two blocks of what Frank called downtown Victoria, Marsh stopped for gas at the Chateau Cafe. It seemed a relief finding that name among all the German businesses up the road: Brumgardt's Grocery, Pfeiffer Appliances . . . But when he stepped inside the cafe, he saw all the same ruddy, blue-eyed faces glancing up from the counter—half of Trish's relatives taking a lunch break.

He signed a traveler's check, then asked about the Englishmen's cemetery, just in case. A stout balding man followed him outside and pointed to a salvage company across the road.

"Drive behind that building and you'll see where they're buried." Then he added, "Of course, the place needs some work."

Marsh swung across the dirt yard of Victoria Salvage, slipped his camera around his neck and climbed from the driver's seat. As he walked past the dusty ruins of cars and tractor tires, he looked back, catching three of the Germans sipping at their coffee, watching him from the doorway of the cafe. He waved and the men ducked from sight.

He stepped through the opening in a sagging barbed-wire fence. Chipped gravestones tilted nearly hidden in tall yellow weeds. Beyond a limestone monument, a splintered flagpole leaned. Marsh moved through the weeds, imagining a faded Union Jack flying at full mast. Then he stopped to part the grass choking a square of granite set flat in the ground.

He read the inscription and whispered, "Mr. Grant." It seemed he'd just bumped into the man himself. He could see George Grant in shirtsleeves, tailing up the moaning Angus in the dark hold of a ship, George Grant smoking a Lebrecht cigar and placing a small leather-bound book in Algie's lap, now nodding from the high saddle of his thoroughbred stallion. Marsh stared at the inscription, not reading the old news of somebody's death. He saw that a man had lived—a man he knew.

Because of this, the big limestone monument seemed almost beside the point. But Marsh snapped a picture on his way out. He focused his camera on a bronze bull and a plaque reading: *To the memory of George Grant, who on May 17, 1873 arrived at this place, introducing the first Aberdeen Angus cattle to United States soil.*

Of course, if Algie hadn't gone into the ship's hold to begin with, those bulls probably wouldn't even have survived to get here. Marsh stepped away, thinking it was just like history to skip over certain things.

For a minute he sat behind the wheel, checking the atlas again. Evie had slipped a handwritten list between the pages. In the midst of everything—Reg's story and SOARS preparing to break camp—Evie had cooked up a scavenger hunt. A little added fun, she said. Marsh thought of the SOARS touring George Grant's estate, roaming every room for a size 38D bra or the leaf from a philodendron plant. He wondered how anyone could be expected to find all those items—why anyone would try. He drove up Cathedral Avenue, feeling no desire to even hunt for Mr. Grant's house. Just coming across George Grant in the cemetery had been enough. It had never occurred to him that a cemetery could actually cause a person to feel so good.

He rolled past Saint Fidelis Cathedral with its twin towers framing blue sky. Any time, Jewel would be stopping there to say a prayer for Princess Grace. As she and Evie made lunch, the old woman had looked up from a jar of mayonnaise and quipped, "Call me a born-again Christian with birth defects."

Marsh glanced into the rearview mirror—that wooden sign above the weeds: HOME OF THE KNIGHTS, 1981 DOUBLE A STATE CHAMPS.

"So long, Knights," he said to the mirror. Then he zipped onto the interstate.

When he reached the town of Hays, he debated pulling over to telephone Richard. But he couldn't think what to say. It seemed he no longer knew anything but Reg's story. He turned north, remembering Alex hollering at him, This is the real world, except you're not in it.

Before him the narrow highway ran straight between fields clipped neat as front lawns and farmhouses that looked more like upper suburbia. He glanced up hedged driveways—a white Buick with a license plate reading ALFALFA. After a while he snapped on the radio, listening for news from the real world. He heard Paul Harvey's parting shot: In Alabama a man and woman had been observed riding nude inside a glass elevator of the Peachtree Hotel. He switched the dial.

It is now believed that Princess Grace of Monaco may have suffered a stroke, causing her to lose control of her vintage Land-Rover . . .

Outside, the land began turning wilder. Marsh saw fewer farmhouses, more black-eyed Susans. He crossed a highway bridge, noticing that the south fork of the Solomon River was down to absolute bottom.

"Not again," he said, as if he'd actually been this way before. Then he glanced to the radio.

Congress was told yesterday that Air Force officials prefer basing the MX missile in the Nebraska panhandle or adjoining areas of Wyoming or Colorado . . .

Marsh thumped the steering wheel. What had happened to the idea of Nevada and Utah? "You people," he muttered. For a moment it seemed this broadcast was coming to him via satellite from some foreign country.

Then he blinked, suddenly pumping the brakes. He stopped along the highway's shoulder and backed up. Beyond the passenger window he saw a dark opening in a knoll of grass. He sat a minute, staring. It seemed he could hear old Iwilla singing, her voice drifting up from the grass: *And what they used was a great big number, oh my Lord, a number forty-four . . .*

But when he climbed outside, Marsh heard nothing but the wind stirring the branches of a cottonwood. Tassled weeds rippled over the dugout, grasshoppers buzzed past his shoes. "Hello," he called into the doorway. Of course, nobody answered—he hadn't really believed anybody would. He stood gazing at the weathered limestone which had been used to face the entrance. Then he ducked inside.

For an instant he couldn't see anything at all. He felt only a deep black coolness and the smell of the earth everywhere around him. He stood until his eyes adjusted to the darkness, until it seemed his feet had always been rooted here. He squinted up at a crumbling swallow's nest and wondered how the idea ever got started about all life emerging from the sea. Because he'd sailed an ocean and never felt so at home as he did right now.

He left the dugout with a strong urge to drive back to Hays, find the first pay phone and tell Richard to change his will to read *buried.* "Back to earth and dust to dust," he said, sliding behind the wheel. Then without warning he thought of Ginny reduced to ashes, hermetically sealed in a lead-lined mausoleum. He swung onto the highway, shaking his head. "Forgive me," he said. But he placed most of the blame on California and those types like Julia Oakes who talked about scattering themselves over mountains and valleys. As if in death they could be everywhere at once.

Listening to the farm report on the radio, Marsh wondered if he'd ever be able to live on that coast again. What did those yogurt-thin people understand about the price of hard wheat or feeder lambs? Marsh himself scarcely knew. But the announcer's words seemed more comprehensible than anything he'd heard on the national news. September wheat had made a disappointing showing on the exchange, down by three and a quarter. Bulls were also off. Corn down five and a half. Marsh wished he'd brought Alex's explorer's notebook with him. It seemed he should be entering these numbers, memorizing the status of soybeans and sorghums.

He turned off the radio, relieved to hear that at least butcher hogs had closed higher. Then he saw the sign, big as a billboard and just ahead. Blue painted sky formed a perfect match with the real horizon. In the sign's prairie foreground, two oxen stood harnessed to a covered wagon. Marsh felt the heat of a distant day—a shimmering heat, and words like a mirage.

NICODEMUS
KANSAS
Welcomes You

Marsh cranked the wheel, leaving the highway for a blacktop road. He drove slowly, as if groping toward a memory. Or maybe it was only a dream he entered—this landscape holding the silence of the billboard. Down the road he glimpsed houses—small and wood frame with shade trees bent from the wind. But no sign of anyone there at all. Then he saw the Kansas Historical Marker sunk into a strip of yellow lawn. He stopped alongside and gazed out.

Across the dry grass the trees looked recently planted. A few picnic tables chained with garbage cans sat at right angles to the highway. The whole place seemed nothing but a roadside rest for travelers.

Marsh pulled the keys from the ignition. For a moment he sat frowning over Evie's scavenger list. Scanning those items, he felt a sudden sadness at the idea of ever finding a six-inch pine cone on this prairie. Finally he folded the list in his pocket and stepped outside.

He aimed his camera at the marker, but couldn't take a picture. There were only words—block letters on a silver plaque. He might've read that brief past tense at the library or in one of Lester's books—just history.

. . . the town's future was blighted when a projected railroad failed to materialize. Nevertheless, these pioneers who built so much with so little hold a proud place.

"Sure," Marsh said. He moved off the strip of lawn and started down the blacktop road. At the corner he came to a limestone building and felt a little more hopeful. But when he peered through the windows, he saw nobody inside.

The church across the road looked vacated years ago, only a rusted water heater standing in its doorway. Marsh turned up the side street toward those quiet houses. Maybe the black people had seen him coming and locked their doors. Maybe he'd missed the sign that said No Whites Allowed. But halfway down the block, he spotted a man ambling out of his driveway.

The black man walked up the road, waving as if he'd been expecting Marsh. "We've got ourselves a hot one today," he called.

As Marsh moved past, the man thrust out his hand. "Vern Butters," he said. He smiled under a bright red baseball cap stenciled with the words Funks Hybrid Seeds. He tilted his dark face at Marsh. "I thought you people always came as a team. Sent you out alone, did they?"

"I'm sort of with a group," Marsh said, feeling a little uneasy. He gazed toward a blue water tower rising above rooftops—the name Nicodemus painted down its side. He wished Reg was here. Reg would know the right thing to say. Or even Frank, who didn't know and didn't care. Frank would just grin, assuming everybody understood the score.

Vern Butters wiped the sweat from his forehead with his cap, then stepped away. "Well, come on over to the house," he said. "I'll show you what I've got in mind."

Marsh stood in the road a moment, then dashed to catch up. "I don't think I'm the person—"

"All I need is the go-ahead," Vern said. He dug into the bib pocket of his overalls and pulled out a pack of chewing gum. He tipped the gum Marsh's way. "That slab's got to be poured before our weather starts in."

Marsh nodded as they turned into Vern's rutted driveway. He thought of the mix-up in Ely—Bud's Radiator Repair, the F.B.I.

Vern trudged beside a sagging white frame house, then pointed into weeds. "We're looking at three feet the other side of the driveway," he said. "I've already ordered the shed—just a metal prefab. And like I said in my letter, the house stays the same. You folks put my place on the Historical Register—that's fine by me. You tell me, stick with white paint, don't change a nail anywhere. I say O.K. I'm not going to raise a flap, even though you've got the town historian with her house blue as that sky up there." Vern shrugged, glancing over. "The thing is, I need this shed."

Marsh stared past him, trying to think if he'd seen a blue house. "Well, I don't know why you can't have it," he said, hardly hearing himself.

"That's all I wanted, was the go-ahead," Vern said. He thumped Marsh on the back as they moved down the driveway. "Oh, it's something all right, being historical. Gets to where it tires a man out having so much attention. That's why your team isn't so bad—you just go for the buildings. It's the oral history nuts, don't have any idea when to let up—especially if they're after the Ph.D.'s."

Marsh stepped from the driveway. "About the blue house . . ."

"You won't find anybody there. Delois moved in with the Senior Citizens back this last November." Vern folded a stick of gum into his mouth, then grinned. "Those oral history people got nothing on me. I tell them before they ever saw daylight, I was a Ph.D. My Daddy, too, and all my folks down the line—every one of them Ph.D.'s." He laid his big lumpy hand on Marsh's arm. "Posthole digger—that's what I say. There's your real Ph.D."

Marsh chuckled, then laughed louder seeing Vern slapping his knee, getting such a kick out of himself.

After a minute Marsh said, "I need to find Delois."

"If it's three o'clock, she could be at choir practice." Vern waved past the row of frame houses. "Try the church first—you don't see her there, go over to Senior Citizens. They might've canceled choir for the Grace Kelly movies—channel three's putting on a marathon. Hasn't been anybody come out of a house since those pictures got started."

Vern swung his head away, aiming his wad of gum into a clump of black-eyed Susans. He followed Marsh out to the road. "Remember to go in easy with Delois and hold your punches. Delois has been talked almost to death. And don't mention that blue paint. Her mind's set on blue—always has been, always will be."

Marsh nodded, already hurrying off. He passed ragged front yards deserted except for a pickup truck here and there—across the way, a Caterpillar tractor parked for a movie break.

Then he saw the blue house. Marsh stared at the pastel stucco, trying to figure how anyone could fail to realize the place wasn't really blue. Unless sky blue had weathered to lavender—that could be a possibility. But it didn't matter. He liked the lavender. When he found Delois, he'd tell her so—give her the go-ahead.

But when he reached the church, Delois wasn't inside. The sanctuary stood empty, though it had clearly survived that denomination at the other end of town. Marsh ran his hand over a polished pew, Gideon Bibles racked beside red-bound hymnals. He leaned for a Sunday bulletin left on a seat. He sat a minute, studying the front of the bulletin—a folded white page with a typed heading: First Missionary Baptist Church of Nicodemus. Then the day's Bible passage.

And a highway shall be there, and a way, and it shall be called The Way of holiness; the unclean shall not pass over it; but it *shall be* for those: the wayfaring men, though fools, shall not err *therein*.

According to the bulletin, the choir had three selections to sing, plus the processional. Marsh looked to the front of the church where a big white piano dwarfed everything—a wooden lectern draped in blue velvet, two plastic potted palms, the white cross wired for light. It seemed the choir was shirking some large responsibility by not practicing today.

Marsh focused his camera, about to snap a picture of the warm low-ceilinged room. Then he dropped his arms. For a moment he felt the intrusion of his own presence. He remembered years ago, his mother folding his fingers in a nursery rhyme. "Here's the church and here's the steeple. Open the doors and see all the people." But the faithful flocks pouring out of his arched hands were only his wiggling fingers—his stubby white, flesh-and-blood people. And this First Missionary Baptist Church had no steeple. He couldn't count himself among that number posted on the Sunday Register: Attendance 25, Offering Today $48.00. Gazing at the Stars and Stripes hanging limp in such an unfamiliar place, he didn't even feel American.

For a while he just sat, as if this was some sort of ultimate test. Then he folded the bulletin into his back pocket and stepped outside.

He crossed the pavement toward a cluster of low, false-brick buildings. Two lawn chairs faced each other on a concrete porch. Over a screen door, Marsh read: Senior Villa. He stepped onto the porch, hearing the loud pop of gunfire from inside and horses squealing. Through the screen he glimpsed long tables, elderly black people seated as if for a meal. But it was too late for lunch despite the big television glowing at the room's other end, striking High Noon.

No one looked up as Marsh opened the screen door and slipped inside. He blinked at the dimness, floral drapes pulled shut. At the end of the room, Grace Kelly was about to fire her one shot through the window of the sheriff's office.

Marsh crept to the nearest metal chair and sat down. He leaned toward an old man in a brown-checked sports coat. "I'm looking for Delois."

Without taking his gaze from the movie, the old man pointed a finger to the table beside them. "She's the blue dress," he said.

Marsh scanned the table. Maybe he'd gone color-blind on this Kansas prairie. The woman's dress looked lavender as her house. She sat stiff in her chair, her face tilted toward the flickering light.

Marsh glanced down at his lap, thinking of a night almost thirty years ago, and Ginny reaching in the dark theater for his hand. Driving home, Ginny said it was too bad Grace had to wear that same dress for the whole movie. She thought Gary Cooper looked more like Grace's father than a bridegroom. But Ginny had been young then, and so had he. This time around, Cooper didn't appear so old. At least Marsh didn't see it.

On the screen, the two newlyweds were riding away to a new life. As their buckboard disappeared over the prairie, Tex Ritter's voice drifted after them, "Wait along, wait along . . ."

Next to Marsh, the elderly man in the sports coat nodded. "Good movie."

Marsh smiled. "They don't make them like that anymore."

"She died, you know." The man glanced up as somebody switched on the lights. His chin wavered at Marsh's shoulder. "Reruns," he whispered. "That's the blessing, comes from TV. You keep holding on like me—keep watching and pretty soon TV's going to show you everything you missed back when. The song says it—you just got to wait along."

Marsh stared at the old man's checked jacket, a gold-colored stickpin piercing his wide tie. It seemed he'd been dressed for the movies since

1950. Marsh looked off, wishing he was still in that year, in the dark, and Virginia clutching his hand. Instead he counted—close as he could—maybe twenty black people glancing his way.

The old man grinned, a wide yellow smile. "You like ice tea?" He waved a shaky hand toward a counter at the side of the room, a kitchen beyond. "Go over, get some tea. You see Delois there—she's the blue dress. Maybe she'll talk, maybe she won't. But if you've been to California, tell her you saw Lake Tahoe. Delois is very fond of that lake."

"I'm *from* California," Marsh said. For a moment it seemed the most astonishing luck that he could say he hailed from that state—that he could say one thing these people might want to hear. He rose to shake the old man's hand. "I've seen Tahoe a hundred times. Been to North Shore, South Shore, been swimming in Emerald Bay."

"That's even better," the black man said, then he chuckled. "I heard they have ice water in that lake. I'm thinking you must be one of those white people belongs to the Polar Bear Club."

"Oh, I am," Marsh said, ready to say anything. Whatever it took.

"I'll be," the man said. His fingers twisted around Marsh's hand. "You jump into ice water. Tell me—you ever go to those redwood trees, drive through that big one with the tunnel in the middle?"

Marsh nodded, waved a hand. "I built my house out of redwood."

"That so. I'm getting the feeling you been all over the place—plus got a house made out of the big trees."

Marsh felt like he might've just hit the lottery. All the lucky numbers—the six-inch pine cone, a size 38D bra. He heard himself raving on, dropping names. Alex's Golden State grizzly, the Golden Gate Bridge and how he'd sailed the *Whither Thou* smack under it.

"A twenty-six-foot sloop," he said.

"A sloop you call it. Isn't that a stunner." The old man let go of Marsh's hand. He tapped one thick black finger on his knee. Then he cocked his head, his eyes narrowing to sharp gleaming slits. His voice dropped, suddenly fierce. "Let me ask you . . . What do you call that big piece of business you left parked out there by the highway?"

Marsh stood straight. He glanced over his shoulder as if he could see the Establishment sitting at the roadside rest—California license plates giving him away from front and rear. He stared at the old man, feeling his chest stiffen, his face turning hot from the black man's cutting smile.

"Used to be, they called those vehicles land yachts." The old man wagged the wide ends of his tie between his fingers, kept his gaze tight on Marsh.

"It isn't mine," Marsh mumbled.

The old black man trembled up. "I drove through the big redwood. I saw Lake Tahoe. I dipped my toe into that south shore." He snatched at Marsh's elbow. "Twenty-five years I worked for Pasadena City. Twenty-five years, I opened the gates to the Rose Bowl. I was the one, unlocked all those doors. And the crowd came in, went out like a thunder. I think maybe you were there."

"Not me," Marsh said, trying to shrug the man's raking hand away.

"I was always standing at the main gate, always right there. So tell me this. Just one time—did you ever see me!"

Marsh pulled himself free. He bumped between metal chairs, dizzied by the old man's seething anger. He stumbled to the counter and Delois frowning up from her tea.

Across the room he heard a lion roar from the television, then music swelling. Beside him, Delois sighed, wheezing into a straw summer purse. Marsh caught a flash of her hand, the thin gold ring, a man's expansion watch loose on her bony wrist. A ballpoint pen slid out of her palm. It rolled over the formica, coming to a stop against his fingers.

Marsh blinked down. He nudged the cheap plastic ballpoint, an advertising special ordered by mail—by the hundred—with stamped messages promoting insurance, or lube jobs, maybe Funks Hybrid Seeds. But in gold capitals he found her name: DELOIS LEBOW, HISTORIAN.

She tapped the counter, her big watch clunking. "Come," she said.

Marsh looked up as Delois turned away, her lavender dress drifting pungent perfume. He slipped the ballpoint into his shirt pocket and moved after her, aware of the movie—another Grace Kelly in progress. Then he stopped short, catching the old black man at the screen door.

The old man shoved out to the porch and held the door wide. Delois walked through, started down the concrete.

Marsh heard the old man's chuckle, a thick sucking sound. The screen door squeaked wider as Marsh slipped past. "Thank you," he said, his voice faltering.

"Not at all," the old man said. "I know for a *fact* you see me now."

Delois turned up a cement walk. As Marsh stepped beside her, she began to speak.

"My father Fennimore Styles was the first baby born in Nicodemus Township, October 10, 1877 . . ."

"You don't have to talk," Marsh said. But it seemed the woman wasn't really talking so much as repeating herself—her words prerecorded, issuing from the thin brown tape of her body.

He shook his head. "I'm not going for the Ph.D."

Delois stopped before the second white door of a Senior Citizen duplex. Her voice trailed off. She frowned over at him, and Marsh saw in her face the remnants of a remarkable beauty. A single deep line creased her high forehead. Her hair rose with the breeze.

"What is it you want?" she demanded.

Marsh heard her voice lifting. In the choir she might sing every part—soprano to bass. She could be six feet tall, though her head came only to his shoulder. Marsh remembered Vern Butters down the road telling him to go in easy, hold his punches.

He shoved his hands into his pockets. "I was just wondering . . ."

"Inside," Delois ordered. She pushed open her front door and pointed to a green couch crowding a narrow front room. "Sit," she said. Then she took two stiff paper fans from the seat of an easy chair and slapped one into his lap. She sank into the deep chair, whipping the fan before her eyes as if to revive herself.

"Lord help you if you ever go for the Ph.D.," she said. "You got to have questions ready, know how to draw people out. Act interested." Delois flapped a disgusted hand at him, the watch sliding toward her elbow. "You don't even have a clipboard."

"No," Marsh said. He reached into his shirt pocket for Delois' red Historian pen.

"Here," she sighed, leaning for a pad of stationery.

Marsh pulled out Evie's scavenger list and turned it blank side up. "I brought my own paper," he said, trying to sound at least half-prepared. In a wobbly scrawl he wrote the time, date, and place. Then he looked at Delois, saw her waiting—high lavender shoulders sinking back in the chair, fan poised.

"My name is Andrew Marsh," he said.

Delois nodded.

The scavenger list fluttered on his knee. He felt the closeness of the room, every wall jammed with family photographs. He glanced to a portable TV, a plastic model of a blimp sitting on top. Finally he said, "I have a friend."

Marsh sat up straighter, smoothed the paper. He thought of Reg smiling from a lawn chair on the blowing prairie. He heard Reg's voice telling the story. Then he heard himself rambling, his eyes resting on the little gray blimp. He described Logan Road and the Exodusters climbing down from the train and Reverend Roundtree hurling his dusty top hat for joy. He gave Delois these details as if she'd never heard.

While he spoke, Delois leaned toward him, blinking across the room. She swept her fan through the warm, still air. "Oh yes," she whispered. "No matter how bad things got, we were always just so proud of the land."

Marsh nodded, listening only to himself, amazed that he could recall with such clarity each event and all those names. He settled into the green sofa as if he'd been sitting there all his life giving interviews, surrounded by aspiring Ph.D.'s and relatives on every wall. He told of the early days in the dugouts and how Pray Without Ceasing had walked into the flooded Solomon before the Freedman's Relief ever arrived. He talked on and on about Algie's worries over becoming a colored person. He described love at first sight and Hole In The Day at the brink of being shoved into the Dead House.

"Merciful Jesus," Delois said. "And then what?"

Marsh folded the scavenger list back into his pocket. "That's about it. Except for Algie bringing the relief."

For a moment Delois shut her eyes. She let her fan drop onto the carpet, then looked up, shaking her gray wavy head. "Well, I do like a story—always have. That's how I got to be Historian, just from listening." She gazed at Marsh, her long fingers clutching the arms of her chair. "Reminds me of the old days hearing you go on so."

"I'm sorry," Marsh said, realizing how much he'd talked. "I guess I've told you everything you already know."

"You told me a pack of lies." Delois raised herself up, then moved toward the rear of the duplex. "This way," she ordered.

In the kitchen she slid a bottle of Orange Crush out of an apartment-sized refrigerator and poured Marsh a glass. "Drink this," she said, as if he needed fortifying. When he started to speak, she shot him a look.

"Now you listen. My daddy was the first one born in Demus, and Cease Jones the first one dead. Those are the facts put down. Then you got other things—secret things whispered round and written in the Gossip Book."

Marsh looked away, Delois' voice hissing in his ears. He frowned at a pine table, a booklet lying there—a beautiful black woman, the words *Avon and You*. Finally he mumbled, "What other things?"

"Such as a sneak sniffing all over another man's wife, licking her bottom day and night like she was a mongrel in heat." Delois cracked a tray of ice cubes against the sink, sending a splintering sound across the room. "And Saro Jones opened her legs up wide for that Vickers man—don't you think she didn't. Opened herself wide as the gates of Hell."

"That's not true," Marsh whispered.

"Every word," Delois said. "I can take you under my bed—show you the Gossip Book kept by my own grandmother. There wasn't anything happened, didn't get into that book."

"Gossip!" Marsh said. He swung around, pointing a finger at Delois. "Maybe your grandmother lied—did you ever think of that?"

"Hush," Delois said, as if he was a child standing there. "You got to know that gossip is just history talking, except right now instead of later. Some folks hear it the first time, some folks got to wait." She touched his arm, her voice dropped low in the boxy kitchen. "One night your Algie Vickers rides straight to Saro's door, starts howling for her to come out. Smart English he had, and white ways. Wasn't a soul didn't know it was him hollering in the pouring rain. And Saro creeps out of bed—poor Cease lying under the sheets with no hands to stop her, him having to keep still like he never heard her go. Well, that was the night Cease Jones threw himself in the river—dead drowned on account of those two."

Marsh dumped his glass into the sink. He thought of Reg on the way here, finally about to meet these people. "Look," he said, "Algie's gone, everybody's gone. There's just an old man—"

Delois turned a faucet, filling an ice tray. "Then the next thing you know, Saro Jones is cheek to cheek with John Niles, president of the town company. But still that Vickers man has got himself inside her. And cock sore she was. She couldn't hardly walk from being rode to a lather. He took her up a tree and over at the graveyard, rode her into the mud like a lizard. Then one day John Niles goes down to Arkansas and lands in jail, never seen again. Some said political business got him— I say politricks, same as the railroad passing us by."

"John Niles was a crook." Marsh pushed around Delois, hearing his voice close to a shout. "Algie brought the relief!"

"He brought nothing but trouble," Delois said, moving after him. "Oh, he had high airs, that Englishman. But he couldn't sweet talk a weed into growing, let alone an ear of corn. Finally joined the Army. Saro Jones followed him up to Nebraska, took her boy Noah with her."

Delois stopped beside her easy chair, one arm propped under her sagging breasts. "Some years later, old Iwilla gets a letter. She asked my grandmother to read it out for her. Seems Saro Jones was burned up in a house fire. One baby—a bastard child—came through. And the Vickers man not there, from what anybody could tell. My grandmother wrote back—said Iwilla didn't want the remains sent down here. Far as I know, that was the last ever heard of those two."

Marsh opened the front door. "You don't know . . ."

"As Jesus is my witness," Delois said. Her voice faded as she bent over a chest of drawers beneath her portable TV.

"I'm talking about the hurt you'll do to an old man."

Delois swayed toward the door, clutching a small cardboard box. "That's how the past does you." She lifted her free hand as if to touch her heart. Her palm shown the palest pink against shirred lavender. "Some days I hurt to remember. Everybody hurts." She opened the little box, her face softening with a slow smile. "But there were a few good things happened right along. Always some of those."

Marsh glanced down at the box, seeing key chains—blue plastic, shaped like the state of Kansas with a single star shining left of center. Nicodemus, the only spot on the map.

"Take one," Delois said, jiggling the box.

"Please," Marsh said. He glanced out the door, looking for the SOARS—Reg up front in the Southwind. Or maybe they'd stop at the campground first. It was getting late. Frank would be wanting to make camp.

Delois pushed the small carton closer, her voice suddenly thinning to the recorded version he'd heard earlier. "There's no charge."

He reached for his wallet anyway, sorting in a rush past dollar bills. "My friend's name is Reg—Reg Vickers." He thrust his hand into the box, buried a twenty at the bottom, then pulled out a key chain. "If you could just tell him the good things . . ."

For a moment Marsh gazed at Delois, her brown eyes rimmed a milky blue, the man's watch flashing at her wrist. Then he pushed out the door and down the cement.

When he reached the street he glanced back, seeing Delois still at her doorway, waving the twenty dollar bill after him. Once again it seemed she rose above her true height, soaring in purple robes, her name gold and her voice rumbling like a kettle drum—oral history. She would never change her story, secrets hidden under her bed and Jesus as her witness. Not for twenty dollars, not for a million. Marsh hurried on past the blue lavender house. No, she wouldn't change that color. Her mind was set.

As he neared Vern Butters' place, he ducked away hoping word hadn't spread about the motor home parked at the roadside rest—those California license plates. He'd had no right, giving Vern the go-ahead. Maybe if he hadn't shown up so full of Reg's story, so sure of himself—the authorized individual.

"Cocksure," Marsh whispered, jogging past the picnic tables.

He hauled himself inside the Establishment, then leaned over the wheel to catch his breath. For an instant back there in Delois' kitchen, he thought she'd said cocksure. But Saro had been sore—couldn't hardly walk, Delois told him. *Cock sore, she was . . . like a mongrel in heat . . .* Marsh felt a heat—a vague ache building —just remembering the words.

He clamped his hands on the wheel and stared out to the highway, already shadowed by late sun. He could wait a little longer, stop Reg right here—tell the old man not to go beyond this point. He'd show Reg the Historical Marker and take a picture. Reg could say he'd been on the spot where his father might've stood.

"Our beloved Algie," Marsh said.

He reached into his pocket for Delois' pen. He sat gazing at her name, shaking his head as if he was still standing in her kitchen. Then finally he started the engine.

He swung down the highway, backtracking the few miles east to Webster State Park—a place Frank had chosen from his thick campground directory. Or maybe the SOARS wouldn't be there, either. Maybe they were still stuck in Victoria and that other part of the story. Marsh wished he'd stayed behind, too. The longer he thought about Algie, the more doubt he felt. Delois had said, He brought nothing but trouble. And now it seemed he was about to bring Reg only grief.

Marsh turned into the state park, thinking Algie should never have become an adult. Maybe nobody should be allowed past childhood. Take the little girl Tiffany, content with one white box. Why couldn't all desire stop right there?

Then he glimpsed Webster Lake—actually a reservoir though the map didn't say so. But there was no mistaking the flat shoreline, the water oddly smooth as if it was also artificial. The whole place looked like false advertising, some bright idea from an office of tourism. Kansas, land of lakes.

Marsh slowed for a faded sign reading Bathhouse and Beach. Maybe it was only the time of night causing this gray desolation, his worry about Reg. He saw the campground ahead, motor homes and trailers parked across the withered field—only a sapling here and there to break the hard-driving breeze off the water. Marsh pulled beside a picnic shelter, forgetting all about picnics. He thought of disaster—group refuge under the open-air roof. He felt a quick fear as if something terrible had already happened . . . Tiffany wandering off, alone in the dark bathhouse, blown into the reservoir with nobody watching. And all his fault.

Then Frank was standing in the sandy road, a fishing rod gleaming bone white against his plaid shirt.

Marsh flung open the driver's door. He dashed to Frank, the wind catching at his legs, sand pitting his face. He grabbed Frank's arm.

"Where's Tiffany?"

Frank grinned, flicking his rod as if to cast clear to the reservoir. "The bullheads are running. Tomorrow morning, crack of dawn, we're out there."

"We're leaving," Marsh said. He shoved past Frank, heading for the Southwind, the dim light burning above its door.

"Hey, wait a minute," Frank hollered, trudging after him.

The little girl looked up from Evie's lap as Marsh burst inside. "Andy!" she said. She scrambled into the Southwind's aisle, stooping for a flashlight on the carpet.

Evie laughed, decked out in her furry bathrobe again. Or maybe she'd worn that getup all day. She shook her head as Tiffany tugged Marsh by the hand. "There's a snake outside in the garbage can—Frank killed it a while ago. Tiffany's been dragging me to gawk at that thing every ten minutes. Looks like it's your turn."

"I need to see Reg first." Marsh bent, easing the flashlight from Tiffany's fingers. "There's a problem."

Frank pushed into the doorway behind him. "I think you'd better tell me what's going on. I've got twenty-eight SOARS lined up to see the colored people tomorrow, and you drive in here raving about leaving."

Marsh glanced down the aisle, the vinyl divider closed across the Southwind's rear. "Is he asleep?"

Evie nodded. "Exhausted. Mr. Grant's house almost did him in. You know what a trooper he is—goes till he drops."

Marsh moved past the dinette, slid the divider open and stepped through. He heard Reg snoring from the white queen-sized bed.

"I need to know," he whispered, leaning over the old man. He laid his hand on Reg's thin shoulders and thought of Saro burned in a fire. One baby had come through, Delois said. A bastard child.

Marsh gazed at the old man, only a sliver of black in the big bed. He wanted to ask, Are you the bastard child? He might've taken Reg in his arms then, carried him from the flames and all over the world to find the missing father nowhere around, far as anybody could tell. Until finally they'd see Algie. He'd be riding a gray horse. Marsh remembered now— that's how the story went. They'd march into the long linen fields. There might be snow . . .

"We'll wear our good coats," Marsh said, close to the old man's ear. Then he drew his hand away and stepped from the room.

Frank followed him as he moved outside. Marsh aimed the flashlight beyond a picnic table—Tiffany already waiting at the battered garbage can. He glanced to Frank. "I heard something today."

He lifted Tiffany so she could see, way down to the bottom of the empty can. The snake lay curled as if alive, basking in the flashlight's glow—except for its mouth wide open and a gash across the pale belly.

Evie leaned at Marsh's shoulder. "Gives me the creeps," she said. "I never saw a snake bleed."

"Excuse me for saying so," Frank muttered, "but your daughter-in-law is just this side of a kook. She did everything but give that rattler mouth-to-mouth recuscitation."

Marsh looked down at the big snake's shimmering skin, iridescent in the light. "That isn't a rattler," he said.

Frank hitched up his pants. "Tell me what you heard."

"It's Algie," Marsh said. He stared into the garbage can as he spoke. He explained about Delois—the way she stood so tall in a dress the color of her house.

"In Nicodemus I think they call it blue." He felt at his shirt pocket, held Delois' Historian pen in the flashlight's beam.

Evie reached around and touched the gold letters. "I'd like to buy one of those."

Marsh tried to take the heat out of Delois' words—all she'd told him in the cramped kitchen, and the Gossip Book under her bed, the relief never coming . . .

Evie shook her head along his shoulder. "It isn't true. That's not like Algie."

"Well, sometimes a person *can* feel sort of a lust," Frank said. "I think what we have here is some hellfire Baptist who's got her Bible all screwed up with this Gossip Book. How I see it— a man gets his hands chopped off, he's liable to walk into a river plain and simple. Sex isn't even in the picture."

Marsh looked over. "But if Reg hears—"

"Maybe we should skip Nicodemus," Evie whispered.

"He won't hear anything." Frank tapped the red ballpoint. "I'll handle this Delois."

Marsh gazed down at her name again, wondering how Frank could turn Delois as in Lois into something sounding like Del*wah*. But it didn't matter—not now with the night blowing tattered clouds across the sky, and on the far horizon, a flash of heat lightning making him yearn for rain.

As he switched off the flashlight, Tiffany wrapped her arms tighter around his neck. "Snake," she whispered.

For a minute they stood in the darkness, only a weak glow from the restrooms across the way and one or two SOARS still awake behind drawn drapes. Marsh glanced up the line, spotting Lester's stepvan, Claire's Micro-Mini. He took hold of Tiffany's hands, let her slide to the grass.

"Where's Alex?"

"Jogging," Evie said. She ran a finger around the garbage can's dented rim. "I guess it sounds silly, but I never thought about a snake having blood."

Marsh turned, looking out to the sandy road. "Which way did she go?"

Evie pointed beyond the field. "There's a boat ramp at the end of the road. We drove down there before dark."

"I want you to know I apologized to her about the snake," Frank said. "There's no hard feelings."

Marsh slipped Delois' pen into his pocket and stepped away.

"The ramp isn't far," Evie called. "She's probably on her way back."

But it seemed miles he ran. He sprinted the dark sandy road—this false shoreline he followed, wishing all the while for whitecaps on the reservoir. And he was out of shape, he knew his limits. But he kept going. He slogged on as if to reach that heat lightning, faint ahead like a spark struck deep at sea. He felt the heat also inside him—the wind entering with its searing voice: *That was the last ever heard of those two.* And he might ache from this tomorrow. Tomorrow the bullheads would be running, thundering from the depths, rumbling like buffalo up the muddy shore. Then the Man Of The West would ride, ride, ride.

"Ride," Marsh panted in the darkness.

Then he blinked sweat from his eyes, struggling to see through the blurred night and Alex coming full speed. Too late. He heard the single sound they made, as if they were just solid bones colliding, now falling. It was a wallop in the dark, enough to slam the breath out of two people. Except he had no breath left, only the soreness he'd felt since the kitchen and the sandy road in his throat.

"My God," Alex whispered, her voice inches away.

Marsh touched his stinging elbow, his right knee. For a minute he lay still as Alex. He closed his eyes and let the wind sweep over him until it seemed he might not be there in the darkness at all. After a minute he shifted to glance at her, sprawled beside him.

"Tell me if you're all right."

"No, I'm not." Her voice trembled, sputtered with sand. "Do you think I'd be lying in this road if I was all right? Do you think I'd be all the way out here in the first place?"

Marsh felt at his shirt pocket. He sat up, trying to make out her face. "I lost my pen."

"Do you think if I was somebody else, I wouldn't be crying right now? And don't stare at me like that." She slapped at his arm. "Go look for your damn pen."

"I'm not myself," he said. He leaned over her and brushed at her cheek. Then down her dusty bra-less shirt, her shorts powdered from the road. He dropped his hand, his fingers still holding the small shape of her breasts. He frowned into the wind, thinking how impossible: a 38D.

"Alex, listen, sometimes a person . . ."

"Oh God," she said. She turned her face toward him, shading her eyes as if from the pitch black night. "You don't have a clue, do you?" She shook her head, looked away. For a while she didn't speak. Finally she sighed, "Frank killed a gopher snake."

"I know," Marsh said. He sat back then, gazing north toward the distant clouds pulsing yellow light. He locked his hands around his knees. "Ginny always wore a bra." He glanced over at Alex lying straight and still, lying so far from anywhere in the world. "Even when her breasts were gone, she wore one."

Alex lifted her head. She nodded at him—kept nodding, tears coursing as if she'd just now felt the fall. "If I had no breasts," she whispered, "I would wear a bra."

Marsh pressed her mouth to stop the words—that admission beyond decent kindness. He kissed her tears, spoke to the darkness in her hair.

"This isn't me."

Then he gathered her T-shirt high, tasting the salty dampness of her belly. He bowed to her arching back, sand clinging everywhere beneath her cotton shorts, across her shoulders, up and down her blazing spine. He felt the strong breeze buffeting him. It seemed the breeze snatched off his clothes. The breeze blew her legs wide open. And it was this wind he rode, while her voice streamed around him.

"Not you, this isn't you."

21

Marsh stood on the top rung of a ladder, the morning sun casting his shadow up the side of Delois Lebow's lavender house. He nodded down to a lone black man who'd wandered over from across the street.

"I think you'd better go get Delois."

As the man hurried off, Marsh started on the lavender stucco under the eaves. He worked slowly, like someone who could take all day. Except there wasn't any time before the SOARS would be rolling down the road and Reg hearing Delois' story.

During the night it occurred to Marsh if he hadn't heard that story first—if Algie hadn't ridden Saro into the mud like a lizard, if he himself hadn't taken the fall to dust and his own son's wife—a morning like this might never have dawned. Instead, he'd been dashed on a reservoir road, then lifted way above himself on this ladder. He felt removed from every action, yet completely in charge. It seemed to him now that he'd been painting houses for years.

Up the highway he'd found a hardware store open early and four gallon pails of whitewash. He dragged a ladder from Delois' backyard. The ladder could've used another extension, but he felt high enough—on a level with treetops and the distant water tower flashing the name Nicodemus.

His hand stayed steady at the boar-bristle brush, even while the black

244

people gathered below him. He paid no attention to their voices rising soft in the morning air. He worked around a second-story window, wishing he'd thought to buy a sash brush.

Except Delois wouldn't come. The black man returned, hollering from the street. "She says she's calling the law."

"I *am* the law," Marsh answered. He squinted up at his job so far and decided he hated stucco, its rough surface bubbling the whitewash. He could see a pale cast of lavender bleeding through. No question about it—the house would need a second coat. "Go tell Delois that Reg Vickers is on his way. Tell her I'm not stopping until she remembers the good things and nothing else, period."

"And get myself killed over a white house," the man shouted back. "Uh-uh."

"I'll do it," somebody said from the foot of the ladder.

Marsh glanced down and saw Vern Butters, the man to whom he'd given the go-ahead. Vern grinned, lifting the bill of his baseball cap.

"Hasn't been a day," Vern said. "Not a day since we got historical, but what Delois isn't lording it over everybody with that blue paint of hers."

"Isn't it the truth," a woman chimed in. She stepped through the small crowd to Marsh's ladder. "Over on your left," she said, "You missed a spot—you've got a little holiday there."

Marsh squinted to see, his eyes dizzied from sunlight blazing on the white stucco.

"He's got holidays all over the place," a man said, then chuckled. "The government sent a house painter out here, don't know the first thing what he's doing."

"It's going to take two coats," another man called. He rapped at the ladder's bottom rung, then signaled with his fingers as if Marsh was incapable of understanding simple language.

Marsh nodded. He slapped paint on the spot he'd missed while the black people shouted more advice. Suddenly it seemed everybody below was supervising the job, telling him to palm the brush, put his whole arm into each stroke. Marsh tried harder. He heard a grumbling over the durability of whitewash. Somebody argued bird shit would last longer. Then there was laughter, except for one woman complaining about her tax dollar wasted as usual on a thing like this.

"First hard rain, and Delois' house goes back to blue," she said.

"Lavender," Marsh whispered, making an effort to use his whole arm.

"Meantime, we're still waiting for the tennis court you promised a year ago April."

Marsh set his paintbrush on the ladder's rung and looked down. He thought of the prostitute Angeline waiting for a Hula-Hoop from her Uncle Sam. And all the hungry Exodusters expecting the Freedman's Relief. "I never promised you anything," he said.

But now the black people were turning away from his ladder. They straggled onto the road, watching the caravan of SOARS taking the far corner. One by one the motor homes, campers, trailers turned up the side street.

Marsh shaded his eyes to see the Southwind in the lead. For a minute it seemed the relief had finally arrived. And Delois would remember only the good things.

"She says okay," Vern Butters called, tramping back across the yard. "She says stop—she's got the message."

Marsh wiped sweat from his forehead and glanced up at the half-white wall. He felt a little disappointed, leaving the job unfinished. No telling what the black people would think of him for just quitting like this. He dipped his brush into the whitewash, going over another missed spot. He had his pride. Then he heard Frank leaning on the Southwind's horn.

Below him, the SOARS sat idling. Alex's van fell second in line. Marsh saw her tanned arm crooked over the driver's window. For a minute he clung to the ladder, as if out of her reach. But Alex was already sliding from the van, hollering for him to come down.

"I hope you realize what you've done," she said as he climbed off the ladder. She pointed to Delois' house, a triangle of white rising like a ship's mainsail against the blowing sky.

Marsh looked away. "I had to do it."

"Oh really," Alex said. "And what about last night—I suppose you had to do that, too!"

He started to answer, then stopped as Frank strode toward them.

"I dropped Reg off at the Senior Citizens." Frank glanced past Marsh to the white stucco. "I thought we agreed I was going to handle this Historian problem."

"It's only whitewash," Marsh said.

"*Only,*" Alex snapped, so close to his ear it seemed he felt her teeth.

"Anyway," Frank said, "you missed a damned good story this morning. Algie brought the relief."

Alex wheeled, storming back to her van. Marsh watched her slamming into the driver's seat. She slapped on a pair of sunglasses, then rolled up the van's windows and punched every lock.

"Of course, I figured Mr. Grant wouldn't live forever," Frank said. "But when Hole In The Day made up his mind to get married—that really threw me. Took off to be with his own people. Disappeared without a word, just like an Indian.

"He was an Indian," Marsh said.

Alex revved the van and swung out of line. Marsh leapt aside as she plowed around the Southwind and lurched into Delois' yard.

"I'd like to know who she's trying to get killed," Frank muttered, watching Alex roar back to the street.

Marsh frowned at his hands, speckled with whitewash. He stepped to the curb—the SOARS caravan strung clear around the corner. From the Southwind, Evie was jabbering about Nebraska and a chuckwagon barbecue. Wherever Algie went next, Evie would be there. For better or worse, Marsh thought.

"You go on," he said to Frank, "I'll wait for Reg."

He moved into the jammed street, thinking he should've told everybody to park at the roadside rest where he'd left the Establishment. The town looked invaded. Even the air felt different, jangled by Frank's amplified voice.

"There'll be an hour's break for lunch and pictures," Frank boomed from his loudspeaker. "All sign-ups for Nebraska report to me."

Marsh dodged away, aware of black people staring from front porches and yards. Of course, anybody knew bird shit would last longer. Those people had ordered him around like he was a one-man reclamation team. They wanted their tennis court, a year overdue. But he'd never given the go-ahead. A tennis court seemed the last thing the place needed— a town without one store doing business. And no pay phone in sight. Otherwise he'd be calling Richard right now, straightening everything out. He'd tell Richard to come get Alex before it was too late. Or better yet, he'd send Alex home.

He rounded the corner, spotting her van parked in front of Senior Citizens. For an instant he considered escaping to the Baptist Church and its safe sanctuary. But then he thought of Reg sitting inside Delois' duplex, sitting on the tweed sofa with photographs on every wall and a little gray blimp. Delois would have given Reg one of those cardboard fans. She'd be telling her story.

"Only the good parts," Marsh said, trudging toward Alex's van. Or was it possible Delois had tricked him off that ladder? Maybe she'd already taken Reg under her bed to the Gossip Book, opened her refrigerator door and said, Now you listen.

Marsh stepped beside the van. Alex yanked off her sunglasses and glared from behind her window.

"You'll suffocate in there," Marsh said, loud against the glass. He glanced toward Delois' duplex and wondered if he should get Reg out of there before things went any farther. He could break down the door if it came to that.

He knocked at Alex's window. "I need to speak to you. Come on, Alex."

She rolled down her window an inch and aimed Delois' red Historian pen through the crack. "I found this on the road. I believe it belongs to you."

"Now that's exactly what I'm talking about. You know yourself it wasn't really me last night." Marsh ducked as the ballpoint shot toward him. He bent to retrieve it from the pavement. "I mean, people make mistakes, they mistake themselves. If we were home nothing like this would've ever happened." He slid the pen into his shirt pocket, then gazed in the direction of the water tower, trees blowing along the parched Solomon River. "There's just something about this place . . . Being all the way out here."

For a moment Alex slumped in the front seat. She looked off, too. Then she unlocked her door and pushed it open. "All right," she grumbled.

So he couldn't tell her, I'm sending you home. She appeared to be in charge, bringing him out of the wind. As he moved into the van, Alex unfolded the back seat so it seemed they'd entered a small room. Waiting room, Marsh thought, glancing toward Delois' duplex.

Alex rummaged in an ice chest, then reached between the legs of her grizzly. Marsh wondered if she could've gained a little weight since the Rockies. Last night her skin had felt soft as the dust and fuller than anyone might believe from just looking. But then, they hadn't been themselves, sprawled there in the road. Marsh pulled his eyes away, fixed them on the grizzly.

"Where do you think Tiffany is." He spoke as if the little girl had struck out on her own, been gone for months.

"She's with somebody responsible for a change," Alex said. She handed him a glass of iced herbal tea and pointed to a pillow.

Marsh propped the pillow against the van's side so he could see out the opposite window to Senior Citizens. Below the window, Alex sipped at her tea, her legs stretched across the floor. The soles of her sneakers grazed his knee. She touched the back of her hand to her forehead, as if checking her temperature, the heat of the day.

"I don't think he'll be much longer," Marsh said, nodding toward the window. "Reg, I mean."

Alex heaved a sigh. "I'm not even going to ask why you were painting that house."

She wore her silky racing shorts and something that looked like a man's summer undershirt—cotton knit scooped low at her chest, under her arms. No bra as usual. And she wasn't going to ask. Not one question.

Marsh could see her pushing everything aside—the whitewash, the dusty reservoir road.

"I honestly don't want to hear," she said.

"Listen Alex, I'm sorry. Jesus," he said, "I don't know how to tell you . . ." He sat back, relieved he could say even this much. It seemed a tribute to the long time they'd known each other. He and Alex could still talk. Although he held her partly responsible for what had happened last night. She'd lain there in the dark, clinging to him like the world was coming to an end.

Alex must've been thinking about this, too. She fidgeted with her sunglasses, turned her head away.

"I'm not sure," Marsh said. "But maybe if a thing happens only once— I mean, even a terrible thing. Well, maybe you can let it go."

Alex gazed around the van, as if hunting for words. When she finally spoke, her voice straggled low. "I guess you heard, Hole In The Day got married."

Marsh nodded. "It's just that I keep thinking of Richard—his feelings. You understand what I'm saying."

But it seemed Alex didn't understand at all. She was moving onto the story he'd missed that morning, talking vaguely about Algie and Hole In The Day, avoiding everything. Making a clean escape.

Marsh slumped against the pillow. He heard Alex humming, trying to remember a song Algie had sung for Hole In The Day. Marsh decided no wonder Alex and Richard had split. Alex didn't *have* any feelings.

"A number forty-four," Alex said, her voice rocking soft.

Outside, a screen door slammed. But Marsh didn't hear. He looked down, feeling Alex's toes keeping time to the song, nudging the rhythm along his leg.

He cupped his hand around her bobbing sneaker.

Alex stopped. "What?"

"Nothing," he said. He drew his hand away, aware of the flutter in his fingers and Alex shaking her head. "You were wiggling your toes, is all."

"Marsh, please." Alex cleared her throat, steering her eyes past him. "If we have to sit here, just let me do this. Don't talk, don't say anything."

Marsh watched her tucking in her undershirt, pressing the iced tea glass to her flushed face.

"I know I'm a wreck. I mean, it's not like I don't know."

"Alex, look . . ." He tried to think of something comforting to say. But there seemed no comfort for either of them. After a minute he said, "All right. Go ahead, just tell me."

Alex reached up and opened the window, then sat back. The breeze took the closeness from the air. The van seemed roomier—big enough for both of them. Alex's voice gained a little with the story. Maybe some sort of comfort in the telling. She used Reg's words, as if they were the only safe ones left. Hole In The Day was going to Pine Ridge to be with his own people. Taking leave, Alex said. She said Hole In The Day wept at Algie's door. He called Algie his *Codah.*

"His sworn comrade," Alex said.

"Right," Marsh said, hardly listening. His mind was wandering to other people—like Richard. His own son. He wanted to pull out his wallet, check to see if Richard's picture was still there. To ask Alex how to go on.

But Alex couldn't go on with anything except somebody else's past. Marsh heard her describing an old rifle, calling it a smoothbore, as if she knew. She said Algie had given the rifle to Hole In The Day. And Hole In The Day had asked to know the number.

"And so Algie told Hole In The Day it was a forty-four." Alex reached over, touched Marsh's arm. "I'm pretty sure there's more with that rifle. Reg almost lost his voice. He's looking worse—you must've noticed."

"Reg," Marsh said, sitting straight. He stared out the window. The old man had been inside the duplex too long—too long for only the good parts.

Marsh tried to stand, his head grazing the ceiling.

Alex reached to stop him. "Wait, there's something else. If I could just tell you—"

"Not now," Marsh said.

He ducked past the grizzly, out the rear of the van. The street was empty. Drapes had been drawn across the windows of Delois' duplex. A note fluttered on her front door. Marsh pinned the scrap of paper with his finger, holding it still in the breeze. *James, Come to the church. Prayer Fellowship today and hot covered dish.*

Alex stepped behind him. She took a deep breath, as if catching up with herself. She rested her hand at his back, gave a little cough. "Who's James?"

"Take your hand off me, Alex."

She leaned around him. "What's this supposed to mean—hot covered dish."

"Nothing," he said. He knocked at the door. "Covered dishes were before your time." He knocked louder. No one answered. He blamed Alex—she'd trapped him in her van, forced him to sit and listen. He pointed to the note, as if to show her what she'd done. "Cooking was before your time, Alex. Covered wagons, covered dishes . . . Real feelings."

She grabbed for his sleeve as he raced back to the curb. He glanced to the church, thinking maybe Reg had gone there. Or he could've just stumbled off with Delois' story still slamming in his ears.

"Real *feelings?*" Alex was suddenly hollering, chasing him across the street. "You think it's just you and Richard. You and Richard all the time. Well, I've got a whole lot more on my mind. God bless it," she shouted. "Listen to me!"

But he had no time to listen. He rushed up to the church, then stopped. He thought of Delois, her brown eyes flashing on him. And the angry man from Senior Citizens—he'd probably be inside, too, asking God to lock all the gates to the Rose Bowl. Let no white man enter.

Marsh swung around as Alex raced up beside him. "Do me a favor— take a look in there and tell me if you see Reg."

"Do *you* a favor?"

"I'll explain later."

"Forget it," she said. She tramped up the church steps. "I'm doing this for Reg."

After a minute she slipped from the church, shaking her head. "Maybe he walked to the roadside rest."

He could've walked into the river, Marsh thought. But Alex knew nothing about the Gossip Book. She had more to think about, more than Marsh or Richard. Marsh felt almost disappointed hearing this. But at least the church had taken all of Alex's anger. She'd gone back to the real world, stirred by the big white piano she'd spotted in the sanctuary, which had somehow put her in mind of religious wars.

"Listen, Alex, I don't know exactly how to say this . . ." Marsh dropped both hands onto her shoulders. "I think you should go home."

He caught her in mid-sentence. She was talking about Christian Democrats and an explosive force equaling a quarter ton of TNT. A man had been sitting in his office in east Beirut. Alex touched her head to Marsh's chest. "He would've been the youngest president they ever had."

"Alex, please." Marsh spoke to the air, because her forehead still rested at his chest, and she wasn't listening but speaking only in these details he didn't want to hear. "Spare me," he said.

"This happened on the same day Princess Grace died."

"Princess Grace," he said, but the name was only a fairy tale, a face in a movie. And Alex would not spare him.

"His brother dug his body out of the building."

"Come to Nebraska," he said.

He caught a roughness in his words, like the forced pronunciation of a foreigner. And in his hands, a fierceness, too. Alex lifted her head.

"Be there," he said. Then, before she could speak, he rushed off the curb and up the road to find Reg.

When he reached the far corner, he came to a halt. He stood a moment, panting for breath and shaking his head because he couldn't for the life of him remember how old Richard was. But he couldn't think about it now. He needed to talk to Reg, get into Nebraska as fast as possible. He should catch up with Tiffany, too. He was losing track of people, losing his grasp, maybe his mind.

"Mind like a steel trap," he said, rushing on. No, that was Jewel with the steel trap. One more person he'd left in the lurch. Because Jewel was going to get trampled on that game show. Beaten by miles—this distance they'd traveled to hear all the facts backwards.

He headed for the roadside rest, then detoured into weeds. A big green harvester bounced down the road. Two black men waved from a high wraparound cab.

The harvester stopped alongside him. A riffraff of wheat swarmed the air like insects trailing an enormous animal.

The young driver pushed open his door and sneezed into the yellow dust. "You lost?" he hollered above the engine's noise. "There's somebody waiting over to the picnic tables—says he thinks there's a missing person. You the one?"

Marsh started to answer, but just then Alex roared past steering wide to avoid the harvester. At the van's rear window the grizzly rocked, claws splayed at the glass like a wave good-bye.

The two men craned in their swivel seats, watching Alex bump onto the highway.

"Where's she going in such a big hurry?" the driver wanted to know.

"Nebraska," Marsh said. He gazed toward the roadside rest and the Establishment. But he couldn't see Reg.

"Now, Nebraska's where you do not want to be lost. They've got 6,000 square miles up there without a paved road. You won't have a chance of anybody finding you."

"Plus you're a quart low on oil." The second man jerked a thumb over his shoulder. "We checked under your hood—thought you might be stopped for engine trouble."

"I'll put some in," Marsh said, stepping back to the road.

"Well, don't be a stranger." The driver grinned. "We've got a lot of history in this town. You might be interested."

"Yes," Marsh said. He moved off, hearing the driver calling after him.

"And when you get back to California, tell everybody we're still here. We're hanging on."

"I will," Marsh hollered. He dashed for the motor home, trying to imagine who in California could be sitting up nights waiting to hear that news.

Reg met him at the side door. The sight of the old man almost took his breath. Alex was right—Reg looked worse. Even dressed up like this—white linen suit, blue shirt, red tie—all this for Delois Lebow. Just to have his nose rubbed in the dirt under Delois' bed. She'd pulled the old man down there, as Jesus was her witness. She'd crumpled that linen suit in her long lavender hands. Reg himself appeared crumpled. Delois had rolled him like a ball, tossed him under her bed.

"I knew it," Marsh snapped, leaping into the Establishment. He wished he'd painted Delois' house with white enamel. He should've rented a spray gun. He slammed the side door shut, hurled Reg's buffalo robe into the passenger seat, then flung himself behind the wheel.

Reg hesitated in the aisle, his shiny hands clutching the dinette counter. His voice quavered.

"I feel I should tell you—"

"It doesn't matter," Marsh said. He dug for his keys, then looked out at the Historical Marker standing cool beside his window. *In July 1877, Negro exodusters* . . . Marsh thought of all the politicians he'd ever watched on TV—men pounding their fists on podiums declaring, Let history show. And he believed he'd seen it all, every morning getting up, on the job, at night before he fell asleep. His face in the mirror, a country created in his image. Marsh turned from the window, sank back in his seat. It seemed he might've been a very good American except for not ever having lived there.

Reg stepped up the aisle. The old man moved with a halting jerkiness, as if he'd lost all balance. Marsh reached to steady him.

"A moment," Reg said, leaning against his seat back. His hand shook, fumbling at his trouser pocket.

"If it's about your father, you don't have to tell me," Marsh said. He sounded like Alex—no questions asked. He started the engine, then sat gripping the steering wheel. He felt the direct force of his hands falling to Alex's shoulders. He'd said, Be there.

Reg eased himself into the passenger seat. He opened his fingers and blinked at the small articles he'd taken from his pocket. "She gave these to me, complimentary. With compliments from Miss Delois Lebow."

Marsh watched the old man arranging the items on the console between them—one red Historian pen, a key chain shaped like Kansas, and a miniature glass vial containing God knew what. Probably poison, Marsh thought. Maybe nerve gas. Sitting there, Reg looked small as a child—susceptible.

Marsh reached across for the old man's seat belt and snapped it.

Reg nodded into his face. "You realize life is far too short. If there was only time . . ."

Marsh revved the engine, shifted into first. "We've got time."

"But there is something—before we go on."

"Just one stop for oil," Marsh said. As they pulled away, he glanced to the rearview. Behind them, the blue water tower rose above dry cottonwoods, sagging houses, Senior Citizens. And two young men, still there—hanging on.

"Those fellows said we were a quart low."

"They believed it was engine trouble." Reg inched his hand under his seat belt, touched his chest. "The trouble is here, of course. The heart hurts."

Marsh jammed the Establishment into second, then third. Kansas blurred along the highway. Soon they'd see Nebraska. They'd cross the Platte River, swing north.

"Listen to me," Marsh said. He caught Reg by the wrist, yanking the old man away from Delois' words. Delois had been the one standing at the door, her fingers gleaming in shirred lavender, her man's watch flashing. *Her* words: Everybody hurts.

"I don't care what she told you." He let go of Reg and swept his hand across the console, scattering every reminder.

Reg leaned over his seat belt. He strained for the floor, straining past his feet toward the red pen, blue key chain, glass vial. He couldn't reach. "They're only small," he whispered. "Small things."

"Leave them," Marsh said.

But Reg was struggling with his seat belt, fingers grappling over his his chest to work free. Marsh couldn't look. He'd seen this once in his imagination—a man tearing at his chest. It was years ago in the hospital waiting room. A nurse came in with a cup of coffee. Someone had just died. The nurse described a man scratching at his chest, as if with a very bad itch. She said, They often do this. It's a sign.

Marsh slammed on the brakes, steering into black-eyed Susans lining the road. "Sit still," he said to Reg. "Sit still, dammit." He slapped the old man's hands away, unfastened the seat belt.

"There's no call for temper," Reg whispered.

"Use your voice, damn you. Are you going to blame your father for—" Marsh leaned past Reg's legs and groped below the dashboard, "for his weakness? Do you think nobody's ever done one terrible thing— not once in their whole life?"

Reg shifted his feet and stared down at the floor. "If it should be broken . . ."

"Just stick to your story, the hell with what she says." Marsh grabbed the little glass vial. It was no bigger than a matchstick. "Let the story be," he said, dumping everything into Reg's lap.

He brushed grains of gravel from his knees, then slumped behind the wheel. Let history show, the story be. Let it be about one decent man who brought relief to the poor and life to the dying Indian. Let it be about one good father, a son . . .

Marsh turned the key in the ignition. "I've done a terrible thing," he said.

But Reg was paying no attention. The old man took the glass vial from his lap, then leaned over the console and held it trembling to Marsh's nose. "You understand this is a sample only. Miss Lebow has the full size."

Marsh swatted at Reg's hand. "Are you listening to me? I'm saying something happened . . ."

Then Marsh gave up. He pulled onto the highway, muttering, "Full size."

Reg nodded. "I believe the name she gave me was White Orchid. She prefers it over the stronger Midnight Rhapsody."

Marsh slowed as they approached the next town. WELCOME TO HILL CITY, HOME OF THE 1981 DOUBLE A STATE CHAMPS. More champions, Marsh thought. He shook his head. "If you ask me, that woman goes beyond all sizes. She's an Amazon."

"She's an Avon lady," Reg said.

"Well, I wouldn't put it past her." Marsh tramped on the gas. "She's capable of almost—" He blinked out the windshield as Reg's words caught up with him. "God no," he said.

But he should've known. He'd seen the little catalog lying on Delois' table. And he could see her now, soaring in her lavender robes, flying high above him with the hot covered dish, bound for Prayer Fellowship where her voice reached octaves. Clear to Heaven—amen and hallelujah—Avon calling.

For a few miles they drove without speaking. Outside, even the wind fell silent as if the sun itself had dropped a non sequitur onto the horizon, putting a sudden end to the conversation and this day.

Marsh thumped the steering wheel, then shrugged—casting around. "I mean, an Avon lady. That should tell you something right there."

But exactly what it was Marsh couldn't say. He no longer knew what they were talking about. He switched the Establishment into cruise control and tried to think. Reg had said, I feel I should tell you . . .

Marsh nodded. "Maybe you'd better tell me."

He reached to pull the visors against the low glare. They'd turned west and a little north, toward the Platte River. In Nebraska they'd find a paved road. Marsh felt sure of this, no matter what anybody said.

He looked over at Reg. "Go ahead—whatever it is, I can take it."

Reg tucked the small glass vial into his shirt pocket. He sat with his hand lingering at the pocket—a spot close to his heart where all the trouble was. After a minute he said, "I believe it is love."

A Waltz Across Miles

And everything comes to One,
As we dance on, dance on, dance on.

—Theodore Roethke
"Once More, The Round"

22

"**L**ove," Evie said. She stretched from her chair, poking a stick into the ashes of last night's campfire.

Muriel let out a little groan. "No fool like an old fool, as the saying goes."

"Well, I think it's sweet," Jewel said.

"He's so cute when he talks about her." Evie tossed the stick aside and smiled at Marsh. "Cute as a bug."

Marsh said nothing, unable to get past the words—cute, sweet—words applying only to the pubescent and the elderly. It seemed romance among the old was regressive. Like Jewel's TV game show "Simon Says"—take two baby steps backwards. Marsh looked off to the boxelders screening Soldiers Creek. He wondered at what age a person might ever be mature enough for love.

He'd spent most of the morning sitting here surrounded by women. Frank and Lester had trekked across the road to the Fort Robinson Lodge. Reg was holed up inside the motor home, attending to what he called intimate personal business. The old man scarcely noticed they'd reached Nebraska. His heart remained in Kansas—in the shimmering hands of Delois Lebow.

Earlier, Frank had taken roll call and declared everybody accounted for. Even Sharon. She'd caught a bus from Grand Junction, announcing Marsh had sent for her. Never mind that in Colorado she'd finally been granted Welfare, or that she'd left Big Hermo's Campground where she was definitely needed, having repaired the faulty movie projector and reorganized the tenters' section. She said the least she could do was come when Marsh called. Any emergency—big or small—he could rely on her. But there no longer seemed to be an emergency. Frank had been wrong—not everyone was accounted for. Alex hadn't arrived.

Marsh poured another cup of coffee, thinking Alex could've been delayed by engine trouble. Maybe she'd broken down on one of those unpaved roads he'd heard about. It seemed he should tell somebody—report a missing person. Only a day ago he'd told Alex to be here.

He looked over at Muriel, but she'd already opened her morning newspaper, grumbling about the NFL's plans to walk out after tomorrow night's game.

Marsh moved from his chair. "I'm a little worried about my daughter-in-law."

"A walkout." Evie clucked her tongue. "Frank's going to have a stroke."

"The President says he hopes and prays the two sides can get together."

"You never know," Jewel said. "There could be a last-hour agreement."

Marsh brushed at a bug scaling his pant leg. Maybe Alex had decided to turn around and head for home. Richard might've heard from her. He could try reaching Richard, he owed his son a phone call—a phone call to say the least.

"I'll be at the fort," he said. "I mean, in case anybody's looking for me."

He walked up the campground road, wondering why he'd been so anxious to get to Nebraska. It made no difference that Algie had joined the cavalry here. Algie still loved Saro, regardless. Hole In The Day had taken off for Pine Ridge to marry one of his own people. Reg wouldn't stop talking about Delois Lebow. Coming to Nebraska only made everything worse, although Marsh blamed Delois in the first place. She'd started it all with her red hot Gossip Book. Back in Kansas, she'd cast some kind of spell, handing out little blue key chains and a glass vial—her red Historian pens aimed at the heart like cupid's arrows.

Marsh felt along his shirt pocket, Delois' ballpoint riding the bull's-eye. He wished Alex had never retrieved the pen from the dust where they'd collided. As he passed the campground restrooms, he considered dropping the ballpoint down a toilet, as if that might return him to normal. But Sharon was stepping from the women's half, calling his name. And some part of him refused to go back to normal—not if the one condition for that return was grief.

"Andy," Sharon hollered, hauling Tiffany behind her.

Marsh stopped to wait.

"Those showers are the pits," Sharon said. "They've got the water pressure so high, it's like standing in front of a firing squad. We're lucky we got out of there with any skin left at all."

Marsh nodded. He'd choose guilt over grief any day. He'd answer to Andy forever, if it came to that.

"Plus, they don't spray for bugs. They've got beetles in sinks, frying on light bulbs. Swear to God," Sharon said. "Haven't they ever heard of dimethyl 3?" She waved a hand toward Tiffany. "I even found beetles in this kid's underpants."

Marsh glanced at Tiffany, her curls wrapped in a towel so she looked like a small swami. He thought about mentioning that until recently, Tiffany hadn't owned any underwear—beetles or not. But Sharon hadn't noticed the shelf full of Tiffany's new clothes. She'd breezed in, dumping the baby—his own namesake—into Claire's lap again. It also seemed that since Grand Junction, Sharon had become a consummate campground authority—the self-appointed last word.

None of this came as any surprise to Marsh. Give Sharon an inch, and she'd take a mile. Except it didn't seem to bother him anymore. And this did surprise him.

"I can't believe you dragged me all the way up here," Sharon said. "I asked you for one simple ride, and ever since you've been taking me places I never wanted to go. Now we're smack in the middle of a full-blown beetle plague."

Marsh bent for Tiffany and scooped her in his arms. He flicked one of the small black and red beetles off her sandal, then turned to Sharon.

"I was wondering if you'd do me a favor and call my son. I think he might've heard from Alex."

"You want me to call up a complete stranger?"

"It's just Richard," Marsh said. He glanced away thinking just Richard.

He hitched Tiffany higher on his shoulder and started toward the lodge. "Never mind," he said as Sharon moved after him. "I'll call Richard myself."

Sharon shoved her baggy T-shirt into her jeans. She claimed to have lost almost all the weight she'd gained during pregnancy. Marsh thought she might've. This morning she looked almost petite. Her brown hair gleamed chestnut in the sun, sizzled clean by the machine-gun shower.

"Oh, all right," she said. "I'll do it. You get on the line and right away you'll be spilling your guts about what happened in Kansas."

"I wouldn't—I mean, there's more to it than that." He walked on, remembering yesterday, Alex shouting, I've got a whole lot more on my mind.

Halfway across the grass, he stopped at a log building chinked with adobe. A sign read: 1874 Guardhouse and Adjutant's Office. He held Tiffany to a barred window through which no light seemed to pass. The guardhouse had obviously been reconstructed, but still bleak and true with empty leg irons chained to the rough-planked floor.

Tiffany squirmed, staring between the iron bars. "Snake," she whispered.

"Not here," Marsh said.

As they crossed the narrow highway that cut through the fort, Marsh stopped a moment, glancing up the road.

Sharon nudged him along. "Maybe you don't realize, but you've dropped into a confessional mode." She stepped toward the pay phone outside the lodge. "According to my ex-mental health worker, it's a total thing with men—sort of the male idea of love. You're just plain lucky I got here when I did."

Marsh let Tiffany slide from his arms. The little girl dashed past the phone and up the wide steps of the lodge. Marsh watched her scrambling for the entrance, stumbling beneath a blue banner which read, Through These Portals Passed The World's Finest Horsemen.

"I love my son," Marsh said.

"Take Rolf for instance." Sharon turned to the phone and slapped a beetle off the receiver. "I'd bet every cent I have that Rolf will be showing up any day to give me the complete blow-by-blow of every godawful thing he's done since he took off in the truck without me or Tiffany, not to mention Andy who happens to be his own flesh and blood baby." Sharon opened her cloth purse, then dug into her pocket. "His own precious seed," she said. She tapped Marsh's arm. "I need a quarter."

He handed her his telephone credit card and Richard's number. Richard would be home today, maybe already watching Sunday football. But not after tomorrow night—tomorrow the NFL was going to walk out. Somehow the thought saddened Marsh, the idea of strong, big-shouldered men—grown men—walking out.

Sharon dialed.

Marsh hung at her side. "I'm just worried about Alex, is all. She's been—"

"Will you stop," Sharon said, clamping her hand over the phone. "Go find Tiffany, do something with yourself. I can't talk to a guy I don't even know and deal with a total wreck at the same time."

"I only wanted to say—"

Sharon jabbed a finger into the air like an alarm. "It's him," she whispered. She grimaced at the receiver, then took a big breath. "Hello—" Her voice jumped loud. "Hello, Richie?"

Marsh jiggled her arm. "His name's Richard."

"Listen, Richie, can you hold a second? Just hang on." Sharon covered the phone again and rolled her eyes at Marsh. "This person is not for real."

"I only wanted to say that I loved her—my wife. I wanted you to know that."

Sharon nodded. "This person definitely sucks blood. I think I'm on the line with some kind of vampire here."

Marsh leaned for the receiver. "Let me talk to him. He's my son, for God's sake."

"No way," Sharon said. She shot him a look, then turned back to the phone.

Marsh stood a minute, trying to hear Sharon's end of the conversation. But her voice had dropped low, her blunt hair falling like a curtain as she chinned the receiver. Marsh glanced to the lodge, its white steps flanked by flags where the world's finest horsemen had passed through. On the columned porch, Tiffany had given up her struggle with the big front door. She'd crawled into a high-backed rocker, her head still turbaned by the towel. Marsh started to return the little girl's wave, then swung around hearing Sharon laugh.

"Whoa," Sharon said, her voice whooping from the receiver.

Marsh stared. He'd never heard Sharon really laugh before, never noticed the throaty itch in her words.

"Easy boy," she was saying into the phone. She tossed her head and grinned straight through Marsh. She sounded in sudden high spirits, mounted and ready to ride. "Easy now."

Marsh couldn't listen. He took the lodge steps two at a time, grabbed Tiffany out of the rocker and sank down, plopping the child into his lap.

"Your mother," he said. He glared toward the pay phone, his new generous feeling ground to nothing beneath the rocker. "Your mother is a t-r-a-m-p."

"Pee," Tiffany whispered, tapping a stubby finger along Marsh's knee.

Marsh shook his head. Sharon probably wouldn't even bother to ask about Alex. He frowned across a clipped parade ground, the Stars and Stripes hanging limp from a silver flagpole. Then he glanced down, saw Tiffany clutching both hands at her crotch.

"Tinkle," he blurted, holding Tiffany at arm's length, dashing for the door.

The child looked up at him as if he had no brains at all. "Pee-pee," she said.

He lurched down a hall, spotted a Women's Room, and shoved Tiffany inside. "Tinkle, pee-pee," he muttered, pacing the hall. Hadn't Sharon ever heard of consistency? After a minute he poked his head into the restroom. Tiffany stood at the doorway, thumb in mouth, underpants bunched around her ankles. Marsh gave her a push toward the white stalls. "Just go, dammit."

Somewhere outside a bugle sounded. A bleary staccato echoed through the corridor—notes falling past a tangled trophy of locked elk horns, a buffalo's dim, massive head. Grave-eyed officers seemed to shift behind glass frames. A pale antelope looked wildly alarmed.

But it was only mess call. Marsh's wristwatch said twelve noon. It seemed Sharon had been on the phone all morning. Inside the Women's Room, Tiffany was still going. Marsh knocked on the restroom door, then glanced up, spotting Frank and Lester walking his way. Frank appeared to have grown a whole head taller since breakfast. He looked on the verge of grabbing a sabre off the wall and joining some regiment. Except the cavalry had galloped off years ago. Fort Robinson had turned into a civilian's tour offering trail rides, jeep rides, hay rides—more rides than an amusement park.

Marsh nodded toward the restroom. "Tiffany," he explained.

"I thought maybe you were waiting your turn." Frank chuckled, whacking him on the back.

"We're just here for lunch," Lester said.

"Mess," Frank corrected.

Lester sighed, his face grim against the white painted walls. "I've spent the last three hours in the museum."

"Post Headquarters," Frank said.

"There's a library in the basement." Lester stepped closer, cupped Marsh's elbow. "It seems the historian woman spoke the truth. I read the post returns—a fire broke out in an abandoned barracks. The wife of Musician Algernon Vickers, Troop K, Ninth Cavalry is listed as having perished in the flames."

"Except the two of them were never married," Frank said.

Marsh looked over as the restroom door opened a crack. "Well, they could've been. We don't know for a fact."

"And there was more," Lester said in his whisper voice. He stood glum as rain, clamped in the solitary gray of his coveralls. "There's just no end."

"It'll have to wait," Marsh said, turning for the door.

"Come to mess," Frank called as he and Lester moved away.

"Mess," Tiffany whispered through the door's crack.

Marsh peered inside. A trail of toilet paper ran from the nearest stall to where Tiffany stood. The little girl's underpants had turned a pale sopping yellow. Crumpled toilet tissue rose in a soggy heap, jamming the door. It looked as if Tiffany had been building a dike to divert whole oceans. For a moment Marsh felt a flicker of pride—the work of a budding engineer. Then he heard a toilet down the way exploding in a full flush, the water pressure way too high.

He yanked Tiffany into the corridor. As he grabbed the towel from her head, the child let out a jerky breath. "Don't cry," he said. She'd been holding up so well until now. Until he reached for her dripping pants. "Only a small accident," he said, seeing her eyes well. He wrapped the wet underpants in her towel and led her up the hallway.

Frank waved from a corner table as they stepped into the pine-paneled restaurant. Sharon had also wandered in, finally off the phone. She sat leaning toward Lester who appeared rattled by her attention. Marsh took the chair at her other side and lifted Tiffany onto his knee. Sharon didn't look over. She was busy holding Lester's hand flat on the restaurant menu, palm up. She tapped a spot near Lester's little finger.

"It looks like you've got two kids, maybe three," she said. "Make it three."

Lester kept his gaze on the far wall—a display of bridles, saddles, custom-made snowshoes for mules. "No children," he said.

"Well, you *should've* had three." Sharon glanced from Frank to Marsh. "Something must've happened."

Something happened, Marsh thought, catching the excited bright blue in Sharon's eyes. He sat closer. "Tell me about the phone call."

But she was bending over Lester's palm again. "I think the trouble's in your love line. You see how it starts to disappear right along there?"

"Somebody better talk to Reg," Frank said. "We finally get here, and he decides to go underground. I knew we shouldn't have let him near that historian."

"That's it, all right," Sharon said. "Your love line just keeps fading and fading away."

Lester fumbled at the pocket of his coveralls and removed his tinted glasses. He bowed his head into the glasses, then slid his hands into his lap. "I once had a disappointment," he said softly.

Sharon sighed. "Those three kids never had a chance."

"That's enough." Marsh nudged her in the ribs. "Just tell me about Richard."

"Don't take it so hard," Frank said to Lester. "We've all had our setbacks one time or another."

Sharon looked up from her menu and shrugged. "Richie got a call. Alex told him she was driving on to the Badlands. I guess she decided to bypass Nebraska."

"Well, that's just great," Frank muttered. "All we need is people skipping ahead." He nodded as a waitress stopped alongside their table. "I'll try the buffalo burger and fries."

"Tiffany and I can split one," Sharon said. "You're supposed to go slow, introducing a new food to a kid. Besides which I told Richie I was back down to my ideal weight."

"His name's Richard." Marsh slapped open his menu and read the day's rations: buffalo taco, braised buffalo tips, buffalo burger . . . "I think I'll just have the Mess Sergeant's Surprise," he said, hoping for some variation.

"Nothing for me," Lester whispered.

Sharon glanced his way. "Listen, it's not your fault if you got a lousy love line. Maybe I shouldn't have told you, but I believe in being totally up front, especially when it's somebody's past, present, and future. That's how I am." She nodded at Marsh. "Richie said I sounded like a very basic person."

"What else did he say?" Marsh shifted Tiffany in his lap, easing her thumb from her mouth. "Just tell me how he is."

Sharon smiled. "He asked me for a date."

Marsh blinked at his place mat, a souvenir guide detailing Officers' Row, stables, the wheelwright's shop . . . Finally he turned, staring at Sharon.

"I guess you'd call it a blind date, being as we don't really know each other. I mean, we haven't been formally introduced or anything."

"It would have to be blind," Frank said. He stopped grinning, catching Sharon's scowl. "If you haven't met, that is . . ."

"Plus there's a problem of distance—me here, Richie there. But you never can tell. Who would've thought I'd wind up in Nebraska?"

"Goes to show, nothing's impossible," Frank said.

Marsh sat back as the waitress stepped beside him with the Mess Sergeant's surprise. "It's impossible," he said.

"Oh really?" Sharon reached over and jerked Tiffany into her lap. "I'd like to know where you get off saying what's possible and what's not. Your own daughter-in-law bypassed you for the Badlands. The *Badlands,* for Christ's sake. Then there's your gentleman friend—a man old as dirt, older than a raisin. All of a sudden he's got the hots for somebody he met exactly one time in Kansas."

The waitress leaned, cutting Sharon's buffalo burger in two. "Well, you won't regret coming to Nebraska," she said. "Our state has just about everything to offer."

"I doubt it," Sharon said. "We're talking horny people here. The whole United States wouldn't be big enough for them."

"Excuse me," the waitress mumbled, her sober face coloring. She turned to Lester, as if he might be the one safe individual. "This fort played a very large part."

"I know," Lester said in his sorrowful voice.

Frank took a bite of his buffalo burger, then swiped his mouth with a napkin. "Just what I figured—every place has some food that's absolutely rotten but they're positive you'd like to eat it." He shrugged at the waitress. "But I guess when in Rome . . ."

The waitress nodded. "Crazy Horse was killed here."

"Yes," Lester whispered.

Marsh glanced over and saw Lester sinking lower in his chair. His face looked faded as his love line. But then, Lester had been in the museum library all morning. He'd read the post returns. He knew about Crazy Horse, the barracks fire—knew this and more. Still, Marsh wondered. What kind of disappointment could it have been to cause such despair?

"Don't think I don't realize," Sharon said. She slid a French fry off Frank's plate and folded it into Tiffany's mouth. "I mean, Richie doesn't exactly sound like my type."

"Not in a million years," Marsh said. He wished Sharon would stop going on about it. The longer she talked, the more clearly he saw his son on the phone asking Sharon for a date—Richard's deadpan eyes, a mocking smile signaling a joke only he could find amusing.

"Will there be anything else?" the waitress asked.

Sharon shook her head. "Knowing me, I'd probably go out with the guy. I tend to be attracted to inappropriate people. My ex-mental health worker says I have this pattern. I like being a victim."

Marsh looked down at his lunch, thick tomato sauce oozing over clotted cheese.

"I hope you enjoy your meal," the waitress said. She placed a little packet of Parmesan at Marsh's plate. "It's our buffalo lasagna."

Marsh stepped from the pay phone and stood a minute, gazing north to the pale buttes rising beyond the parade ground. For the first time in days there was no wind, and he kept thinking he should feel relieved. Every morning, every hour, he'd faced the same drilling breeze. It seemed he'd chased Muriel's golf cap all over Kansas and half of Nebraska. He'd rescued plastic tablecloths tangled like kites in the branches of trees. He'd prevented mass suicides of lawn chairs hurtling toward campground pools. Across these plains, the wind provoked boundless chaos. Marsh himself had never felt such hatred for his hair. He held the wind partially responsible for what had happened with Alex.

Yet he missed that familiar warm breeze. He started down a lane bordering the parade ground, thinking even the trees looked lonely. They flanked the lane in military fashion, straight as picket lines. They'd been planted to break the wind. They stood now, limbs locked as if against the next charge, braced like seasoned soliders when the enemy has become strangely quiet.

During lunch, Marsh had thought about going after Alex. He'd left his Mess Sergeant's Surprise and headed back to camp. Reg was still shut inside the motor home. On the Establishment's door, Evie had posted a notice in red felt pen: *If this rig is rocking, don't bother knocking.* Marsh ripped the note away, but he hadn't knocked. He'd dashed to the Southwind and flipped through Frank's campground directory. He copied the three numbers listed for the Badlands, then returned to the lodge and dialed from the pay phone. Alex had registered at Pinnacle View Campground. The office manager told Marsh she'd checked in that morning, then gone out. "There's an afternoon fossil walk," the manager said. Marsh had left the lodge number, just in case. But he didn't think Alex would call.

At the corner he turned, continuing around the parade ground. He stepped beside a long, low-slung building set back on the grass. A sign placed near the entrance read: Musicians' Barracks.

Marsh dug into his pocket for the paper place mat he'd kept from lunch. He studied the blue map printed on the paper, then moved down Officers' Row. Tree-shaded houses faced the clear expanse of parade ground, their backs turned from the wild prairie and steep rugged buttes. Wooden markers bearing names of officers stood white as picket fences outside every door. Capt. Guy V. Henry, Lt. M.A. Batson, Capt. Henry J. Nolan . . .

He supposed it could be the stillness—the low silver sky causing the air to feel close and hushed—this stillness turning old trees secretive and all the grass darkest green. But it seemed the markers gave current addresses, these men here, behind windows draped in cavalry blue and tied with golden cords. They sat diagramming field drills, skimming post returns. Their high-polished boots stood at ease by the door. While up the road, the musicians tuned their instruments, then struck their perfect pitch. And the note they sounded was for all the world Male—honorable and heraldic—a note held forever. A note more tender than a woman's love. Marsh thought so, he believed so. He walked on in the full company of men, and for just an instant it seemed for all the world like coming home.

Historical markers dotted the lane. Marsh saw that Crazy Horse had passed this way en route to the guardhouse. The year was 1877. But that was before Algie had enlisted. Marsh stepped away, studying the date on a sign where the post chapel had stood. Then an ordnance store. And finally, the site of a cavalry barracks once used to hold a band of Cheyenne.

The marker said, Cheyenne Outbreak. Marsh skimmed the words, looking for a year. *Northern Cheyenne taken into custody . . . Imprisoned in this log barracks, they escaped on January 9, 1879 . . . Last ones killed or captured . . .*

Algie had fallen in love at first sight. Sometime during those early years he'd taken up teaching in Mr. Grant's schoolhouse. Marsh stared at the marker, wondering if Algie, hero of the great Indian Wars, had ever seen action at all. It seemed he'd encountered no one but Hole In The Day, a praying Indian—his sworn comrade.

This barracks destroyed by fire on March 22, 1898 . . .

Marsh headed back toward the lodge. It wouldn't hurt to check for a message, or maybe he'd try calling Alex again. Then he remembered the post returns. Listed as having perished in the flames, Lester said. Seems Saro Jones was burned up in a house fire—that was Delois speaking. Marsh could hear her voice thundering oral history over his head. He looked up and saw the low clouds suddenly streaking lavender, Delois storming the whole sky. One baby—a bastard child—came through.

Marsh grabbed Delois' ballpoint from his pocket and raced back to the marker. He scribbled the year on his place mat, then made a dash for Post Headquarters. He streaked past a tennis court, a magpie pecking at the serve line. A silver squirrel bolted across his path, two cottontails took cover under a cannon. The still air hovered like twilight. A frog leapt down the wooden steps as Marsh trudged up.

A woman met him at the door, catching him by surprise. He'd expected a man. But the woman seemed in charge, nodding from under a felt trooper's hat.

"It's determined to rain," she said. She pivoted, dealing postcards into a wire rack like a deadeye. "Our exhibit rooms begin to your right. If you'll give us a second of your time and sign our register on your way out . . ."

"I'd like to see the post returns," Marsh said. He spoke to her back, the yellow triangle of a neckerchief against her deep blue shirt. Except for her shoes—penny loafers flashing dimes—she looked dressed for a field campaign. On her sleeve she wore a corporal's double chevron, a half-inch stripe raced the length of her trousers.

"Glory," she said, doing an about-face. "You make the second one today. And this is supposed to be our slow season." She disappeared around a doorway marked Museum Office. "Things come in stupefying streaks," she called. "Never rains but it pours."

Marsh waited. He signed the register, then stepped to a painting of a long-legged sorrel displayed on a mint green wall. An arrow directed visitors up a staircase, beneath the yellow banner of Company C. Marsh stopped at the entrance to Exhibit Room One, a rifle mounted there and a small card reading: The Sharps Rifle, Caliber .44, Model 1873.

The woman emerged from the office, jingling keys on a braided leather quirt. She led Marsh through a hallway, then marched him down basement steps.

"I wish our curator hadn't gone home with his sciatic nerve," she said. "We don't get that many people interested in the details."

"Well, I am," Marsh said. He blinked along the dim stairwell, ducking an insulated furnace pipe overhead. "I understand this fort played quite a part."

"Believe it or not," the woman said, as if she didn't quite. "The excitement just never stops."

She flicked light switches right and left as they moved deeper into the basement. At the end of a cement corridor, she pulled up and sorted through her keys. Then she leaned to a dark varnished door and flung it open.

"Enter, thrill-seeker," she said.

Marsh watched her veering around the musty room, pulling the chain on an overhead lamp, snatching the plastic hood from a microfilm screen.

"Will you be having any desire for the copy machine?" she asked, finger aimed on the button.

"I'm not sure," he said. Shelves lined the walls, crammed higher than his head with books. Across the concrete floor, filing cabinets stood shoulder to shoulder—deep-drawered, mouths shut.

He glanced up at the furnace pipe mazing the ceiling, wrapped white as a shroud. Up there—above ground—he heard the rain suddenly battering, the tramp of every infantry, the cavalry's pounding charge. Men by the hundreds, thousands, and he would never find just one. It would take months and years of post returns, a million miles of microfilm parading names and dates. And the returns still coming in. There was no end.

"I hope to heaven you're not camping in this rain," the woman said.

Marsh stared at the microfilm reader. "There's a group of us," he mumbled, realizing he didn't have the first idea how to use that machine.

"They tell me the boxelder bugs are on the rampage down there. I can't figure what it is, gets into those bugs. Some years you don't see a solitary one."

The woman looked down, shaking her head over a notebook lying beside the reader. "I hope this Mr. Harmon has a good memory for facts. He spent the morning down here, then blundered off without his notes."

Marsh stepped to the table. Outside, the rain beat harder. Between the officers' slick adobe quarters, Crazy Horse was passing without incident to the guardhouse. The Northern Cheyenne fled, falling across the parade ground like hail. Saro having perished in flames no storm could ever put out.

"Leave them," he said as the woman turned away with Lester's notes.

"Mr. Harmon's in my group, we're looking for the same person. A musician, Algernon Vickers. Troop K, Ninth Cavalry."

The woman gave a nod. "Yes, I know the name."

"Lester Harmon," Marsh said. "I'll see that he gets his notes."

"Algernon Vickers," she said. "I could've told you. He was the last one. In history we keep track of things like that—things like the first one killed, the last. Those names are always written down."

"But Algie—Mr. Vickers—didn't die here. He has a son, they went to California." They'd crossed the divide, Algie had stood on his head. "I've seen a photograph," Marsh said.

"I didn't mean killed *per se.*" The woman reached into her trouser pocket and pulled out a gold badge that read Volunteer Guide. She pinned the badge to her shirt, as if assuming her official capacity.

"Musician Algernon Vickers," she said, handing Marsh the notebook. "On detached service, Company K, Ninth Cavalry. Conspicuous bravery in action with Indians. White Clay Creek, 1890."

Marsh flipped open the notebook. "Hold on," he said, scribbling to keep up.

"He was the last black soldier to receive a Medal of Honor in the west, the last one ever to win it on American soil."

Marsh stopped writing. "Algie?"

"You're lucky that soldier was the last one, otherwise you'd be going blind trying to spot him in the returns. I lost my twenty-twenty over Spencerian penmanship. Our files are chock-full."

Marsh caught the woman's blue sleeve. "I need to see them—the files."

The volunteer heaved a sigh, picking through her keys again. "It's just a blessing we had so many illiterates in those days. Can you imagine history if everybody'd known how to write?"

She stepped to the oak cabinets, moving from one to the other, her shoulders squared, as if inspecting troops at a dress parade. "I doubt you'll want to go past 1898," she said. "Your man left with the Ninth that year—got orders for Chickamauga, then Cuba. Troop C led the charge up San Juan Hill. The rest, as they say, is history." She turned to leave, then glanced back at him.

"I'd stay and give you a hand if I wasn't manning the fort by myself."

"That's all right," Marsh said, following her to the door. "Except there is one thing—about White Clay Creek. Where is it exactly?"

"Just over the border, near Pine Ridge." The volunteer reached around the doorway, ran a finger down a shelf of books and pulled one out. "There's a map here from the Engineer's Office, Department of the Platte. General Brooke had it made for the Sioux Campaign. Have you been to the Badlands yet?"

"No," Marsh said. He glanced down as she handed him the book. *Pine Ridge 1890: An Eyewitness Account of the Events Surrounding the Fighting at Wounded Knee.*

"Well, it isn't far. You'll want to make the trip."

"Yes," Marsh said, staring at the book. He thought of Hole In The Day gone to Pine Ridge to be with his people.

"That's where everything happened." The woman stepped from the room. "Believe me, you won't be disappointed."

Marsh watched her striding away, down the long basement corridor. "Is there a list?" he called after her. "A list of the dead."

But the volunteer marched on. "As you were," she barked, then vanished up the stairs.

For a minute Marsh stood at the doorway, not knowing where to begin. It seemed everything had happened right here in the basement—just now, the story told to him in not so many words. And he would be disappointed. He felt it, he felt almost sick as if with a dull low-grade fever that would never have kept him home. He'd already come this far.

He moved to the microfilm table. He didn't sit so much as perch on his chair, watching for the returns—the name of the last black man to flash across the screen. He placed the book on the table, then turned to Lester's notes. But Lester had written nothing after the first entry. *White Clay Creek. December 30, 1890. Medal of Honor, Sioux Campaign. Pine Ridge, South Dakota.*

Marsh reached down and pulled up his socks. It had been college—that long since he'd spent a rainy afternoon in a library. But not ever so quiet as this. Back in camp, Tiffany might be taking a nap with her big white box. Reg probably hadn't set foot outside the Establishment, not in this weather. Why hadn't Reg who knew all the details—why hadn't he mentioned Algie's Medal of Honor—the last one ever on American soil.

Finally Marsh opened the book—a collection of newspaper reports filed by a man who'd been on the spot. A man who knew how to write.

Today at 2 o'clock the Ninth Cavalry, Major Henry in command, moved out toward the Badlands. A shout from 1,000 throats shook the air, while the gallant colored boys rode by. It is believed that Major Henry, with his brunettes, will close up from the north and southwest and Major Whiteside, with his battalion of the Seventh Cavalry, will edge in simultaneously.

Marsh skimmed down the pages, one after another.

The hostiles would neither surrender nor return with the friendlies. More than a dozen of the supposedly friendly Indians have turned traitor. There seems great fear that others will join the hostile camp some miles north.

It is now very cold and a storm is expected, which will cause much suffering . . .

Marsh pushed the book aside. He wondered if Reg had even been told this part of the story. Maybe Algie had stopped short, bypassing the winter of 1890. Otherwise who would've known the Ninth was anywhere near Wounded Knee? And where did it say that Company C led the charge up San Juan Hill? When those Rough Riders finally crested the hill, did they find the black Ninth already there—Algie greeting them with the Light Cavalry Overture adapted for French horn?

For a moment Marsh had the feeling he'd inadvertently tuned in to some cable TV channel on the microfilm screen—a network presenting Black Week In Review, Black Entertainment Now, Black Business, Black Shoppers' Guide, and Avon and You. Black people thronged the screen, doing everything. They'd thought up the New Deal—someone had been telling Marsh that. Before Roosevelt. Any second he'd be hearing how the first person to walk on the moon was actually black, except nobody knew.

Marsh shoved from his chair, crossed the room, and threw open the files. He started anywhere, because it didn't matter now. He knew nothing. A folder of old clippings fell at his feet. He bent, gathering them up.

We were favored last evening with a treat by the Ninth Cavalry Band who got up a lively minstrel show of original Darky Melodies performed by original Darkies.

Marsh slapped the folder shut. He dropped it into a drawer and kept going. He picked through files until his eyes blurred, looping and sliding with all the words that had ever been written by those who knew how. Until he found Algie's file—a man raised on the King's English, conspicuous in action, the last black man. A file held together by a big rubber band.

I am sorry to report that William Sibbitt of our command died last night. We all turned out and buried him with the honors of war. The surgeon said homesickness was the most the matter with him. He called all the time for his mother.

The folder bulged with letters, erratic notes on foolscap, scraps with a single sentence, one crumpled receipt from the sutler's store. Other papers—official documents, recipes, musical compositions—had been printed in a tight careful hand.

> Specification—In this, that he, Sergeant Algernon Vickers, Regimental Band, on detached service Company K, 9th Cavalry, did blatantly disobey an order relative to the key in which he was commanded to play Stable Call. This on or about the 8th day of September, 1890, at the hour of 3:45 P.M..

Marsh stepped to the copy machine and pushed the button. He fed the machine by hand, glad for something to do—something mindless and mechanical. But his eyes kept catching.

> I have written seven more letters for Relax Hale who is hoping for a furlough at month's end. There is a girl digging leeks in Indiana who he wants in the worst way to see.

> Escort Duty Monday last. Did not locate Hole In The Day while at the agency, but understand his health abides.

> Outfit all drunk.

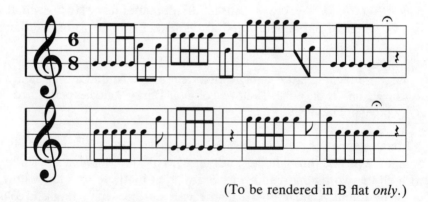

(To be rendered in B flat *only*.)

Marsh crammed the file back into its drawer, then slipped ten dollars from his wallet and left it beside the machine. He climbed the dim basement steps, nearly colliding with the volunteer corporal on her way down.

"I see you had the presence of mind to remember your notes," she said.

Marsh juggled the thick stack of copied papers, trying to shake her hand. "You've been a very big help."

"At ease," she said and waved him out the door.

Marsh started down the lane, relieved the rain had finally stopped. He was already past the old firehouse before he realized he'd been walking in the wrong direction. He blamed the library. He felt disoriented by decades—by dress parades and Stable Call. The sight of a single car parked outside the blacksmith's shop startled him. The woman in the museum had been wrong. He'd lost his presence of mind. And Algie wasn't the last black man. The last one could only be Reg who'd remained behind and grown so old he'd become the true father. Because Algie would never age. Because his name had been written down and because he was gone forever, he would always need fathering.

For a minute Marsh quit walking. He gazed north beyond the glistening buttes and the far gray sky, where the army had moved out and a thousand shouts shook the air as they rode by, and it seemed to him that all of history held an enormous grieving—one long walk backwards down a trail of tears where everything behind you still lay ahead.

Or maybe it was just this place where original darkies had performed, where everyone but Crazy Horse knew the route led only to the guardhouse. Or this day still waiting for wind. But it would be evening soon. Dusk already filled the cavernous doorway of the stallion stable. Rain had plowed the wide corrals, turned them black and loamy. To the south, the pine hills wallowed into the pale White River. The buttes became vulnerable, revealing their weaknesses in shadows where some nocturnal animal might find the passage north. A man could travel through.

Marsh backtracked up the road, surprising a prairie dog busy digging out from the rain. He walked directly to the pay phone. He rummaged through his pants pocket for the number, then dialed. The office manager answered. She told him to please hold the line, they owned a go-cart precisely for this purpose. She'd bring Alex straight to the phone. Marsh waited, deciding he'd never liked anyone on such short notice as this office manager who got right to the point, no questions asked, when he himself didn't know the point, or exactly what the purpose was.

"Hello?" Alex said, as if just anyone might be calling her at Pinnacle View Campground in the Badlands.

"It's me," Marsh said. He shoved Algie's papers onto the narrow shelf beneath the phone. "I thought you'd be here."

"Oh, Marsh—"

He believed she was going to burst out in tears. He knew her so well. He glanced across the parade ground to the walled buttes. It seemed she stood right behind them, crying into the Badlands.

"I needed to think," she said.

"What's wrong with talking—just tell me." He heard his voice rising like an argument, but it was only fear. After all they'd been through, to reach a place they couldn't get past. He wanted to explain about how sometimes between death and passion there could be a confusion. Because it struck him that it had never been love—not even lust—but grief slamming them on that dark reservoir road. "We should be talking," he said. "Instead you're up there wandering around looking at fossils."

"I never went on the fossil walk. I mean, I couldn't."

Marsh felt her sigh, the absent breeze in his ear.

"I had to go to Pine Ridge." Alex paused. When she spoke again, Marsh had to plug his free ear to catch her voice. "Hole In The Day was killed."

Marsh stared at the phone, trying to follow this quick change in the conversation. He rested his hand on the crisp stack of papers. "I know," he said.

It seemed he'd always known, but had just now heard. Hole In The Day was killed. Alex had to go to Pine Ridge. This might've happened only an hour ago.

"There's more," Alex said. "Maybe you should come, when are you coming?"

Marsh nodded, thinking, always more. "I was in the library today. There are some things—"

"It's just so hard here." He heard her voice crack. "I thought leaving home might help, I really did."

"Calm down," he said. He tried to smile. "Just how bad can the Badlands actually be?"

"It's not them," she said. "This has nothing to do with them."

Marsh straightened his papers, took a deep breath. "Okay, it's not the Badlands. You say it's not Richard, not me. Tell me exactly what's bothering you."

"I can't. I have to figure this out by myself."

"No you don't," Marsh said. He remembered miles back—Reg saying, It's a pity you couldn't find someone to go with you.

"Anyway," Alex said. "I hope you won't mention anything about Hole In The Day. To Reg, I mean."

"I'm pretty sure he knows," Marsh said.

"Well, regardless."

Marsh considered asking about Algie then. He could ask if she'd been to White Clay Creek. But he felt a silence falling around that question, falling around everything. He couldn't ask. And Alex was already telling him good-bye. There was a constellation watch at the National Park. The stars would be coming out any minute. She said she needed to go, it might help.

"Yes," Marsh said, glancing from the phone booth. But clouds still clotted the Nebraska sky.

He hung up and headed across the parade ground. He pictured stars blazing all over the Badlands. He wondered if it was possible to glimpse the northern lights from there. What would that latitude be? He wished he'd thought to bring his charts from the *Whither Thou*. Except those maps wouldn't do him any good. He'd strayed too far inland. It seemed he had only Algie's story to go by, not even the glimmer of a star for help.

But no matter. He carried the story with him, slap-slapping against his arm. Tonight he'd put all the pages in order, read them start to finish, from every latitude and longitude. Then spread out his plotting sheets and set a course. He'd get things straight with Alex, put his own house in order. Then he'd take Reg all the way to the end. After which, the rest was history. I doubt you'll want to go past 1898, the museum volunteer had told him. Marsh had written that year on the back of his place mat.

He crossed the road, then stopped. He unfolded the blue place mat from his pocket and stared at the date. It was the year Algie had gone to Cuba. He'd been charging up San Juan Hill when the barracks burned. A bastard child had come through. Marsh squinted into the darkening air, struggling to do the subtraction in his head. Finally he reached for Delois' pen. He smoothed the place mat on Algie's stack and scribbled the numbers. In the twilight, he borrowed from the eight, took another from the nine. He found the remainder and proved it the way he'd been taught in school.

Then he started over the grass. He'd almost reached the guardhouse when he heard the bugle sound. Somewhere off to his left, a frog quit singing. Locusts high in trees suddenly ceased their buzz, like every power line for miles going down. A full minute, and not a single leaf or any living thing stirred. Because the call was Retreat—a call from labor. All men could leave the field. The flag was at rest, no horse without pasture. Only this sound for one whole minute lasting forever—a sound rising and falling, calling everywhere, all is well, the day is done. Come home.

And so Marsh kept walking, passing the bleak guardhouse, the adjutant's office. Until he reached the campground. He found Reg sitting in front of a smoking campfire, logs sizzling from the rain. Reg had written Delois Lebow a letter that looked like an entire box of stationery. The letter wouldn't fit into an envelope—at least that's what Marsh thought the trouble was. Reg sat sputtering along with the fire, creasing deckle-edge stationery on his madras plaid knee. There also seemed to be some new problem with the boxelder beetles. Evie had stripped the Southwind of anything that could be moved. Picnic tables were heaped with towels, sheets, plastic plates, cups, saucers, flatware for six, an all-season full-figure wardrobe. A very big garage sale appeared to be taking place. Tiffany was apparently selling everything, except her white box without which she would've been altogether naked. Across the way, Sharon stood hollering for Claire to climb out of her Micro-Mini, but then somebody dashed by shouting, Don't bother. Claire didn't have any intention of being seen until Princess Grace was buried, and it had already been almost a whole week with Grace lying there under glass in the cathedral. In state. Of course, Claire seldom showed her face anyway. Jewel could be seen, though. In three days she was leaving for her upcoming appearance on national TV. She'd wandered over to tell Marsh she was trying a new hairstyle—experimenting for the camera. As she spoke, Frank suddenly rushed by, lugging a gallon can of white gas. He said thank God Muriel had managed to save the crepe paper for the Anti-Freeze Dance. "Canceled by rain," he shouted, lumbering away. Marsh hadn't even known the dance was scheduled for tonight.

"I need your opinion," Jewel said in her faint, sweet voice. She turned before the campfire so Marsh could inspect her hair—a wisp swept high and blue-gray. "How do you like it up?" she asked.

Marsh couldn't say. He couldn't imagine what to make of it—not just Jewel's hair, but everything that seemed to be happening here. He'd answered the bugle call, he'd left the field. But there was no retreat. Somehow he didn't mind. He felt strangely honored that Jewel had asked his opinion. He gave her a nod, and she smiled.

And then—he would never be able to tell the reason why—he stepped past Jewel to the billowing smoke. His eyes watered instantly, but he bent closer, feeding the fire. First his paper place mat, then Algie's recipe for Fort Robinson punch, Algie's plea for a married man's quarters, three pages providing proof positive that the lowly Osage orange should enjoy the status of a tree. The flames leapt up, grew brighter. Forty-two original bugle calls of such confusing intricacy as to cause a nation's downfall. All to be played in B flat. A diary entry written from a place called Harney Springs. *The blizzard is increasing. We made a forced march of eighty miles and did not see a sign of the hostiles. Twenty men were tied in their saddles owing to snow blindness. Our instruments are jammed. The spittle freezes in my throat.*

Tiffany dropped her big white box, she was so taken by the flames. Sharon stopped hollering, Claire stared out her window. *For a better part of this month, the bread has been bitter and unwholesome.* Evie drew up a chair. *Did not locate Hole In The Day, but understand his health abides.*

The fire blazed on and on in the darkness. For a while it seemed the flames would never go out. Marsh let the last paper slide from his hand. *For Jove himself sits in the azure skies, And laughs below at lovers' perjuries. . . .*

And then the fire began to dwindle. Blue flames lapped here and there, streamed to nothing but smoke. The papers settled into ashes, making the soft shushing sound of so many fallen leaves. The night deepened again. There were no stars.

Marsh turned away, smelling smoke in his clothes, his face still burning from the heat. He stepped beside Reg's chair and eased down on his haunches. He gazed into the snuffed fire, resting his hand on Reg's knee. "We're going to the Badlands," he said.

"I know," Reg said. "The story is all in my head. And in my heart— it goes without saying."

Reg tucked the deckle-edge letter inside his shirt. He gripped Marsh's hand. He'd been sitting too close to the flames. His dark clutching fingers looked charred. Marsh felt the tight seal of the old man's hand, as if something had been decided, the last hour agreement reached.

Marsh nodded. "Without saying." He glanced away then, his eyes blurred from the drifting smoke. It seemed he spoke only to himself, the words riding low on his breath. "You are eighty-four."

23

"After the fire, she was buried here," Reg said. "The boy Noah and two girls, age six and three with her."

Marsh gazed across the grass to cottonwoods choking the junction of Soldiers Creek and the White River. Spring floods had swept the low-lying cemetery, washing over sunken graves. The dead had been re-moved. Saro was gone, no stone marked the spot. Reinterred in California, Reg said. But it was impossible for Marsh to picture Saro there.

Reg hooked his hands at the cemetery fence and peered over. He looked even smaller, as if he'd been sinking with this bottom land.

"There was a tetchy little dog, burned to a crisp. She ran to fetch him, otherwise she might have lived. Ever after, my father refused to utter that animal's name."

"Maybe we should drive into town and mail your letter," Marsh said. It couldn't be good—all this talk Reg had kept going since breakfast. Marsh wished for yesterday, and the old man still locked inside the Establishment. Instead, Reg had woken up determined to tour the fort. Marsh trailed the old man around, steering him clear of Post Head-quarters and the musty basement library. What Reg knew and what he didn't still went without saying. Marsh wasn't sure what he himself knew except Hole In The Day had been killed. But there was something more. And Marsh thought it could be found in Algie's papers—all those pages he'd copied, then burned without ever reading them through.

Reg spread his arms. "The place of my birth," he said. "Not to mention the final resting place."

"Not yours," Marsh said.

Reg nodded back at the empty cemetery as Marsh turned him away. "Two courageous men of the Ninth rested there, decorated with this country's highest military laurel."

Marsh looked over thinking now would be the time to ask about Algie, the last black man. He thought about the returns, Algie's bulging folder sitting like some kind of evidence in the filing cabinet.

"Of course, I myself will never rest." Reg chuckled, sun glinting his hair. Wiry curls spun straight up from the crown of his head. He needed a haircut. They both did. "Although at my age it is best to be always ready—booted and spurred, so to speak."

They walked the dirt road leading to camp. Since yesterday's rain the breeze had turned cool and mild. Earlier, somebody mentioned that snow had fallen in Yellowstone, the mountain goats and elk were moving down. Frank, Evie, Jewel—everybody had already broken camp and headed north for the Badlands. Alex would be waiting. Marsh had asked Sharon to keep an eye on her until he got there. He was hoping maybe Sharon could talk to her.

Reg looked up as they passed beneath a trestle of the Burlington Northern. For an instant his face ran to shadows. He seemed to have no features except darkness. "Some days every part of me quakes—you may have noticed."

"Yes," Marsh said, thinking eighty-four years.

They stepped across the campsite which looked barren now that everyone else had left. Reg leaned at a picnic table, winded from the walk.

"It would appear that I am preparing to dislodge," he said.

"You just have your days, is all." Marsh unfolded a lawn chair, brushing boxelder beetles off the seat. The rain had driven the beetles into tight formation. They swarmed in bunches of red and black, like the clicking jewel colors in a kaleidoscope. Beetles were everywhere. Marsh swept them from the plastic tablecloth. They flowered on the towel he'd hung out to dry. He tossed them like bouquets. Then he began packing up to leave.

He unhooked the electricity and water, then started the motor home's engine. Across the way, Reg was still in his chair, smoking his concluding cigarette. Marsh spread Reg's buffalo robe over the passenger seat. Maybe the old man could catch some sleep before the Badlands. He grabbed Reg's hat—a billed cap webbed for ventilation. Then he slid outside.

Reg had already nodded off. In the dust beside his chair, the cigarette was burning itself out, smoke yellowing the clear sweet air. Marsh hung the cap on Reg's knee. The old man didn't stir.

Marsh moved to the Establishment, deciding to wait a little. Reg needed the rest. Marsh cut the engine, then leaned against the bumper. He brushed a beetle from his sleeve and glanced at his watch. He looked off toward the fort, thinking he could be there and back in less than ten minutes. Ten minutes tops.

He took off on foot, leaving the Establishment in case Reg woke up.

The volunteer corporal glanced up as he burst into Post Headquarters. "Back for more," she said, reaching for her keys.

Marsh followed her down the basement steps out of breath, his voice a rush.

"Slow down," the volunteer said. She unlocked the library door. "Are you telling me you lost that whole pile of notes from yesterday?"

"Lost," Marsh said.

The volunteer jammed her hands on her trig blue hips. "You men," she said. She pivoted and flung open the cabinets. Then she tramped away.

Marsh gave himself five minutes. He slipped everything out of Algie's folder. He grabbed blank paper from the copy machine and slapped it on top of the stack. Upstairs he heard footsteps roaming the exhibit rooms, the volunteer rattling off dates in her loud gymnasium voice.

He shoved the empty folder into a cabinet. Then he clamped Algie's file under his arm and made a dash up the basement stairs. The volunteer marched out of Exhibit Room One, leading a group of chattering Camp Fire Girls.

"I knew that copier was fast," she said, nodding to his arm. "But this is a miracle."

Marsh shifted the papers away from her gaze and dug into his pocket.

"You must've been on automatic feed." The volunteer ran her thumb across her tongue, sorting through the bills he'd pushed into her hand. "Way too much."

"A donation," he said edging for the door. "I'm sort of in a hurry. Someone's waiting—we're leaving for the Badlands."

"In that case I'll accept on behalf of the Historical Society and because I like you. I don't know why, but I do." She huffed after him, the Camp Fire Girls straggling behind. "You'll want to be careful of the roads up there," she called. "They never get repaired—nobody can decide who's responsible."

Marsh hesitated on the museum steps, feeling apprehended by her helpfulness. It seemed he should just give up, turn over Algie's papers, turn himself in. "Thanks," he said after a moment. "I'll be careful."

She nodded and gave him a brisk salute. "Company dismissed," she bellowed. "And as they say in history—Godspeed!"

Then he was home free. He fled across the parade ground, thinking it was a miracle. That's what the volunteer had told him. Although he couldn't imagine any place in history where it said Godspeed.

He dodged around the Establishment, seeing Reg still in the lawn chair, the blue cap still perched on the old man's knee. It seemed Reg hadn't moved a muscle. Marsh stepped over to wake him, then swayed back. A rosette of boxelder beetles studded the toe of Reg's white patent loafer. Beetles were climbing Reg's arms, beetles swarmed his lap. Marsh would've brushed them off, he would've said something then. But he couldn't speak. He stared down, thinking the old man had just nodded off. He kept thinking this. Then he shoved his hands in his pockets and felt something like the fear of God, except he'd put the fear there himself—a tremble at the end of his fingers, then a rush to his head.

He hunched beside the chair. He rested Algie's papers on his knees and watched for some movement. Except for the rustling cottonwoods it seemed there had never been such a quiet morning. A silver squirrel skittered under the picnic table—that's how quiet. The little beetles kept coming. Reg sat with his hands upturned and open on the plastic arms of the chair. His fingers curled only slightly. If anyone had walked by just then, they might've seen something of a surrender in that gesture. But Marsh saw how like a nest. Two nests, beetles nesting in Reg's hands.

If somebody would come along now, Marsh wished somebody would. Because it seemed he needed to be told. Somebody to say, the elderly gentleman—that one sitting there. You must know, you don't need to be told.

Marsh yanked to his feet. He dashed to the motor home and slapped Algie's papers onto the console. For a moment he leaned over the wheel, trying to think—thinking nobody ever got home free. What you take, you lose. A man steps away for ten minutes—ten minutes, tops. He glanced to the clock on the dash, remembering the hospital, the doctor looking up to note the exact time. Ten minutes. And the world falls apart. Marsh felt it giving way in his hands, his chest. Everything dislodging.

He bunched the mangy buffalo robe in his arms. He hauled it outside for no reason. Except to think that sooner or later Reg was going to have to be moved.

The buffalo robe kicked dust as he dragged it across the campsite. Somebody ought to come by. He didn't know how to go about getting Reg out of the chair. He couldn't push his mind past the boxelder beetles zipping everywhere. It seemed they'd been summoned to do the job, transport this weight. Beetles clutched at Reg's elbows. They braced the old man's shoulders. They'd beaded his shoes for the journey.

Marsh glanced up, saw one renegade breaking from the pack. The beetle scrambled the curve of Reg's ear, then veered across his face.

"No," Marsh said in a voice that wasn't his. He dropped the buffalo robe and leaned to flick the beetle away. But Reg's eyes had flown open.

"You mustn't touch me."

Marsh bolted straight.

The old man's dim yellow eyes slid side to side—beetles swarming his ropy arms. "As you can see, I'm commending myself."

"I thought—" Marsh stopped short. He decided maybe if he turned his back. He did this. He walked over to the Establishment and folded the buffalo robe inside. Then he stepped back to the chair.

Reg was still sitting absolutely quiet, commending himself.

"I thought—" Marsh frowned at the picnic table, keeping his eyes clear. "I thought you'd fallen asleep, you nodded off."

"I, for one, believed I was dead," Reg said.

Marsh glanced over, then away. "I don't know," he said. "It could've been a dream—maybe you died in a dream."

"No, no," Reg said. "In my dream I was alive."

"Stop right there," Marsh said. He circled the chair—dizzy, looking down from all angles.

"This could be a rehearsal," Reg said, "what with the insects. Or perhaps a little sinking spell."

Marsh ran his hand through his hair. "Well, maybe so," he said finally. Beetles ringed his knees as he knelt beside Reg's chair. "But if you were—just assuming you could be—dead, I mean. And somebody came along and decided to move you . . . ."

"I'd prefer that you carried me."

"That's what I thought," Marsh said.

He touched Reg's hand. The beetles flew up, red and black, spangling the air. Wherever he pointed a finger, beetles took to the sky. Reg struggled to his feet and Marsh lifted him.

Reg clutched his hat to his chest. "You realize I'm not dead."

"Never mind," Marsh said.

He cradled Reg high. The old man's gabardine legs dangled limp over Marsh's right arm. A shock of gray curls mounted a riot at Marsh's chin. Only a minor snag. Reg himself weighed all of nothing.

Marsh started across the campsite. With every step, a hundred beetles shot from his feet. Along the creek, all the trees stirred.

Reg raised his head. "I don't imagine you know any songs."

"A few," Marsh said. "I know a few."

"I would like the 'Tennessee Waltz.' "

Marsh stopped a moment, tried to think.

"A last request," Reg said. "You remember that some of my people came from Tennessee."

"I remember," Marsh said. He took a deep breath.

" 'I was dancing with my darling . . .' "

"I dreamed about a shore," Reg said.

" 'When an old friend . . .' "

"And a wave rolled in and washed up a glass eye. The eye looked at me."

Marsh stepped beside the motor home. "Just a dream."

"A very blue eye," Reg said. He raised a finger, made a little circle in the air. "If you could spin me once."

"One spin," Marsh said.

" 'I remember the night,' " Reg said.

" 'I remember the night, and the Tennessee waltz . . .' "

He arranged Reg in the passenger seat, then slid behind the wheel. Reg's hand fell absently to the console and Algie's file.

"Only a letter home," Marsh said, turning the pile facedown.

" 'The beautiful Tennessee waltz,' " Reg said.

As they pulled away, Marsh glanced to the rearview mirror. He saw the empty campground, the lawn chair still sitting there, holding out its plastic arms. He tried to keep the chair in sight until they met the highway. And then there was only the rising road.

For a while they followed railroad tracks. They crossed Squaw Creek, then the creek called Dead Horse. A feed lot locked the smell of manure in the air. Small metal signs announced the last green rows of summer corn. Trojan Seed, Jericho Hybrid . . .

Marsh switched on the radio, hunting the farm report. He hoped for a comeback of soybeans and an upward swing for feeder lambs. But he heard only that the President's wife had flown to Monaco wearing a black dress and hat. She'd been joined by Princess Diana who trailed a dark veil. Princess Caroline wore a black mantilla. The coffin was carried through the palace square by twelve members of the Order of Black Penitents. The prince's face had been contorted with grief.

And Marsh could not shake the thought of Reg's death. The old man was asking now for an envelope, his hands fussing over the fat fold of deckle-edge stationery.

"A large envelope," Reg said.

Marsh nodded. They crested a slight grade, overtaking a train laboring the rails with Wyoming coal. Dark, binned cars rattled on and on through the prairie, and Marsh saw the cortege—all the black penitents.

"Miss Lebow reminded me of my color," Reg said.

"We'll find an envelope in the Badlands," Marsh promised. Reg had only to say the word—his every word a last request.

"Over the years it seems I've formed something of an impression that I might be white."

Marsh glanced over, remembering Hole In The Day whispering *Wasicum Sapa*.

"A black white man," Reg said.

"You're wrong," Marsh said, though he'd believed it and had always wanted it. "You never were."

Reg shook his head. His voice dropped hoarse. "I expect you've heard the talk circulated about my mother and father."

"Just gossip," Marsh said, keeping his eyes fixed on the road.

He wasn't surprised to see that the town of Rushville had won a championship. It seemed no team in all of Kansas or Nebraska had ever lost a title game. Every town a winner—Home of the 1981 Double A State Champs.

"But if there were even a small grain of truth . . ."

"Well, there isn't," Marsh said. "And that's the beginning and end of it."

Reg sank back, turned his head away.

The town lay to either side of the railroad tracks, its old brick buildings dwarfed by Co-op elevators. At the next corner, a billboard invited them to take a turn south and tour a museum dedicated to the Evolution of the Gas Pump. Marsh hit the turn signal, swinging the Establishment in the opposite direction, toward open country and a painted four-leaf clover rising from wheat stubble. THE TROOPERS WELCOME YOU. SHERIDAN COUNTY 4-H.

Reg blinked out at the sign. He coughed into a handkerchief, then raised himself up. "They gathered here," he said. "Five companies of infantry and three troops from the Ninth Horse. And Hole In The Day with them as scout."

"A scout," Marsh said. He let up on the gas a moment, thinking somewhere ahead, Hole In The Day had been killed.

Reg set his long letter aside, his voice growing stronger with the miles. "At the first hint of trouble, Hole In The Day had volunteered. They were sworn comrades, after all—he and Algie. Hole In The Day rode in on his little piebald pony, carrying a message for Major Henry. It seemed a band of hostiles had fled into the Badlands, to a place called the Stronghold. At the Stronghold, the hostiles were continuing their dance while awaiting the Messiah's second coming. You remember how preoccupied those people were with dancing."

Marsh nodded. Even now, Muriel might be hanging the crepe paper she'd rescued from the rain. And tonight there would be dancing—a dance called Anti-Freeze, signaling summer's end.

"The troops moved under cover of darkness. My father carried only one blanket—that blanket so thin he called it the *Chicago Herald*. The young private Relax Hale rode beside him. It was a silent march with no stop for rest." Reg waved toward a straggle of pines wandering up a ravine. "Of course, the hostiles were scarcely expecting anyone other than the Messiah."

"No," Marsh said. But they were nearing the border regardless. Marsh figured it might be dark by the time they reached the campground. There was still the reservation to cross and the road ahead didn't look all that promising. Only a while ago, the volunteer corporal had warned him to be careful.

"Naturally, Hole In The Day knew the lay of the land. Years before, he'd been given the Bump of Locality." Reg lifted his cap and tapped a spot near the back of his head. "Precisely here," he said. "The bump." For a minute the old man was quiet. He frowned, sighing down at his cap. "I wonder why it is that the only worthwhile hat patterns were devised in the Middle Ages."

"I'll find you another hat," Marsh said. He looked over, noticing how the deepest blue had claimed caverns in the old man's dark, pleated face. "I was wondering," he cleared his throat, kept his eyes on the road, "wondering how you might want to be buried. You know—just in the event."

"I am a Republican," Reg said, as if that settled everything.

Outside, the Establishment cast its chunky shadow due east in the late sun. They were driving through shallow hills. The highway never curved, but took the hills straight on. Up, then down—Marsh spotted an intersection below.

Reg tugged the cap over his head, then leaned to touch Marsh's arm. "There was an infantry lieutenant, rode with them as well. A strapping man with a fair face and deep-set eyes. I myself would glimpse that face. But it would be years and miles from here. In another war."

Marsh slowed as they approached the intersection.

Reg looked up, clutching the dash. "You mustn't stop," he said. "A stop could be extremely dangerous."

But there was no intersection. Only this highway passing one white flaking gas station whose pumps had never evolved. Then a small dingy market bearing the name Jack and Jill. To the right, a liquor store with dense barred windows advertising Cheap Spirits. And battered cars everywhere—cars that looked beyond all help, too far gone for gasoline. But across the back of a crumpled hatchback Gremlin, a bumper sticker seemed to be trying to look on the bright side. You're In Indian Country. Trying with an exclamation point. *You're In Indian Country!*

Marsh pulled his eyes away, shifted into second. "What was the lieutenant's name?"

"John Pershing," Reg said, settling back. "You see, we are in modern history."

The bashed business section ended and Marsh speeded up. He felt relieved, as if they'd just driven through the scene of some terrible accident before any ambulances arrived. But all the fatalitites had occurred around the next bend. At first the red markers seemed only road reflectors. Marsh counted eight signs lining the grassy shoulder—red crossed out with a black X on the spot. The words: THINK! WHY DIE?

Reg turned, peering over his high swivel seat. "How many?"

"Eight," Marsh said. He jumped, startled as a horn sounded from behind. The hatchback Gremlin from the business section sped around, grazed the shoulder, then recovered.

Marsh dropped back, giving the Gremlin a long lead into Pine Ridge. Dull brown houses announced the town. A stop sign leaned at a corner.

Reg shook his head. "Don't stop."

"It's the law," Marsh said, nodding to the sign. But the law had been riddled with bullets.

Marsh eased on through. Across the street, Yellow Bird's Gas Station was doing a booming broken-down business. Music blared from its skewed doorway. Marsh glanced to the Establishment's radio—they'd picked up the same signal, the same twanging heartbreak song.

The Sioux Nation Shopping Center resembled a warehouse—corrugated metal painted turquoise. The parking lot, a salvage yard. A poster fluttered from a splintered power pole: GOD SEES ALL YOU DO. But no one cared. It seemed these people believed they were invisible. Maybe because this wasn't any place for a person to be—not in modern history. Not even the Middle Ages. Nobody appeared to have a clue as to exactly what time it was.

Marsh slammed the brakes as a man in a sleeveless T-shirt stumbled into the street. The man was feeling no pain.

Reg pulled his visor low over the windshield, though the sun gave no glare.

"In just a couple minutes," the radio announced, "it'll be somewhere around four-thirty."

They drove on, leaving outskirts of rusted tin roofs, an abandoned station wagon, hood up, glass shattered, a pea green trailer in a dirt yard.

Another mile and Marsh saw the hatchback Gremlin sail off the road. A couple tumbled out of the front seat. A man dressed like a cowboy grappled with a heavy woman in bell-bottom slacks. They crawled to their feet, swaying at the Gremlin's sprung door. Marsh slowed, the man looked up, weaved sideways, waved him by.

Reg put his hand to his face. "Are they injured?"

"No," Marsh said.

For a while the road angled east, then swung north again. At the turn, a crumpled mailbox dangled from a post. The row of signs said, Think! Why Die?

"How many?" Reg asked.

"Five," Marsh said.

Outside the sun was falling, but the radio signal grew stronger. Marsh squinted to find the transmitter above pine hills. Buffalo grass overran the road. Barbed wire buckled into tattered fields. Fenceposts had been reduced to sticks, the stripped low branches of pale ash.

"Lucille lost some keys down at Wamblee," the radio said. "Turning to sports, Wes just called from half-time. Things have got off to a pretty bad start over there. Billy High Horse missed the conversion, and a center snap to He Crow got intercepted somewhere along the five-yard line."

Marsh rolled down his window as they hit open road. "Monday night football," he said.

". . . Wes says it's the first game jitters."

"Still early in the season," Marsh said, nodding to Reg. A big green sign flashed by the old man's window. MASSACRE OF WOUNDED KNEE.

Reg pushed the lock at his door.

On a dry knoll, Marsh saw the small yellow cemetery with three trees. Behind it, the Mission of Sacred Heart.

"Hang on for news," the radio said. "We've got Marvin Shields and Jim Has The Pipe hitchhiking over from Yankton to talk to us about becoming a sovereign nation. So if you see those guys, stop and give them a lift."

Marsh glanced to the radio, remembering Hole In The Day, sick and walking all the way from Yankton to be baptized a Catholic. The thought of it seized him—just the thought—grabbed him tight in the face. His hand slammed down, striking the wheel.

"They're hitchhiking," he said. He heard his voice. He was hollering at Reg, as if the old man was all to blame. "Damn you," he said, shouting at a silent black army that gave no rest. "Damn you." He dashed his hand toward the windshield. "Eleven people have been killed out there. If I see those two, I'm stopping. Do you hear?"

Reg shook his head. "By my count thirteen."

"If I see them—" Marsh caught a glint of glass, the bottle lobbed from a streaking pickup.

"Drive on," Reg said. "They are not injured."

Marsh tramped the gas. A sign read four miles to Porcupine, eight miles to Big Foot's Grocery. But the last sign said Big Foot Surrenders.

> East 1/2 mile from this point on the old Cherry
> Creek-Pine Ridge Trail, Chief Big Foot and his
> Minneconjou band, with some forty braves of
> Sitting Bull's Hunkpapa band, were intercepted
> and surrendered on December 28, 1890. Big
> Foot, who was ill . . .

And then twilight fell. At the back of a wagon, Chief Big Foot lay coughing into a white flag of truce, Sitting Bull already dead. The troops moved into the field. All the birds came out. Meadowlarks wheeled, soared up and over the Establishment. A great blue heron lifted its wings. The radio fell back on music, still waiting for those two hitchhikers. Otherwise it was a silent march.

Marsh gave up counting how many had been killed. They rounded a bend, and the Badland wall suddenly rose before them. Somebody was singing. *You got to keep running . . .* Marsh turned up the radio, he needed the saddest song possible. But they'd almost lost the signal. *Got to try and make it to the Stronghold . . .*

"We're going there," Reg said.

Marsh snapped off the radio.

Reg nodded in the quiet. "You and I." He reached across the console and grasped Marsh's hand.

Marsh steered with his left.

"We are in this together," Reg said.

They crossed the reservation boundary. In the distance, lights shone from the town of Interior. A few more miles and they met the White River again, this time north. The same shallow river, holding another campground in its grassy crook. Marsh turned at the arrow leading to Pinnacle View. He didn't stop at the campground office, but followed the gravel lane past a swimming pool and a strip of asphalt with a basketball hoop sunk at one end.

He pulled to a stop and gazed out. Music drifted from a speaker mounted above the basketball hoop. Colored lights gleamed through the loose net. Butcher paper ran the length of the big Southwind's side: FOURTH ANNUAL ANTI-FREEZE DANCE. ALL CAMPERS WELCOME.

At the opposite end of the court, Evie was setting up an open bar on two picnic tables. Muriel commanded a stepladder, tacking up the last of fluted crepe paper with a staple gun. Lester aimed a flashlight while Muriel fired away. No sign of Alex, but Marsh spotted her van parked beside Claire's Micro-Mini.

He glanced over as Reg fumbled to open the passenger door. A stray boxelder beetle clung to the back of the old man's head. Marsh brushed it away, then caught another one struggling out from under Reg's blue cap. He sat back thinking he should've taken a cue from Evie—aired the house, evacuated everything to picnic tables.

"They're here," he said, gripping the steering wheel. Maybe it was only the panic still with him from morning, the sight of Reg in the lawn chair. This last trace of beetles. Or the black and red warnings planted along the road. A death count trailing them all the way.

He pushed the old man back against the seat. "You don't look so good," he said. "Wait here, I'll only be a minute."

He slid outside, the pure night air hit him full in the face.

Reg rolled down his window. "I promise you, I've never felt better."

But Marsh wasn't taking any chances. He crossed the basketball court, nearly bumping into Tiffany at the free-throw line. The little girl smiled up from a froth of white lace. Embroidered daisy chains slipped off her small shoulders, bunched at her feet.

Marsh stopped to straighten the white ribbon hanging below her waist. "I told you that dress was way too big."

Tiffany didn't care. She spread her pale arms, she wanted to dance.

"Save the next one," he said.

He stepped around Claire's Micro-Mini, through the light of a television flickering from the screen door. He tapped at the screen.

"You can come out," he called. "It's all over—Princess Grace got buried." But the old woman never turned his way.

"Laid to rest," he whispered, walking on. He peered into Alex's van, seeing only the giant grizzly standing guard with a T-shirt flung over its arm.

He found Alex sitting three doors down in the Southwind. She didn't even glance up as he climbed inside. She was hard at work writing some sort of protest letter to a publishing company. A young Sioux woman sat across the dinette table, frowning over a thick paperback book.

While Alex struggled with correct wording, the young woman drummed her fingers. She leaned around a bottle of Cutty Sark.

Marsh reached for the whiskey, seeing the Gremlin sailing, the bottle lobbed from a truck.

But Alex yanked the whiskey away.

The young woman rolled her deep brown eyes at Alex and turned to Marsh. "Tipsy," she said, making a see-saw with her hand.

Alex took a swallow from a plastic highball glass, then proceeded to cross out a whole paragraph.

"Listen, Alex," Marsh said, "I left Reg in the motor home. I need you to take a look at him."

"Pursuant to the Black Hills Treaty of 1868," Alex read in a loud voice, her number 2 pencil meandering over a yellow legal pad.

"The Black Hills should come last," the young woman said. She sank her full arms onto the table, blew dark hair from her forehead. She wore a green blouse and a green cotton skirt. "The hills are my final point."

The young woman shoved her paperback book aside and took Alex's hand, helping it across the yellow pad. She reminded Marsh of a very large Girl Scout. "The first thing I want to say is, we have *never* eaten a baby's afterbirth."

"Cut the noise," Frank hollered from the Southwind's rear. He sat in his leatherette lounger, watching the Giants take on the Green Bay Packers. But it seemed more like a wake—Frank looking grim, the hushed voices of the play-by-play. Another hour, and the NFL was walking out. Still early in the game, but all over.

A commercial flashed on and Frank groaned back in his chair, jabbing the remote control. "Oh, what's the use," he muttered.

As he spoke, Sharon ducked around the vinyl divider. She nudged Jewel into the aisle.

"What do you think?" Jewel asked, plumping bone white wisps at her ears.

"We're trying it in a modified wedge," Sharon said. She shook a can of hairspray, then blasted Jewel up the aisle.

"Good-bye ozone layer," Alex mumbled, her eyes drifting over the yellow pad. "Good-bye everything . . . adios, so long."

"Maybe I'd better do the writing," the young woman said.

Jewel nodded at Marsh. "Wanda goes to college."

Marsh turned to the young woman. "Alex isn't usually like this. She doesn't drink." He gave Sharon a look. "I thought you were going to have a talk with her."

"Her full name's Wanda Blue Going," Jewel said. "She works part-time in the campground office."

"I never drink," Alex said.

Sharon hurled the hairspray onto the counter. "I'd like to see you try talking to her."

"I think my ride's here," Wanda said, looking hopeful.

Just then, Evie banged inside and grabbed the bottle of Cutty Sark. "Better get into your costume," she called to Frank. "We're almost ready for you."

She glanced at Marsh on her way out the door. "Frank's giving us a little kickoff."

Marsh stepped after her. He fidgeted at the bar while Evie filled plastic tumblers with ice. Out on the court, Tiffany twirled in place, her feet twined with daisies. A big red double-decker bus sat parked in the lane. Marsh thought maybe it was Wanda's ride.

He caught Evie's elbow. "I was wondering if you'd come with me a minute. I've been sort of worried about Reg."

"Don't tell me he's heard about Hole In The Day." Evie shook a finger in Marsh's face. "That daughter-in-law of yours better watch it—sneaking around putting two and two together. You and I both know that kind of addition never adds up to the right answer."

"Look," Marsh said. "There was fighting—a lot of people got killed."

"Killed," Evie said. She slammed down her ice bucket and wheeled away. "*Killed* isn't the half of it!"

For a moment Marsh stood staring after her. A needle skipped over a record. The Sons of the Pioneers loped into the Navajo Trail. Marsh poured himself a straight shot, then moved across the court to get Reg.

He opened the passenger door and handed Reg his whiskey.

"This isn't necessary," Reg said as Marsh hoisted him from the passenger seat.

"Just humor me," Marsh said, shifting the old man's weight in his arms. "I've had a rough day."

Reg sipped at the drink, a little whiskey sloshing his sweater. "I scarcely think your day can match mine, considering I'm the one who could've been dead."

"That isn't the half of it," Marsh said. He thought about putting the question to Reg. What is the sum of two and two? But the young Indian woman was walking toward them, her head bent over the big paperback.

"I think your ride's here," Marsh said.

The young woman glanced at the red bus and laughed. The night breeze filled her skirt. "That's the camping bus from Yugoslavia. They stop every year to look at the Badlands."

Reg craned over Marsh's arm. "Who is this person?"

"Wanda," Marsh said.

"Blue Going," Wanda said, gazing down at Reg. It seemed nothing surprised her—not even an old man speaking from the cradle of his presumed death.

"They also come to see us," she added. "They're interested in my people."

"Is that so," Marsh said. He glanced down at the chunky bestseller, remembering miles ago and somebody saying, They get it from reading.

Across the way, Frank edged to center court, about to launch into his kickoff. Frank looked a little nervous. He appeared to be wearing no clothes.

"I myself am eager to reach the Stronghold," Reg said.

"The road will be bad now." Wanda turned, watching a mangled Cutlass Supreme crunch up the gravel. She waved, then nodded back at Reg. "My great great grandfather used to go to the Stronghold. He lived in the old free years."

At the other side of the court, Muriel manned the stereo. She pulled a record from its sleeve, then spoke into Frank's portable microphone.

"Excuse us," Marsh said. But Wanda was already walking away, heading for her ride.

Evie unfolded extra chairs. Campers wandered to the sidelines, the double-decker bus pulled closer. Marsh lowered Reg into a canvas lounger and snapped it to the sitting position. Then he sank down beside the old man.

Frank waited, scuffing his calloused foot at the center line. He wore a white tablecloth pinned into an enormous diaper. Two small cardboard wings arched at his back. Muriel dropped the record onto the turntable, and Frank raised a little toy bow and arrow over his head.

From the loudspeaker, a voice broke into song, but it seemed the words came straight from Frank. *Cupid, draw back your bow* . . . Frank notched his suction-tipped arrow and let fly. The Yugoslavians leaned out of their bus. Wanda's ride stared from the Cutlass Supreme. *Cupid, please hear my cry* . . . Frank cupped his ear. He sloped across the court, all jiggling skin—one very big man gone thin in the legs.

Marsh clamped his hands over his face, trying to hang on to his grin. When he looked up, Frank had lurched into a jerky cha-cha.

The crowd clapped time, the wowed Yugoslavians hit the horn. Frank leaned into his audience like a teasing superstar. He kissed a complete stranger. He bounced one-two-three and plastered Marsh with a wet smack, then whispered, "Bet you didn't think I had it in me."

Marsh couldn't stop laughing. Beside him, Reg was howling. Marsh grabbed the whiskey from Reg's hands and clicked him into the flat position. Reg lifted his head. He came up chuckling, but Marsh shoved him down thinking if laughter could kill a man.

The song faded out. Frank hopped to his backside and gave a deep bow. The crowd whistled, yelled hubba-hubba. Frank's diaper shone like the moon. Then Tommy Dorsey struck up The Music Goes Round And Round, and all the blazing Badlands stars spun themselves dizzy.

The Yugoslavians spilled from their bus, reeling over. Marsh watched the Cutlass Supreme pull away—he let Reg out of his sight for just that instant. And the old man was gone, out of the lounger and onto the dance floor. But fortunately Reg wasn't moving any major part of his body, only bobbing his chin.

Muriel slapped on one oldie after another. Tears On My Pillow cried from the loudspeaker. Alex stumbled over, mumbled something, then collapsed into the vacant lounger and pulled her yellow legal pad over her face.

Evie danced by with a box of cornmeal. "Makes for a smoother surface," she said, showering the asphalt. Then she smiled down at the lounger and poured the rest of the box on Alex. But Alex never twitched a muscle.

Frank had disappeared, probably watching the last half before the walkout. But Jewel seemed to prefer The Stroll over any walkout. She stuttered across the court with her game show notes, followed by Sharon who looked utterly miffed.

"Do you believe this," Sharon said, giving Marsh's chair a swift kick. "Muriel thinks The Beatles are too recent."

Marsh jerked his thumb toward the Establishment. "Go open that door—the beetles in person."

"Not funny," Sharon said.

But Marsh thought so. He felt a breeziness tapping his feet. It seemed the night had suddenly been let loose, the Badland walls tumbling down. Somewhere in the Stronghold, Wanda's people had never stopped dancing—dancing for the Messiah's second coming and a new world. But the new world was an old one, a home where buffalo roamed and every lost loved one returned. Marsh set his drink in the grass. He hadn't touched a drop. The music kept spinning regardless—spinning round and round in one long everlasting revolution. And all the people everywhere stood up to dance. Not for a new world. Just the old free years.

Marsh looked down, brushed a few grains of cornmeal off Alex's smooth surface. "The next slow song—how about it?"

"I can't move," Alex moaned. She squinted out from under her legal pad, one eye only. "I think I could be dying."

Marsh sat back, deciding Sharon was right. There was just no talking to Alex.

Above the hoop, The Penguins lilted into Earth Angel, The G-Clefs sang I Understand Just How You Feel. Then Along Came Jones in the form of a Yugoslavian. The young foreigner leaned over Alex, speaking in a language beyond any hope of translation, except maybe love.

Marsh shook his head at the gushing Yugoslavian. "She doesn't feel like dancing." He pointed to Alex, trying to make himself understood.

But the young man was already turning to him, smiling and nodding toward the dance floor, then grabbing Marsh's flustered hands.

"Thank you very much," Marsh said as the Yugoslavian yanked him onto midcourt, "but no thank you. Not me." Then he gave up. "Thank you very much."

And then they were pumping through cornmeal, lifting their knees in what seemed a combination jitterbug and some sort of stomping folk dance. Turquoise beads bounced at the Yugoslavian's white shirt and he let out a sound that came close to a yodel, and Marsh was grinning, wishing Frank were around. He'd dance smack up to Frank and say, Bet you didn't think I had it in me.

Then Sharon cut in. She jammed her face under the Yugoslavian's chin and they clinched in a dangerous dip while a deep voice wailed about lonely garden walls. Below the net, Tiffany was still spinning in a knot of daisies. She spotted Marsh and dove for his pant leg, nabbing him on the rebound.

Marsh scooped the little girl in his arms. As they swayed across the freethrow line, he wondered if it would really bother him if Tiffany grew up to be exactly like Sharon. By the time they reached Muriel's card table, he decided he probably wouldn't mind all that much.

Muriel sat hiding under a Masters Classic golf cap. She nursed a drink, her head sunk over the turntable.

Marsh nodded at Muriel's tote bag crammed with records. "I'd like to request a song." He smiled into Tiffany's hair, thinking of airwaves and dedications going out. "For somebody special."

"I'm not taking any more requests," Muriel grumbled. She downed the last of her screwdriver, then shoved back her hat. "Frank just passed the word—the Giants lost to the Packers. Jim Lofton ran eighty-three yards off a double reverse."

"I was thinking maybe Daddy's Little Girl by the Mills Brothers," Marsh said. "Nothing recent."

"Then he walked off the field." Muriel slumped lower in her chair. "Flat walked out."

The last chords of Deep Purple fell through the air. But Muriel just sat. After a minute, Marsh reached over and lifted the needle. Out on the court, the crowd waited.

Marsh let Tiffany slide from his arms. He reached for Muriel's tote bag and started flipping through. Then his eyes caught.

All of a sudden Muriel looked up and whacked his hand. "Drop that record. I'm still in charge here."

"It's just the Tennessee Waltz," Marsh said.

Muriel eyed the dog-eared jacket. "Is it Patti Page or Brenda Lee?"

"Patti Page," Marsh said. He bent, giving Tiffany's chin a tap. "You and me—the next one after this. I promise."

Reg was standing at the bar, streamers of pink and white crepe paper dangling above his head.

"Listen," Marsh said, pushing beside him.

Reg pursed his lips and squinted through streamers to the night sky. "I can't hear . . ."

"Listen."

The song seemed to be traveling from miles away. No introduction, only the full lyric waltzing closer across the dark plains.

"We're lucky it was Patti Page," Marsh said. "I don't think Muriel would've played anybody else."

"Well, that would have been a shame," Reg said.

"Especially since some of your people came from Tennessee."

"And seeing that it was my last request."

Reg buttoned his mohair sweater, adjusted the cuffs, then dropped his hands to his sides. "I expect you'll want to sweep me up and give me a little spin."

Marsh looked down at the old man preparing to go limp in a quarter inch of cornmeal. All around them, couples swayed by. Sharon swooped Tiffany, Evie steered Frank through the box step. Every Yugoslavian seemed to know at least one of the words.

For a minute Reg stood nodding his head, keeping time. "Although if I were allowed a second last request . . ." He turned, smiling at Marsh. "It would be to remember this night."

"I'm not taking any last requests," Marsh said. Because it seemed more like a second coming—something close, with Reg standing there on his own two feet. Not Algie glimpsed riding across a white field, or the regimental band sounding the call. Only the Tennessee Waltz after so many years. And an old man coming back reminded of his color.

Marsh rested his left hand at Reg's shoulder. He raised his right. "You lead."

24

Alex's little one-man tent stood empty. A morning breeze rippled the canvas walls. Marsh had expected to find her asleep, or at least unable to move after last night's whiskey. He stepped away, sipping at a very strong cup of coffee intended for her.

The basketball court looked almost normal again, only a tag of crepe paper wagging from the backboard. The red double-decker bus had pulled out earlier—Yugoslavians off to scout the Badlands.

Marsh dashed the last of Alex's coffee onto the gravel and headed for the campground office. Maybe he was only feeling a natural letdown—the dance over, most of the SOARS gone with the cool change of weather. And Jewel leaving tomorrow for Studio City. Jewel and her entourage—all of them heading off to "Simon Says." It seemed the campground had already been deserted. Except for Claire. The drapes remained drawn across the windows of her Micro-Mini, as if nothing was really over. Princess Grace not buried after all, and the walkout had never happened.

Frank was waiting for him as he stepped through the office door. "It's about time—those foreigners have almost an hour lead on us."

"This isn't a race," Marsh said. He glanced to the check-in counter. Wanda Blue Going arranged souvenirs on the glass, keeping busy while Alex followed her around with the yellow legal pad. In a corner, Jewel, Evie, and Muriel crowded a small table strewn with shopping bags.

Evie looked up, waved Marsh over.

"The main thing is, we stick together," Frank said, following him across the office. The first real autumn chill, and Frank was wearing plaid shorts. Clunky binoculars hung at his chest. The shorts bagged around his pink knees. "Once we hit the reservation, we don't leave our rigs for any reason—no walking around in the open. The manager was in a while ago, said sometimes they take pot shots."

"I don't believe that for a minute," Evie said.

Frank frowned at his watch. "Now all we need is Reg."

"We dropped Sharon and the kids at park headquarters." Evie pulled a beaded change purse from a bag, then smiled at Marsh. "Sharon says she's not really interested in the Badlands."

"Well, I hope she'll give some thought to Los Angeles," Jewel said. "Otherwise, I don't know how I'll ever manage this hair."

Marsh blinked down, trying to catch up with the morning. "Not California," he said. He scrambled to calculate the distance between Los Angeles and Richard.

"Don't worry," Evie said, turning to Jewel. "I told Sharon about Welfare out there. It's a wonderful opportunity for her."

"Hold on," Marsh said. He figured anything less than four hundred miles would put Sharon within striking range. "Did it occur to you that I happen to live in California?"

Muriel nodded up at him from under her golf cap. "I think you're what's called the added incentive."

Frank jammed his hands to his hips, rocked on his toes. "I'm giving Reg five more minutes to get himself in here. He isn't ready to go by then, we leave without him."

"We can hardly do that," Jewel said. "He's the only one who knows what happened."

Evie gave Jewel a quick look, then dove into her paper bags. Marsh watched her pulling prices from unglazed pottery. He thought of Algie's papers. He'd stashed them under the driver's seat, avoiding them after all he'd done. Back at the fort, the volunteer corporal might've already discovered the missing file, reported his name from the guest register.

"Where is he," Marsh said. "Reg, I mean."

Frank waved toward a restroom door marked BRAVES. "He mentioned something about changing clothes."

Marsh turned for the restroom. At the check-in counter, Wanda Blue Going had disappeared below the glass. Marsh saw only her square brown hands arranging agate key chains on a velvet tray.

As he passed the counter, Alex caught his arm. "I think we should skip White Clay Creek." She nodded, jumpy at his face, her sunny skin gone pale and skimmed with sweat. "You know—" The legal pad slipped from her hands onto the counter. "Because of Hole In The Day."

"Alex, for Christ's sake," Marsh said, because he didn't believe it was just White Clay Creek or Hole In The Day. Not even a hangover. "For Christ's sake, get hold of yourself." He gripped her shoulders, feeling the heat of her yellow T-shirt bunched in his hands. He wanted to give her a shake, shake some sense into her.

But Frank was stepping between them asking, "Anything wrong?"

"Nothing," Marsh said. He let his breath out slow, shook his head at Alex's yellow shirt, the words: Free Dick Marshall.

"One of my people," Wanda said, rising from the counter. She nodded at the T-shirt. "Jailed by the United States Government."

"*Your* people," Frank muttered.

Alex wheeled, heading toward a white door marked SQUAWS.

Marsh nudged beside Frank at the counter. "My daughter-in-law's having a few problems. Marital," he mumbled. He glanced to a display of postcards on the glass. The Badlands at dusk, at dawn. A panoramic view captioned: *Ten thousand acres of hell with the fires gone out.*

After a minute he turned to Wanda. "About the Stronghold . . ."

"The road needs to dry," Wanda said. "We had a rain here—wait another day."

"Another day and everybody will be gone," Marsh said.

"It's a gumbo road," Wanda said.

Frank leaned over the counter, frowning as Wanda scooped up a pile of small fringed moccasins. "Your whole trouble is you can't get it through your head that you're an American, same as the rest of us— we're all Americans."

At the crowded table, Evie, Muriel, and Jewel scraped from their chairs as if to be counted in. They moved across the room in a crackle of paper bags. Alex barged from the restroom, her hair dripping. Actually, everything dripping—blue jeans, T-shirt, the works.

"I showered," she said gravely.

Lester appeared at the BRAVES door. He wore his usual gray, with the exception of black steel-toe boots laced high. He held the restroom door open and Reg stepped out.

The old man moved as if by inches, slowed under the weight of Algie's shaggy campaign coat. He wore Algie's muskrat cap with the flaps up. He was dressed for a winter campaign, dressed for a storm that would cause much suffering. Above his heart, the Medal of Honor gleamed. It seemed Reg had just this minute raised that shine, and polished his own face, as well. His eyes glittered in a mass of fur. The dark folds of his cheeks, his chin glistened. His wild hair sprung from his cap like the crown of a buffalo. He looked for all the world like a Buffalo Soldier.

But Wanda didn't even notice. She was staring at Frank. "You people," she said. She flung the moccasins onto the counter, then shoved straight, flashing her long jet hair. She shook her head at Frank, shook so hard her whole body shimmered green. For a moment it seemed she was wearing nothing but leaves. She pressed both hands to the glass.

"You'll never know what it's like being an American."

Alex swung her van into a dirt turnaround and stopped before the sign reading: Massacre of Wounded Knee. From the Southwind, Frank aimed his camera. He'd snapped on his telephoto lens, so he didn't need to leave his rig for any reason. Not that much appeared to be happening out there in the open. There was only the green sign crowding words on both sides. . . . *A shot was fired, and all hell broke loose . . . Persuit by the 7th Cavalry resulted in the killing of more men, women, and children . . . This site marks the last armed conflict between the Sioux Indian and the United States Army.*

Muriel, Evie, and Jewel peered out the Southwind's side door. "As if things weren't bad enough," Evie said, shaking her head at Marsh. "Now they've gone and spelled pursuit with an *e*."

"Shut that door," Frank ordered.

Alex pulled her explorer's notebook off the dash, studying the directions Wanda had given her. Alex wasn't the person Marsh would've chosen to put behind the wheel, though the shower seemed to have helped. He also wished Lester hadn't climbed into the back seat of the van with him. Having Lester along was like spelling pursuit with an e.

"Well, at least the Ninth Cavalry wasn't here," Marsh said, feeling a little relieved.

Reg smiled from the front. "Although if Algie had been present he might've taken some satisfaction seeing Charles' death finally avenged."

Frank hit the Southwind's horn, waving Alex into the lead.

As they pulled away, Reg gazed back at the cemetery knoll. "That battle resulted in a total of twenty-three Medals of Honor."

Lester looked over at Marsh, his tinted glasses darkening as the sun rose higher. "It was a whitewash."

"Come, come," Reg said.

They took the road south, with Frank close behind. Marsh spotted very few cars on the narrow highway—probably too early in the day for drunk drivers. But around every bend, people were traveling the road on foot. Where these people were headed, Marsh didn't know. He thought of the Stronghold. Or maybe the radio station had finally issued its signal for a sovereign nation. At the back of Alex's van, the giant grizzly appeared to sense trouble on the way. The bear rocked right and left, mounting a rear skirmish as the van swept curves.

"However, the battle at Wounded Knee was *not* the final confrontation," Reg said.

The old man nodded around the front seat, his muskrat cap sliding lower on his forehead. Marsh wondered how he managed the slightest move, every part of him weighted in fur. For a moment it seemed Alex's Wildlife Project had been funded after all. She'd hit the road with one muskrat, a bear, and a buffalo. Marsh thought of Ginny's sable hanging in the Establishment. He wished he'd brought the fur along. His drip-dry 100% combed cotton clothes struck him as too tame. He knew it had something to do with the wind—always that. And the people traveling on foot, just walking around in the open.

Reg lifted the matted collar of his campaign coat to his chin. "The Ninth Horse was camped some fifty miles distant. Hole In The Day rode in with a scouting report from the Stronghold. It seemed the last hostiles were finally prepared to give up dancing."

Lester shook his grim head. "We starved them out."

"Thus bloodshed was avoided," Reg said. He wasn't listening, just rambling on. "Naturally, Hole In The Day rejoiced. You realize there was still no word as to what had happened at Wounded Knee. That night Algie prepared to drop into his first deep sleep in a month. But then, as the story goes, little did he know . . ."

Except Marsh knew. He'd realized it the moment he saw the medal gleaming on the old man's coat. The rest of this story would be told— that part Marsh had thought might go without saying.

Alex braked at a junction. She hesitated, frowning east and west, then touched her forehead to the steering wheel. For a minute it seemed they might still avoid the last armed confrontation.

But just then, Frank gave a blast of the Southwind's horn.

Alex swung west. For a while they drove in quiet. Finally Alex slowed, turning into a paved drive. A sign announced Red Cloud School, The Holy Rosary Mission. Old brick buildings bordered flower beds and a parking lot. Alex stopped beside a row of cars that had somehow managed to escape all bent fenders and shattered glass.

"I need to check my directions," she said. She opened her door, then glanced across the seat to Reg. "I mean, if you're sure you want to go on."

"I am," Reg said.

Frank pulled up next to them. Across the cement parking lot, a buzzer sounded, jabbing the air in three quick bursts. Children spilled out of a flat-roofed addition.

"Recess," Frank hollered, climbing from the Southwind.

But it felt more like a reprieve. Marsh watched Alex disappearing between a tangle of jump-ropers and marble-shooters. No battlefield, only a rush of children on a schoolground.

"Might as well stretch our legs," Marsh said. He smiled at Lester. "Being as we're not anywhere out in the open."

But Lester didn't budge.

Marsh slid outside, a cool breeze hit him stiff in the chest. He reached into the back seat for his windbreaker, then glanced at Lester. "I hope you realize what you're doing to yourself. You keep this up, and it'll put you under."

"I know it will." Lester bowed his head, removed his tinted glasses. He looked up, suddenly showing his age, his watery eyes. "I'm sorry," he whispered. He turned from Marsh, as if ashamed. "It's just that in my later years I've become very concerned about humanity."

Marsh stared into the van. "Listen," he said, gripping Lester's arm. "Do you think you're the only one who cares—the only one who has it in you? Is that what you think?" But Lester wouldn't look around. Marsh let go of him and slammed the door. Halfway across the parking lot he stopped and glanced back, waiting a minute. Then he dashed inside the flat-roofed building.

Alex and Frank stood in a hallway, talking to an elderly man wearing a black clerical shirt tucked into baggy Levi's. Except Frank wasn't paying much attention, absently eyeing a photograph of a very serious Mother Teresa mounted beside crayon drawings on the wall.

"Brother William," Alex said as Marsh stepped over. She turned back to the elderly man. "The day after Wounded Knee, a battle took place near here. We're looking for White Clay Creek."

"Well, you've come to the right person," Brother William said with a smile. "That period happens to be my specialty."

Marsh looked away thinking of Delois Lebow, thinking everywhere a Historian, every team a state champ. With the possible exception of this place. He remembered somebody calling from half-time. *Things have got off to a pretty bad start . . .*

Brother William shoved his hand up a sprig of his white hair. "The engagement at White Clay Creek is most often called the Drexel Mission Battle. Our mission was founded under that name through donations of the famous Drexels of Philadelphia. I believe they made furniture."

Frank glanced from Mother Teresa's photograph. "Listen, Father, we have people waiting."

"It's Brother," Alex said.

"This won't take long," Brother William said, turning to Frank. "Early on the morning of the 29th, our own Father Craft traveled over to Wounded Knee to assist in calming Big Foot's people. Around nine o'clock, a shot was fired into the air." Brother William raised his white eyebrows and shrugged. "I suppose the discharging of a gun must have been the breaking of a military rule of some sort. At any rate . . ."

Marsh nodded. All hell broke loose.

"Our mission overflowed with hysterical people. The hostiles who'd been riding in from the Stronghold turned right around when they heard the news from Wounded Knee. They rushed up the banks of White Clay Creek. Many more left the agency and fled north. Two missionary ladies from the Episcopalians deserted their posts for our doorstep. They appeared at the gates, carrying a yellow canary in a silver cage. Father Craft returned from the battle site in the back of a wagon. While he was attending to the dying, an Indian rammed a knife into his back, collapsing his right lung. Fortunately, Father Craft recovered. But if he stopped smoking cigarettes for two days because of that wound, we have no record of it."

Brother William chuckled, pausing a moment. He laid his hand at Frank's antsy back. "I see you're interested in our Mother Teresa."

"Not really," Frank said, turning from the photograph. "Well, I mean everybody's interested. She won the Pulitzer Prize here a while ago."

"It was the Nobel," Alex said. She ducked away, as if this was her opening. She headed for the door, then glanced at Brother William. "If you could just tell me how far past the mission before we make the left turn . . ."

"Not more than two and a half miles." Brother William removed the photograph from the wall and held it toward Frank. "Perhaps you'd like to have this."

"That's all right," Frank said, shoving his hands into his pockets. "I was just looking."

"Take it," Brother William said. He wedged the black and white photo under Frank's arm. "I have another—I'm a very big fan of Mother Teresa. We're more or less in the same business."

Frank nodded. "Indians." He sidled through the doorway, clamping the photograph with his elbow.

"All God's people," Brother William said. "I traveled to see Mother Teresa when she came for the Eucharistic Congress. She's been praying for us."

"That's nice," Frank said.

They stepped out to the parking lot. Evie was snapping pictures with Frank's camera. She aimed for the children at recess, but the telephoto lens kept forcing her farther away.

Brother William smiled clear across the parking lot as if to reach her. Then he turned to Frank and Marsh. "Mother Teresa says the whole world understands our suffering."

"I don't know," Frank said, "these kids you've got here look pretty happy to me."

"She means everybody, this country of ours." Brother William reached over and patted Frank's arm. He might've been consoling one of the children under his care. "I think this country's getting tired—just plain worn out from greatness."

Frank frowned at the old man. He looked a little nonplussed. "Well, she's a damned good sport, Mother Teresa. I mean, a darned good sport. You probably don't remember when those two disc jockeys called her up from L.A."

Marsh looked off, seeing Evie standing at the top of a little hill, still trying to fit everybody in. She seemed to be hollering down to the parking lot, though nobody could hear her from that distance.

"Our cemetery," Brother William said. He pointed toward Evie, a white cross rising behind her. Then he hung one arm around Marsh's shoulder.

"There's a man buried at White Clay Creek. He left our fold to ride with the hostiles—the only known casualty among the Sioux that day. His Christian name was Ezra Holiday, although it seems in the end he felt the need to be redeemed by his own people."

Marsh hardly heard. At the back of Alex's van, there was a sudden commotion. A crowd of children bunched close, jumping to see above each other's heads.

Brother William nodded to the children, their long-sleeved shirts fringed with bright ribbons. "We normally hold recess later, but today's an exception. At 2:30 the camping bus arrives from Yugoslavia. Would you believe—they come to see us every year."

"I know," Marsh said.

Alex loped over with her explorer's notebook. She opened it to the last page and planted herself in front of Brother William. "Two and a half miles, turn left," she said, scribbling the directions as she spoke.

"It will be your first opportunity after the bridge," Brother William said. "Take the dirt trail, you'll see an old cabin. Stay to your left. You want the box canyon."

"After the bridge," Alex said, underlining the words, "the box canyon."

Brother William glanced down at her notebook. "That's where the Seventh Cavalry ran into trouble on White Clay Creek."

"Okay, let's hit it," Frank hollered. He hauled himself into the Southwind and slid the photograph of Mother Teresa on the dash.

Brother William stepped beside the children bobbing at the rear of the van. He rested his hands on a small pair of ribboned shoulders.

A little girl looked up. "Buffalo," she said.

"Yes," Brother William said. He turned to Marsh. "The Seventh Cavalry came close to another Battle of Little Bighorn on that creek. But the Buffalo Soldiers rode to save them." Brother William pointed toward the stone columns flanking the mission drive. "The black troopers charged past our gates, every one of them howling to make your eyes cross."

"Excuse me," Marsh said. He squeezed between the knot of children to the van.

Reg leaned at the van's rear door, as if somebody had propped him there. Children pressed at the old man's fur sides. A little girl stroked his shaggy sleeve. Directly behind him, the grizzly seemed to be looking on.

"It was a very long time ago," Reg was saying in a loud voice. He spoke slowly, separating the words so it seemed he might be addressing Yugoslavians and small children alike. "When you were hungry, I fed you. I kept you warm. Now put on your thinking caps and raise your hands. Do you know me?"

Marsh glanced up, seeing Evie still aiming from the hill. He hoped she could fit everybody in. He waved, trying to get her attention.

Brother William waved back. "Howling like banshees," he called across a dozen wagging hands.

"Yes," Reg said. "I am your old uncle, the buffalo."

Then a boy struggled forward, taller than the rest. For a moment the boy just stood and stared. Finally he lifted one finger and dropped it into Reg's black hand.

Reg smiled. He turned his hand this way and that, but the boy's finger stayed put.

"You see, this is my skin," Reg said.

Then he nodded over his matted shoulder. He lifted his hand to the razor claws hovering above his head. "And this," he said, "is a bear."

The bridge was nothing more than a low cement grid. Marsh couldn't spot White Clay Creek for a tangle of trees choking the shallow gully. "You want the first left," he said to the back of Alex's head.

"Will you stop," Alex said.

"I was only—"

"God bless it, leave me alone." Alex bumped onto the dirt road, then glanced into the rearview mirror, watching for the Southwind to make the turn.

Outside his window Marsh saw the old cabin Brother William had mentioned. Alex stayed to her left. Behind them, the Southwind strained up the winding trail in first gear.

For the past few miles, Reg had been tapping the dash, humming the

"Yellow Rose of Texas." But once he worked his way into the song, the words came out all different.

So out we marched with splendid cheer
the Badlands to explo'e;
With Major Henry at our head we never
feared the foe . . .

Alex's shoulders sagged at the wheel. "Explo," she said.

"Only for the sake of the rhyme," Reg said.

Beside Marsh, Lester's face went tight. "For the sake of a country that never cared if they lived or died."

Marsh jabbed Lester in the ribs. Then he turned to gaze out. It was the way Alex had spoken the word, dropping the sound loose and low—and Marsh saw black men muffled in fur, joined to make a frontier army, joined from Missouri, Arkansas, and Tennessee.

"So out they rode," Reg said. "They left the Badlands and traveled into a facing wind. It was fifteen below. They lived on field rations that had reached the age of twenty-seven years—that food nearly as old as Algie himself. They carried single shot carbines. Everything old, all of it expired. By the time the next day dawned, they'd ridden a hundred miles. It was the morning after Wounded Knee. When they reached the agency, our men fairly fell from their saddles. And how to say what confusion—tired as he was, my father couldn't sleep."

Reg looked into the back seat. He held up his hand. "These two fingers, frozen fast in a glove. And Relax Hale gone mad, don't you know. Snow-blind, my father said. And the break-bone fever—that too. The ground icy where they sat. And Relax Hale rummaging through a mess kit of Civil War rations. Then, from the direction of White Clay Creek, the sudden pop of gunfire. It was at that moment Algie noticed Hole In The Day had vanished. Algie reached for his saddle, but he couldn't budge it from the ground. The feverish Relax Hale had swung one leg over the pommel as if to ride. A mission bell sounded. A half-breed rushed across the square, holding his bandaged nose. Then the Episcopalian rector appeared—a thin slip of a man known to the Indians as Ant Body. This man, Ant Body, passed by carrying an empty bird cage. A woman followed, her face streaming tears. And then the call to Boots and Saddles. My father leaned again for his saddle. But Relax Hale was mounted there, attempting to dig Indians out of his ear with a little tin fork."

All at once the dirt road lurched up a steep grade. Marsh glanced back, worried the Southwind might high-center on that stretch. He craned to see past the rocking grizzly. He wished they'd left the bear at the mission. He was tired of looking at it—suddenly tired of everybody. Behind them, Frank gunned the engine, making a roar that seemed the whining machinery of the wind itself, flattening prairie grass and bowing trees.

Finally they topped the grade. Below them lay the box canyon. The valley floor looked almost man-made, turning sharp corners with White Clay Creek. A single cottonwood stood at the south end. Marsh figured maybe three hundred yards across the canyon.

Alex pulled over, leaving room for the Southwind.

Frank scanned the bluffs through his binoculars, then swept his arm out the window. "Okay," he called, as if everybody had just been waiting for him to give the signal.

Everybody except Reg. He'd already struggled from the van and started down the slope toward the valley floor.

It wasn't a difficult walk, but Marsh wondered if Jewel should try. He took her arm, then noticed she'd changed her shoes. The cracked white shoes looked old and orthopedic, but Jewel kept smiling at her feet.

She nodded at Marsh. "I used to be a nurse."

"I never knew," Marsh said. But he wished she hadn't told him. Somehow this detail only made him more worried about Jewel's chances on the game show.

Just ahead, Reg led the way with Alex beside him. Frank had put Evie in charge of the telephoto lens while he manned the binoculars. Muriel had prodded Lester out of the van. She lugged a baseball bat, trailing its wide end through soapweed and pale oat grass. In case of snakes, she said.

Marsh tightened his grip on Jewel's arm. "I was thinking about the game show. They might ask you who was the first to ride up San Juan Hill. Where did the last armed conflict take place? Things like that."

Jewel paused to knot a chiffon scarf under her chin, protecting her modified wedge.

"There are answers, and then again there are answers. Do you understand what I'm getting at?"

Jewel fumbled with the sheer ends of her scarf. "Well, if you're looking for the honest truth, the truth is I do have a very bad case of the butterflies."

"Hold it," Evie called.

Marsh turned Jewel toward Evie's camera. He sighed into the breeze. "Don't worry," he said finally. "You'll do just fine."

He led Jewel on, maneuvering her past a stand of prickly pears. Wild grass streamed around them. The afternoon air held a sheen like champagne.

Halfway down the slope, Reg stopped to drop the flaps of his muskrat cap. He pointed to the canyon floor.

"The Seventh Cavalry rode through here in a reconnaissance of force. But almost directly the entire command found itself trapped. Sniping hostiles gained the high ground, firing from all directions. Colonel Forsyth ordered a Hotchkiss wheeled into position. Then he sent two scouts—one after the other—tearing back to the agency with a call for help.

Reg dashed his hand into the air. "So saddle up, men! Lively now!" The Ninth Cavalry leapt into action. Fours left, trot! And a lucky thing it wasn't a gallop, because Algie's mount could manage little better than a broken-down walk. In the column ahead, Relax Hale babbled and bounced, riding all over his horse. But then, Relax Hale had never expected a battle. You recall he'd joined the frontier army after hearing that mush was never served west of the Missouri.

Well, there's a sight for you—two hundred bone weary vagabonds called to the rescue of four hundred. Quick—Major Henry flung out a mounted skirmish line. And Algie among them. Those troops made a spirited lunge up the east side, covered by the Hotchkiss. That powerful long tom plowed shells across the ridge. Meantime, Troops D and F raised a dismounted attack on the bluffs opposite. Sixty men faced about, hurled themselves *ventre á terre*, and blazed away, scattering hostiles like chaff.

The canyon rang. *Sound* to Arms was the call. It is all in the word— a rattling of pistols, the carbine's sharp ping, a deep rumble of the Hotchkiss carrying the bass. And instantly the landscape sprang alive in a rush of men and horses. And savages falling everywhere back. Falling and falling and skipping from here to there like fleas.

The big Hotchkiss pounded on, raising so much white dust it seemed a fog had descended. My father claims he had no idea he'd reached the crest of the ridge. He could not see past his horse's ears. He never knew that only a moment before, Relax Hale had lost the top of his head. Somewhere below, or perhaps just ahead, he heard a man's voice drifting through the white fog. 'My God, I am killed.' It was a simple observation, this—as simple as sudden death itself."

Reg paused a minute. He turned, gazing after Alex. She'd broken from his side and started down the slope. Marsh stepped away, about to follow. But Reg called him back.

The old man lifted his fur flaps from his ears. "I need you to hear this."

"It's enough," Marsh said. "We've gone far enough."

They stood just above the valley. There was no booming artillery, not a sound left. Nothing to hear, nothing to see. Nothing but an old man dressed up for winter combat—below them, the canyon floor, empty except for one tree. But Evie snapping pictures regardless. Then Lester, who'd suffered the one disappointment encompassing all of humanity, that disappointment turning him every shade of gray. And Jewel smiling at her nurse's shoes. She could be seen, but not until next Tuesday and at the most, only for thirty minutes. And Muriel—What was Muriel really doing with that baseball bat?

Marsh glanced off across the valley, a quick anger stinging him in the face. It should be tomorrow, they should all be gone.

"Hole In The Day lost his life," Reg said.

Marsh turned and grabbed the bat from Muriel's hand. He stepped away, stepped into the swing; he swung like the longest home run ever. And it seemed the one thing he'd been wanting to do for months on end. The bat sailed out from the slope and over the valley. Marsh believed he saw it land all the way on the other side. He heard the thunk, then the explosion of white dust.

Evie moved beside him. She wrapped her big arms around him and hugged him with the strength of ten men. "I know, I know," she said. "I feel the same way. But it was war."

Marsh shook his head, because he couldn't think of anybody dying except from sickness—just sickness.

"It was an accident," Reg said. "He rode out of the falling dust, as if from nowhere. At first, only his horse could be seen. And not the little scouting pony, but a long-legged black. The big horse pirouetted along the top of the ridge, with its full black tail tied up for battle in the savage way. The Indian wore greasy buckskins. He wheeled the black horse with his knees, a carbine glinted in his hands. The horse danced in a skirmish meant to raise an army. But no warriors rode behind. Only this one, without a war cry. Without taking a shot.

And then Algie saw his face. My father called out. He shouted for Hole In The Day to turn back. But Hole In The Day pressed on. He rode just inches from Algie's eyes, but never once looked over. Then Hole In The Day set the black horse charging down the ridge. Algie leapt to follow, riding into his own covering fire. At once his horse buckled under him. He ducked behind the fallen animal. Above and below—everywhere around him—Algie felt the heat of bursting shells. Yet for a moment it seemed Hole In The Day might ride the distance without ever catching a bullet. He'd nearly reached the smoking Hotchkiss. And it was exactly there—at such close range—that Hole In The Day finally took aim and shot the gunner down.

The Hotchkiss fell suddenly silent. At the same instant, Hole In The Day spun off his horse, face first. Algie never knew from which direction that shot was fired. He understood only that Hole In The Day had been hit, and he must go to the man lying there, because they had been boys together.

'We were boys,' Algie cried, the tears leaping in his eyes.

And Hole In The Day answered, 'My friend.' He said, 'My friend, pass by me. I am going to fall down now.'

But you realize he was already down. And not enough life blood left in him to ever go around.

Algie pulled off his neckerchief, as if that scrap of cloth could stop the flow. Then his gaze caught on the rifle. It was an old carbine. A smoothbore, remember. Algie lifted the rifle.

Hole In The Day turned his face, all of his face powdered with dust. He labored to speak. Algie knelt close, hearing the gulping consumptive breath of a man both diseased and mortally wounded—twice consumed.

Hole In The Day whispered, 'The number . . .'

Algie shook his head over the rifle. He thought of two mountains and someone blown down, and what they'd used was a great big number. Algie wanted to answer a hundred, a million trillion. He wished for a number no ear had ever heard. But the number he gave was one.

'One,' he said.

And it seemed the greatest comfort just then. Because Hole In The Day closed his eyes. His mouth dropped open and his last breath tumbled out. He said, 'God is great.'

'Yes,' Algie said, though he did not, nor would he ever in all the years to come, believe so.

And then my father stumbled away. He'll tell you that for the next space of minutes he lost his own life. Just below him, the artillery gunner slumped over the Seventh Cavalry's quiet Hotchkiss. The rest of Forsyth's command had passed safely through the lines. Major Henry had withdrawn his troops from the bluffs. But Algie could still see the scudding shadows of hostiles across the canyon. The wounded gunner had been hit in his pocket watch. A small gold spring clung to his cheek. Three gingersnaps lay at his feet.

Algie lifted the moaning corporal from the big gun. He lowered the young man to the ground, thinking for an instant of Charles, though this person bore no resemblance beyond a fairness of skin. And of course, this man would survive. He would live to tell the tale of a pocket watch scattered throughout his anatomy. And how an older black sergeant with delicate hands and the most absent manner had swung the long tom's nose to the west and pulled the lanyard again and again. Fifty shells a minute pumped into the clay outcrops of the bluffs. Until the very last dash of Indians called it a day.

"A last day," Reg said. "And one last Medal of Honor. One last black man left in the valley who could not for the life of him remember firing a single round from a Hotchkiss. Nor could he recall his own name."

Reg lifted the muskrat cap from his head. He swept his arm east, then west, as if doffing his cap to those directions. "And I myself have lived to tell the tale."

For a moment it was quiet, only the wind whistling off the bluffs. Then Evie raised her camera, catching Reg with his cap clutched to his chest. Muriel wandered off to find her baseball bat. Marsh moved down the slope. At the bottom, Alex stood beneath the lone tree. She seemed to be embracing its crooked trunk, holding on against the blowing green sea of the valley.

Alex shook her head as Marsh stepped under the cottonwood. She parted the tall grass at her feet, and he looked down. A rough stone pitched from the grass.

> Here lies the body of Ezra Holiday
> who was accidentally shot
> on the banks of White Clay Creek
> while defending his country
> he was shot with one of the large
> Springfield rifles with a breech
> loader it was one of the old-fashion
> kind single cartridge and of such is
> the kingdom of heaven.

25

Frank nodded to the picture of Mother Teresa. He'd propped the photograph against a bottle, so it seemed the centerpiece of the black formica table.

"All I want is your opinion," Frank said. "Forget who she is—you don't know anything about her. You're just going down the street and she walks past. Now, would you say she looks like a man, or what?"

"That does it," Sharon said, shoving back in her chair. "I thought we were supposed to be having some laughs here. You drag me out for a few beers—our last night, which ended over an hour ago according to that clock on the wall. And the only thing you can talk about is this poor woman."

Marsh glanced to the bar and a clock mounted in the corner. He wondered how Sharon could even make out the time through the haze hanging around them. On his first trip to order drinks, he'd noticed a sign taped to a mirror: Smoking Is Allowed Everywhere In This Room. But it seemed more like a command.

After the long afternoon at the box canyon, they'd driven into town— Frank, Lester, Marsh, and Sharon. For a few beers. Marsh had lost track of the exact number along with the time. Other than Sharon, nobody seemed to care one way or the other. Frank had picked this place because of a painted board outside the door that said No Indians Allowed. The words were faded and obviously no longer in effect. There were five

Indians at the bar, a younger couple sitting near a door leading to the restrooms. Earlier, there'd been more of a crowd—some card players and a little dancing. But those people had taken off before the night got rough. Not that anything had actually happened. There was only a feeling—a sort of lurch into carelessness. Marsh caught it in the loose watery eyes of the men shaking dice at the bar. His own presence—this table of white strangers—seemed to have stopped bothering the regulars except in the area of their shoulders. They'd bumped their backs closed, but now and then a shoulder twitched or rolled as if with an awareness of being watched.

"Don't stare," Marsh said, poking Sharon.

"Well, if you'd just go over and ask them one simple question. It's not like they're going to bite."

Lester removed his tinted glasses. "Did it occur to you that maybe these people don't have a phone?"

"I suppose that would give you a real thrill," Sharon said.

"Anyway," Frank said, nudging the photograph straighter, "these two disc jockeys got the idea to call her up and tell her about the Raiders going to the Super Bowl. And the call went through, all the way to Calcutta."

Marsh nodded. This made twice tonight Frank had told his story about Mother Teresa and the disc jockeys. And at least the hundredth time Sharon had nagged him about finding a phone. She seemed determined to let Richard know she was on her way to California. Blind date or not, she said, a person needed a little advance notice. But Marsh couldn't believe she actually intended to go to California. On top of which it didn't matter if she ever informed Richard.

"Listen, Sharon—we're talking somewhere around four hundred miles between San Francisco and Los Angeles. Do you realize how far that is?"

But Sharon was still glaring at Lester. "Even poor people have telephones. *I* had a phone, for God's sake. Your problem is, you don't want anybody to be happy."

"It's one of his hang-ups," Frank said, glancing from Mother Teresa. His eyes had turned red and droopy as a bloodhound's. "Phones, hang-ups, get it?"

"Los Angeles isn't even close," Marsh said.

Sharon reached for Lester's beer. "I've spent practically my whole life around your type. You get off on other people's trouble. You ought to go find yourself a job at Welfare."

Frank slumped back, shaking his head at the photograph. "What's the deal with this woman anyway—claiming the whole world's worried about us. I don't mind saying I resent the hell out of that. I didn't come up here to have somebody I don't know from Adam tell me I'm suffering."

"Right on," Sharon said. "That's exactly what I'm talking about."

The bartender moved by showering a box of sweeping compound onto the cement floor. "Last call," he said.

"We'll take another round," Frank said.

Marsh gazed off to the jukebox. An old man stood studying the selections. Marsh hadn't seen him come in, or maybe he'd been there all along. At the table nearby, a coffee mug sat beside a bottle of Jim Beam. Smoke streamed from a plastic ashtray.

"How about some music," Marsh said. It was their last night, they were supposed to be having some laughs. Or at least feeling relieved, the end of the story finally told.

Sharon waved him off. "Just get our drinks."

Marsh started across the room, then detoured to the jukebox. He was glad Reg and Alex had turned in early, before this so-called celebration.

"Last call for a song," he said, glancing back.

"Find out about the phone," Sharon said.

The old Indian swayed from the jukebox, tucking his shirttail into dirt-crusted Levi's. His cowboy boots were bandaged with silver electrician's tape holding flapping soles. It seemed the man was drinking both whiskey and coffee, plus smoking an ashtray full of cigarettes all at once.

"I didn't mean to horn in," Marsh said. But the old Indian just smiled, revealing a crooked collection of brown-stumped teeth.

At least ten years had passed since anyone had thought to update the jukebox. Marsh dug for a quarter. He'd almost settled on "Moon River" when he felt the Indian right behind him—so near he caught the foulness of a hot breath at his neck.

"Thank you," the Indian said as Marsh swung around. "Thank you for saying hello to me."

"I'm sorry," Marsh said. Because he hadn't given the man anything like a hello. He dropped his quarter into the jukebox, aware of the Indian still hovering. So just for the sake of it, he asked about the phone.

The old Indian smiled again, as if at the sound of Marsh's voice. He pointed toward the restroom door. Then he whispered, "Nobody has a word for me." He nodded, touching one stained brown finger to his lips like a secret. "They don't speak to me, because I am a thief."

Marsh blinked at the man, speechless. He backed away and sank down at the table. In his absence, Frank had gone for the beers. Fortunately,

Frank still had his wits about him. He'd had the sense to get their drinks and was talking about settling the whole question once and for all by calling up Mother Teresa to find out exactly what kind of suffering she'd been shooting her mouth off about. Whereas Marsh couldn't begin to think of what to say.

Sharon ducked close. "I saw the entire thing," she said. "That Indian walked smack up behind you and smelled the back of your head. Like you were an animal or something."

"Strange people," Frank said, flipping through his wallet. "And we wonder why they didn't get into the melting pot. Well, there's your answer."

Marsh looked up as if it was really here—the answer staring him in the face.

"They just never went in for the right things. That's always been their big problem."

Sharon took a swig of Lester's beer. "Talk about weird."

Frank pulled out his telephone credit card and tossed it onto the table. "What did I tell you. Is that my international number on the bottom line, or isn't it?"

"Over there," Marsh mumbled, "the phone." He pointed to the restroom door, not caring anymore. Let them call India, California, wherever.

Sharon reached for the credit card. "I'll pay you back," she said to Frank. "Just as soon as I start my job out west. I'm thinking of going into hair."

"This won't take long," Frank said. He turned to Lester. "What time do you think it is in Calcutta?"

Lester shook his bowed head. "Please," he whispered. "I don't know everything."

"Doesn't matter," Frank said, lumbering away. He pulled Sharon to his side, as if protecting her from the men still bunched at the bar. "There's bound to be somebody awake over there."

Marsh watched them disappear around the restroom door. For a minute he thought about playing his selection on the jukebox. He'd paid his quarter. But he lacked all energy. He noticed the old Indian was gone—the coffee mug, whiskey, ashtray gone, too. Cleared out, Marsh thought. But it didn't matter. The Indian had picked up his scent. It seemed wherever he went from now on, that man would always be able to find him.

Across the room, the bartender flipped the lights off, then on again.

Lester lifted his gray cuff and looked at his watch. "They've got five minutes."

"I think Frank's had one too many," Marsh said. "This has been some kind of day—what a day."

"It's been almost unbearable," Lester said.

"I don't know," Marsh said. "Maybe it wouldn't be so bad—I mean, Sharon coming to California."

"I held my tongue," Lester said. "We all did."

Marsh nodded. "I could keep Tiffany a while longer, until Sharon—" He glanced up as the lights snapped out overhead. At the bar, the men were reaching for their jackets. They groped in the dim glow of a yellow bulb burning above the restroom door.

"Everybody except you," Lester said, his voice growing even softer in the darkness. "And Reg. I honestly don't believe he knew the truth of what happened, either."

Marsh shoved into his windbreaker. He gathered Sharon's raggedy red sweater out of her chair. He saw the stone hidden in grass. Hole In The Day accidentally shot while defending his country. But what country? Marsh turned to Lester, gripped his arm. "All right, I'm asking—what happened?"

As they moved outside, Frank brushed behind them. "The operator said something about circuits piling up, jammed up, I don't know what all in hell was going on over there."

"I left a message on his answering machine," Sharon said, slipping her sweater from Marsh's hand.

"It was written in the post returns," Lester whispered. "And in the file, written in Algie's own words. Written everywhere you looked."

Frank fumbled for his keys and unlocked the Southwind. "Anyway, the operator says she'll keep trying. She's going to call me back when the line's clear."

For a moment there was only the slamming of doors, one after another—a sound much louder in the dark. A car rattled onto the highway ahead of them. The car weaved in the opposite direction, missing its right taillight, its headlight.

Lester was holding Marsh's hand. They crammed the little sofa behind the driver's seat. Marsh hunched in the middle with Sharon yawning into his shoulder, Lester gripping his hand. They bunched up front like the last people riding the last late night bus. But they didn't have far to go, only across the White River.

"I've never talked into an answering machine before," Sharon said, her voice miles away. "I just hope I sounded all right."

Marsh squeezed Lester's hand. "You sounded fine."

"In Algie's own words, it was no accident. He fired the shot and Hole In The Day came off the horse, face first. Hole In The Day was riding with the Sioux, yes. But any other man could've killed him."

Marsh nodded. "Is it cold in here, are you cold? Your hand's cold," he said to Lester.

"I'm turning on the heat," Frank said. He fiddled at the dashboard, then groaned. "Oh Christ. She's going to call me back and I'm not even there. Is that stupid, or what?"

Lester let go of Marsh's hand. "Are you listening to me? Are you? In his own words, he killed his own friend."

"I hear you," Marsh said.

They crossed the shallow river and turned into the campground. Frank stopped alongside the Establishment. "I can't believe I gave the operator that number."

Marsh climbed outside, pulling Sharon with him.

"Wait a minute," Frank said. "Did one of you pick up that picture?"

Marsh shook his head.

Frank squinted off across the dark campground. "I must be going out of my mind."

"Try plastered," Sharon said.

But Marsh had never felt so sober. "Get some rest," he said, nodding up to Frank's window. "Sleep in."

"You'd better believe it," Sharon said. "Tough luck if the kids wake up early. I'm sleeping right through them."

"Keep quiet," Marsh whispered. He stepped into the Establishment and led Sharon up the aisle. He grabbed a flashlight from the glove box, then beamed it under the driver's seat.

Sharon tapped his shoulder. "The kids—where are they?"

Marsh gathered up the file, every scrap of paper written in Algie's own words. "The kids are at Claire's," he said, nudging Sharon ahead of him. He glanced to the sofa bed, Reg's snore whistling up from the sheets.

As Sharon ducked toward the bathroom, Marsh caught a handful of her sweater. "This will only take a minute. I want you to come with me."

"Not on your life," Sharon said.

But he was already pushing her out the door.

They picked their way past picnic tables and campfires without even a glow left. It didn't matter—a fire was out of the question. Marsh had tried that once before.

"Out here in the pitch black middle of the night," Sharon grumbled. "I think you'd better tell me exactly what we're supposed to be doing."

Marsh stopped at the edge of the campground and aimed the flashlight into scrub brush. "We have to get rid of these papers, is all."

"Oh God," Sharon said, stumbling behind him. "Not Algie again."

The brush gave way to a mud flat stretching to the river. There seemed to be no current, hardly any water at all.

"N.O.," Sharon said as Marsh handed her the flashlight. "I mean it. No way am I going into that river."

"Hold these a minute," Marsh said. He shoved Algie's papers under her arm. Then he began emptying his pockets.

"Anyway, people are always killing their friends. You know that."

"The key to my house," Marsh said. "It's the one with the square head."

Sharon nodded. "Domestic violence is the leading crime."

"You might need to jump-start my car. It hasn't been driven for a while. This small key is for the gas cap."

"Hang on," Sharon said. She shot the flashlight into his face. "You're making me a little bit nervous here."

"It's just that you'll probably get to California before I do." He dug for his wallet, his right hip pocket, his left. "But I'd like to take Tiffany." He rummaged through his pockets again—pants, shirt, windbreaker.

Sharon sighed, watching him searching everywhere. "What now?"

For a moment his hands kept up a frantic hunt, while his mind snapped into reverse. Earlier, he'd paid for at least three rounds of drinks. Then Frank had said, Put away your wallet. Your money's no good here. After that, Marsh lost track of the beers and the time, his money hadn't been any good. But the jukebox had accepted his quarter.

He glanced down at Sharon. She'd seen the entire thing. "I think I've been robbed."

"No," Sharon breathed.

"Yes," Marsh said.

She shook her head, he nodded. They stood like this—nodding and shaking their heads. Marsh had never felt so naive. And Sharon wasn't any better. She thought they should do something, but she couldn't decide what.

"At this hour," she said.

"It'll have to wait," Marsh said, feeling strangely relieved.

He grabbed Algie's file and started across the muddy flat of the river. He felt his way in the darkness, heard the squish of tepid water entering his shoes. It had been weeks ago—in the darkness. He'd sat beside her hospital bed and said Forgive me, I have no past except for you. This grief is all I have, is more than I can bear.

Water swilled at his legs, so shallow he might've waded to the other side. He thought if he could tell her now, to say he didn't know where, he would never know where to put all the missiles, or this story given from father to son, this man's book his past, this burden of history, his story to bear. In the darkness beside her bed he'd searched his mind for

secrets until it seemed he was the one in need of absolution, this unburdening his dying confession.

He stood waist deep and prayed for the scales of darkness to be lifted
away. Mother Teresa was praying for him, all God's children. The President was praying for the NFL.

Sharon hollered for him to be careful. She called, "Watch out for
snakes!"

Marsh waved the papers over his head. He asked for some light.

And then he let everything go.

26

This is what Marsh remembered: an Indian smelling the back of his head, a breath filming his neck, rusted teeth. The Indian was wearing an old flannel shirt and cowboy boots wrapped in electrician's tape. A black horse appeared on the ridge. Then Hole In The Day plunged face first. He whispered, God is great. I am a thief, the Indian said. Behind the restroom door, a telephone rang and rang. Mother Teresa's photograph stood propped on a table. A stranger sat down. Now try again. You got the whole thing wrong from start to finish, but there's still time. Think back. What were you carrying in your wallet? Tell me in your own words, who fired the shot? Do you know who is calling? Marsh tried to answer, but he didn't know the number. The international number. The number is one, Algie said. Marsh reached for the phone.

Just then, Tiffany scrambled over his chest. She lifted the curtain at the sleeping loft window and peeked out. Sunlight slanted across the blankets. A boxelder beetle struggled along the metal sill.

Sharon stepped up the Establishment's aisle with a cup of coffee. "Did you hear me? I was saying you've got to report this to the police."

Marsh rolled over, still trying to answer the call. But it was no use. The phone had stopped ringing. He lifted his head and Tiffany dove for him. On the dinette table below, the baby sat in its plastic infant seat. Marsh's namesake, decked out in the yellow stretch suit from Kansas.

"I thought we were going to sleep through them," Marsh mumbled from his pillow.

"We did," Sharon said. She pushed the coffee mug into his hand. "Frank says he wants to leave by ten. He's got this idea about having lunch in the Black Hills. You know—Mount Rushmore, the Avenue of Flags."

Tiffany nodded against Marsh's cheek. She whispered, "Mincher goff."

Marsh swung his stiff legs over the edge of the loft and dropped into the aisle. Dried mud lumped up in his crotch. His shirt felt gritty as the river bottom.

"You should've been on the phone first thing. Talk about passive behavior—my ex-mental health worker should get a load of you." Sharon moved down the aisle, collecting odds and ends—the baby's pacifier, a red clip from Tiffany's hair. Reg's buffalo robe lay on the sofa, the old man up before everybody else as usual.

"I'll call," Marsh said. It seemed he'd been struggling to get to the phone all night long. But he hadn't been carrying much cash in his wallet. And he doubted the old Indian would have any luck trying to use his preferred member credit cards. His driver's license did worry him, though. Plus the pictures of Ginny and Richard. He felt their loss more than anything. Not one, but two people vanished.

And now Sharon about to head out the door. She checked the wardrobe closet one last time, pulled out a little pink sock and slapped it on top of Tiffany's new clothes. "I don't know how we ended up with so much stuff. But I guess when you start from zero."

"Hold on," Marsh said, feeling a sudden panic. He lifted the baby from its infant seat. His keys were lying on the dinette table. He hurried after Sharon, clutching the baby to his chest, the keys heavy in his hand. Last night he'd given Sharon the key to his house, given her a complete rundown from the square head to the gas cap. He thought he'd made everything clear.

Sharon clomped outside, dragging Tiffany and two bulging paper bags. "I can't believe you slept in those clothes," she said as Marsh hustled beside her. "You look like 'The Creature from the Black Lagoon.' "

"Listen, I want you and the kids to come with me."

Sharon shook her head. "Frank needs me to help drive. He says it's going to take all his energy trying to de-program Jewel."

"I'm asking you to come—it's important." He looked off, trying to think how to convince her, hunting for some sensible reason. But all he could say was, "What about your blind date?"

"It's off," Sharon said. She rested the paper bags on a picnic table, then turned to him. "I had breakfast with your daughter-in-law this morning—at least we were supposed to be having breakfast. One minute I was eating scrambled eggs and the next thing I was holding Alex's head over the toilet bowl. So here we go again, I said to myself. Another unwed mother, and I'm supposed to go out with the jerk who knocked her up? No way—I have my standards.''

"For your information, Alex and Richard are married," Marsh said. "Or they have been. Married, I mean." He sank down on the bench, shifted the baby to his knee. "Wait a minute—" He stared up at Sharon. "Are you saying pregnant?"

"Five weeks," Sharon said. "With child. P.G. Anyway, it got me thinking. Do you realize last night I couldn't even remember where my own kids were? I had this flash like you see on TV: Parents, Do You Know Where Your Children Are?" Sharon hauled the bags off the table and started to move on. "Well, you can guess how that made me feel."

But Marsh would never have guessed. This seemed the worst possible moment for Sharon to decide to become a good mother. Suddenly there was Alex to think about. But he couldn't begin to comprehend it—Alex of all people. And Richard. My God, Richard, he thought. Although for an instant Marsh almost believed it could've been him—himself a new father on the reservoir road. He supposed that idea should make him feel worse than ever. Instead he felt oddly grateful, as if the random wind had blown a stray seed into him. He jammed the baby higher on his shoulder and grabbed Tiffany's hand. And all of it seemed true—he had so many children.

"I have this feeling I might be turning over a new leaf," Sharon said. She reached over and pulled the baby from his arms. "You know— becoming more responsible."

"Will you cut it out," Marsh said. "Don't talk like that."

They started up the row of campsites—Lester's rickety stepvan, the big Southwind, Muriel's Airstream. Then Claire's Micro-Mini with all the drapes finally pulled open. Everybody looked ready to roll.

Marsh turned at Claire's door. "I'll be right back."

Claire was sitting behind the wheel, her face in a magazine that asked: Who Tampered With The Brakes On Princess Grace's Death Car? It seemed nothing would ever be laid to rest. This question alone could keep Claire holed up for another two weeks.

"I need you to come to my house," Marsh said. He glanced down the aisle, the old woman's refrigerator crammed with all the missing children on milk cartons. He thought of the baby at Claire's breast. "My daughter-in-law's pregnant and she doesn't have the first idea."

Claire nodded, though he couldn't tell whether it was at him, or the magazine—the exclusive inside story.

"I just wanted you to know," Marsh said, leaning to Claire's spongy ear. And then he said, "Be seeing you." But somehow he didn't believe he ever would.

He stepped out the door, nearly bumping into Frank.

"It's none of my business," Frank said, pointing an oil stick at him. "But when was the last time you did your laundry?"

Marsh tucked in his shirt and followed Frank under the Southwind's hood. "Do me a favor—see that Sharon has enough cash to make it to my house. I'll pay you back. It's just that I've lost my wallet."

Frank nodded, slamming the hood. "Well, if you happen to come across that picture of Mother Teresa while you're looking."

"Plus my daughter-in-law's pregnant and I need to get her home. She's been acting . . . well, I think she's having a hard time."

Frank gave a shrug. "Female hormones," he said. "Anyway, congratulations. That makes two of us—grandfathers."

Then everybody was wandering over to say goodbye. Except Frank kept interrupting with the grandfather news. Evie gave Marsh a hug. Muriel allowed as how she wouldn't have minded children, but then there'd been all that business with her fallopian tubes. "Whatever they may be," she muttered. Naturally, Jewel saw the entire new development as a good omen.

Marsh turned to Jewel. In the midst of everything, he'd almost forgotten the game show. He looked off, searching for some last word of advice. But the only thing he could come up with was the truth. And everybody knew where that would lead.

"Don't worry," Jewel said. She opened her chiffon scarf, ballooning it in the breeze. It seemed she might float away—drift clear to California. "I'll do the very best I can."

"Yes," Marsh said. "Just do your best."

"And be myself."

Evie stepped between them with the SOARS Directory. "In case you want to find us," she said, suddenly choked up in a goodbye.

Marsh slid the directory under his arm. He thought of The Fountain of Youth R.V. Resort, Thanksgiving, everybody bringing large electric roasters, and life beginning when the dog finally died and the children grew up. But Marsh couldn't see that happening any time soon. They didn't even have Tiffany completely toilet-trained yet.

Evie sighed. "I wish we could stay until Reg gets back, but Frank wants to see the Presidents. Plus I told Tiffany we'd play miniature golf in Custer. Plus they're predicting possible snow."

"You know what they say." Frank grinned. "The first flake that hits you is God's fault. The second one's yours."

Marsh glanced up. "Where'd he go—Reg. Where is he?"

"He went with your daughter-in-law," Muriel said. "They're planning to meet you here at noon."

"I don't think Reg wanted to be around when we pulled out. He seemed sort of down." Evie gave Marsh a look. "It worries me. You know—because of the other."

Marsh nodded. He saw how it could happen—how the events of a life, a story told in its entirety—how all this could be discarded in a river. And a name would literally become mud. Because Marsh himself felt nameless, his wallet gone, his clothes stiff with the river's white clay. Reg had said, Sometimes you fail to remember where one person ends and you begin. Marsh turned to Evie thinking, When life begins.

"My house," he said, "for Thanksgiving."

"I don't know," Frank said. "We've got one heck of a busy schedule." He screwed his mouth, as if trying to think exactly what the schedule was. Finally he said, "We'll try and fit you in."

"Maybe you'd better make it next week," Marsh said. He gazed across the campsites. Alex's van was gone, her one-man tent, the Coleman lantern missing, too. "Tell me—" He looked to Lester, because Lester always knew. "Did they say where they were going?"

Evie smiled. "To the Stronghold. Wanda drew them a map. It looked like a cave drawing—little x's, little cows . . ."

But Marsh was already racing for the campground office.

Sharon stepped out the office door, lugging a fresh supply of disposable diapers, the baby strapped to her chest. She nudged Tiffany toward him.

"Give Andy a kiss," she said.

Marsh tried to move past. "Reg and Alex are out at the Stronghold and I need to catch them. Wanda must be—" He glanced down to Tiffany brushing at his sandy knees.

He bent and the little girl swept his face with a blank mouth, as if it was all the same to her. Hello, good-bye—a simple ride from here to there with a stop for miniature golf.

But Sharon knew all about leaving. Back in Utah, she'd told him: You need the kiss good-bye. Still, she startled him, crumpling into his shoulder.

"It's all right," he said. He inched his hand into his pocket, aware of the baby squished in its sack. He squeezed out the keys and jangled them into the baby's bag. He looked Sharon in the eye. "You have my only set. If you're not at my house, I won't be able to get in."

"That's a complete lie," Sharon said, jutting straight.

Marsh dodged around her. "I'm depending on you."

"Oh brother," Sharon hollered after him.

But Marsh could tell he'd made an impression. Especially for a person who might be turning over a new leaf.

He stepped inside the office, straight to the check-in counter. He didn't look around as Frank hit the Southwind's horn.

The campground manager was standing at the counter, which seemed a surprise. Marsh pictured her as never there—just always off somewhere riding her go-cart.

"I'm looking for Wanda. . . . Blue Going," he added.

And then he heard the sound of all the horns—everyone honking onto the road like geese streaming a flyway.

The manager waved her hand toward the restroom marked SQUAWS. The door stood propped open with a bucket, a sandwich board barred the entrance. Closed for Cleaning. But Marsh ducked past.

Wanda was sitting under the blasting nozzle of an automatic hand dryer. It seemed she'd washed her hair along with everything else in the room. She sat cross-legged, her skirt plumped out, her blue-black hair flying all ends in the nozzle's hot air.

"I have to find the Stronghold," he said. "You sent two people—" Just then, the blower shut off, and Marsh heard himself shouting about snow and a gumbo road and Alex pregnant besides and what a crazy thing to do, letting them drive off like that.

He lowered his voice. "I need to find them."

Wanda peeled off her rubber gloves and parted the damp hair from her eyes. She fished a fat yellow pen out of her skirt. "Hand me a paper towel."

She was going to draw him a map, Marsh could see that. "Oh, no you don't," he said. For a moment he couldn't think of anything more archaic than a paper towel—just the idea of it.

Wanda stared up at him. She looked him over as if he might be her next big job. Everything from head to foot, Closed For Cleaning. "Well, all right," she said finally. "Give me a minute and I'll show you the way."

They drove west and then south, crossing in and out of the national park. You Are Now Entering, You Are Now Leaving, You Are Now . . . Boundaries confused the land. But Wanda seemed to know where every line had been drawn. Marsh had the feeling there was almost nothing Wanda didn't know. Except distances. Whenever he asked her how much farther, she just said, "Soon." Otherwise, she was an expert. She gave advance warning of potholes and sudden dips. She told him that around the next bend he might see a golden eagle. And he did. She said snow was not possible, but he could expect an overnight frost with low-lying fog in the Black Hills. When he asked her who maintained the roads, she shrugged, "Just God."

She said, "You are now entering the reservation."

Not again, Marsh thought. And again, the sluggish White River. Just past the river, they scudded onto gravel and a sign reading: Passable Only When Dry. Marsh felt a sudden play in the steering wheel and tightened his grip. They hadn't passed a car for miles. There was nothing except flat grass country edging toward the Badlands. Then the road took a long curve and Marsh realized they were climbing. A small rough sign said, Cuny Table Cafe. Marsh glanced out, hoping for Alex's van. But the sagging brown cafe appeared to be doing no business at all.

Wanda nodded. "You want the next right."

But it seemed a turn into nowhere. Marsh eased the Establishment through an open barbed-wire gate. They bumped over a dirt path choked with wheat stubble. Before long, the wheat gave way to prairie grass. Then the path quit almost entirely, becoming two ruts grown over with weeds. Marsh could've turned around then, some part of him kept saying he should.

Clay mud still clogged the ruts. The Establishment slipped and slewed, then caught on dense grass. Marsh was barely touching the gas pedal. He wondered why Wanda hadn't warned him. They had no business being all the way out here in a motor home. Alex and Reg didn't have any business, either—one old man and a woman in Alex's condition.

But it didn't matter anymore, because the road had stopped altogether. It ended directly out the windshield with a small herd of cattle.

Wanda reached over and hit the Establishment's horn. "Just drive on through," she said.

"Right," Marsh said, creeping forward. There seemed no choice now. The SOARS were probably at the Black Hills, he'd told everybody goodbye. He'd never phoned about his wallet. He let it all go. But if this was the point of no return, he believed the point must be zero. Sharon had said, I guess when you start from zero . . .

The cattle bawled into the tall grass—lean, poor-looking animals with alarmed runny eyes and crooked horns. Beyond them, the grassland ran flat forever. The clouds had lifted a little, leaving a silver ribbon of light across the horizon. It felt like sea level, like the wide-open ocean itself.

They left the last traces of road and started through the pale-tipped grass. Birds flew up wheeling and musical. A wave of grasshoppers clicked over the windshield. Long bluestem swept beneath the chassis with the shish of quiet surf. And Marsh thought there could be no map for this. How had Wanda given directions when it was all grass and sky—the final landmark a herd of range cattle that never stayed put.

Marsh flicked at a grasshopper buzzing his face. "I think they must be lost."

He himself was just drifting, waiting for Wanda to show him the way. The speedometer moved only when they took a hidden bump, he was driving so slow. Nothing registered except noise—the Establishment gone loose without a road. Cupboards jiggled, the roof creaked. At the rear, the wardrobe closet rocked open and banged against a wall.

And then a sudden thunk—a swift deep sound like a ball stopped hard in a mitt.

Marsh hit the brakes.

"It was a bird," Wanda said, leaning to the dash.

And Marsh felt his own heart snagged low. "It's no use," he said. He stared at the brittle grasshoppers collecting on the windshield wipers, needling antennaes groping up the glass. The wind rattled at his door. The clock on the dash kept ticking. And Marsh put his hand to his face, ashamed of his eyes—that he could've cried for a bird stunned dead in the grille, or the sight of himself dredged from the river, or for Hole In The Day caught in the fire of an old friend, for an unborn child and Alex and Reg no bigger than dots on this landscape, or the stone men looking out from the Black Hills with the eyes of giants five hundred feet tall. For a country worn out with greatness, he might've cried.

He said, "Where are we?"

Wanda brushed a boxelder beetle off her sleeve. "We're almost there," she said. "Do you want me to drive?"

"Yes," Marsh said.

Wanda climbed out. For a minute she rambled through the grass, this way and that. Then she returned and took the wheel.

"I found their tracks," she said, steering to the right. "There's somebody with them."

Marsh nodded. It seemed he'd known about Wanda all along. She possessed the Bump of Locality.

She followed the tracks, two sets running side by side, flattening the grass a deeper green.

Marsh pressed to the windshield, wondering who else could be out here. Frank had said, They take pot shots.

He glanced to Wanda. "Do you think there could be trouble? I mean, do you have any idea who might be with them?"

"There were some men from Wyoming. They were looking for uranium, but I heard they left. If it's not them, I don't know." Wanda shook her head. "This isn't such a good place anymore. I usually don't go driving around without protection. Things can happen."

"Jesus," Marsh said.

"It's just that my people—"

"I know, I know, drive faster, can't you go a little faster. Jesus Christ," Marsh said.

"My mother says it's a sickness with us. The no-motion disease—that's what she says it is."

Marsh shoved into the aisle, remembering the old rifle stuck away in the closet. "Keep driving," he said to Wanda. "There's a gun."

"Get it," Wanda said. And then she said, "Never mind."

Marsh sank into the dinette, trying to quiet his jangling hands. Then he looked out the window and lost his breath.

They were driving across a narrow neck of grass—a land bridge giving way to steep chalk cliffs on either side. The bridge didn't seem wide enough. Marsh clung to the window, seeing rivulets of dirt plunging off behind them.

Then suddenly the land opened out again. Just ahead, a man motioned them on. A red Toyota truck sat parked behind him. The man looked unusually small, up to his waist in grass. He wore a black cowboy hat and dark glasses the size of saucers.

Wanda leaned out, speaking to the man for a minute. Then she gave a soft laugh and put the motor home into gear. "That was Clarence from the cafe," she said as they rolled forward. "He's always been short, but not that short. He's standing in a rifle pit."

Marsh gazed back at the Indian half-hidden in the trench. They must've reached the Stronghold. No cavalry could've ridden past that land bridge. Marsh moved to the passenger seat, feeling a little safer himself, just knowing Clarence was back there standing guard.

He shifted straight. "What about Reg and Alex?"

"They stopped at the cafe and said they were lost. So Clarence led them in his truck. He says he was courteous, but he believes they're crazy people."

"Well, they're not," Marsh said, although he wondered about anybody who'd take off for a place like this.

Wanda shrugged. "I drew them a map and they still got lost. Now Clarence says those two think they're doing something out here, but they're not doing anything at all."

"They're just looking," Marsh said. "Mr. Vickers wanted to come to the Stronghold, because his father—"

"Because his father never did," Wanda said, a sudden firmness in her voice. "This was one place they couldn't get to us."

"No," Marsh said. He gazed off remembering Lester saying, We starved them out. Yet only a moment ago, Marsh had gone for the gun— gone for it as if he'd been packing a weapon all his life.

And of such is the kingdom of Heaven, he thought. This lofty place so near the top of the sky. He knew they'd been climbing, but he hadn't realized how high—not until they crossed the bridge and rolled onto this grassy tabletop.

At the far edge of the table, he spotted Alex's van. And then he saw them—those two who believed they were doing something. But from here, Marsh couldn't say what it was. They seemed to be just wandering around in the grass—Alex drifting one way, Reg another. They might've been picking flowers from a field in mid-air. Because it was possible that the world had pitched a flowering roof above the depths of hell where the lights had gone out centuries ago.

"There are two springs with good water," Wanda said. She bumped across the table, cutting a swath toward Alex's van. "Now they say there's uranium. That's why they've got all these flags everywhere."

But Marsh kept thinking he was seeing flowers—here and there a glimpse of white fluttering in tall grass. He knew the milkweed's blossom and the spongy tops of yarrow. There was a weed called snow-on-the-mountain. He thought that's what Reg and Alex held in their hands—fistfuls of late-blooming prairie flowers.

Wanda pulled beside the van and set the emergency brake. "They say the uranium's world class."

Marsh wasn't listening. They'd stopped at the table's edge. The land sheered off abruptly, plunged to nothing on three sides. Far below, the Badlands heaved to the horizon. Marsh leaned to the windshield and looked down into the ruins of ages. He saw the pale channels of extinct rivers, the great crumbling catacombs of lost leaves—a maze of nobs and spires from which no man would ever find his way.

He opened his door and slid out. Instantly the grass rushed up his legs. Wind caught him like a parachute, spun him around to Alex.

He blinked at her, seeing miles back—Sharon standing in the rain, belly bulging under the old fringed poncho. He'd said, I thought you were pregnant. But it was Alex here in the wind, clutching white flags, the wind filling her eyes.

He touched her face. "I should've known."

It seemed Alex couldn't speak. She bunched the flags to her chest and brushed the hair from her welling eyes. She shook her head, held out her hand, and said nothing.

But then Reg was stepping beside them saying, "My father . . . four regiments of black men."

The old man pointed off over the Badlands. He was still wearing Algie's campaign coat, but no hat. His hair flew. In his left hand, he held a dozen little white flags. It seemed he alone had gained the Stronghold. He'd marched a hundred forced miles and climbed to the top. He walked the ramparts in a flourish of flags. If Evie was around, she would never have missed this shot.

"Wait here," Marsh said, turning for the Establishment.

He opened the glove box and fumbled over Reg's long letter to Delois Lebow. For some reason, Marsh thought they'd mailed it. But then, there had been the problem of an envelope.

I am all alone in the world. That was the letter's last line. *Sincerely.*

"Liar," Marsh said, pulling out his camera.

He trudged over to Alex and Wanda. They ambled through the grass, yanking up flags as if they could erase every claim.

Marsh snapped their picture. Someday he would look back and see Wanda Blue Going with her face turned away, and Alex five weeks along.

He moved beside Alex. "If you could take one of me with Reg . . ." He watched as she bent for another flag, then laid his hand at her shoulder. "You know this won't work. Somebody will just come back and do it all over again."

Alex looked up and cleared her throat. Finally she found her voice. "I'd like to see them try."

"Alex please," he said. Then he gave up. Alex believed she was doing something, firing off protests on sheets of legal pad, uprooting flags. Too late, Marsh thought. Too late for a world long gone, a child already pushing off across the amniotic waters. But Alex seemed too busy to realize. Her hands were full.

"Hold these," she said.

Marsh gathered up the flags. He squeezed next to Reg, and Alex took aim. But it seemed she might never snap the picture. For a moment Marsh wondered if photographs could be forbidden—a place so concealed, with the wind moaning up the chalk cliffs like a warning. Alex kept shaking her head, then raising the camera for another try.

"If you could see yourselves," she said. "If you could just see."

But Marsh knew how it looked. He knew. They were two grown men standing on a sod table in the sky. They needed haircuts. Their clothes were crumpled and covered with dust. They'd traveled a long way for this, but they weren't smiling. They held the little white flags.

"I can't do it," Alex said. She thrust the camera into Wanda's hands. "I mean, look at them. They're just too much. Too sad, too something . . . too I don't know."

So Wanda took the picture, one from a distance and then up close.

Reg swayed toward her. He faced Wanda as if she was filming some documentary interview aired live and all over the world. "Don't tell me," he said. His voice snapped, but not with anger. His eyes flared, as if an idea was trying to burst out of them. Reg looked into the camera, looked straight at Wanda. "Don't ever tell me I don't know what it's like to be an American. Do you think I don't realize . . ." The flags quivered, he was holding them so tight. "Ask any man what we did." Reg glanced up. He sank his trembling hand on Marsh's arm. "Ask him."

Marsh felt the old man nodding at his shoulder. He stared down, searching for a way out of the words, finding no way. "It was written in the post returns," he said, his voice a shudder in the wind. "Written everywhere you looked." He saw it now in Reg's face—a face carved deep with all the secrets of what had been required. This photograph would never lie. There were no stone men gazing from the shrine of democracy. Only this dark, reamed face giving everything away.

"Somewhere," Reg whispered, "there is a place in history."

"A place in hell," Wanda muttered behind the camera.

"Stop there," Marsh said. Because if any man deserved such an end, he believed it must be him. This place in history, his.

He turned to Reg. "Let's go home," he said.

For a moment they leaned together, and it was then Wanda snapped the picture—the two of them leaning against the wind, leaning like bridesmaids over their white bouquets.

"Let's just go home."

"Home?" Reg said. He stumbled toward the Establishment, dropping his flags into the grass.

Alex stooped to pick them up.

Then Wanda ambled over and led Alex away. "Just leave me at Clarence's truck," she said.

Marsh turned, watching Alex and Wanda climbing into the van. At the van's rear window, the grizzly looked ready to ride, claws raised in another good-bye. Marsh dashed to the Establishment. "Follow me," he hollered.

But Wanda and Alex were already driving off. Marsh swung the Establishment around, tailing them up the Stronghold.

In the passenger seat, Reg clutched the dash with both hands. His windblown hair stood straight up, as if he'd suffered a terrible scare. "I knew and I didn't know," he said. His voice scraped, caught with every bump. "I wonder—is it enough for a man to go into the world and bring back a story? Otherwise he had nothing left, my father. And nobody to give the story to, except myself—a boy."

Just before the land bridge, Marsh stopped. He waited for Wanda to get out of the van. "It was enough," he said, turning to Reg. Because it seemed more than just a story. Before they'd ever driven a mile, Reg had said, It's your idea that keeps you going on.

Marsh turned off the ignition. Wanda was taking forever. For a moment he gazed back to the Stronghold, that fortress with the sky falling all around. He saw the tracks they'd made through the long grass. But it could've been years ago, a path narrowing behind him and already fading.

"Toward the last," Reg said, "my father went to the bank to withdraw his life savings. There was a man standing behind the window, asked him did he want it in heads or tails. That was a joke my father told. The joke of a dying man, a colored man gone down to the Bank of America. So I need to know, can a man be sent to hell for loving white people? Tell me—is that the mistake of the world?"

"No," Marsh said, thinking the mistake had been his—for years never seeing anyone coming toward him, never believing it could ever be just love.

Reg squinted down at the medal pinned to Algie's coat. "Well, there's the sadness if you ask me now. For a man to win the war, to reach the end of the frontier with only himself. To become, as they say, his own consolation prize."

"I think you're forgetting," Marsh said. He touched the old man's hand, as if to jog his memory. "Your father always had you."

After a minute he started the engine and let it idle, still waiting. Then he stared out at the land bridge. He saw Wanda and Alex shoving from the van. They marched around to the rear door. Wanda flung open the door, Alex crawled inside. Marsh watched Wanda yanking at the grizzly's legs. Then Alex scrambled out, grasping the head. They carried the bear between them like a ladder. They raised it at the bridge.

Reg blinked out the windshield, then let his head fall back. Across the way, Clarence stepped from the rifle pit and removed his hat. He looked mystified.

Wanda and Alex slapped dust from their hands. Then they waved Marsh forward. He steered past the van and started across the bridge.

As he rolled by, Alex shot him a glance, as if she expected an argument. "Don't say a word."

"I'm not," Marsh said. And he wasn't. He drove on, unable to speak or take his eyes from the narrow bridge. But he could feel the bear rearing after him from the Stronghold—a slash of claws and snarling teeth. No good-bye, but who goes there. *Who goes?*

27

Marsh thought they could still make it as far as Cheyenne. They'd crossed the border, catching Highway 85— a straight shot south on a good improved road. The speed limit felt like a hundred miles an hour after the slow crawl across the reservation. But then, God had nothing to do with maintenance here. It seemed women were now in charge.

For the past ten minutes, a young woman in a fluorescent bib had been flagging traffic just outside Marsh's window. It was a small road crew—one grader and an oil truck manned by females. But Alex didn't seem thrilled by this Equal Opportunity. She idled behind Marsh, drumming her fingers over the steering wheel. Ever since the Stronghold, Reg had been drifting in and out of sleep. The old man was awake now, but not saying anything.

Marsh snapped on the radio, looking for company. He heard that NBC hoped to televise Canadian League Football in the wake of the walkout. CBS would run a Sunday talk show to help fans through the crisis. Except Marsh didn't think he'd survive until Sunday. He'd been feeling the crisis for miles—not the strike, but this return trip.

It wasn't true, what they said about never being able to go home again. The trouble was: you could. And you almost always would. No walk-out ever lasted. Sooner or later—maybe years from now, or just a few hours back—the idea hit you. You might be standing at the end of the Earth, standing high up where nobody could reach you. The Messiah

334

could be coming to bring a new world. And you'd still say, Let's go home.

Marsh looked over at Reg. He remembered cottages shaded in hedgerows, damp redwoods. "I've been wondering—do you think you'll want to go back to Heather Hills?"

"Not if I know myself," Reg said.

Outside, a station wagon rolled toward them, its hazard lights flashing and a neon green tennis ball bobbing from the aerial. The station wagon led a string of cars up the detour route. The last car held honeymooners. The driver's side foamed with shaving cream and the message: Hot Springs Tonight, Deadwood Tomorrow.

For a minute Marsh wished he was heading back their way. He could return to the town of Interior, locate the old Indian and maybe even his wallet. Instead he sat at the end of a long day, stalled in the state of Wyoming. It seemed he'd hit bottom. His pockets were empty, he didn't even have a license to drive.

Reg slid his Chesterfields off the dash. "I've been considering a move to Norman's house. You recall he left his place to me."

But Marsh remembered only that Norman was dead. And no man should have to go back and find nothing left but himself.

He glanced to the radio, the last chord of a country song, then a voice announcing it was official—the official end of summer. "The daylight period today will be shorter by two minutes."

"Norman's house won't work," he said. He gazed off, filled with a sudden melancholy over the loss of two minutes. Behind the thick clouds, he saw the sun flicker as if already subtracting from itself. "I think you'd better come to my house—at least for the time being."

"Aptly put," Reg said, "given my advanced years."

"You know that's not what I meant." Marsh folded his arms over the steering wheel. "The thing is, I've done this whole trip with you. Now all I'm saying is come with me." As if he actually knew where he was going.

But just then, the station wagon pulled in front of them, hazard lights blinking around the command: PILOT CAR—FOLLOW ME.

Outside Marsh's window the flagger spun her Stop sign to Slow.

Marsh moved forward, Alex bumping close on his tail. They'd collected a half dozen cars and a whining diesel. The Pilot Car set the pace, ferrying them down the detour. It seemed the pilot had supplied her own vehicle for the job. Her license plates were personalized, her bumper sticker said Put The MX On The President's Ranch. The best idea Marsh had heard yet.

He believed he might follow this woman forever. He liked the look of her dusty arm crooked out the window, the yellow beacon of her flashing lights. Her car was the color of the desert—of pale sagebrush and pronghorn antelope ranging to the west. Behind them, the distant Black Hills already blurred in the predicted low fog. But the pilot's hair was blonde and shining like the Golden West as she rounded the turn. The wind blew from that direction. It lobbed the tennis ball Marsh's way, and he leaned to the dash. Any second, he expected to hear the pilot's voice on the radio. *Divert where? You're exactly where you're supposed to be, so keep coming buddy. Just keep coming.* And she would lead him across. She manned the escort boat he'd never seen. So Marsh kept going. He followed her until they met the highway again. Then she swung aside and waved him on.

The road led to Cheyenne, but all the signs said Little America. Billboards talked about nothing else. The land became one long advertisement delivered line by line, closing the distance to The World's Largest Gas Pumps Open Day and Night . . . Credit Cards Welcome . . . 150 Deluxe Rooms and Colored TV . . . Get Your Free Legend.

A PROMISE KEPT, THE DREAM COME TRUE—LITTLE AMERICA JUST AHEAD.
Marsh took the exit.

Alex thought they were stopping for gas. She pulled to one of the world's largest pumps and slid out of her van.

The big diesel from the detour geared down, its air brakes hissing. The driver nodded to Marsh, rolling past, a Boston bull terrier in his lap.

Beyond the parking lot, flags flew from the greens of a nine-hole golf course. The Stars and Stripes whipped above cedar-sided buildings. The complex sprawled in a ranch style meant to appear rustic. It looked only new.

Marsh shut off the engine, then rummaged through the glove box and pulled out his travelers checks along with Reg's letter to Delois Lebow. It seemed that here they might find the world's largest envelope.

He walked around to the passenger door and helped Reg out. "Little America," he said. "On me."

But the young man working the hotel lobby refused to accept his checks. Two pieces of identification were required. Marsh offered his signature. He recited his date of birth, his social security number, without any luck.

Finally Reg took out his slick billfold and clattered plastic cards onto the counter.

"I'd like to know what we're doing here, anyway," Alex said.

For an instant Marsh wondered the same thing. Alex's hair hung in a tangle. Her sneakers bristled with sand burs and tufted bluestem. She looked like the wrath of God, just back from the Stronghold. Reg had decided against wearing his campaign coat, but the mangy smell of buffalo lingered on. Marsh himself stood smeared in the chalk clay of the White River.

"What we are doing is humoring a certain individual who shall go nameless," Reg said, signing a credit slip.

Marsh shrugged. He slid a brochure from the counter, along with the promised free legend.

Across the lobby, a banner welcomed a convention of insurance underwriters. Some of the group were waiting to register. The men beamed in shirtsleeves, shiny faces. One man stood with his arm around golf clubs, another patted the back of a woman. "My better half," the man said with a chuckle.

Marsh looked away, stunned by the sight. It felt like a hundred years since he'd come across a married couple. When he glanced over again, he saw the woman gazing off with just the slightest smile. But then, he'd understood about women all along, about Ginny. The better half.

Finally he turned back to the counter. "I just figured we could use one night—clean sheets, no dishes to wash." No hookups, he thought. Plus Alex in her condition. "A hot bath wouldn't hurt us."

"Not until I eat something," Alex said. She started across the plush lobby then turned, waiting for them.

They followed her through an arcade of shops. Shelves glittered with French crystal, Wyoming jade, Black Hills gold. Eskimo dolls and glazed peasants flanked Wedgwood teacups. Bronze cowboys lassoed balky steer. In a corner, The Thinker sat on a Peruvian rug, his chin sunk into his hand, a Pendleton shirt draped over his shoulder.

Alex promised to be ill. She said one look at all this was enough, even on an empty stomach.

Marsh paid no attention, browsing along the shelves. Everybody was buying—truckers, tourists, a knot of underwriters wearing nametags that said Howdy Partner. All of them, buying like a sale's last big day. And it could've been. Outside the sun was setting on the official end. So just for the sake of it, Marsh grabbed a handtooled leather purse.

Reg pulled out his credit cards and smiled at the saleswoman. "My friend here doesn't have any identification."

"I'll pay you back," Marsh said.

"Never," Reg said, taking Marsh's arm. "What's mine is yours. When I cross the Great Divide, I'm leaving everything to you."

"No, you're not."

"Plus Norman's estate."

"Well, I won't take it," Marsh said, craning over the crowd for Alex. He didn't want to be left anything. Not left again. His own consolation prize.

They found Alex near the restaurant. She stood staring at a tall glass case. The case housed an enormous penguin. Probably the world's largest, standing sedate in swanky black and white.

"It was supposed to be brought back alive," Alex said. "They carried it all the way from the South Pole, but it died en route." She turned, nodding at Marsh, nodding the way she did when something touched her. For a moment he almost expected tears. But then, Alex wasn't one for crying. Of course, she didn't drink either. She wouldn't touch red meat.

"Go ahead and get us a table," she said, dashing off.

Marsh stared after her, worried she might really be sick. In the restaurant they saved her a chair facing the golf course. Marsh opened the tassled menu over her plate. After a minute she returned with her explorer's notebook. She looked perfectly fine. She sprawled into her chair, glanced down, ordered Baron of Beef.

Their waitress nodded. "And what for the gentlemen?"

Reg slid his wire-rimmed glasses back into his pocket. "I believe the trout."

"We'll have the trout," Marsh said.

The dining room looked Victorian—the Old West dressed up in chandeliers and a crimson carpet. Their places were set with two spoons, two knives, three forks and starched white napkins folded like fans. Reg appeared pleased with the whole arrangement. Except for the butter knife which he claimed should never be used for formal dining.

"I have it from my father," he said.

Marsh nodded, thinking of everything passed on, Norm mumbling in the hospital, My father taught me . . .

Beside him, Alex was explaining that the penguin had been captured on Admiral Byrd's expedition. It stood three feet tall and weighed 130 pounds. Alex wrote this down. She ate everything with her salad fork. She'd been on the range too long. She was eating for two, but it seemed like an army. After a moment she set her fork aside. She studied the hotel's brochure, then read in a loud voice:

" 'How did an exceptional western resort come to be named after an explorer's base camp in the Antarctic? Therein lies a tale . . .' "

At the next table, two underwriters looked over as if to hear.

Marsh reached into his shirt pocket for his free legend. He unfolded it, thinking therein would lie the tale. But he found only a chart listing distances. Little America to Abilene, Little America to Belfast, to Barcelona, to Cairo. The list ran on and on.

Reg unfolded his glasses, trailing his finger down the long columns. "It's just as I told you," he said, finally sitting back. He nodded at Marsh. "In the beginning, all the world was—"

"America."

They spoke the name together—in the same instant—so it seemed this was the true beginning, and they'd discovered the world. For miles, they'd carried the name on the tips of their tongues. They crossed rivers and the wide fields of battle. They buried their dead at every turn. It was Thursday. They reached this place September 23, 1982. Two gentlemen traveling home from the frontier.

Marsh crumpled his napkin beside his plate. "Order me a cup of coffee. I've got to phone Richard."

"Don't," Alex said, catching his arm. "Please don't. I haven't told him yet. I mean, with the way things have been . . ."

Just then the waitress sidled up with their check on a little red tray. Reg reached for his credit cards.

Marsh eased away from Alex. "I promise I won't say anything."

"Your purse," Reg called after him.

Marsh glanced to the paper bag he'd left beside his chair. "Give it to Alex, have some dessert. I'll only be a minute."

The pay phones were mounted side by side on a paneled wall, ruling out any possibility for a private conversation.

"You're the third collect call tonight," Richard said. "Hasn't anybody out there heard of money?"

"Sorry," Marsh said. "My card's lost and I couldn't remember my charge number." He looked up, distracted by a truck driver leaning at the phone on his left.

He lowered his voice. "My wallet's missing."

"I know," Richard said. "Somebody called from the interior."

"It's a town," Marsh said. "Interior."

"Anyway, they're going to send your wallet once they wind up the investigation. Of course, they want to talk to you."

Marsh thought of the Indian breathing at his neck. An admitted thief. What more did they need? "Well, I'm not talking to anybody, I'm not pressing charges."

"It doesn't matter," Richard said. "The guy's dead. They found him outside some bar. He had your wallet on him—no cash, just a bunch of credit cards."

"Wait a minute." Marsh covered the mouthpiece as if he could stop Richard's words. Beside him, the truck driver yammered about the rotten condition of his rear differential.

"Stabbed," Richard said. "They figure he was jumped for your wallet. How much money were you carrying?"

"I guess maybe twenty dollars, thirty maybe."

"Jesus Christ," Richard said.

"Look, it's pretty rough out here." Marsh closed his eyes, rubbed the bridge of his nose. He could see Wanda Blue Going shaking her head saying, You people, you'll never know what it's like. "You don't have any idea," he said.

"I've been around," Richard snapped. "I know what kind of holes—"

"Wrong," Marsh said. He glanced over as Alex and Reg nudged beside him. Alex had slung the purse over her shoulder, hand-tooled leather shaped like a saddle. Miniature stirrups dangled at her elbow, her hand gripped the pommel.

Marsh turned back to the phone. "I'm telling you, Richard, it's tough. You've never been here. You've never even gotten a postcard from here."

But Richard was still talking about the wallet, wanting to know did he have his driver's license. "Do you?" Richard's voice rose, he was practically shouting on the other end. "Do you have a picture of a nun in front of you? Because they've got one. They think it's yours."

Marsh shook his head, feeling a heat, his temper pulsing just under his skin. "There was a picture of you, Richard—and Ginny. Your mother."

"Were you in that bar praying for her? Is that what you were doing?"

Alex tapped his shoulder, giving him a look. "You promised," she whispered.

But Marsh wished he hadn't. He wanted to blurt everything out. To say praying yes. To holler into the phone, Start now! Pray for the living, for the place you've never been, pray for God's sake that we have it in us.

"They've got the idea you were out there looking for uranium," Richard said. "They thought you were from Wyoming."

"We're *in* Wyoming, dammit." Marsh took a deep breath, tried to calm himself. He leaned away from the phone, seeing Reg wandering off, Alex disappearing into a shop across the lobby. "Alex and I," he mumbled. "Something happened . . ." But he believed there must be more than this—more than a life lived between guilt and grief. Finally he said, "We're on our way home."

"I heard," Richard said. "That woman called—another collect. She said she was going to let you into the house. I assume your keys are missing, too."

"Her name's Sharon," Marsh said.

"You don't need to remind me. She spelled it for me—spelled Sharon, like I was some idiot."

Marsh nodded, hearing Sharon's voice. He saw her dialing the number, phoning collect to cancel a date she would never have had, spelling her name—her name written a hundred times over on the dotted Welfare line.

"Anyway, here's the point," Richard said. "It could've been me. Think about it—I could've let you in."

"You," Marsh said. For a moment his voice faded, only a scratch on the line. "Richard, you . . ." He stopped to think. He looked down at his hand and thought of how you opened the door and saw all the people—all the people opening his hands. "Go over to the house," he said.

"You could've asked me."

"I'm asking now, Richard. I want you to go over there and do something."

"Do what?" Richard said.

"I'd like you to—" After she died, he'd tried to make that list—an endless number of chores needing his attention. But all he could come up with was:

"Air the house."

"Oh God," Richard said.

"Just do it," Marsh said, although he himself didn't know exactly how. "I'll explain everything later."

On the other end, he heard Richard asking was he nuts. Richard had his court dates, he was a busy man. And besides, he grumbled, the windows were probably stuck, you could expect that from an older place.

Marsh listened. At least Richard seemed to have some idea. He was muttering about spot removers, litigation against hazardous chemicals, what dry cleaning did to drapes.

"Do your best. We've got to try," Marsh said. "I'll be there."

He hung up, then stood a minute, seeing no sign of Reg and Alex. Finally he stepped to the hotel desk and picked up a postcard and a room key. He asked for an envelope. "The largest you have."

The desk clerk wanted to know if a padded envelope would do, and Marsh nodded. For Delois Lebow, yes—it should be padded.

In the coffee shop he slid onto a stool and contemplated how to word the postcard. Dear Richard, You're going to be a father. Alex is five weeks along, with child, P.G. We've got to try our best. Dear Richard, Greetings from Little America. We've got to try. But none of the words sounded right. He slipped the postcard into his pocket and listened to truckers talking about the walkout. He drank two cups of coffee, not caring if it kept him awake. It was after ten. He hoped Reg would be asleep.

Their rooms were adjoining—he and Reg in 105, Alex 104. He wondered why the ground floors in places like this always started at 100. What was wrong with 1? The number is one, Algie had said. Tonight one old Indian was dead.

Reg had already taken a bath and turned in, leaving a fake gold lamp burning between their king-sized beds. A gilded eagle spread its wings on the mantel above a shallow fireplace. Otherwise the room was hotel French provincial—burnished headboards and a cream carpet. Marsh didn't look into the bathroom. He knew it would be flecked gold.

He pulled back the industrial clean sheets, then sat on the edge knowing he'd never climb in. Behind the blinds, it could be daylight. He felt nothing of the wide campground nights—no sound of the wind, or soft clacking cottonwoods. He listened for the buzz of locusts, maybe a cricket somewhere. A frog. He heard only ventilation droning through Reg's snore. There was no air.

After a minute he leaned over Reg. "I'll just be outside."

He was almost to the door, when he heard Reg give a little cough.

The old man lifted his head, squinting in the lamp's light. Marsh moved to snap it off, but Reg whispered, "Wait." The sheets slipped down the dark knobs of his shoulders. He nodded across the room, blinking his gummy eyes open. "This place," he said. "Where is this?"

"Little America," Marsh said, switching off the lamp.

Reg shook his head against the pillows. "And me in my feeble state of nature."

"Go back to sleep. I'll bring you clean clothes in the morning."

"I have never wanted to be found naked," Reg whispered.

Marsh smiled over the bed. "Well, I've found you." But he knew what the old man meant. He tucked the sheets at Reg's chest and heard a stirring, the sound of a faint breeze through prairie grass. "Listen, if it'll make you feel better, I'll get your pajamas."

But Reg was snoring again by the time Marsh stepped outside. He crossed the parking lot, thinking he should've let the old man know, It will always be me. In life, in death, I'll find you. Except the night seemed to hold some lingering question as to exactly who had found who.

He climbed into the Establishment. The wardrobe closet was open, the door hanging wide from the bumpy drive to the Stronghold. Everything inside the closet was a jumble—clothes fallen to the floor, shoes tossed anywhere. But he welcomed the smell of dust. He brushed at a boxelder beetle clinging to Algie's muskrat cap, and it seemed like all outdoors. No matter that across the parking lot, the world's largest pumps stood flooded in light. Here, there was only the night prairie. And Marsh wide awake in the middle of it, his mind suddenly speeding.

He moved to the sink and cranked open the louvered window. Then he started in. He sorted dirty socks in one pile—socks feathered with the grass of Kansas, Nebraska, South Dakota. He ran his hand along the closet's top shelf, the stack of Tiffany's new clothes cleared out. But he found the other pink sock. He folded the sock, thinking of Tiffany sweeping his face with a kiss. Tomorrow he'd hunt for a gift, maybe a pair of fringed moccasins. He dropped the sock onto his pile, then pulled out Reg's extra large blue pajamas—Reg now sleeping in his state of nature where he never wanted to be found.

Marsh separated the pastels from the darks, the way he'd seen Ginny do it so many times. He sifted sand from the cuffs of four pairs of dirty trousers, shook his head at the drab khaki color called fatigue. He turned his pockets inside out and felt joy turning in him, like motes in a shaft of light—all the small, shining activities of the world.

Delois' red Historian pen tumbled into his hand. What had he done with her padded envelope? Evie's scavenger list was still folded in a shirt, along with a church bulletin from the Baptists dated September 12. *The wayfaring men, though fools . . .* He noticed that the Northern California Racing Association had sent him another letter. Or maybe this was the same one, crossing the finish line again and again. But never mind. He left the letter unopened, thinking he might just forward it to Delois. He had a strong feeling there could be some kind of prize involved.

He unbuckled Algie's haversack, then unzipped the garment bag holding Ginny's sable. He plunged his hand into the bag and caught her fresh cool scent. He remembered those first few months when she was carrying Richard, how she'd felt so full of zip. He'd wake up to find her waxing the kitchen floor, the washer and dryer rocking with overloads. It would be two or three in the morning.

No Avon Lady had ever called on her. But he added the coat to Delois' pile anyway. He left it to oral history—one sable of heraldic color. Then he reached for the haversack and turned it upside down. A tin fork fell to the carpet, along with the little book Norm had given him in the hospital.

Marsh straightened the loose pages of the book, then gathered up Reg's big blue pajamas. For a minute he sat at the dinette table, under the brightest light. He traced the monogram on the blue pajama pocket— letters as complicated as any Spencerian hand. The pajamas had once been Norman's. Marsh had figured as much. But it seemed the book would never belong to anyone but Algie. *Presented to me by Mr. George Grant, April 25, 1873.*

Marsh ran his finger down the table of contents. He turned the dogeared pages, paper brittle and thin as an old Bible. Well, it was a Bible of sorts—this guidebook missing half its pages. But maybe still enough to go by:

Supplies for 110 Days

150 pounds of flour or equivalent in hard bread; 250 pounds bacon or pork, and enough fresh beef to be driven on the hoof; 15 pounds

coffee, 20 pounds sugar, also a quantity of saleratus or yeast powders for the making of bread. Should salt become scarce and the necessity arise, a dash of gunpowder sprinkled on mule steak will suggest the presence of both salt and pepper.

Marsh would remember this. If all else failed and the necessity arose. His knees cracked as he slid out of the dinette. He stood deep in dirty clothes, he figured at least four loads. There was always a point in housecleaning, where everything looked worse than when a person started. Marsh saw that he'd reached that point.

He slung Norm's pajamas over his shoulder and tucked the book under his arm. Then he high-stepped the piles and moved outside. He hardly noticed the parking lot, except to think he'd chosen a very level spot for making camp. He believed Frank would be proud. Overhead, clouds were finally breaking up. It seemed if he looked long enough he'd see the hunting owls coasting in front of the stars. He walked along, thrilled by the breeze lifting his hair.

It was his intention to locate the padded envelope. He'd help Reg into the blue pajamas so the old man would never be found. But out on the nine-hole golf course he glimpsed a light shining. For some reason he thought of people digging worms. A job done by night, although the light didn't move, even as he walked closer. It just kept glowing, casting Alex's shadow up the wall of her one-man tent.

He crossed the sand trap, then up a little rise.

"I couldn't sleep," Alex said as he lifted the canvas flap. She sat cross-legged on a sleeping bag, her Coleman lantern hanging from a loop above.

"I guess it wasn't such a great idea," he said, ducking inside. "Clean sheets and a hot bath."

"Well, I see you didn't take one." She nodded to the pajamas draped on his shoulder. "Where's Reg?"

"Inside," he said. He crawled next to her, the thermal sleeping bag billowing around his knees.

Alex could spend a night at 50 below and survive. Marsh found this a comfort, considering the baby. But then, this wasn't really the Antarctic, no explorer's frigid base camp. And that child had already survived so much—a thousand miles and more, the spin-out, a fall on a reservoir road.

"I didn't tell Richard," he said. He set the little frontier guide between them. "About anything."

Alex stared down at the book. "Listen, I need to say this. I want you to know I'm not really sorry it happened—I mean, what happened in Kansas. And I'll tell Richard about the baby. I will. It's just that it's been—well, so hard." She glanced over, letting her hands fall into her lap. "Sharon says I've been practicing denial."

Marsh nodded, thinking about Sharon's ex-mental health worker. It almost seemed this other person had been driving with them, explaining the downward cycle, the spontaneous moment, and no free love. Somehow Marsh felt he might even have been helped.

"Look," he said, "maybe there's another way for you and Richard. You don't have to get a divorce."

"I do," Alex said. But it sounded more like a marriage vow. She fell silent then, staring out the nylon screen window behind him. After a minute she said, "I guess you noticed they have scented toilet paper in those rooms."

"I wouldn't put it past them," Marsh said. He wadded Norm's giant pajamas small as possible, hunting for a place they'd fit. It occurred to him that nobody in the world should ever own a one-man tent.

"Not to mention how stuffy they keep everything in there."

Marsh brushed at his lap, mud caking his knees.

"Being in that place made me wonder if I'd ever be able to walk into an actual room in an actual house again."

"I think you will."

"I don't know," Alex said. She hitched her dark hair behind her ears and gazed up at the light. Marsh saw her face change, a little telltale tuck at the corner of her mouth. She was thinking about home, thinking ahead.

"Turn out the lantern," he said. Because he knew that sometimes it was better to be afraid in the dark. He'd learned this years ago, lying beside Virginia. He wished now that he'd raised a tent for her on a knoll of grass. Just once for his wife. The lantern would flare, then fade slowly the way it did now—a glow dimming to the moon and stars.

Alex sighed in the darkness. "I have to tell you—I hate that purse you gave me. I'm sorry, but I really do."

"It was just an impulse," he said, drawing the sleeping bag around her.

"But I was thinking maybe Jewel should go on the show with it. You know, for good luck."

"Close your eyes—rest," he said. "You're going to need your strength."

He leaned back on his elbows, listening to the highway, the soft sound of cement moving like incoming tide. A breeze swept across the close darkness. Tonight this darkness would last two minutes longer.

"Don't fall asleep on me," Alex whispered.

"I'm not," he said. "I'm just thinking." He was trying. He folded his hands in his sandy lap and thought of the man killed for the sake of his wallet. He imagined the whole story—secrets hidden under beds and damp basements holding the files and tangled ribbons of microfilm—all the words ever written. And how somewhere along the line, the worst always came out. He sat considering the here and now. Because it occurred to him that knowing the worst could never again be left to another time.

"Thinking about what?"

"Nothing," he said. He shifted to look at her, then smiled. "Well, maybe that you might've gained a little weight."

"I should hope," Alex said. She nodded up. "I hope so much—"

"Yes," Marsh said. "It's such good news, the greatest news. I just can't say . . ."

He looked off, wishing Ginny knew, wishing he could've said something to Richard. Although he'd let almost everybody else know about the baby. He tried to think exactly who he'd told—first Claire, then Frank, Jewel, Evie. But they were practically relatives by now. It seemed years he'd woken up with them, eaten every meal, the table set . . . He blinked down at Alex.

"I need to know—how many casseroles did you put into my freezer?"

"You had about three weeks of not having to cook." Alex reached behind her for a pillow. "Except that was for you by yourself. Before you invited half the country to stay in your house."

"It'll never be enough," Marsh said. He sat back, glad that at least he could offer very level parking.

Alex thumped the pillow, then pulled it over her head. "Tomorrow an early start," she mumbled.

"Yes," Marsh said. He smiled in the darkness, imagining his neighbor staring at his full house from her picture window. Most likely somebody would call up to complain. They'd probably mention zoning.

Marsh glanced over, feeling Alex stir as if with a dream. For a while he kept very still, so as not to wake her. He sat stiff as a mummy, grit clinging everywhere. Finally he moved, creeping his hands over his shirt. He fumbled with the buttons, his zipper spilled sand. He pried off his shoes. He shoved everything off, pushed up like somebody surfacing.

For a minute he lingered in the state of nature. He gazed out the tent screen to the tips of evergreens piercing the sky. Then a rush of wind along the canvas. He struggled with Norm's pajamas, thinking tomorrow an early start. Then he eased onto the sleeping bag and crossed his huge pajama arms. But only for a minute. He needed to take the pajamas to Reg. Never mind that he was in them. He would deliver the pajamas, deliver himself to the man who had found him.

"Sshhh," he said, hearing Alex mumbling in her sleep.

Alex was going to need her strength. They all were. He was sure three weeks of food would never be enough. The guidebook had clearly stated: Supplies for 110 Days. Marsh stared up at the tent's low roof, trying to figure exactly how many weeks that amounted to. After a minute he shut his eyes. Then he heard a frog. Only for a minute. And then all the frogs started in. Or maybe he'd drifted off. Because he was crossing the frontier. In the distance he glimpsed Richard airing the house. And everybody coming, on their way. It was a place somewhere in history— just how far Marsh couldn't say. He carried the book with him, but nothing had been written, there was nothing to follow. He kept thinking if he could find the instructions. Even a word. Just one word to leave on the trail for anybody else who might be looking. He searched the book, frantic. He tore out every blank page.

Then the wind snapped the canvas and Marsh came fully awake. He sat up, squinting to get his bearings. Then he ducked outside. He raced over the greens, past the monumental pumps and a field of parking stripes, the sky pale with the thin light of stars and dawn sending every soft murmuring clear and strangely far, as if even a syllable meant more. He saw the truckers moving for their high cabs, going darkly by the dawn's early light, he heard a word traveling, caught the smell of diesel in the air, his feet slapping bare, blue pajamas billowing.

He stopped at #105, stopped to catch his breath and hitch up his bottoms. Then he opened the door. He crossed the gold provincial room, his cold bed still waiting and Reg still sleeping. He flung himself beside the old man. Reg bounced, raised his head from the king-sized pillow. He looked at Marsh amazed, taking everything in, his mouth hanging. Speechless.

And for that, Marsh was grateful. He slung his arm around the old man, then pulled the sheets over the world's largest pajamas. Nothing needed to be said, he had the word in him. The word was Godspeed.

ACKNOWLEDGMENTS

"Gratitude is Heaven itself," William Blake said, and it's this feeling I wish to express to friends who offered encouragement and help with this work: Jane Howard, Ruth Costello, Barbara Grossman, Nancy Nicholas, Ronda Gomez, Ruth Hall, Molly Friedrich, and—as ever and always—Allan Gurganus. The work was expertly guided to publication by Alice Mayhew and George Hodgman.

Certain excerpts were drawn from *The Prairie Traveler* by Capt. Randolph B. Marcy, U.S. Army (Harper & Bros., 1859) and *Pine Ridge, 1890: An Eyewitness Account of the Events Surrounding the Fighting at Wounded Knee*, edited by Alexander Kelley and Pierre Bovis (Pierre Bovis, 1971). Other books most relied on: *In Search of Canaan, The Buffalo Soldiers, The Last Days of the Sioux Nation, The Black West,* and *The Wounded Knee Interviews of Eli S. Ricker.* The state and local Historical Societies of Kansas and Nebraska provided access to valuable archive material.

My appreciation to the National Endowment for the Arts. And to those who assisted with research along the way, especially: Jan and Tom Brady, Don Eldridge, Nancy Stevens, Annette Schulte, Teresa Wooden Knife, Frank Schubert, Vance Nelson, and Dora Hale.

And to Tom, Janai, Megan, and Matthew, who traveled every road with me.